In the Time of the Butterflies

Also by Julia Alvarez

Fiction

How the García Girls Lost Their Accents

Poetry

Homecoming
The Housekeeping Book

Pulú Pelegrin • Mario Guerra • Virgilio Martínez Reina • Emilio Reyes • Desiderio Arias • Salomón Haedad • sús María Patiño (Chichí) • Agustín Darío Patiño (Tía) • César Perozo • Faustino Perozo • Manuel de Jesús .e. • Julio Brache • José Roca • Tiberio Santillana • o Pou • José Morel • **Rufino de la Cruz** • Nicolás • Montaño Deschamps • Santiago Lozao • Rigoberto Romeo Hernández • Ramón Silverio Sandoval • Luis viñón (Quero) • Enrique Litghow • Fernando Suárez carpio Soler • Jesús de Galíndez • Gloria Viera • o Bergés (Grillito) • Chichí Valera • Hugo Cabrera ne • Ercilio García Bencosme • Roberto Monagas • cía Pintor • Martín Taveras • Eugenio de Marchena César Augusto Batista Turbides • Joaquín Herrera • • Rafael Moore Garrido • Luis Rafael Quezada (Lulú) trella • Yuyo Alfau • Agustín Alfau • Ney Pimentel ánchez • Nono Moreno Martínez • Octavio Peña González Pardi • Eugenio Perdomo • Camilo Disla Enrique Jiménez Moya • José Horacio Rodríguez • Manuel Torres • Chichí Montes de Oca • Luis Ricardo y • **Minerva Mirabal de Tavárez** • Manuel González • Salcedo • Alejandro Selva • Jesús Bienvenido del María Helú • Félix Mario Ceballos • Ramón Montes amón Camilo • Guido Cabral • Tintin Grullón • a • Mauricio Báez • Pipí Hernández • Andrés Requena Jaime Tineo • Roberto Reid • Huáscar Tejeda • Cáceres (Tunti) • Miguel Angel Báez Díaz • Elpidio cía • Danilo Valdez Borges • Ricardo Vasallo Alfonso Herasme Peña • Aldo D'Alessandro Tavares • Justino n de los Santos • Amaro Ventura • Luis Eugenio gés (Grillito) • Miguel Alvarez Fadul • Belliard Sosa •

JULIA ALVAREZ

In the Time
of the
Butterflies

Algonquin Books
of Chapel Hill
1994

Published by
Algonquin Books of Chapel Hill
Post Office Box 2225
Chapel Hill, North Carolina 27515-2225
a division of
Workman Publishing Company, Inc.
708 Broadway
New York, New York 10003

Library of Congress Cataloging-in-Publication Data
Alvarez, Julia.
In the time of the butterflies : a novel / by Julia Alvarez.—1st ed.
p. cm.
ISBN 1-56512-038-8
1. Dominican Republic—History—1930–1961—Fiction.
2. Women revolutionaries—Dominican Republic—Fiction.
I. Title.
PS3551.L84515 1994
813'.54—dc20   94–15004
CIP

10 9 8 7 6 5 4 3 2 1
First Edition

This work of fiction is based on historical facts referred to in the author's Postscript on pages 323–324.

For Dedé

In Memoriam

PATRIA MERCEDES MIRABAL
February 27, 1924–November 25, 1960

MINERVA MIRABAL
March 12, 1926–November 25, 1960

MARIA TERESA MIRABAL
October 15, 1935–November 25, 1960

RUFINO DE LA CRUZ
November 10, 1923–November 25, 1960

Contents

In the Time of the Butterflies

I

1938 to 1946

CHAPTER ONE

Dedé

1994
and
circa 1943

She is plucking her bird of paradise of its dead branches, leaning around the plant every time she hears a car. The woman will never find the old house behind the hedge of towering hibiscus at the bend of the dirt road. Not a *gringa dominicana* in a rented car with a road map asking for street names! Dedé had taken the call over at the little museum this morning.

Could the woman please come over and talk to Dedé about the Mirabal sisters? She is originally from here but has lived many years in the States, for which she is sorry since her Spanish is not so good. The Mirabal sisters are not known there, for which she is also sorry for it is a crime that they should be forgotten, these unsung heroines of the underground, et cetera.

Oh dear, another one. Now after thirty-four years, the commemorations and interviews and presentations of posthumous honors have almost stopped, so that for months at a time Dedé is able to take up her own life again. But she's long since resigned herself to Novembers. Every year as the 25th rolls around, the television crews drive up. There's the obligatory interview. Then, the big celebration over at the museum, the delegations from as far away as Peru and Paraguay, an ordeal really, making that many little party sandwiches and the nephews and nieces not always showing up in time to help. But this is March, *¡María Santísima!* Doesn't she have seven more months of anonymity?

3

"How about this afternoon? I do have a later commitment," Dedé lies to the voice. She has to. Otherwise, they go on and on, asking the most impertinent questions.

There is a veritable racket of gratitude on the other end, and Dedé has to smile at some of the imported nonsense of this woman's Spanish. "I am so compromised," she is saying, "by the openness of your warm manner."

"So if I'm coming from Santiago, I drive on past Salcedo?" the woman asks.

"*Exactamente*. And then where you see a great big anacahuita tree, you turn left."

"A . . . great . . . big . . . tree . . . ," the woman repeats. She is writing all this down! "I turn left. What's the name of the street?"

"It's just the road by the anacahuita tree. We don't name them," Dedé says, driven to doodling to contain her impatience. On the back of an envelope left beside the museum phone, she has sketched an enormous tree, laden with flowers, the branches squirreling over the flap. "You see, most of the *campesinos* around here can't read, so it wouldn't do us any good to put names on the roads."

The voice laughs, embarrassed. "Of course. You must think I'm so outside of things." *Tan afuera de la cosa.*

Dedé bites her lip. "Not at all," she lies. "I'll see you this afternoon then."

"About what time?" the voice wants to know.

Oh yes. The gringos need a time. But there isn't a clock time for this kind of just-right moment. "Any time after three or three-thirty, four-ish."

"Dominican time, eh?" The woman laughs.

"*¡Exactamente!*" Finally, the woman is getting the hang of how things are done here. Even after she has laid the receiver in its cradle, Dedé goes on elaborating the root system of her anacahuita tree, shading the branches, and then for the fun of it, opening and closing the flap of the envelope to watch the tree come apart and then back together again.

———

In the garden, Dedé is surprised to hear the radio in the outdoor kitchen announce that it is only three o'clock. She has been waiting expectantly since after lunch, tidying up the patch of garden this American woman will be able to see from the *galería*. This is certainly one reason why Dedé shies from these interviews. Before she knows it, she is setting up her life as if it were an exhibit labeled neatly for those who can read: THE SISTER WHO SURVIVED.

Usually, if she works it right—a lemonade with lemons from the tree Patria planted, a quick tour of the house the girls grew up in—usually they leave, satisfied, without asking the prickly questions that have left Dedé lost in her memories for weeks at a time, searching for the answer. Why, they inevitably ask in one form or another, why are you the one who survived?

She bends to her special beauty, the butterfly orchid she smuggled back from Hawaii two years ago. For three years in a row Dedé has won a trip, the prize for making the most sales of anyone in her company. Her niece Minou has noted more than once the irony of Dedé's "new" profession, actually embarked upon a decade ago, after her divorce. She is the company's top life insurance salesperson. Everyone wants to buy a policy from the woman who just missed being killed along with her three sisters. Can she help it?

The slamming of a car door startles Dedé. When she calms herself she finds she has snipped her prize butterfly orchid. She picks up the fallen blossom and trims the stem, wincing. Perhaps this is the only way to grieve the big things—in snippets, pinches, little sips of sadness.

But really, this woman should shut car doors with less violence. Spare an aging woman's nerves. And I'm not the only one, Dedé thinks. Any Dominican of a certain generation would have jumped at that gunshot sound.

———

She walks the woman quickly through the house, *Mamá's bedroom, mine and Patria's, but mostly mine since Patria married so young, Minerva and María Teresa's.* The other bedroom she does not say was her father's after he and Mamá stopped sleeping together. There are the three pictures of the girls, old favorites that are now emblazoned on the posters every November, making these once intimate snapshots seem too famous to be the sisters she knew.

Dedé has placed a silk orchid in a vase on the little table below them. She still feels guilty about not continuing Mamá's tribute of a fresh blossom for the girls every day. But the truth is, she doesn't have the time anymore, with a job, the museum, a household to run. You can't be a modern woman and insist on the old sentimentalities. And who was the fresh orchid for, anyway? Dedé looks up at those young faces, and she knows it is herself at that age she misses the most.

The interview woman stops before the portraits, and Dedé waits for her to ask which one was which or how old they were when these were taken, facts Dedé has at the ready, having delivered them so many times. But instead the thin waif of a woman asks, "And where are you?"

Dedé laughs uneasily. It's as if the woman has read her mind. "I have this hallway just for the girls," she says. Over the woman's shoulder, she sees she has left the door to her room ajar, her nightgown flung with distressing abandon on her bed. She wishes she had gone through the house and shut the doors to the bedrooms.

"No, I mean, where are you in the sequence, the youngest, the oldest?"

So the woman has not read any of the articles or biographies around. Dedé is relieved. This means that they can spend the time talking about the simple facts that give Dedé the illusion that hers was just an ordinary family, too—birthdays and weddings and new babies, the peaks in that graph of normalcy.

Dedé goes through the sequence.

"So fast in age," the woman notes, using an awkward phrase.

Dedé nods. "The first three of us were born close, but in other ways, you see, we were so different."

"Oh?" the woman asks.

"Yes, so different. Minerva was always into her wrongs and rights." Dedé realizes she is speaking to the picture of Minerva, as if she were assigning her a part, pinning her down with a handful of adjectives, the beautiful, intelligent, high-minded Minerva. "And María Teresa, *ay, Dios*," Dedé sighs, emotion in her voice in spite of herself. "Still a girl when she died, *pobrecita*, just turned twenty-five." Dedé moves on to the last picture and rights the frame. "Sweet Patria, always her religion was so important."

"Always?" the woman says, just the slightest challenge in her voice.

"Always," Dedé affirms, used to this fixed, monolithic language around interviewers and mythologizers of her sisters. "Well, almost always."

She walks the woman out of the house into the *galería* where the rocking chairs wait. A kitten lies recklessly under the runners, and she shoos it away. "What is it you want to know?" Dedé asks bluntly. And then because the question does seem to rudely call the woman to account for herself, she adds, "Because there is so much to tell."

The woman laughs as she says, "Tell me all of it."

Dedé looks at her watch as a polite reminder to the woman that the visit is circumscribed. "There are books and articles. I could have Tono at the museum show you the letters and diaries."

"That would be great," the woman says, staring at the orchid Dedé is still holding in her hand. Obviously, she wants more. She looks up, shyly. "I just have to say, it's really so easy to talk to you. I mean, you're so open and cheerful. How do you keep such a tragedy from taking you under? I'm not sure I am explaining myself?"

Dedé sighs. Yes, the woman is making perfect sense. She thinks of an article she read at the beauty salon, by a Jewish lady who survived a concentration camp. "There were many many happy years. I remember those. I try anyhow. I tell myself, Dedé, concentrate on the positive! My niece Minou tells me I am doing some transcending meditation, something like that. She took the course in the capital.

"I'll tell myself, Dedé, in your memory it is such and such a day, and I start over, playing the happy moment in my head. This is my movies—I have no television here."

"It works?"

"Of course," Dedé says, almost fiercely. And when it doesn't work, she thinks, I get stuck playing the same bad moment. But why speak of that.

"Tell me about one of those moments," the woman asks, her face naked with curiosity. She looks down quickly as if to hide it.

Dedé hesitates, but her mind is already racing backwards, year by year by year, to the moment she has fixed in her memory as zero.

She remembers a clear moonlit night before the future began. They are sitting in the cool darkness under the anacahuita tree in the front yard, in the rockers, telling stories, drinking guanabana juice. Good for the nerves, Mamá always says.

They're all there, Mamá, Papá, Patria-Minerva-Dedé. Bang-bang-bang, their father likes to joke, aiming a finger pistol at each one, as if he were shooting them, not boasting about having sired them. Three girls, each born within a year of the other! And then, nine years later, María Teresa, his final desperate attempt at a boy misfiring.

Their father has his slippers on, one foot hooked behind the other. Every once in a while Dedé hears the clink of the rum bottle against the rim of his glass.

Many a night, and this night is no different, a shy voice calls out of the darkness, begging their pardon. Could they spare a *calmante* for a sick child out of their stock of kindness? Would they have some tobacco for a tired old man who spent the day grating yucca?

Their father gets up, swaying a little with drink and tiredness, and opens up the store. The *campesino* goes off with his medicine, a couple of cigars, a few mints for the godchildren. Dedé tells her father that she doesn't know how they do as well as they do, the way he gives everything away. But her father just puts his arm around her, and says, "Ay, Dedé, that's why I have you. Every soft foot needs a hard shoe.

"She'll bury us all," her father adds, laughing, "in silk and pearls." Dedé hears again the clink of the rum bottle. "Yes, for sure, our Dedé here is going to be the millionaire in the family."

"And me, Papá, and me?" María Teresa pipes up in her little girl's voice, not wanting to be left out of the future.

"You, *mi ñapita*, you'll be our little coquette. You'll make a lot of men's—"

Their mother coughs her correcting-your-manners cough.

"—a lot of men's mouths water," their father concludes.

María Teresa groans. At eight years old, in her long braids and checkered blouse, the only future the baby wants is one that will make *her*

own mouth water, sweets and gifts in big boxes that clatter with something fun inside when she shakes them.

"What of me, Papá?" Patria asks more quietly. It is difficult to imagine
Patria unmarried without a baby on her lap, but Dedé's memory is playing dolls with the past. She has sat them down that clear, cool night
before the future begins, Mamá and Papá and their four pretty girls, no
one added, no one taken away. Papá calls on Mamá to help him out
with his fortune-telling. Especially—though he doesn't say this—if
she's going to censor the clairvoyance of his several glasses of rum.
"What would you say, Mamá, about our Patria?"

"You know, Enrique, that I don't believe in fortunes," Mamá says
evenly. "Padre Ignacio says fortunes are for those without faith." In her
mother's tone, Dedé can already hear the distance that will come
between her parents. Looking back, she thinks, *Ay*, Mamá, ease up a little on those commandments. Work out the Christian math of how you
give a little and you get it back a hundredfold. But thinking about her
own divorce, Dedé admits the math doesn't always work out. If you
multiply by zero, you still get zero, and a thousand heartaches.

"I don't believe in fortunes either," Patria says quickly. She's as religious as Mamá, that one. "But Papá isn't really telling fortunes."

Minerva agrees. "Papá's just *confessing* what he thinks are our
strengths." She stresses the verb *confessing* as if their father were actually being pious in looking ahead for his daughters. "Isn't that so, Papá?"

"*Sí, señorita*," Papá burps, slurring his words. It's almost time to go
in.

"Also," Minerva adds, "Padre Ignacio condemns fortunes only if you
believe a human being knows what only God can know." That one can't
leave well enough alone.

"Some of us know it all," Mamá says curtly.

María Teresa defends her adored older sister. "It isn't a sin, Mamá, it
isn't. Berto and Raúl have this game from New York. Padre Ignacio
played it with us. It's a board with a little glass you move around, and it
tells the future!" Everybody laughs, even their mother, for María Teresa's
voice is bursting with gullible excitement. The baby stops, suddenly, in
a pout. Her feelings get hurt so easily. On Minerva's urging, she goes on

in a little voice. "I asked the talking board what I would be when I grew up, and it said a lawyer."

They all hold back their laughter this time, for of course, María Teresa is parroting her big sister's plans. For years Minerva has been agitating to go to law school.

"*Ay, Dios mío*, spare me." Mama sighs, but playfulness has come back into her voice. "Just what we need, skirts in the law!"

"It *is* just what this country needs." Minerva's voice has the steely sureness it gets whenever she talks politics. She has begun talking politics a lot. Mamá says she's running around with the Perozo girl too much. "It's about time we women had a voice in running our country."

"You and Trujillo," Papá says a little loudly, and in this clear peaceful night they all fall silent. Suddenly, the dark fills with spies who are paid to hear things and report them down at Security. *Don Enrique claims Trujillo needs help in running this country. Don Enrique's daughter says it's about time women took over the government.* Words repeated, distorted, words recreated by those who might bear them a grudge, words stitched to words until they are the winding sheet the family will be buried in when their bodies are found dumped in a ditch, their tongues cut off for speaking too much.

Now, as if drops of rain had started falling—though the night is as clear as the sound of a bell—they hurry in, gathering their shawls and drinks, leaving the rockers for the yardboy to bring in. María Teresa squeals when she steps on a stone. "I thought it was *el cuco*," she moans.

As Dedé is helping her father step safely up the stairs of the *galería*, she realizes that hers is the only future he really told. María Teresa's was a tease, and Papá never got to Minerva's or Patria's on account of Mamá's disapproval. A chill goes through her, for she feels it in her bones, the future is now beginning. By the time it is over, it will be the past, and she doesn't want to be the only one left to tell their story.

CHAPTER TWO

Minerva

1938, 1941, 1944

Complications
1938

I don't know who talked Papá into sending us away to school. Seems like it would have taken the same angel who announced to Mary that she was pregnant with God and got her to be glad about it.

The four of us had to ask permission for everything: to walk to the fields to see the tobacco filling out; to go to the lagoon and dip our feet on a hot day; to stand in front of the store and pet the horses as the men loaded up their wagons with supplies.

Sometimes, watching the rabbits in their pens, I'd think, I'm no different from you, poor things. One time, I opened a cage to set a half-grown doe free. I even gave her a slap to get her going.

But she wouldn't budge! She was used to her little pen. I kept slapping her, harder each time, until she started whimpering like a scared child. I was the one hurting her, insisting she be free.

Silly bunny, I thought. You're nothing at all like me.

It started with Patria wanting to be a nun. Mamá was all for having a religious in the family, but Papá did not approve in the least. More than once, he said that Patria as a nun would be a waste of a pretty girl. He only said that once in front of Mamá, but he repeated it often enough to me.

Finally, Papá gave in to Mamá. He said Patria could go away to a convent school if it wasn't one just for becoming a nun. Mamá agreed.

So, when it came time for Patria to go down to Inmaculada Concepción, I asked Papá if I could go along. That way I could chaperone my older sister, who was already a grown-up señorita. (And she had told me all about how girls become señoritas, too.)

Papá laughed, his eyes flashing proudly at me. The others said I was his favorite. I don't know why since I was the one always standing up to him. He pulled me to his lap and said, "And who is going to chaperone *you?*"

"Dedé," I said, so all three of us could go together. He pulled a long face. "If all my little chickens go, what will become of me?"

I thought he was joking, but his eyes had their serious look. "Papá," I informed him, "you might as well get used to it. In a few years, we're all going to marry and leave you."

For days he quoted me, shaking his head sadly and concluding, "A daughter is a needle in the heart."

Mamá didn't like him saying so. She thought he was being critical because their only son had died a week after he was born. And just three years ago, María Teresa was born a girl instead of a boy. Anyhow, Mamá didn't think it was a bad idea to send all three of us away. "Enrique, those girls need some learning. Look at us." Mamá had never admitted it, but I suspected she couldn't even read.

"What's wrong with us?" Papá countered, gesturing out the window where wagons waited to be loaded before his warehouses. In the last few years, Papá had made a lot of money from his farm. Now we had class. *And*, Mamá argued, we needed the education to go along with our cash.

Papá caved in again, but said one of us had to stay to help mind the store. He always had to add a little something to whatever Mamá came up with. Mamá said he was just putting his mark on everything so no one could say Enrique Mirabal didn't wear the pants in his family.

I knew what he was up to all right. When Papá asked which one of us would stay as his little helper, he looked directly at me.

I didn't say a word. I kept studying the floor like maybe my school lessons were chalked on those boards. I didn't need to worry. Dedé always was the smiling little miss. "I'll stay and help, Papá."

Papá looked surprised because really Dedé was a year older than me. She and Patria should have been the two to go away. But then, Papá thought it over and said Dedé could go along, too. So it was settled, all three of us would go to Inmaculada Concepción. Me and Patria would start in the fall, and Dedé would follow in January since Papá wanted the math whiz to help with the books during the busy harvest season.

And that's how I got free. I don't mean just going to sleepaway school on a train with a trunkful of new things. I mean in my head after I got to Inmaculada and met Sinita and saw what happened to Lina and realized that I'd just left a small cage to go into a bigger one, the size of our whole country.

First time I met Sinita she was sitting in the parlor where Sor Asunción was greeting all the new pupils and their mothers. She was all by herself, a skinny girl with a sour look on her face and pokey elbows to match. She was dressed in black, which was odd as most children weren't put in mourning clothes until they were at least fifteen. And this little girl didn't look any older than me, and I was only twelve. Though I would have argued with anyone who told me I was just a kid!

I watched her. She seemed as bored as I was with all the polite talk in that parlor. It was like a heavy shaking of talcum powder in the brain hearing all those mothers complimenting each other's daughters and lisping back in good Castilian to the Sisters of the Merciful Mother. Where was this girl's mother? I wondered. She sat alone, glaring at everybody, as if she would pick a fight if you asked her where her mother was. I could see, though, that she was sitting on her hands and biting her bottom lip so as not to cry. The straps on her shoes had been cut off to look like flats, but they looked worn out, was what they looked like.

I got up and pretended to study the pictures on the walls like I was a lover of religious art. When I got to the Merciful Mother right above Sinita's head, I reached in my pocket and pulled out the button I'd found on the train. It was sparkly like a diamond and had a little hole in back so you could thread a ribbon through it and wear it like a romantic lady's choker necklace. It wasn't something I'd do, but I could see the button would make a good trade with someone inclined in that direction.

I held it out to her. I didn't know what to say, and it probably wouldn't have helped anyway. She picked it up, turned it all around, and then set it back down in my palm. "I don't want your charity."

I felt an angry tightness in my chest. "It's just a friendship button."

She looked at me a moment, a deciding look like she couldn't be sure of anybody. "Why didn't you just say so?" She grinned as if we were already friends and could tease each other.

"I did just say so," I said. I opened up my hand and offered her the button again. This time she took it.

After our mothers left, we stood on line while a list was made of everything in our bags. I noticed that along with not having a mother to bring her, Sinita didn't own much either. Everything she had was tied up in a bundle, and when Sor Milagros wrote it out, all it took was a couple of lines: *3 change of underwear, 4 pair of socks, brush and comb, towel and nightdress.* Sinita offered the sparkly button, but Sor Milagros said it wasn't necessary to write that down.

"Charity student," the gossip went round. "So?" I challenged the giggly girl with curls like hiccups, who whispered it to me. She shut up real quick. It made me glad all over again I'd given Sinita that button.

Afterwards, we were taken into an assembly hall and given all sorts of welcomes. Then Sor Milagros, who was in charge of the tens through twelves, took our smaller group upstairs into the dormitory hall we would share. Our side-by-side beds were already set up for the night with mosquito nets. It looked like a room of little bridal veils.

Sor Milagros said she would now assign us our beds according to our last names. Sinita raised her hand and asked if her bed couldn't be next to mine. Sor Milagros hesitated, but then a sweet look came on her face. Sure, she said. But when some other girls asked, she said no. I spoke right up, "I don't think it's fair if you just make an exception for us."

Sor Milagros looked mighty surprised. I suppose being a nun and all, not many people told her what was wrong and right. Suddenly, it struck me, too, that this plump little nun with a bit of her gray hair showing under her headdress wasn't Mamá or Papá I could argue things with. I was on the point of apologizing, but Sor Milagros just smiled her gap-toothed smile and said, "All right, I'll allow you all to choose your own beds. But at the first sign of argument"— some of the girls had already sprung towards the best beds by the window and were fighting about who got there first—"we'll go back to alphabetical. Is that clear?"

"Yes, Sor Milagros," we chorused.

She came up to me and took my face in her hands. "What's your name?" she wanted to know.

I gave her my name, and she repeated it several times like she was tasting it. Then she smiled like it tasted just fine. She looked over at Sinita, whom they all seemed partial to, and said, "Take care of our dear Sinita."

"I will," I said, standing up straight like I'd been given a mission. And that's what it turned out to be, all right.

———————

A few days later, Sor Milagros gathered us all around for a little talk. Personal hygiene, she called it. I knew right away it would be about interesting things described in the most uninteresting way.

First, she said there had been some accidents. Anyone needing a canvas sheet should come see her. Of course, the best way to prevent a mishap was to be sure to visit our chamber pots every night before we got in bed. Any questions?

Not a one.

Then, a shy, embarrassed look came on her face. She explained that we might very well become young ladies while we were at school this year. She went through a most tangled-up explanation about the how and why, and finished by saying if we should start our complications, we should come see her. This time she didn't ask if there were any questions.

I felt like setting her straight, explaining things simply the way Patria had explained them to me. But I guessed it wasn't a good idea to try my luck twice in the first week.

When she left, Sinita asked me if I understood what on earth Sor Milagros had been talking about. I looked at her surprised. Here she'd been dressed in black like a grownup young lady, and she didn't know the first thing. Right then, I told Sinita everything I knew about bleeding and having babies between your legs. She was pretty shocked, and beholden. She offered to trade me back the secret of Trujillo.

"What secret is that?" I asked her. I thought Patria had told me all the secrets.

"Not yet," Sinita said looking over her shoulder.

It was a couple of weeks before Sinita got to her secret. I'd forgotten about it, or maybe I'd just put it out of my mind, a little scared what I might find out. We were busy with classes and making new friends. Almost every night someone or other came visiting under our mosquito nets or we visited them. We had two regulars, Lourdes and Elsa, and soon all four of us started doing everything together. It seemed like we were all just a little different—Sinita was charity and you could tell; Lourdes was fat, though as friends we called her pleasantly plump when she asked, and she asked a lot; Elsa was pretty in an I-told-you-so way, as if she hadn't expected to turn out pretty and now she had to prove it. And me, I couldn't keep my mouth shut when I had something to say.

The night Sinita told me the secret of Trujillo I couldn't sleep. All day I hadn't felt right, but I didn't tell Sor Milagros. I was afraid she'd stick me in the sickroom and I'd have to lie in bed, listening to Sor Consuelo reading novenas for the sick and dying. Also, if Papá found out, he might change his mind and keep me home where I couldn't have any adventures.

I was lying on my back, looking up into the white tent of the mosquito net, and wondering who else was awake. In her bed next to mine, Sinita began to cry very quietly as if she didn't want anybody to know. I waited a little, but she didn't stop. Finally, I stepped over to her bed and lifted the netting. "What's wrong?" I whispered.

She took a second to calm down before she answered. "It's José Luis."

"Your brother?" We all knew he had died just this last summer. That's how come Sinita had been wearing black that first day.

Her body began to shake all over with sobs. I crawled in and stroked her hair like Mamá did mine whenever I had a fever. "Tell me, Sinita, maybe it'll help."

"I can't," she whispered. "We can all be killed. It's the secret of Trujillo."

Well, all I had to be told was I couldn't know something for me to *have* to know it. So I reminded her, "Come on, Sinita. I told you about babies."

It took some coaxing, but finally she began.

She told me stuff I didn't even know about her. I thought she was always poor, but it turned out her family used to be rich and important. Three of her uncles were even friends of Trujillo. But they turned against him when they saw he was doing bad things.

"Bad things?" I interrupted. "Trujillo was doing bad things?" It was as if I had just heard Jesus had slapped a baby or Our Blessed Mother had not conceived Him the immaculate conception way. "That can't be true," I said, but in my heart, I felt a china-crack of doubt.

"Wait," Sinita whispered, her thin fingers finding my mouth in the dark. "Let me finish.

"My uncles, they had a plan to do something to Trujillo, but somebody told on them, and all three were shot, right on the spot." Sinita took a deep breath as if she were going to blow out all her grandmother's birthday candles.

"But what bad things was Trujillo doing that they wanted to kill him?" I asked again. I couldn't leave it alone. At home, Trujillo hung on the wall by the picture of Our Lord Jesus with a whole flock of the cutest lambs.

Sinita told me as much as she knew. I was shaking by the time she was through.

According to Sinita, Trujillo became president in a sneaky way. First, he was in the army, and all the people who were above him kept disappearing until he was the one right below the head of the whole armed forces.

This man who was the head general had fallen in love with another man's wife. Trujillo was his friend and so he knew all about this secret. The woman's husband was a very jealous man, and Trujillo made friends with him, too.

One day, the general told Trujillo he was going to be meeting this woman that very night under the bridge in Santiago where people meet to do bad things. So Trujillo went and told the husband, who waited under the bridge for his wife and this general and shot them both dead.

Very soon after that, Trujillo became head of the armed forces.

"Maybe Trujillo thought that general was doing a bad thing by fooling around with somebody else's wife," I defended him.

I heard Sinita sigh. "Just wait," she said, "before you decide."

After Trujillo became the head of the army, he got to talking to some people who didn't like the old president. One night, these people surrounded the palace and told the old president that he had to leave. The old president just laughed and sent for his good friend, the head of the armed forces. But General Trujillo didn't come and didn't come. Soon, the old president was the ex-president on an airplane to Puerto Rico. Then, something that surprised even the people who had surrounded the palace, Trujillo announced he was the president.

"Didn't anyone tell him that wasn't right?" I asked, knowing *I* would have.

"People who opened their big mouths didn't live very long," Sinita said. "Like my uncles I told you about. Then, two more uncles, and then my father." Sinita began crying again. "Then this summer, they killed my brother."

My tummy ache had started up again. Or maybe it was always there, but I'd forgotten about it while trying to make Sinita feel better. "Stop, please," I begged her. "I think I'm going to throw up."

"I can't," she said.

Sinita's story spilled out like blood from a cut.

One Sunday this last summer, her whole family was walking home from church. Her whole family meant all Sinita's widowed aunts and her mother and tons of girl cousins, with her brother José Luis being the only boy left in the entire family. Everywhere they went, the girls were assigned places around him. Her brother had been saying that he was going to revenge his father and uncles, and the rumor all over town was that Trujillo was after him.

As they were rounding the square, a vendor came up to sell them a lottery ticket. It was the dwarf they always bought from, so they trusted him.

"Oh I've seen him!" I said. Sometimes when we would go to San Francisco in the carriage, and pass by the square, there he was, a grown man no taller than me at twelve. Mamá never bought from him. She claimed Jesus told us not to gamble, and playing the lottery was gambling. But every time I was alone with Papá, he bought a whole bunch of tickets and called it a good investment.

José Luis asked for a lucky number. When the dwarf went to hand him the ticket, something silver flashed in his hand. That's all Sinita saw. Then José Luis was screaming horribly and her mother and all the aunts were shouting for a doctor. Sinita looked over at her brother, and the front of his white shirt was covered with blood.

I started crying, but I pinched my arms to stop. I had to be brave for Sinita.

"We buried him next to my father. My mother hasn't been the same since. Sor Asunción, who knows my family, offered to let me come to *el colegio* for free."

The aching in my belly was like wash being wrung so tightly, there wasn't a drop of water left in the clothes. "I'll pray for your brother," I promised her. "But Sinita, one thing. How is this Trujillo's secret?"

"You still don't get it? Minerva, don't you see? Trujillo is having everyone killed!"

I lay awake most of that night, thinking about Sinita's brother and her uncles and her father and this secret of Trujillo that nobody but Sinita seemed to know about. I heard the clock, down in the parlor, striking every hour. It was already getting light in the room by the time I fell asleep.

In the morning, I was shaken awake by Sinita. "Hurry," she was saying. "You're going to be late for Matins." All around the room, sleepy girls were clapping away in their slippers towards the crowded basins in the washroom. Sinita grabbed her towel and soap dish from her night table and joined the exodus.

As I came fully awake, I felt the damp sheet under me. Oh no, I thought, I've wet my bed! After I'd told Sor Milagros that I wouldn't need an extra canvas sheet on my mattress.

I lifted the covers, and for a moment, I couldn't make sense of the dark stains on the bottom sheet. Then I brought up my hand from checking myself. Sure enough, my complications had started.

¡Pobrecita!
1941

The country people around the farm say that until the nail is hit, it doesn't believe in the hammer. Everything Sinita said I filed away as a terrible mistake that wouldn't happen again. Then the hammer came down hard right in our own school, right on Lina Lovatón's head. Except she called it love and went off, happy as a newlywed.

Lina was a couple of years older than Elsa, Lourdes, Sinita, and me; but her last year at Inmaculada, we were all in the same dormitory hall of the fifteens through seventeens. We got to know her, and love her, which amounted to the same thing when it came to Lina Lovatón.

We all looked up to her as if she were a lot older than even the other seventeens. She was grownup-looking for her age, tall with red-gold hair and her skin like something just this moment coming out of the oven, giving off a warm golden glow. Once when Elsa pestered her in the washroom while Sor Socorro was over at the convent, Lina slipped off her gown and showed us what we would look like in a few years.

She sang in the choir in a clear beautiful voice like an angel. She wrote in a curlicued hand that was like the old prayerbooks with silver clasps Sor Asunción had brought over from Spain. Lina taught us how to roll our hair, and how to curtsy if we met a king. We watched her. All of us were in love with our beautiful Lina.

The nuns loved her too, always choosing Lina to read the lesson during silent dinners or to carry the Virgencita in the Sodality of Mary processions. As often as my sister Patria, Lina was awarded the weekly good-conduct ribbon, and she wore it proudly, bandolier style, across the front of her blue serge uniform.

I still remember the afternoon it all started. We were outside playing volleyball, and our captain Lina was leading us to victory. Her thick plaited hair was coming undone, and her face was pink and flushed as she flung herself here and there after the ball.

Sor Socorro came hurrying out. Lina Lovatón had to come right away. An important visitor was here to meet her. This was very unusual since we weren't allowed weekday visitors and the sisters were very strict about their rules.

Off Lina went, Sor Socorro straightening her hair ribbons and pulling at the pleats of her uniform to make the skirt fall straight. The rest of us resumed our game, but it wasn't as much fun now that our beloved captain was gone.

When Lina came back, there was a shiny medal pinned on her uniform just above her left breast. We crowded around her, wanting to know all about her important visitor. "Trujillo?" we all cried out. "*Trujillo* came to see you?" Sor Socorro rushed out for a second time that day, hushing and rounding us up. We had to wait until lights-out that night to hear Lina's story.

It turned out that Trujillo had been visiting some official's house next door, and attracted by the shouts from our volleyball game below, he had gone out on the balcony. When he caught sight of our beautiful Lina, he walked right over to the school, followed by his surprised aides, and insisted on meeting her. He wouldn't take no for an answer. Sor Asunción finally gave in and sent for Lina Lovatón. Soldiers swarmed about them, Lina said, and Trujillo took a medal off his own uniform and pinned it on hers!

"What did you do?" we all wanted to know. In the moonlight streaming in from the open shutters, Lina Lovatón showed us. Lifting the mosquito net, she stood in front of us and made a deep curtsy.

Soon, every time Trujillo was in town—and he was in La Vega more often than he had ever been before—he stopped in to visit Lina Lovatón. Gifts were sent over to the school: a porcelain ballerina, little bottles of perfume that looked like pieces of jewelry and smelled like a rose garden wished it could smell, a satin box with a gold heart charm inside for a bracelet that Trujillo had already given her with a big L charm to start it off.

At first the sisters were frightened. But then, they started receiving gifts, too: bolts of muslim for making convent sheets and terrycloth for their towels and a donation of a thousand pesos for a new statue of the Merciful Mother to be carved by a Spanish artist living in the capital.

Lina always told us about her visits from Trujillo. It was kind of exciting for all of us when he came. First, classes were cancelled, and the whole school was overrun by guards poking through all our bedrooms. When they were done, they stood at attention while we tried to tease smiles out of their on-guard faces. Meanwhile, Lina disappeared into the parlor where we had all been delivered that first day by our mothers. As Lina reported, the visit usually started with Trujillo reciting some poetry to her, then saying he had some surprise on his person she had to find. Sometimes he'd ask her to sing or dance. Most especially, he loved for her to play with the medals on his chest, taking them off, pinning them back on.

"But do you love him?" Sinita asked Lina one time. Sinita's voice sounded as disgusted as if she were asking Lina if she had fallen in love with a tarantula.

"With all my heart," Lina sighed. "More than my life."

Trujillo kept visiting Lina and sending her gifts and love notes she shared with us. Except for Sinita, I think we were all falling in love with the phantom hero in Lina's sweet and simple heart. From the back of my drawer where I had put it away in consideration for Sinita, I dug up the little picture of Trujillo we were all given in Citizenship Class. I placed it under my pillow at night to ward off nightmares.

For her seventeenth birthday, Trujillo threw Lina a big party in a new house he had just built outside Santiago. Lina went away for the whole week of her birthday. On the actual day, a full-page photograph of Lina appeared in the papers and beneath it was a poem written by Trujillo himself:

> She was born a queen, not by dynastic right,
> but by the right of beauty
> whom divinity sends to the world only rarely.

Sinita claimed that someone else had written it for him because Trujillo hardly knew how to scratch out his own name. "If I were Lina—" she began, and her right hand reached out as if grabbing a bunch of grapes and squeezing the juice out of them.

Weeks went by, and Lina didn't return. Finally, the sisters made an announcement that Lina Lovatón would be granted her diploma by government orders *in absentia*. "Why?" we asked Sor Milagros, who was still our favorite. "Why won't she come back to us?" Sor Milagros shook her head and turned her face away, but not before I had seen tears in her eyes.

That summer, I found out why. Papá and I were on our way to Santiago with a delivery of tobacco in the wagon. He pointed out a high iron gate and beyond it a big mansion with lots of flowers and the hedges all cut to look like animals. "Look, Minerva, one of Trujillo's girlfriends lives there, your old schoolmate, Lina Lovatón."

"Lina?!" My breath felt tight inside my chest as if it couldn't get out. "But Trujillo is married," I argued. "How can he have Lina as a girlfriend?"

Papá looked at me a long time before he said, "He's got many of them, all over the island, set up in big, fancy houses. Lina Lovatón is just a sad case, because she really does love him, *pobrecita*." Right there he took the opportunity to lecture me about why the hens shouldn't wander away from the safety of the barnyard.

Back at school in the fall during one of our nightly sessions, the rest of the story came out. Lina Lovatón had gotten pregnant in the big house. Trujillo's wife Doña María had found out and gone after her with a knife. So Trujillo shipped Lina off to a mansion he'd bought for her in Miami where he knew she'd be safe. She lived all alone now, waiting for him to call her up. I guess there was a whole other pretty girl now taking up his attention.

"*Pobrecita*," we chorused, like an amen.

We were quiet, thinking of this sad ending for our beautiful Lina. I felt my breath coming short again. At first, I had thought it was caused by the cotton bandages I had started tying around my chest so my breasts wouldn't grow. I wanted to be sure what had happened to Lina Lovatón would never happen to me. But every time I'd hear one more secret about Trujillo I could feel the tightening in my chest even when I wasn't wearing the bandages.

"Trujillo is a devil," Sinita said as we tiptoed back to our beds. We had managed to get them side by side again this year.

But I was thinking, No, he is a man. And in spite of all I'd heard, I felt sorry for him. *¡Pobrecito!* At night, he probably had nightmare after nightmare like I did, just thinking about what he'd done.

Downstairs in the dark parlor, the clock was striking the hours like hammer blows.

The Performance
1944

It was our country's centennial year. We'd been having celebrations and performances ever since Independence Day on February 27th. Patria had celebrated her twentieth birthday that day, and we'd thrown her a big party in Ojo de Agua. That's how my family got around having to give some sort of patriotic affair to show their support of Trujillo. We pretended the party was in his honor with Patria dressed in white, her little boy Nelson in red, and Pedrito, her husband, in blue. Oh yes, the nun thing had fallen through.

It wasn't just my family putting on a big loyalty performance, but the whole country. When we got to school that fall, we were issued new history textbooks with a picture of you-know-who embossed on the cover so even a blind person could tell who the lies were all about. Our history now followed the plot of the Bible. We Dominicans had been waiting for centuries for the arrival of our Lord Trujillo on the scene. It was pretty disgusting.

All through nature there is a feeling of ecstasy. A strange other-worldly light suffuses the house smelling of labor and sanctity. The 24th of October in 1891. God's glory made flesh in a miracle. Rafael Leonidas Trujillo has been born!

At our first assembly, the sisters announced that, thanks to a generous donation from El Jefe, a new wing had been added for indoor recreation. It was to be known as the Lina Lovatón Gymnasium, and in a few weeks, a recitation contest would be held there for the entire school. The theme was to be our centennial and the generosity of our gracious Benefactor.

As the announcement was being made, Sinita and Elsa and Lourdes and I looked at each other, settling that we would do our entry together. We had all started out together at Inmaculada six years ago, and everyone now called us the quadruplets. Sor Asunción was always joking that when we graduated in a couple years, she was going to have to hack us apart with a knife.

We worked hard on our performance, practicing every night after lights out. We had written all our own lines instead of just reciting things from a book. That way we could say what we wanted instead of what the censors said we could say.

Not that we were stupid enough to say anything bad about the government. Our skit was set way back in the olden days. I played the part of the enslaved Motherland, tied up during the whole performance until the very end when Liberty, Glory, and the narrator untied me. This was supposed to remind the audience of our winning our independence a hundred years ago. Then, we all sang the national anthem and curtsied like Lina Lovatón had taught us. Nobody could get upset with that!

The night of the recitation contest we could hardly eat our dinners, we were so nervous and excited. We dressed in one of the classrooms, helping each other with the costumes and painting our faces, for the sisters did allow makeup for performances. Of course, we never washed up real good afterwards, so that the next day we walked around with sexy eyes, rosy lips, and painted-on beauty marks as if we were at a you-know-what-kind-of-a-place instead of a convent school.

And the quadruplets *were* the best, by far! We took so many curtain calls that we were still on stage when Sor Asunción came up to announce the winners. We started to exit, but she motioned us back. The place broke into wild clapping, stomping, and whistling, all of which were forbidden as unladylike. But Sor Asunción seemed to have forgotten her own rules. She held up the blue ribbon since no one would quiet down to hear her announce that we had won.

What we did hear her say when the audience finally settled down was that we would be sent along with a delegation from La Vega to the capital to perform the winning piece for Trujillo on his birthday. We looked at each other, shocked. The nuns had never said anything about this added performance. Later as we undressed in the classroom, we discussed turning down the prize.

"I'm not going," I declared, washing off all the goop on my face. I wanted to make a protest, but I wasn't sure what to do.

"Let's do it, oh please," Sinita pleaded. There was such a look of desperation on her face, Elsa and Lourdes readily agreed, "Let's."

"But they tricked us!" I reminded them.

"Please, Minerva, please," Sinita coaxed. She put her arm around me, and when I tried to pull away, she gave me a smack on the cheek.

I couldn't believe Sinita would really want to do this, given how her family felt about Trujillo. "But Sinita, why would you want to perform for *him*?"

Sinita drew herself up so proud she looked like Liberty all right. "It's not for him. Our play's about a time when we were free. It's like a hidden protest."

That settled it. I agreed to go on the condition that we do the skit dressed as boys. At first, my friends grumbled because we had to change a lot of the feminine endings, and so the rhymes all went to pot. But the nearer the big day approached, the more the specter of Lina haunted us as we did jumping jacks in the Lina Lovatón Gymnasium. Her beautiful portrait stared across the room at the picture of El Jefe on the opposite wall.

We went down to the capital in a big car provided by the Dominican Party in La Vega. On the way, Sor Asunción read us the epistle, which is what she called the rules we were to observe. Ours was the third performance in the girls'-school division. It would begin at five, and we would stay to the conclusion of the La Vega performances, and be back at *el colegio* for bedtime juice. "You must show the nation you are its jewels, Inmaculada Concepción girls. Is that perfectly clear?"

"Yes, Sor Asunción," we chorused back absently. But we were too excited about our glorious adventure to pay much attention to rules. Along the way, every time some cute fellows passed us in their fast, fancy cars, we'd wave and pucker up our mouths. Once, a car slowed, and the boys inside called out compliments. Sister scowled fiercely at them and turned around to see what was going on in the back seat of the car. We looked blithely at the road ahead, quadruplet angels. We didn't have to be in a skit to give our best performance!

But as we neared the capital, Sinita got more and more quiet. There was a sad, wistful look on her face, and I knew who she was missing.

Before long we were waiting in an anteroom of the palace alongside other girls from schools all over the country. Sor Asunción came in, swishing her habit importantly and motioned for us. We were ushered into a large hall, bigger than any room I'd ever been in. Through a break in a row of chairs, we came to the center of the floor. We turned circles trying to get our bearings. Then I recognized him under a canopy of Dominican flags, the Benefactor I'd heard about all my life.

In his big gold armchair, he looked much smaller than I had imagined him, looming as he always was from some wall or other. He was wearing a fancy white uniform with gold fringe epaulets and a breast of medals like an actor playing a part.

We took our places, but he didn't seem to notice. He was turned towards a young man, sitting beside him, also wearing a uniform. I knew it was his handsome son, Ramfis, a full colonel in the army since he was four years old. His picture was always in the papers.

Ramfis looked our way and whispered something to his father, who laughed loudly. How rude, I thought; after all, we were here to pay them compliments. The least they could do was pretend that we didn't look like fools in our ballooning togas and beards and bows and arrows.

Trujillo nodded for us to start. We stood frozen, gawking, until Sinita finally pulled us all together by taking her place. I was glad I got to recline on the ground, because my knees were shaking so hard I was afraid that the Fatherland might faint right on the spot.

Miraculously, we all remembered our lines. As we said them out loud, our voices gathered confidence and became more expressive. Once when I stole a glance, I saw that the handsome Ramfis and even El Jefe were caught up in our performance.

We moved along smoothly, until we got to the part when Sinita was supposed to stand before me, the bound Fatherland. After I said,

Over a century, languishing in chains,
Dare I now hope for freedom from my woes?
Oh, Liberty, unfold your brilliant bow,

Sinita was to step forward, show her brilliant bow. Then, having aimed imaginary arrows at imaginary foes, she was to set me free by untying me.

But when we got to this part, Sinita kept on stepping forward and didn't stop until she was right in front of Trujillo's chair. Slowly, she raised her bow and took aim. There was a stunned silence in the hall.

Quick as gunfire, Ramfis leapt to his feet and crouched between his father and our frozen tableau. He snatched the bow from Sinita's hand and broke it over his raised knee. The crack of the splintering wood released a hubbub of whispers and murmurs. Ramfis looked intently at Sinita, who glared right back at him. "You shouldn't play that way."

"It was part of the play," I lied. I was still bound, reclining on the floor. "She didn't mean any harm."

Ramfis looked at me, and then back at Sinita. "What's your name?"

"Liberty," Sinita said.

"Your real name, Liberty?" he barked at her as if she were a soldier in his army.

"Perozo." She said it proudly.

He lifted an eyebrow, intrigued. And then, like a hero in a storybook, he helped me up. "Untie her, Perozo," he ordered Sinita. But when she reached over to work the knots loose, he grabbed her hands and yanked them behind her back. He spit these words out at her: "Use your dog teeth, bitch!"

His lips twisted into a sinister little smile as Sinita bent down and untied me with her mouth.

My hands freed, I saved the day, according to what Sinita said later. I flung off my cape, showing off my pale arms and bare neck. In a trembly voice I began the chant that grew into a shouting chorus *¡Viva Trujillo! ¡Viva Trujillo! ¡Viva Trujillo!*

On the way home, Sor Asunción scolded us. "You were not the orna-
ments of the nation. You did not obey my epistle." As the road darkened, the beams of our headlights filled with hundreds of blinded
moths. Where they hit the windshield, they left blurry marks, until it
seemed like I was looking at the world through a curtain of tears.

CHAPTER THREE

This little book belongs to María Teresa

1945 to 1946

Feast Day of the Immaculate Conception
Saint's Day of our school!

Dear Little Book,

Minerva gives you to me today for my First Communion. You
are so pretty with a mother of pearl cover and a little latch like a
prayerbook. I will have such fun writing on your tissue-thin
pages.

Minerva says keeping a diary is also a way to reflect and reflection
deepens one's soul. It sounds so serious. I suppose now that I've got
one I'm responsible for, I have to expect some changes.

Sunday, December 9

Dear Little Book,

I have been trying to reflect, but I can't come up with anything.

I love my new shoes from my First Communion. They're white
leather with just a little heel like a grownup young lady. I practiced a
lot beforehand, and I must say, I didn't wobble once on my way to the
altar. I was so proud of myself.

Mamá and Dedé and Patria and my little nephew Nelson and my
little niece Noris came all the way from Ojo de Agua just to watch me
make my First Communion. Papá couldn't come. He is too busy with
the cacao harvest.

Wednesday, December 12

Dear Little Book,

It is hard to write in you here at school. First, there is hardly any free time except for prayers. Then, when I do take a minute, Daysi and Lidia come up sneaky and grab you. They toss you back and forth while I run after them trying to catch you. Finally, they give you back, giggling the whole time like I'm being silly keeping a diary.

And you might not know this, Little Book, but I always cry when people laugh at me.

Feast Day of Santa Lucía

Dear Little Book,

Tonight, we will have the candle lighting and all our eyes will be blessed on account of Santa Lucía. And guess what? I have been chosen to be Santa Lucía by all the sisters! I'll get to wear my First Communion dress and shoes all over again and lead the whole school from the dark courtyard into the lit-up chapel.

I have been practicing, walking up and down the Stations of the Cross with a blessed look on my face, not an easy thing when you are trying to keep your balance. I think saints all lived before high heels were invented.

Saturday, December 15

Dear Little Book,

What does it mean that I now *really* have a soul?

All I can think of is the picture in our Catechism of a valentine with measles. That is the soul when it commits mortal sins. Venial sins are lighter, like a rash instead of measles. A rash that goes away even without Confession if you say an Act of Contrition.

I asked Minerva what it means to her, having a soul. We had been talking about Daysi and Lidia and what I should do.

Minerva says a soul is like a deep longing in you that you can never fill up, but you try. That is why there are stirring poems and brave heroes who die for what is right.

I have that longing, I guess. Sometimes before a holiday or a birthday party, I feel like I'm going to burst. But Minerva says that's not exactly what she meant.

Sunday, December 16

Dear Little Book,

I don't know if you realize how advanced I am for my age?

I think it's because I have three older sisters, and so I've grown up quick. I knew how to read before I even started school! In fact, Sor Asunción put me in fourth, though really, I should have been in third with the other tens.

My penmanship is also very pretty as you will have noticed. I've won the writing prize twice, and I would have this week, too, but I decided to leave some i's undotted. It doesn't help with the other girls if you are best all the time.

At first, Mamá didn't even want me to leave home. But she agreed it made sense for me to come since this is Minerva's last year at Inmaculada Concepción, and so I would have family here to look after me my first year.

Don't tell anyone: I don't like it here that much. But after we talked Mamá into letting me board, I have to pretend. At least, Minerva is here with me even if she sleeps in another hall.

And you are here with me too, my dear Little Book.

Thursday, December 20

My dear Little Book,

Tomorrow, Minerva and I take the train home for the holidays. I can't wait! My soul is full of longing all right.

I long to see Papá, whom I haven't seen in three whole months!

And my rabbits, Nieve and Coco. I wonder how many new ones I have?

And Tono and Fela (they work for us) making a fuss over me.

And my room (I share with Minerva) with the windows you throw open on the garden with its bougainvillea arch like the entrance to a magic kingdom in a storybook.

And to be called Mate. (We're not allowed nicknames here. Even Dedé was called Bélgica, which no one has *ever* called her.)

I guess I will miss some things here.

Like dear Sor Milagros who always helps me braid my hair with ribbons. And Daysi and Lidia who have been so nice lately. I think it helped that Minerva had a talk with them.

But I will NOT miss waking up at six and early morning Matins and sleeping in a big dormitory hall with rude sleepers who snore and Rest & Silence every day and wearing a navy blue serge uniform when there are so many nicer colors and fabrics in the world.

And the chocolate not made with enough chocolate.

Sunday, December 23
Home!

My dear,

Minerva explained everything to me in detail and with diagrams as we were coming home on the train. I was not one bit surprised. First, she had already told me about cycles, and second, we do live on a farm, and it's not like the bulls are exactly private about what they do. But still, I don't have to like it. I am hoping a new way will be found by the time I am old enough to be married.

Oh dear, everyone is calling me to come see the pig Tío Pepe brought for tomorrow's Christmas Eve party.

To be continued, Little Book.

Later

Back to the train coming home. A young man started following us around, saying Minerva was the most beautiful woman he'd ever seen. (She's always getting compliments when we walk on the street.)

Just as Minerva and I were going to sit down, this young man dashes forward and wipes our seat with his handkerchief. Minerva thanks him, but doesn't really give him the time of day. At least not the time he wants, which is the invitation to sit with us.

We thought we'd gotten rid of him. We were riding along, the *thing* lesson being done, and here he comes again with a cone of roasted cashews he bought for us at the last stop. He offers it to me, although I'm not to accept tokens from strange men either.

And yet, and yet . . . those cashews smell so yummy and my stomach is growling. I look up at Minerva with my sad puppy dog look, and she gives me the nod. "Thank you very much," I say, taking the cone, and suddenly, the young man is sitting to my left, and peering at the lesson on my lap.

"What a lovely drawing," he says. I could have died! There it was, the *thing* and its two balls. Minerva and I giggled so hard, I started choking on a cashew, and the young man smiled away, thinking he had said something very clever!

Christmas Eve

My dearest, darling Little Book!

I am so excited! Christmas and then New Year's and then Three Kings—so many holidays all at once! It is hard to sit still and reflect! My soul just wants to have fun!

My little niece and nephew are staying through Three Kings' Day. Yes, at ten, I am an aunt twice over. My sister Patria has those two babies and is pregnant with a third one. Noris is so cute, one year old, my little doll. Nelson is three and his is the first boy's thing I've seen close up, not counting animals.

First Day of 1946

Little Book,

I pulled out *Regular* from under my pillow for my New Year's fortune. Mamá frowns that this isn't allowed by the pope, but I have to think fortunes really do tell the truth. My first day of the year wasn't *Good* and it wasn't *Bad*, just *Regular*.

It started out with Patria scolding me for telling Nelson ghost stories. I know that Patria is pregnant and not feeling all that well. Still, doesn't she remember she used to play Dark Passages with me when I was only four?

And it was Fela who told me the zombie story. I just repeated it.

It takes the joy out of making my resolves, but here they are.

<u>Resolves of María Teresa Mirabal for 1946:</u>

I resolve not to scare Nelson with scary stories.

I resolve to be diligent with my tasks and not fall asleep when I say my prayers.

I resolve not to think of clothes when I am in church.

I resolve to be chaste, as that is a noble thing to do. (Sor Asunción said we should all resolve this as young ladies in the holy Catholic and Apostolic church.)

I resolve not to be so tenderhearted as even Minerva says crying will bring on prematuring wrinkles.

I think that is enough resolves for a *regular* year.

Friday, January 4

Dearest Little Book,

We went all the way to the shops in Santiago. They were swamped. Everyone shopping for Three Kings. We had a list made up with things we needed. Papá had given me some money for helping him out at the store. He calls me his little secretary.

I talked Mamá into letting me buy another pair of shoes. She didn't see why I needed a second pair since she just got me my First Communion ones. But these newest ones are *patent leather*, and I have *always* wanted patent leather shoes. I must admit Minerva helped with some of the convincing.

Minerva is so smart. She always finds ways around Mamá.

Like today, Minerva found this cute red-and-white checkered swimsuit with a little skirt. When she went to buy it, Mamá reminded Minerva of her *promesa*. Last night at dinner, Minerva announced that this year she's giving up swimming in our lagoon in exchange for divine help in becoming a lawyer. Minerva drops hints as big as bombs, Papá always says.

"I don't plan to use it," Minerva explained to Mamá. "But how can my *promesa* have any bite unless I have a pretty suit to tempt me?"

"You are going to argue with Saint Peter at the gate," Mamá said. But she was smiling and shaking her head.

Minerva's new
swimsuit

My new shoes

(The bows are
snap-ons)

(The bag
doesn't come
with it)

Saturday, January 5

Dear Little Book,

Cousin Berto is so dear. His older brother Raúl, too, but Berto is
especially special-minded, if that is a word.

Yesterday when Tía Flor was up with the boys, Mamá was bemoan-
ing that her rose bushes were so scrabbly and saying she wasn't going
to be seeing much of her favorite flowers this year. Right after breakfast this morning, Berto appears with a big basketful of the most beautiful roses for her he had picked himself. Tía's garden has been
blooming every variety. Berto had arranged them so specially in the
basket. He had picked them with long stems too. Isn't that unheard of
for a boy?

The whole house is as sweet as a perfume shop this morning.

Three Kings Day

Dear Little Book,

I had such a time deciding between the patent leather and white
leather for church today. I finally settled for the white pair as Mamá
picked those out for my First Communion, and I wanted her to feel
that they were still my favorites.

Afterwards at Three Kings dinner with all the uncles and cute cousins, there was a funny little moment. Tío Pepe reminded us of the big parade next Sunday for Benefactor's Day, and Minerva said something like why don't we go celebrate at the cemetery. The room went silent as a tomb, all right.

I guess I do have a reflection. Why should we celebrate Benefactor's Day in the cemetery? I asked Minerva, but she said it was just a bad joke, forget she said so.

Benefactor's Day

My dear Little Book,

We're expecting Tío Pepe any moment. He is coming in the old wagon and taking us to the celebrations in Salcedo. After the parade, there's going to be recitations and a big party over at the town hall. Papá is going to say the speech for the Trujillo Tillers!

This time I'm inaugurating my patent leather shoes and a baby blue poplin dress with a little jacket to match. Patria made them for me with fabric I picked out.

While we're waiting, I am taking these few minutes to wish El Jefe Happy Benefactor's Day with all my heart. I feel so lucky that we have him for a president. I am even born the same month he is (October) and only nine days (and forty-four years!) apart. I keep thinking it shows something special about my character.

Monday, January 14

Dear best friend Little Book,

Back at school after the holidays, and I am so homesick. Really, I am writing to keep myself from crying.

Daysi is now best friends with Rita. They both live in Puerto Plata, so they became best friends over the holidays. Maybe Lidia will be my best friend now. She is not coming back until after the Virgencita's feast day on the 21st as her whole family is making the pilgrimage to Higüey.

We are having Rest & Silence before lights-out. We must keep quiet and not visit with each other, but think only of our immortal souls.

I am so tired of mine.

Monday, February 18

Dear Little Book,

This morning without warning, I was summoned to the principal's office, and my heart dropped when I saw Minerva there, too. At first, I thought someone had died in our family until I noticed Minerva eyeballing me as if to say, watch what you say, girl.

Sor Asunción comes right out and says your older sister has been caught sneaking out of school. Then, before I can even put that in my head, she asks me if our Tío Mon, who lives in La Vega, is ill, yes or no. I take one look at Minerva's sick-looking face and I nod yes, our Tío Mon is ill, and then I invent with *sarampión*, last I heard.

Minerva's face recovers. She flashes our principal an I-told-you-so look.

I guess I even improved upon her lie. Now Minerva could explain her sneaking out. *Sarampión's* so contagious, the sisters would've never let her visit if she'd asked.

Thursday, February 21

Dear Little Book,

I've been worrying about Minerva sneaking out and lying about Tío Mon. Today, after our courtyard rosary, I cornered her behind the statue of the Merciful Mother. What is going on? I asked, but she tried to brush me off with a joke, "Now, little sister, you don't want us to talk behind the Virgin's back, do you?"

I said yes, yes I do. So Minerva said I was too young to be told some things. That made me angry. I told her that if I was going to commit a Mortal sin, as lying to a religious can't be Venial, the least Minerva could do was tell me what I was risking my immortal soul for.

She seemed pretty impressed with my arguing back at her like that. She's always telling me to stand up for myself, but I guess she didn't figure I'd stand up to her.

She promised to tell me later when we can have a more private conversation.

Sunday, February 24

Little Book,

The whole school went to the Little Park of the Dead today. Minerva and I had a chance to talk and she told me everything. Now I am worried to death again. I swear my older sister will be the death of me!

It turns out she and Elsa and Lourdes and Sinita have been going to some secret meetings over at Don Horacio's house! Don Horacio is Elsa's grandfather who is in trouble with the police because he won't do things he's supposed to, like hang a picture of our president in his house. Minerva says the police don't kill him because he is so old, he will soon die on his own without any bother to them.

I asked Minerva why she was doing such a dangerous thing. And then, she said the strangest thing. She wanted me to grow up in a free country.

"And it isn't that already?" I asked. My chest was getting all tight. I felt one of my asthma attacks coming on.

Minerva didn't answer me. I supposed she could see that I was already upset enough. She took both my hands in hers as if we were getting ready to jump together into a deep spot in the lagoon of Ojo de Agua. "Breathe slowly and deeply," she intoned, "slowly and deeply."

I pictured myself on a hot day falling, slowly and deeply, into those cold layers of water. I held on tight to my sister's hands, no longer afraid of anything but that she might let go.

Monday, February 25

Dearest Little Book,

It is so strange now I know something I'm not supposed to know. Everything looks just a little different.

I see a *guardia*, and I think, who have you killed. I hear a police siren, and I think who is going to be killed. See what I mean?

I see the picture of our president with eyes that follow me around the room, and I am thinking he is trying to catch me doing something wrong. Before, I always thought our president was like God, watching over everything I did.

I am not saying I don't love our president, because I do. It's like if I were to find out Papá did something wrong. I would still love him, wouldn't I?

Sunday, March 3

Oh dear! Little Book!

Tío Mon appears today for visiting hours with some letters and a parcel for us, and almost the first words out of Sor Asunción's mouth are "And how are you feeling, Don Ramón?" I just about died of flabbergastedness, if that is a word. Minerva, who is much quicker on her feet, just hooked her arm in his and whisked him away saying, "Tío Mon, a nice stroll will do you good." Tío Mon looked a little confused, but Minerva had him through the arm as well as around her little finger, so off he goes.

About the letters he brought me. Dear Little Book, here I am ten years old and already getting beaus. Berto wrote again. I've shown Minerva all his letters and she smiles and says they are "sweet, boyish letters."

I confess I didn't show her his last one.

It's not that it was mushy, but I felt sort of shy about it. Berto wrote so sympathizingly about my homesickness and signed himself, "your Stronghold."

I do like the sound of that.

Tuesday, April 30

Dearest Little Book,

This new friend of Minerva's, Hilda, is really rude. She wears trousers and a beret slanted on her head like she is Michelangelo. Minerva met her at one of her secret meetings at Don Horacio's house. Very soon this Hilda was always at Inmaculada. I think the sisters felt sorry for her because she is some kind of orphan. Rather, she made herself an orphan, I am sure. Her parents probably just died of shock to hear that girl talk!

She says the most awful things like she isn't sure God exists. Poor Sor Asunción. She keeps giving Hilda little booklets to read that will explain everything. I've seen what happens to those little booklets the minute our principal turns her back. The nuns have let her get away with her fresh ways for a while, but today, they finally put their foot down.

Sor Asunción asked Hilda if she wouldn't like to join us for Holy Communion, and Hilda said that she liked a heartier menu!

So, she was asked to leave and not come back. "She has a very poor attitude," is how Sor Asunción explained it, "and your sister and her friends are catching it." Although I hated to hear anyone criticize Minerva, I had to agree about Hilda.

Friday, June 27

My dear secret Little Book,

All week guards have been coming in and out, looking for Hilda. Minerva has told me the whole story.

Hilda appeared a few nights ago at Inmaculada wanting to hide! What happened was she hid some secret papers in the trunk of a car she borrowed, and she ran out of gas on the highway. A friend came to pick her up, and they got some gas in a can at a station, but when they were on the way back, they saw police swarming around the car. The trunk was pried open. Hilda got her friend to drop her off at Inmaculada where she woke up Minerva and her friends. They all argued what to do. Finally, they decided they had to ask the sisters for help.

So, late that night, they knocked on the convent door. Sor Asunción appeared, in her night dress, wearing a nightcap, and Minerva told her the problem.

Minerva said she still doesn't know if Sor Asunción agreed to help Hilda out of the goodness of her heart or because this was a perfect lesson to teach that fresh girl. Imagine! Hilda, who doesn't even believe in God!

The police have been here again today. They passed right by Sor Hilda with her hands tucked in her sleeves and her head bowed before the statue of the Merciful Mother. If I weren't so scared, I'd be laughing.

41

Thursday, July 4
Home at last!

Dear Little Book,

Minerva graduated this last Sunday. Everyone went to La Vega to watch her get her diploma. Even Patria with her stomach big as a house. She is expecting any day now.

We are home for the summer. I can't wait to go swimming. Minerva says she's taking me to our lagoon and diving right in herself in her "temptation" swimsuit. She says why keep her *promesa* when Mamá and Papá still won't let her go to law school in the capital?

I'm going to spend the summer learning things I *really* want to learn! Like (1) doing embroidery from Patria (2) keeping books from Dedé (3) cooking cakes from my Tía Flor (I'll get to see more of my cute cousin Berto, and Raúl, too!!!) (4) spells from Fela (I better not tell Mamá!) (5) how to argue so I'm right, and anything else Minerva wants to teach me.

Sunday, July 20

Oh Little Book,

We all just got back from the cemetery burying Patria's baby boy that was born dead yesterday.

Patria is very sad and cries all the time. Mamá keeps repeating that the Lord knows what he does and Patria nods like she doesn't half believe it. Pedrito just cracks his knuckles and consoles her by saying that they can have another one real soon. Imagine making such a gross promise to someone who is already having a hard enough time.

They are going to stay with us until she feels better. I am trying to be brave, but every time I think of that pretty baby dead in a box like it doesn't have a soul at all, I just start to cry.

I better stop till I get over my emotions.

Wednesday, in a hurry

My dearest Little Book, Oh my dearest,

Minerva asks if I'm ready to hand you over. I say, give me a minute to explain things and say goodbye.

Hilda has been caught! She was grabbed by the police while trying to leave the convent. Everyone in Don Horacio's meeting group has been told to destroy anything that would make them guilty.

Minerva is burying all her poems and papers and letters. She says she hadn't meant to read my diary, but it was lying around, and she noticed Hilda's name. She says it was not really right to read it, but sometimes you have to do something wrong for a higher good. (Some more of that lawyer talk she likes so much!) She says we have to bury you, too.

It won't be forever, my dear Little Book, I promise. As soon as things are better, Minerva says we can dig up our treasure box. She's told Pedrito about our plan and he's already found a spot among his cacao where he's going to dig a hole for us to bury our box.

So, my dearest, sweetest Little Book, now you know.

Minerva was right. My soul has gotten deeper since I started writing in you. But this is what I want to know that not even Minerva knows.

What do I do now to fill up that hole?

Here ends my Little Book

Goodbye
for now, not forever
(I hope)

43

CHAPTER FOUR

Patria

1946

From the beginning, I felt it, snug inside my heart, the pearl of great price. No one had to tell me to believe in God or to love everything that lives. I did it automatically like a shoot inching its way towards the light.

Even being born, I was coming out, hands first, as if reaching up for something. Thank goodness, the midwife checked Mamá at the last minute and lowered my arms the way you fold in a captive bird's wings so it doesn't hurt itself trying to fly.

So you could say I was born, but I wasn't really here. One of those spirit babies, *alelá*, as the country people say. My mind, my heart, my soul in the clouds.

It took some doing and undoing to bring me down to earth.

From the beginning, I was so good, Mamá said she'd forget I was there. I slept through the night, entertaining myself if I woke up and no one was around. Within the year, Dedé was born, and then a year later Minerva came along, three babies in diapers! The little house was packed tight as a box with things that break. Papá hadn't finished the new bedroom yet, so Mamá put me and Dedé in a little cot in the hallway. One morning, she found me changing Dedé's wet diaper, but what was funny was that I hadn't wanted to disturb Mamá for a clean one, so I had taken off mine to put on my baby sister.

"You'd give anything away, your clothes, your food, your toys. Word got around, and while I was out, the country people would send their kids over to ask you for a cup of rice or a jar of cooking oil. You had no sense of holding on to things.

"I was afraid," she confessed, "that you wouldn't live long, that you were already the way we were here to become."

Padre Ignacio finally calmed her fears. He said that maybe I had a calling for the religious life that was manifesting itself early on. He said, with his usual savvy and humor, "Give her time, Doña Chea, give her time. I've seen many a little angel mature into a fallen one."

His suggestion was what got the ball rolling. I was called, even I thought so. When we played make-believe, I'd put a sheet over my shoulders and pretend I was walking down long corridors, saying my beads, in my starched vestments.

I'd write out my religious name in all kinds of script—*Sor Mercedes*— the way other girls were trying out their given names with the surnames of cute boys. I'd see those boys and think, Ah yes, they will come to Sor Mercedes in times of trouble and lay their curly heads in my lap so I can comfort them. My immortal soul wants to take the whole blessed world in! But, of course, it was my body, hungering, biding its time against the tyranny of my spirit.

At fourteen, I went away to Inmaculada Concepción, and all the country people around here thought I was entering the convent. "What a pity," they said, "such a pretty girl."

That's when I started looking in the mirror. I was astonished to find, not the child I had been, but a young lady with high firm breasts and a sweet oval face. She smiled, dimpling prettily, but the dark, humid eyes were full of yearning. I put my hands up against the glass to remind her that she, too, must reach up for the things she didn't understand.

At school the nuns watched me. They saw the pains I took keeping my back straight during early mass, my hands steepled and held up of my own volition, not perched on the back of a pew as if petition were conversation. During Lent, they noted no meat passed my lips, not even a steaming broth when a bad catarrh confined me to the infirmary.

I was not yet sixteen that February when Sor Asunción summoned me to her office. The flamboyants, I remember, were in full bloom. Entering that sombre study, I could see just outside the window the brilliant red flames lit in every tree, and beyond, some threatening thunderclouds.

"Patria Mercedes," Sor Asunción said, rising and coming forward from behind her desk. I knelt for her blessing and kissed the crucifix she held to my lips. I was overcome and felt the heart's tears brimming in my eyes. Lent had just begun, and I was always in a state during those forty days of the passion of Christ.

"Come, come, come"—she helped me up—"we have much to speak of." She led me, not to the stiff chair set up, interrogative style, in front of her desk, but to the plush crimson cushion of her window seat.

We sat one at each end. Even in the dimming light I could see her pale gray eyes flecked with knowing. I smelled her wafer smell and I knew I was in the presence of the holy. My heart beat fast, scared and deeply excited.

"Patria Mercedes, have you given much thought to the future?" she asked me in a whispery voice.

Surely it would be pride to claim a calling at my young age! I shook my head, blushing, and looked down at my palms, marked, the country people say, with a map of the future.

"You must pray to the Virgencita for guidance," she said.

I could feel the tenderness of her gaze, and I looked up. Beyond her, I saw the first zigzag of lightning, and heard, far off, the rumble of thunder. "I do, Sister, I pray at all times to know His will so it can be done."

She nodded. "We have noticed from the first how seriously you take your religious obligations. Now you must listen deeply in case He is calling. We would welcome you as one of us if that is His Will."

I felt the sweet release of tears. My face was wet with them. "Now, now," she said, patting my knees. "Let's not be sad."

"I'm not sad, Sister," I said when I had regained some composure. "These are tears of joy and hope that He will make His will known to me."

"He will," she assured me. "Listen at all times. In wakefulness, in sleep, as you work and as you play."

I nodded and then she added, "Now let us pray together that soon, soon, you will know." And I prayed with her, a *Hail Mary* and an *Our Father*, and I tried hard but I could not keep my eyes from straying to the flame trees, their blossoms tumbling in the wind of the coming storm.

———————

There was a struggle, but no one could tell. It came in the dark in the evil hours when the hands wake with a life of their own. They rambled over my growing body, they touched the plumping of my chest, the mound of my belly, and on down. I tried reining them in, but they broke loose, night after night.

For Three Kings, I asked for a crucifix for above my bed. Nights, I laid it beside me so that my hands, waking, could touch his suffering flesh instead and be tamed from their shameful wanderings. The ruse worked, the hands slept again, but other parts of my body began to wake.

My mouth, for instance, craved sweets, figs in their heavy syrup, coconut candy, soft golden flans. When those young men whose surnames had been appropriated for years by my mooning girlfriends came to the store and drummed their big hands on the counter, I wanted to take each finger in my mouth and feel their calluses with my tongue.

My shoulders, my elbows, my knees ached to be touched. Not to mention my back and the hard cap of my skull. "Here's a *peseta*," I'd say to Minerva. "Play with my hair." She'd laugh, and combing her fingers through it, she'd ask, "Do you really believe what the gospel says? He knows how many strands of hair are on your head?"

"Come, come, little sister," I'd admonish her. "Don't play with the word of God."

"I'm going to count them," she'd say. "I want to see how hard His work is."

She'd start in as if it were not an impossible task, *"Uno, dos, tres . . ."* Soon her gratifying fingering and her lilting voice would lull me to sleep again.

———————

It was after my conference with Sor Asunción, once I had begun praying to know my calling, that suddenly, like a lull in a storm, the cravings stopped. All was quiet. I slept obediently through the night. The struggle was over, but I was not sure who had won.

I thought this was a sign. Sor Asunción had mentioned that the calling could come in all sorts of ways, dreams, visitations, a crisis. Soon after our conference, school was out for Holy Week. The nuns closed themselves up in their convent for their yearly mortifications in honor of the crucifixion of their bridegroom and Lord, Jesus Christ.

I went home to do likewise, sure in my bones that I would hear His calling now. I joined in Padre Ignacio's Holy Week activities, going to the nightly novenas and daily mass. On Holy Thursday, I brought my pan and towels along with the other penitents for washing the feet of the parishioners at the door of the church.

The lines were long that night. One after another, I washed pairs of feet, not bothering to look up, entranced in my prayerful listening. Then, of a sudden, I noticed a pale young foot luxuriant with dark hair in my fresh pan of water, and my legs went soft beneath me.

I washed that foot thoroughly, lifting it by the ankle to soap the underside as one does a baby's legs in cleaning its bottom. Then, I started in on the other one. I worked diligently, oblivious to the long lines stretching away in the dark. When I was done, I could not help looking up.

A young man was staring down at me, his face alluring in the same animal way as his feet. The cheeks were swarthy with a permanent shadow, his thick brows joined in the center. Underneath his thin *guayabera*, I could see the muscles of his broad shoulders shifting as he reached down and gave me a wad of bills to put in the poor box as his donation.

Later, he would say that I gave him a beatific smile. Why not? I had seen the next best thing to Jesus, my earthly groom. The struggle was over, and I had my answer, though it was not the one I had assumed I would get. For Easter mass, I dressed in glorious yellow with a flamboyant blossom in my hair. I arrived early to prepare for singing

Alleluia with the other girls, and there he was waiting for me by the choir stairs.

Sixteen, and it was settled, though we had not spoken a word to each other. When I returned to school, Sor Asunción greeted me at the gate. Her eyes searched my face, but I would not let it give her an answer. "Have you heard?" she asked, taking both my hands in her hands.

"No, Sister, I have not," I lied.

April passed, then came May, the month of Mary. Mid-May a letter arrived for me, just my name and Inmaculada Concepción in a gruff hand on the envelope. Sor Asunción called me to her office to deliver it, an unusual precaution since the sisters limited themselves to monitoring our correspondence by asking us what news we had gotten from home. She eyed me as I took the envelope. I felt the gravity of the young man's foot in my hand. I smelled the sweat and soil and soap on the tender skin. I blushed deeply.

"Well?" Sor Asunción said, as if she had asked a question and I was tarrying in my answer. "Have you heard, Patria Mercedes?" Her voice had grown stern.

I cleared my throat, but I could not speak. I was so sorry to disappoint her, and yet I felt there was nothing to apologize for. At last, my spirit was descending into flesh, and there was more, not less, of me to praise God. It tingled in my feet, warmed my hands and legs, flared in my gut. "Yes," I confessed at last, "I have heard."

I did not go back to Inmaculada in the fall with Dedé and Minerva. I stayed and helped Papá with minding the store and sewed frocks for María Teresa, all the while waiting for him to come around.

His name was Pedrito González, the son of an old farming family from the next town over. He had been working his father's land since he was a boy, so he had not had much formal schooling. But he could count to high numbers, launching himself first with his ten fingers. He read books, slowly, mouthing words, holding them reverently like an altar boy the missal for the officiating priest. He was born to the soil, and there was something about his strong body, his thick hands, his shapely mouth that seemed akin to the roundness of the hills and the rich, rolling valley of El Cibao.

And why, you might ask, was the otherworldly, deeply religious Patria attracted to such a creature? I'll tell you. I felt the same excitement as when I'd been able to coax a wild bird or stray cat to eat out of my hand.

We courted decorously, not like Dedé and Jaimito, two little puppies you constantly have to watch over so they don't get into trouble— Mamá has been telling me the stories. He'd come over after a day in the fields, all washed up, the comb marks still in his wet hair, looking uncomfortable in his good *guayabera*. Is pity always a part of love? It was all I could do to keep from touching him.

Once only did I almost let go, that Christmas. The wedding was planned for February 24th, three days before my seventeenth birthday. Papá had said we must wait until I was seventeen, but he consented to giving me those three days of dispensation. Otherwise, we would be upon the Lenten season, when really it's not right to be marrying.

We were walking to our parish church for the Mass of the Rooster, Mamá, Papá, my sisters. Pedrito and I lagged behind the others, talking softly. He was making his simple declarations, and I was teasing him into having to declare them over and over again. He could not love me very much, I protested, because all he said was that he loved me. According to Minerva, those truly in love spoke poetry to their beloved.

He stopped, and took me by the shoulders. I could barely see his face that moonless night. "You're not getting a fancy, high-talking man in Pedrito González," he said rather fiercely. "But you are getting a man who adores you like he does this rich soil we're standing on."

He reached down and took a handful of dirt and poured it in my hand. And then, he began kissing me, my face, my neck, my breasts. I had to, I had to stop him! It would not be right, not on this night in which the word was still so newly fleshed, the porcelain baby just being laid by Padre Ignacio—as we hurried down the path—in His crèche.

You'd think there was nothing else but the private debates of my flesh and spirit going on, the way I've left out the rest of my life. Don't believe it! Ask anyone around here who was the easiest, friendliest, simplest of the Mirabal girls, and they'd tell you, Patria Mercedes. The day I married, the whole population of Ojo de Agua turned out to wish me well. I burst out crying, already homesick for my village even though I was only moving fifteen minutes away.

It was hard at first living in San José de Conuco away from my family, but I got used to it. Pedrito came in from the fields at noon hungry for his dinner. Afterwards we had siesta, and his other hunger had to be satisfied, too. The days started to fill, Nelson was born, and two years later, Noris, and soon I had a third belly growing larger each day. They say around here that bellies stir up certain cravings or aversions. Well, the first two bellies were simple, all I craved were certain foods, but this belly had me worrying all the time about my sister Minerva.

It was dangerous the way she was speaking out against the government. Even in public, she'd throw a jab at our president or at the church for supporting him. One time, the salesman who was trying to sell Papá a car brought out an expensive Buick. Extolling its many virtues, the salesman noted that this was El Jefe's favorite car. Right out, Minerva told Papá, "Another reason not to buy it." The whole family walked around in fear for a while.

I couldn't understand why Minerva was getting so worked up. El Jefe was no saint, everyone knew that, but among the *bandidos* that had been in the National Palace, this one at least was building churches and schools, paying off our debts. Every week his picture was in the papers next to Monsignor Pittini, overseeing some good deed.

But I couldn't reason with reason herself. I tried a different tack. "It's a dirty business, you're right. That's why we women shouldn't get involved."

Minerva listened with that look on her face of just waiting for me to finish. "I don't agree with you, Patria," she said, and then in her usual, thorough fashion, she argued that women had to come out of the dark ages.

She got so she wouldn't go to church unless Mamá made a scene. She argued that she was more connected to God reading her Rousseau than when she was at mass listening to Padre Ignacio intoning the Nicene Creed. "He sounds like he's gargling with words," she made fun.

"I worry that you're losing your faith," I told her. "That's our pearl of great price; you know, without it, we're nothing."

"You should worry more about *your* beloved church. Even Padre Ignacio admits some priests are on double payroll."

"*Ay,* Minerva," was all I could manage. I stroked my aching belly. For days, I'd been feeling a heaviness inside me. And I admit it, Minerva's talk had begun affecting me. I started noting the deadness in Padre Ignacio's voice, the tedium between the gospel and communion, the dry papery feel of the host in my mouth. My faith was shifting, and I was afraid.

"Sit back," Minerva said, kindly, seeing the lines of weariness on my face. "Let me finish counting those hairs."

And suddenly, I was crying in her arms, because I could feel the waters breaking, the pearl of great price slipping out, and I realized I was giving birth to something dead I had been carrying inside me.

After I lost the baby, I felt a strange vacancy. I was an empty house with a sign in front, *Se Vende,* For Sale. Any vagrant thought could take me.

I woke up in a panic in the middle of the night, sure that some *brujo* had put a spell on me and that's why the baby had died. This from Patria Mercedes, who had always kept herself from such low superstitions.

I fell asleep and dreamed the Yanquis were back, but it wasn't my grandmother's house they were burning—it was Pedrito's and mine. My babies, all three of them, were going up in flames. I leapt from the bed crying, "Fire! Fire!"

I wondered if the dead child were not a punishment for my having turned my back on my religious calling? I went over and over my life to this point, complicating the threads with my fingers, knotting everything.

We moved in with Mamá until I could get my strength back. She kept trying to comfort me. "That poor child, who knows what it was spared!"

"It is the Lord's will," I agreed, but the words sounded hollow to my ear.

Minerva could tell. One day, we were lying side by side on the hammock strung just inside the *galería.* She must have caught me gazing at our picture of the Good Shepherd, talking to his lambs. Beside him hung the required portrait of El Jefe, touched up to make him look better than he was. "They're a pair, aren't they?" she noted.

That moment, I understood her hatred. My family had not been personally hurt by Trujillo, just as before losing my baby, Jesus had not taken anything away from me. But others had been suffering great losses. There were the Perozos, not a man left in that family. And Martínez Reyna and his wife murdered in their bed, and thousands of Haitians massacred at the border, making the river, they say, still run red—¡Ay, Dios santo!

I had heard, but I had not believed. Snug in my heart, fondling my pearl, I had ignored their cries of desolation. How could our loving, all-powerful Father allow us to suffer so? I looked up, challenging Him. And the two faces had merged!

I moved back home with the children in early August, resuming my duties, putting a good face over a sore heart, hiding the sun—as the people around here say—with a finger. And slowly, I began coming back from the dead. What brought me back? It wasn't God, *no señor.* It was Pedrito, his grief so silent and animal-like. I put aside my own grief to rescue him from his.

Every night I gave him my milk as if he were my lost child, and afterwards I let him do things I never would have before. "Come here, *mi amor,*" I'd whisper to guide him through the dark bedroom when he showed up after having been out late in the fields. Then I was the one on horseback, riding him hard and fast until I'd gotten somewhere far away from my aching heart.

His grief hung on. He never spoke of it, but I could tell. One night, a few weeks after the baby was buried, I felt him leaving our bed ever so quietly. My heart sank. He was seeking other consolations in one of the thatched huts around our *rancho*. I wanted to know the full extent of my losses, so I said nothing and followed him outside.

It was one of those big, bright nights of August when the moon has that luminous color of something ready for harvest. Pedrito came out of the shed with a spade and a small box. He walked guardedly, looking over his shoulder. At last, he stopped at a secluded spot and began to dig a little grave.

I could see now that his grief was dark and odd. I would have to be gentle in coaxing him back. I crouched behind a big ceiba, my fist in my mouth, listening to the thud of soil hitting the box.

After he was gone to the yucca fields the next day, I searched and searched, but I could not find the spot again. *Ay, Dios*, how I worried that he had taken our baby from consecrated ground. The poor innocent would be stuck in limbo all eternity! I decided to check first before insisting Pedrito dig him back up.

So I went to the graveyard and enlisted a couple of *campesinos* with the excuse that I'd forgotten the baby's Virgencita medallion. After several feet of digging, their shovels struck the small coffin.

"Open it," I said.

"Let us put in the medal ourselves, Doña Patria," they offered, reluctant to pry open the lid. "It's not right for you to see."

"I want to see," I said.

I should have desisted, I should not have seen what I saw. My child, a bundle of swarming ants! My child, decomposing like any animal! I fell to my knees, overcome by the horrid stench.

"Close him up," I said, having seen enough.

"What of the medal, Doña Patria?" they reminded me.

It won't do him any good, I thought, but I slipped it in. I bowed my head, and if this was prayer, then you could say I prayed. I said the names of my sisters, my children, my husband, Mamá, Papá. I was deciding right then and there to spare all those I love.

And so it was that Patria Mercedes Mirabal de González was known all around San José de Conuco as well as Ojo de Agua as a model

Catholic wife and mother. I fooled them all! Yes, for a long time after losing my faith, I went on, making believe.

————

It wasn't my idea to go on the pilgrimage to Higüey. That was Mamá's brainstorm. There had been sightings of the Virgencita. She had appeared one early morning to an old *campesino* coming into town with his donkey loaded down with garlic. Then a little girl had seen the Virgencita swinging on the bucket that was kept decoratively dangling above the now dry well where she had once appeared back in the 1600s. It was too whimsical a sighting for the archbishop to pronounce as authentic, but still. Even El Jefe had attributed the failure of the invasion from Cayo Confites to our patron saint.

"If she's helping him—" was all Minerva got out. Mamá silenced her with a look that was the grownup equivalent of the old slipper on our butts.

"We women in the family need the Virgencita's help," Mamá reminded her.

She was right, too. Everyone knew my public sorrow, the lost baby, but none my private one, my loss of faith. Then there was Minerva with her restless mind and her rebellious spirit. Settle her down, Mamá prayed. Mate's asthma was worse than ever and Mamá had transferred her to a closer school in San Francisco. Only Dedé was doing well, but she had some big decisions ahead of her and she wanted the Virgencita's help.

So, the five of us made our plans. I decided not to take the children, so I could give myself over to the pilgrimage. "You sure you women are going on a pilgrimage?" Pedrito teased us. He was happy again, his hands fresh with my body, a quickness in his face. "Five good-looking women visiting the Virgin, I don't believe it!"

My sisters all looked towards me, expecting I would chide my husband for making light of sacred things. But I had lost my old strictness about sanctity. God, who had played the biggest joke on us, could stand a little teasing.

I rolled my eyes flirtatiously. "*Ay, sí,*" I said, "those roosters of Higüey!"

A cloud passed over Pedrito's face. He was not a jealous man. I'll say

it plain: he was not a man of imagination, so he wasn't afflicted by suspicions and worries. But if he saw or heard something he didn't like,
even if he had said it himself, the color would rise in his face and his
nostrils flare like a spirited stallion's.

"Let them crow all they want," I went on, "I've got my handsome
rooster in San José de Conuco. And my *two* little chicks," I added. Nelson and Noris looked up, alerted by the play in my voice.

We set out in the new car, a used Ford Papá had bought for the store, so
he said. But we all knew who it was really for—the only person who
knew how to drive it besides Papá. He had hoped that this consolation
prize would settle Minerva happily in Ojo de Agua. But every day she
was on the road, to Santiago, to San Francisco, to Moca—on store business, she said. Dedé, left alone to mind the store, complained there were
more deliveries than sales being made.

María Teresa was home from school for the long holiday weekend in
honor of El Jefe's birthday, so she came along. We joked about all the
commemorative marches and boring speeches we had been spared by
leaving this particular weekend. We could talk freely in the car, since
there was no one to overhear us.

"Poor Papá," María Teresa said. "He'll have to go all by himself."

"Papá will take very good care of himself, I'm sure, " Mamá said in a
sharp voice. We all looked at her surprised. I began to wonder why
Mamá had suggested this pilgrimage. Mamá, who hated even day trips.
Something big was troubling her enough to stir her far from home.

It took us a while to get to Higüey, since first we hit traffic going to
the capital for the festivities, and then we had to head east on poor
roads crossing a dry flat plain. I couldn't remember sitting for five hours
straight in years. But the time flew by. We sang, told stories, reminisced
about this or that.

At one point, Minerva suggested we just take off into the mountains
like the *gavilleros* had done. We had heard the stories of the bands of
campesinos who took to the hills to fight the Yanqui invaders. Mamá had
been a young woman, eighteen, when the Yanquis came.

"Did you sympathize with the *gavilleros*, Mamá?" Minerva wanted to know, looking in the rearview mirror and narrowly missing a man in an ox cart going too slow. We all cried out. "He was at least a kilometer away," Minerva defended herself.

"Since when is ten feet a kilometer!" Dedé snapped. She had a knack for numbers, that one, even in an emergency.

Mamá intervened before those two could get into one of their fights. "Of course, I sympathized with our patriots. But what could we do against the Yanquis? They killed anyone who stood in their way. They burned our house down and called it a mistake. They weren't in their own country so they didn't have to answer to anyone."

"The way we Dominicans do, eh?" Minerva said with sarcasm in her voice.

Mamá was silent a moment, but we could all sense she had more to say. At last, she added, "You're right, they're all scoundrels—Dominicans, Yanquis, every last man."

"Not every one," I said. After all, I had to defend my husband.

María Teresa agreed, "Not Papá."

Mamá looked out the window a moment, her face struggling with some emotion. Then, she said quietly, "Yes, your father, too."

We protested, but Mamá would not budge—either in taking back or going further with what she had said.

Now I knew why she had come on her pilgrimage.

———

The town was jammed with eager pilgrims, and though we tried at all the decent boarding houses, we could not find a single room. Finally we called on some distant relations, who scolded us profusely for not having come to them in the first place. By then, it was dark, but from their windows as we ate the late supper they fixed us, we could see the lights of the chapel where pilgrims were keeping their vigil. I felt a tremor of excitement, as if I were about to meet an estranged friend with whom I longed to be reconciled.

Later, lying in the bed we were sharing, I joined Mamá in her goodnight rosary to the Virgencita. Her voice in the dark was full of need. At the first Sorrowful Mystery, she said Papá's full name, as if she were calling him to account, not praying for him.

"What's wrong, Mamá?" I whispered to her when we were finished. She would not tell me, but when I guessed, "Another woman?" she sighed, and then said, "*Ay*, Virgencita, why have you forsaken me?"

I closed my eyes and felt her question join mine. Yes, why? I thought. Out loud, I said, "I'm here, Mamá." It was all the comfort I had.

The next morning we woke early and set out for the chapel, telling our hosts that we were fasting so as not to give them any further bother. "We're starting our pilgrimage with lies," Minerva laughed. We breakfasted on water breads and the celebrated little cheeses of Higüey, watching the pilgrims through the door of the cafeteria. Even at this early hour, the streets were full of them.

The square in front of the small chapel was also packed. We joined the line, filing past the beggars who shook their tin cups or waved their crude crutches and canes at us. Inside, the small, stuffy chapel was lit by hundreds of votive candles. I felt woozy in a familiar girlhood way. I used the edge of my mantilla to wipe the sweat on my face as I followed behind María Teresa and Minerva, Mamá and Dedé close behind me.

The line moved slowly down the center aisle to the altar, then up a set of stairs to a landing in front of the Virgencita's picture. María Teresa and Minerva and I managed to squeeze up on the landing together. I peered into the locked case smudged with fingerprints from pilgrims touching the glass.

All I saw at first was a silver frame studded with emeralds and agates and pearls. The whole thing looked gaudy and insincere. Then I made out a sweet, pale girl tending a trough of straw on which lay a tiny baby. A man stood behind her in his red robes, his hands touching his heart. If they hadn't been wearing halos, they could have been a young couple up near Constanza where the *campesinos* are reputed to be very white.

"Hail Mary," María Teresa began, "full of grace . . ."

I turned around and saw the packed pews, hundreds of weary, upturned faces, and it was as if I'd been facing the wrong way all my life. My faith stirred. It kicked and somersaulted in my belly, coming alive. I turned back and touched my hand to the dirty glass.

"Holy Mary, Mother of God," I joined in.

I stared at her pale, pretty face and challenged her. Here I am, Virgencita. Where are you?

And I heard her answer me with the coughs and cries and whispers of the crowd: *Here, Patria Mercedes, I'm here, all around you. I've already more than appeared.*

II

1948 to 1959

CHAPTER FIVE

Dedé

1994
and
1948

Over the interview woman's head, Dedé notices the new girl throwing plantain peelings outside the kitchen shed. She has asked her not to do this. "That is why we have trash baskets," she has explained. The young maid always looks at the barrel Dedé points to as if it were an obscure object whose use is beyond her.

"You understand?" Dedé asks her.

"*Sí, señora.*" The young girl smiles brightly as if she has done something right. At Dedé's age, it is hard to start in with new servants. But Tono is needed over at the museum to take the busloads through the house and answer the phone. Tono has been with them forever. Of course, so had Fela until she started going wacky after the girls died.

Possessed by the spirits of the girls, can you imagine! People were coming from as far away as Barahona to talk "through" this ebony black sibyl with the Mirabal sisters. Cures had begun to be attributed to Patria; María Teresa was great on love woes; and as for Minerva, she was competing with the Virgencita as Patroness of Impossible Causes. What an embarrassment in her own backyard, as if she, Dedé, had sanctioned all this. And she knew nothing. The bishop had called on her finally. That's how Dedé had found out.

It was a Friday, Fela's day off. As soon as the bishop had left, Dedé headed for the shed behind her house. She had jiggled the door just so to unlock it—a little trick she knew—and *¡Dios mío!* The sight took her breath away. Fela had set up an altar with pictures of the girls cut out from the popular posters that appeared each November. Before them, a table was laid out, candles and the mandatory cigar and bottle of rum. But most frightening was the picture of Trujillo that had once hung on Dedé and Jaimito's wall. Dedé was sure she had thrown it in the trash. What the devil was *he* doing here if, as Fela argued later, she was working only with good spirits?

Dedé had pulled the door to, letting the old lock catch again. Her head was spinning. When Fela returned, Dedé offered her two alternatives. Either stop all this nonsense and clean out that shed, or. . . . She could not bring herself to state the alternative to the stooped, white-haired woman who had weathered so much with the family. She hadn't had to. The next morning, the shed was indeed empty. Fela had moved her operation down the road to what was probably a better spot—an abandoned storefront on the bus route to Salcedo.

Minou was furious when she heard what Dedé had done to Fela. Yes, that's the way she had phrased it, "What have you *done* to her, Mamá Dedé?"

"It was disrespectful to your mother's memory. She was a Catholic, Minou, a Catholic!"

Minou would have none of it. Dedé had already told her too much about her mother's falling out with the church. Sometimes Dedé worries that she has not kept enough from the children. But she wants them to know the living breathing women their mothers were. They get enough of the heroines from everyone else.

Now, Minou stops by at Fela's whenever she comes to visit her aunt. It gives Dedé goose bumps when Minou says, "I talked to Mamá at Fela's today, and she said . . ."

Dedé shakes her head, but she always listens to what the old woman has to say.

The strangest time was when Minou came from Fela asking after Virgilio Morales. "Mamá says he's still alive. Do you know where he is, Mamá Dedé?"

"Didn't your mother tell you?" Dedé asked sarcastically. "Don't spirits know the whereabouts of all of us?"

"You sound upset, Mamá Dedé," Minou observed.

"You know I don't believe in all this spirit business. And I think it's a disgrace that you, the daughter of—"

Minou's eyes flashed with anger, and Minerva herself stood before Dedé again. "I'm my own person. I'm tired of being the daughter of a legend."

Quickly, the face of her sister fell away like water down a slanted roof. Dedé held out her arms for her dear niece-daughter. Dark mascara tears were coursing down Minou's cheeks. Didn't she, Dedé, understand that feeling of being caught in a legacy. "Forgive me," she whispered. "Of course, you have a right to be yourself."

Afterwards, Dedé confessed that she did know where Lío Morales now lived. Someone had pointed out the house to her the last time she was in the capital. The comfortable bungalow was just blocks from the dictator's huge wedding cake palace that the mobs had long ago burned down.

"So what's the message you're to deliver?" Dedé asked as casually as she could.

"Message?" Minou looked up, surprised. "I was just to say hello and how much Mamá thought of him."

"Me, too," Dedé said, and then to clarify, "Tell him I said hello, too."

"So when did all the problems start?" The interview woman's voice calls Dedé back to the present moment. Again, Dedé feels as if the woman has been eerily reading her thoughts.

"What problems?" she asks, an edge to her voice. Whatever feelings she once had for Lío never became a problem for anyone, even for herself. She had taken care of that.

"I mean the problems with the regime. When did these problems start?" The woman speaks in a soft voice as if she suspects she is intruding.

Dedé apologizes. "My mind wanders." She feels bad when she can't carry off what she considers her responsibility. To be the grande dame of the beautiful, terrible past. But it is an impossible task, impossible! After all, she is the only one left to manage the terrible, beautiful present.

"If it is too much, I can stop now," the woman offers.

Dedé waves the offer away "I was just thinking about those days. You know, everyone says our problems started after Minerva had her run-in with Trujillo at the Discovery Day dance. But the truth is Minerva was already courting trouble two or three years before that. We had this friend who was quite a radical young man. You might have heard of Virgilio Morales?"

The woman narrows her eyes as if trying to make out a figure in the distance. "I don't think I ever read about him, no."

"He was thrown out of the country so many times, the history books couldn't keep up with him! He came back from exile in '47 for a couple of years. Trujillo had announced we were going to have a free country—just like the Yanquis he was trying to butter up. We all knew this was just a show, but Lío—that's what we called him—may have gotten swept up in the idea for a while. Anyhow, he had family in this area, so we saw a lot of him for those two years before he had to leave again."

"So he was Minerva's special friend?"

Dedé feels her heart beating fast. "He was a special friend of mine and my other sisters too!" There she has said it, so why doesn't it feel good? Fighting with her dead sister over a beau, my goodness.

"Why was the friendship the beginning of problems?" The woman's head tilts with curiosity.

"Because Lío presented a very real opportunity to fight against the regime. I think that, after him, Minerva was never the same." And neither was I, she adds to herself. Yes, years after she had last seen Lío, he was still a presence in her heart and mind. Every time she went along with some insane practice of the regime, she felt his sad, sober eyes accusing her of giving in.

"How do you spell his name?" The woman has taken out a little pad and is making invisible zeroes trying to get her reluctant pen to write. "I'll look him up."

"I'll tell you what I remember of him," Dedé offers, stroking the lap of her skirt dreamily. She takes a deep breath, just the way Minou describes Fela doing right before the sisters take over her body and use her old woman's voice to assign their errands.

She remembers a hot and humid afternoon early in the year she got married. She and Minerva are at the store plowing through an inventory. Minerva is up on a stool, counting cans, correcting herself, adding "more or less," when Dedé repeats the figure before she writes it down. Usually, Dedé cannot bear such sloppiness. But today she is impatient to be done so they can close up and drive over to Tío Pepe's where the young people have been gathering evenings to play volleyball.

Her cousin Jaimito will be there. They have known each other all their lives, been paired and teased by their mothers ever since the two babies were placed in the same playpen during family gatherings. But in the last few weeks, something has been happening. All that had once annoyed Dedé about her spoiled, big-mouthed cousin now seems to quicken something in her heart. And whereas before, her mother's and Jaimito's mother's hints were the intrusion of elders into what was none of their business, now it seems the old people were perceiving destiny. If she marries Jaimito, she'll continue in the life she has always been very happy living.

Minerva must have given up calling down numbers and getting no response. She stands directly in Dedé's line of vision, waving. "Hello, hello!"

Dedé laughs at getting caught daydreaming. It is not like her at all. Usually it is Minerva whose head is somewhere else. "I was just thinking . . ." She tries to make up something. But she is not good at quick lies either. Minerva is the one with stories on the tip of her tongue.

"I know, I know," Minerva says. "You were thinking about Einstein's theory of relativity." Sometimes she can be funny. "You want to call it quits for today?" The hopeful expression on her face betrays her own wishes.

Dedé reminds them both, "We should have gotten this done a week ago!"

"This is so silly." Minerva mimics their counting. "Four crumbs of *dulce leche*; one, two, let's see, seven ants marching towards them—" Suddenly, her voice changes, "Two visitors!" They are standing at the door, Mario, one of their distributors, and a tall, pale man behind him, his glasses thick and wire-rimmed. A doctor maybe, a scholar for sure.

"We're closed," Dedé announces in case Mario is here on business. "Papá's at the house." But Minerva invites them in. "Come and rescue us, please!"

"What's wrong?" Mario says, laughing and coming into the store. "Too much work?"

"Of the uninspiring kind," Minerva says archly.

"But it needs to be done—our end-of-the-year inventory is now our new year's unfinished business." Saying it, Dedé feels annoyed at herself all over again for not having finished the job earlier.

"Maybe we can help?" The young scholar has stepped up to the counter and is gazing at the shelves behind Dedé.

"This is my cousin," Mario explains, "just come from the capital to rescue ladies in distress."

"You're at the university?" Minerva pipes up. And when the young man nods, Mario goes on to brag for his cousin. Virgilio Morales has recently returned from Venezuela where he earned his medical degree. He is now teaching in the faculty of medicine. Every weekend he comes up to the family place in Licey.

"What a serious name Virgilio." Dedé blushes. She is not used to putting herself forward in this way.

The young man's serious look fades. "That's why everyone calls me Lío."

"They call you Lío because you're always in one fix or another," Mario reminds his cousin, who laughs good-naturedly.

"Virgilio Morales . . ." Minerva muses aloud. "Your name sounds familiar. Do you know Elsa Sánchez and Sinita Perozo? They're at the university."

"Of course!" Now he is smiling, taking a special interest in Minerva. Soon the two of them are deep in conversation. How did that happen? Dedé wonders. The young man, after all, had headed straight for her, offering his help.

"How are you, Dedé?" Mario leans confidentially on the counter. He tried courting her a few months back before Dedé set him straight.

Mario is just not, not, well, he's not Jaimito. But then neither is this young doctor.

"I wish we could get this done." Dedé sighs, capping her pen and closing the book. Mario apologizes. They have interrupted the girls in their work. Dedé reassures him that it was slow going before the visitors arrived.

"Maybe it's the heat," Mario says, fanning himself with his Panama hat.

"What do you say we all go for a swim in the lagoon?" Minerva offers. The young men look ready to go, but Dedé reminds Minerva, "What about volleyball?" Jaimito will be looking for her. And if she's going to end up with Mario, which is no doubt the way things will settle, she'd rather be with the man she intends to marry. So there.

"Volleyball? Did someone say volleyball?" the young scholar asks. It is nice to see a smile on his pale, serious face. It turns out he has played on several university teams.

Minerva gets another great idea. Why not play volleyball, and then, when they are hot and sweaty, go jump in the lagoon.

Dedé marvels at Minerva's facility in arranging everyone's lives. And how easily she assumes they can get permission from Papá. Already the volleyball evenings are becoming a problem. Papá does not feel that two sisters make the best chaperones for each other, especially if they are both eager to go to the same place.

Back at the house, while the young men visit with Mamá in the *galería*, Minerva argues with their father. "But Papá, Mario's a man you do business with, a man you trust. We're going to Tío Pepe's, our uncle, to play volleyball with our cousins. How much more chaperoned can we be?"

Papá is dressing before his mirror. He has been looking younger, more handsome, something. He cranes his neck, looking over Minerva's shoulder. "Who is that young man with Mario?"

"Just some cousin of Mario's here for the weekend," Minerva says too offhandedly. Dedé notes how Minerva is avoiding mentioning Lío's association with the university.

And then the coup de grâce. "Why don't you come with us, Papá?"

Of course, Papá won't come along. Every evening he tours his property, hearing reports from the *campesinos* about what's been done that day. He never takes his girls along. "Men's business," he always says. That's what he's getting ready to do right now.

"You be back before it's dark." He scowls. This is the way Dedé knows he's granted them permission—when he begins talking of their return.

Dedé changes quickly, but not fast enough for Minerva. "Come on," she keeps hurrying Dedé. "Before Papá changes his mind!" Dedé is not sure her buttons are all buttoned as they head down the driveway to where the young men now wait beside their car.

Dedé feels the stranger's eyes on her. She knows she looks especially good in her flowered shirtwaist and white sandal heels.

Lío smiles, amused. "You're going to play volleyball dressed like that?" Suddenly, Dedé feels foolish, caught in her frivolity as if she were a kitten knotted in yarn. Of course, she *never* plays. Except for Minerva in her trousers and tennis shoes, the girls all sit in the *galería* cheering the boys on.

"I don't play," she says rather more meekly than she intends. "I just watch."

The truth of her words strike Dedé as she remembers how she stood back and watched the young man open the back door for whoever wanted to sit by him. And Minerva slipped in!

She remembers a Saturday evening a few weeks later.

Jaimito and his San Francisco Tigers are playing poorly against the Ojo de Agua Wolves. During a break, he comes up to the *galería* for a cold beer. *"Hola, prima,"* he says to Dedé as if they are *just* cousins. She is still pretending not to give him the time of day, but she checks herself in every reflecting surface. Now her hands clench with tension in the pockets of her fresh dress.

"Come on and play, cousin." He tugs at her arm. After all, Minerva has long been working up a sweat on the Ojo de Agua side of the net. "Our team could use some help!"

"I wouldn't be much help," Dedé giggles. Truly, she has always considered sports—like politics—something for men. Her one weakness is her horse Brío, whom she adores riding. Minerva has been teasing her how this Austrian psychiatrist has proved that girls who like riding like sex. "I'm all flan fingers when it comes to volleyball."

"You wouldn't have to play," he flirts. "Just stand on our side and distract those wolves with your pretty face!"

Dedé gives him the sunny smile she is famous for.

"Be nice to us Tigers, Dedé. After all, we did bend the rules for you Wolves." He indicates over his shoulder where Minerva and Lío are immersed in an intent conversation in a corner of the *galería*.

It is true. Although Lío is not from Ojo de Agua, the Tigers have agreed to let him play for the weakling team. Dedé supposes that the Tigers took one look at the bespectacled, pale young man and decided he wouldn't be much competition. But Lío Morales has turned out to be surprisingly agile. The Ojo de Agua Wolves are now gaining on the San Francisco Tigers.

"He's had to be quick," Jaimito has quipped. "Escaping the police and all." Jaimito and his buddies knew exactly who Virgilio Morales was the first night he came to play volleyball. They were split between admiration and wariness of his dangerous presence among them.

Jaimito hits on a way of getting Dedé to play. "Girls against guys, what do you say?" he calls out, picking up a fresh bottle of beer. Used to keeping tabs at the family store, Dedé has made note of three large ones for Jaimito already.

The girls titter, tempted. But what about mussing their dresses, what about spraining their ankles on high heels?

"Take off your heels, then," Jaimito says, eyeballing Dedé's shapely legs, "and whatever else is in your way!"

"You!" Her face burns with pleasure. She has to admit that she is proud of her nice legs.

Soon, shawls are flung on chairs, a half dozen pairs of heels are kicked off in a pile at the bottom of the steps. Dress sleeves are rolled up, ponytails tightened, and with squeals of delight, the Amazons—as they've christened themselves—step out on the slippery evening grass. The young men whistle and hoot, roused by the sight of frisky young women, girding themselves, ready to play ball. The cicadas have started their trilling, and the bats swoop down and up as if graphing the bristling excitement. Soon it will be too dark to see the ball clearly.

As they are assigning positions, Dedé notices that her sister Minerva is not among them. Now, when they need her help, the pioneer woman player deserts them! She looks towards the *galería*, where the two empty chairs facing each other recollect the vanished speakers. She is wondering whether or not to go in search of Minerva when she senses Jaimito's attention directed her way. Far back, almost in darkness, he is poised to strike. She hears a whack, then startled by the cries of her girlfriends, she looks up and sees a glowing moon coming down into her upraised hands.

Wasn't it really an accident? Dedé ponders, rewinding back to the exact moment when she belted that ball. It had sailed over everyone's heads into the dark hedges where it landed with the thrashing sound of breaking branches, and then, the surprising cry of a startled couple.

Had she suspected that Minerva and Lío were in the hedges, and her shot was an easy way to flush them out? But why, she asks herself, why would she have wanted to stop them? Thinking back, she feels her heart starting to beat fast.

Nonsense, so much nonsense the memory cooks up, mixing up facts, putting in a little of this and a little of that. She might as well hang out her shingle like Fela and pretend the girls are taking possession of her. Better them than the ghost of her own young self making up stories about the past!

There was a fight, that she remembers. Lío came out of the hedges, the ball in his hand. Jaimito made a crude remark, carried away by his three-plus beers and growing uneasiness with Lío's presence. Then the picture tilts and blurs the memory of Lío throwing the ball at Jaimito's chest and of it knocking the breath out of him. Of Jaimito having to be held by his buddies. Of the girls hurrying back to their high heels. Of Tío Pepe coming down the steps from inside, shouting, "No more volleyball!"

But before they could be ushered away, the two men were at the quick of their differences. Jaimito called Lío a troublemaker, accusing him of cooking up plots and then running off to some embassy for asylum, leaving his comrades behind to rot in jail. "You're exposing us all," Jaimito accused.

"If I leave my country, it's only to continue the struggle. We can't let Chapita kill us *all*."

Then there had been the silence that always followed any compromising mention of the regime in public. One could never be sure who in a group might report what to the police. Every large household was said to have a servant on double payroll.

"I said no more volleyball tonight." Tío Pepe was looking from one to the other young man. "You two shake and be gentlemen. Come on," he encouraged. Jaimito stuck out his hand.

Oddly enough, it was Lío, the peace lover, who would not shake at first. Dedé can still picture the long, lanky body holding in tension, not saying a word, and then, finally, Lío reaching out his hand and saying, "We could use men like you, Jaimito." It was a compliment that allowed the two men to coexist and even to collaborate on romantic matters in the months ahead.

Such a small incident really. A silly explosion over a foul volleyball. But something keeps Dedé coming back to the night of that fight. And to the days and nights that followed. Something keeps her turning and turning these moments in her mind, something. She is no longer sure she wants to find out what.

—————

No matter what Mamá said later, she was at first very taken with Virgilio Morales. She would sit in the *galería*, conversing with the young doctor—about the visit of Trygve Lie from the United Nations, the demonstrations in the capital, whether or not there was government in Paradise, and if so what kind it would be. On and on, Mamá listened, spoke her mind, Mamá who had always said that all this talking of Minerva's was unhealthy. After Lío had left, Mamá would say, "What a refined young man."

Sometimes Dedé felt a little peevish. After all, her beau had been along, too. But not a word was said about that fine young man Jaimito. How handsome he looked in his Mexican *guayabera*. What a funny joke he had made about what the coconut said to the drunk man. Mamá had known him since he was a kindred swelling of her first cousin's belly. What was there to say about him but, "That Jaimito!"

Dedé and Jaimito would wander off, unnoticed, stealing kisses in the garden. They'd play How Much Meat, Butcher?, Jaimito pretending to saw off Dedé's shoulder, and instead getting to touch her sweet neck and bare arms. Soon they'd hear Mamá calling them from the *galería*, a scold in her voice. Once when they did not appear immediately (the butcher had been wanting the whole animal), Mamá put a limit to how much Jaimito could come calling—Wednesdays, Saturdays, and Sundays only.

But who could control Jaimito, only son of his doting mother, unquestioned boss of his five sisters! He appeared on Mondays to visit Don Enrique, on Tuesdays and Thursdays to help with any loading or unloading at the store, on Fridays to bring what his mother had sent. Mamá sighed, accepting the coconut flan or bag of cherries from their backyard tree. "That Jaimito!"

Then one Sunday afternoon Mate was reading Mamá the newspaper out loud. It was no secret to Dedé that Mamá couldn't read, though Mamá still persisted in her story that her eyesight was bad. When Dedé read Mamá the news, she was careful to leave out anything that would worry her. But that day, Mate read right out how there had been a demonstration at the university, led by a bunch of young professors, all members of the Communist party. Among the names listed was that of Virgilio Morales! Mamá looked ashen. "Read that over again, slowly," she commanded.

Mate reread the paragraph, this time realizing what she was reading. "But that isn't our Lío, is it?"

"Minerva!" Mamá called out. From her bedroom, the book she was reading still in hand, appeared the death of them all. "Sit down, young lady, you have some explaining to do."

Minerva argued eloquently that Mamá herself had heard Lío's ideas, and she had even agreed with them.

"But I didn't know they were communist ideas!" Mamá protested.

That night when Papá came home from doing his man's business about the farm, Mamá took him to her room and closed the door. From the *galería* where Dedé visited with Jaimito, they could hear Mamá's angry voice. Dedé could only make out snatches of what Mamá was saying—"Too busy chasing . . . to care . . . your own daughter." Dedé looked at Jaimito, a question in her face. But he looked away. "Your mother shouldn't blame your father. She might as well blame me for not saying anything."

"You knew?" Dedé asked.

"What do you mean, Dedé?" He seemed surprised at her plea of innocence. "You knew, too. Didn't you?"

Dedé could only shake her head. She didn't really know Lío was a communist, a subversive, all the other awful things the editorial had called him. She had never known an enemy of state before. She had assumed such people would be self-serving and wicked, low-class criminals. But Lío was a fine young man with lofty ideals and a compassionate heart. Enemy of state? Why then, Minerva was an enemy of state. And if she, Dedé, thought long and hard about what was right and wrong, she would no doubt be an enemy of state as well.

"I didn't know," she said again. What she meant was she didn't understand until that moment that they were really living—as Minerva liked to say—in a police state.

A new challenge sounded in Dedé's life. She began to read the paper with pointed interest. She looked out for key names Lío had mentioned. She evaluated and reflected over what she read. How could she have missed so much before? she asked herself. But then a harder question followed: What was she going to do about it now that she did know?

Small things, she decided. Right now, for instance, she was providing Minerva with an alibi. For after finding out who Lío was exactly, Mamá had forbidden Minerva to bring him into the house. Their courtship or friendship or whatever it was went underground. Every time Jaimito took Dedé out, Minerva, of course, came along as their chaperone, and they picked up Lío along the way.

And after every outing, Dedé would slip into the bedroom Minerva shared with Mate when their little sister was home from school. She'd lie on Mate's bed and talk and talk, trying to bring herself down from the excitement of the evening. "Did you eat parrot today?" Minerva would say in a sleepy voice from her bed. That one had nerves of steel. Dedé would recount her plans for the future—how she would marry Jaimito; what kind of ceremony they would have; what type house they would buy; how many children they would have—until Minerva would burst out laughing. "You're not stocking the shelves in the store! Don't plan it all. Let life surprise you a little."

"Tell me about you and Lío, then."

"*Ay*, Dedé, I'm so sleepy. And there's nothing to tell."

That perplexed Dedé. Minerva claimed she was not in love with Lío. They were comrades in a struggle, a new way for men and women to be together that did not necessarily have to do with romance. Hmm. Dedé shook her head. No matter how interesting-minded she wanted to be, as far as she was concerned, a man was a man and a woman was a woman and there was a special charge there you couldn't call revolution. She put off her sister's reticence to that independent streak of hers.

Dedé's own romance with Jaimito acquired a glamorous, exciting edge with Lío and Minerva always by their side. Most nights when there was no place "safe" to go—a new thrilling vocabulary of danger had entered Dedé's speech—they'd drive around in Jaimito's father's Chevy or Papá's Ford, Jaimito and Dedé and Minerva visible, Lío hidden in the back of the car. They'd go out to the lagoon, past a military post, and Dedé's heart would beat fast. They would all talk a while, then Minerva and Lío would grow very quiet, and the only sounds from the back seat were those coming from the front as well. Intent whispers and little giggles.

Maybe that's why Jaimito went along with these dangerous sallies. Like most people, he avoided anything that might cause trouble. But he must have sensed that engaging in one illegality sort of loosened other holds on Dedé. The presence of Lío gave her the courage to go further with Jaimito than ever before.

But without a plan Dedé's courage unraveled like a row of stitches not finished with a good, sturdy knot. She couldn't bear reading in the papers how the police were rounding up people left and right. She couldn't bear hearing high-flown talk she didn't understand. Most of all she couldn't bear having her head so preoccupied and nothing useful to do with her hands.

One night, she asked Lío right out: "How is it you mean to accom-. plish your goals?"

Thinking back, Dedé remembers a long lecture about the rights of the *campesinos*, the nationalization of sugar, and the driving away of the Yanqui imperialists. She had wanted something practical, something she could use to stave off her growing fears. *First, we mean to depose the dictator in this and this way. Second, we have arranged for a provisional government. Third, we mean to set up a committee of private citizens to oversee free elections.* She would have understood talk like that.

"*Ay*, Lío, " she said at last, weary with so much hope, so little planning. "Where is it you get your courage?"

"Why, Dedé," he said, "it's not courage. It's common sense."

Common sense? Sitting around dreaming while the secret police hunted you down! To keep from scolding him, Dedé noted that she liked his shirt. He ran his hand down one side, his eyes far away, "It was Freddy's," he said in a thick voice. Freddy, his comrade, had just been found hanging in his prison cell, a supposed suicide. It seemed weird to Dedé that Lío would wear the dead man's shirt, and even weirder that he would admit it. In so many ways, Lío was beyond her.

Lío's name started to appear regularly in the papers. His opposition party had been outlawed. "A party for homosexuals and criminals," the papers accused. One afternoon, the police came to the Mirabal residence, asking after Virgilio Morales. "We just want him to clear up a little matter," the police explained. Mamá, of course, swore she hadn't seen Virgilio Morales in months, and furthermore, that he wasn't allowed in her house.

Dedé was scared, and angry at herself for being so. She was growing more and more confused about what she wanted. And uncertainty was not something Dedé could live with easily. She started to doubt everything—that she should marry Jaimito and live in Ojo de Agua, that she should part her hair on the left side, that she should have water bread and chocolate for breakfast today like every day.

"Are you in your time of the month, *m'ija?*" Mamá asked her more than once when Dedé set to quarreling about something.

"Of course not, Mamá," Dedé said with annoyance in her voice.

She decided not to read the papers anymore. They were turning her upside down inside. The regime was going insane, issuing the most ludicrous regulations. A heavy fine was now imposed on anyone who wore khaki trousers and shirts of the same color. It was against the law now to carry your suit jacket over your arm. Lío was right, this was an absurd and crazy regime. It had to be brought down.

But when she read the list to Jaimito, she did not get the reaction she expected. "Well?" he said when she was through and looked up at him.

"Isn't it ridiculous? I mean, it's absurd, insanely ridiculous." Unlike her golden-tongued sister, Dedé was not eloquent with reasons. And my God, what reasons did she need to explain these ridiculous insanities!

"Why are you so worked up, my love?"

Dedé burst into tears. "Don't you see?"

He held her as she cried. And then in his bossy, comforting voice, he explained things. Same-color khaki outfits were what the military wore, and so a dress distinction had to be made. A jacket over the arm could be hiding a gun, and there had recently been many rumors about plots against El Jefe. "See, my darling?"

But Dedé didn't see. She shut her eyes tight and wished blindly that everything would turn out all right.

One night not long after that, Lío told them that as soon as his contact in the capital could arrange for asylum, he and several others would be going into exile. Minerva was deathly quiet. Even Jaimito, who wouldn't give a rotten plantain for risky politics, felt Lío's plight. "If he'd just relax, and stop all this agitating," he argued later with Dedé, "then he could stay and slowly work his changes in the country. This way, what good is he to everyone far away?"

"He doesn't believe in compromise," Dedé defended Lío. The anger in her voice surprised her. She felt somehow diminished by Lío's sacrifice. *Ay*, how she wished she could be that grand and brave. But she could not be. She had always been one to number the stars.

Jaimito tried convincing Dedé to his way of thinking. "Don't you see, my heart, all life involves compromise. You have to compromise with your sister, your mother has to compromise with your father, the sea and land have to compromise about a shoreline, and it varies from time to time. Don't you see, my life?"

"I see," Dedé said at last, already beginning to compromise with the man she was set to marry.

She remembers the night Lío went into hiding.

It was also the night she finally agreed to marry Jaimito.

They had been to a gathering of the Dominican party in San Francisco—Jaimito's idea. Belonging to *the* party was an obligation unless, of course, like Lío you wanted trouble for yourself and your family. Needless to say, Lío had not come along. Minerva had reluctantly chaperoned Dedé and Jaimito and brought her *cédula* to be stamped.

The evening was deadly. There were readings by high-ranking women in the party from *Moral Meditations*, an awful book just published by Doña María. Everyone knew the dictator's wife hadn't written a word of it, but the audience clapped politely. Except Minerva. Dedé prodded her with an elbow and whispered, "Think of it as life insurance." The irony of it—she had been practicing for her future profession!

They came directly home, sobered by the travesty in which they had participated. The three of them sat on the *galería* with the gas lamp off to keep the bugs down. Jaimito began what Minerva called her "interrogation."

"Has your friend invited you to go with him?" Jaimito had sense enough not to mention Lío's name out loud in Mamá's house.

There was a pause before Minerva spoke up. "Lío"—and she mentioned the name distinctly without a cowardly lowering of her voice— "is just a friend. And no, he hasn't invited me to leave with him, nor would I go."

Again Dedé wondered over her sister's reserve about Lío. Here was

Minerva risking her life for this young man, why not just admit she was in love with him?

"They were looking for him today at my house," Jaimito whispered. Dedé could feel her own shoulders tightening. "I didn't want to worry you, but they took me down to the station and asked me a bunch of questions. That's why I wanted us to all go tonight. We've got to start behaving ourselves."

"What did they want him for?" This time Minerva did lower her voice.

"They didn't say. But they did want to know if he had ever offered me any kind of illicit materials. That's what they called it."

Jaimito paused a long moment so that the two women were beside themselves. "What did you say?" Dedé's voice broke from a whisper.

"I told him he had."

"You what?" Minerva cried out.

"I confess." Jaimito's voice was playful. "I told them he'd given me some girlie magazines. Those guards, you know how they are. They all think he's a queer from what the papers have been saying. If nothing else, he climbed a little in their regard today."

"You are too much!" Minerva sighed, getting up. There was tiredness but also gratitude in her voice. After all, Jaimito had stuck his neck out for a man whose politics he considered foolhardy. "Tomorrow, we'll probably read in the papers how Virgilio Morales is a sex maniac."

Dedé remembers a sudden stillness after Minerva left, different from their usual silences. Then Jaimito returned to the topic of Minerva and Lío. It was almost as if they had become for Jaimito, too, a shadow couple by which he could talk of his own deepest, most hidden wishes.

"Do you think she's hiding something?" Jaimito asked Dedé. "Do you think they have crossed the Río Yaque?"

"*Ay,* Jaimito!" Dedé chastised him for suggesting such a thing about her sister.

"They haven't exactly been discussing Napoleon's white horse in the back seat!" Jaimito was now lifting up her hair for access to the pale, hidden parts of her neck.

"Neither have we been discussing Napoleon's white horse in the front seat," Dedé reminded him, pushing him gently away. The kissing was bringing on waves of pleasure she feared would capsize her self-control. "And we haven't crossed the Río Yaque, and we aren't going to!"

"Ever, my sky, ever?" he asked, putting on a hurt voice. He was patting his pockets for something. Dedé waited, knowing what was coming. "I can't see in this dark," he complained. "Light the lamp, will you, my own?"

"And wake up everyone, no!" Dedé felt her heart fluttering. She wanted to delay his asking. She had to think. She had to make sure that she was choosing right.

"But I have something I want you to see, my love." Jaimito's voice was full of excitement.

"Let's go out back. We can get in Papá's car and turn on the inside light." Dedé could never bear to disappoint him.

They stumbled down the driveway to where the Ford was parked, a big black hulking shape in the dark. Mamá would not be able to see them from her front bedroom window. Dedé eased open the passenger door and turned on the ceiling light. Across from her, Jaimito was grinning as he slid into the driver's seat. It was a grin that carried Dedé all the way back to the day her naughty cousin had put a lizard down her blouse. He had been grinning like that when he approached her, his hands behind his back.

"My lamb," he began, reaching for her hand.

Her heart was beating loud. Her spoiled, funny, fun-loving man. Oh, what a peck of trouble she was in for. "What have you got there, Jaimito Fernández?" she said, as he slipped the ring on her hand. It was his mother's engagement ring that had been shown to Dedé on numerous visits. A small diamond set at the center of a gold filigree flower. "Ay, Jaimito," she said, tilting it to catch the light. "It's lovely."

"My heart," he said. "I know I have to ask your father for your hand. But no matter what Minerva says, I'm modern. I believe the woman should be asked first."

That's when they heard the alerting little cough from the back of the car. She and Jaimito looked at each other in shock. "Who's there?" Jaimito cried out. "Who?" He had turned himself around so he was kneeling on the front seat.

"Relax, it's just me." Lío whispered from the back of the car. "Turn off the light, will you?"

"Jesus Christ!" Jaimito was furious, but he did turn off the light. He sat down again, facing the front as if he and his girl were alone, talking intimacies.

"Look, I'm sorry," Lío explained. "The heat's on. Mario's house is surrounded. My ride to the capital is stopping at the anacahuita tree at dawn. I have to hide out till then."

"So you come here and endanger this whole family!" Jaimito twisted around in his seat, ready to throttle this reckless man.

"I was hoping to get this to Minerva."

A hand slipped an envelope between Jaimito and Dedé. Before Jaimito could grab it, Dedé had it. She put it away in her pocket. "I'll take care of it," she promised.

"Now you've done what you came to do, you're not staying here. I'll give you a goddamn ride." Jaimito's father's Chevy was parked in front of the house by the gate.

"Jaimito, be smart, listen." Lío's whispers were eerie, a disembodied voice from the dark interior of the car. "If you're on the road in the middle of the night, of course you'll be stopped, and your car searched."

Dedé agreed. When Jaimito was finally convinced, she walked him down the drive to his car. "So what do you think, my love?" he asked as she was kissing him goodbye.

"I think you should go home, and let him catch the ride he's already arranged."

"I'm talking about my proposal, Dedé." Jaimito's voice was that of a hurt little boy.

It wasn't so much that she had forgotten as it was the inevitability of that proposal. They had been headed for it since they had patted mud balls together as toddlers in the backyard. Everyone said so. There was no question—was there?—but that they would spend the rest of their lives together.

He kissed her hard, his body insisting that her body answer, but

Dedé's head was spinning away with questions. "Yes, my love, of course, but you must go. I don't want you to be stopped on the road."

"Don't worry about me, my darling," Jaimito said bravely, emboldened by her concern. But he left soon after a last lingering kiss.

Alone, Dedé breathed in the cool air and looked up at the stars. She would not count them tonight, no. She twisted the ring around and around her finger, glancing towards the car at the bottom of the drive. Lío was there, safe! And only she knew it, only she, Dedé. No, she would not tell Minerva. She wanted to hold the secret to herself just this one night.

In the bedroom she had once shared with Patria, the lamp was burning low. Dedé took out the letter from her pocket and stared at the poorly sealed envelope. She toyed with the flap and it came easily undone. Slipping the letter out, she read haltingly, telling herself after each paragraph she would stop.

Lío was inviting Minerva to take asylum with him! She should drive down to the capital on the pretense of seeing the exhibit at the Colombian embassy and refuse to leave. What a risk to ask her sister to take! Why, the embassies were surrounded these days, and all the recent refugees had been intercepted and put in prison where most of them had disappeared forever. Dedé could not expose her sister to this danger. Especially if, as Minerva claimed, she did not even love this man.

Dedé took the chimney off the lamp, and with a trembling hand, fed the letter to the flame. The paper lit up. Ashes fluttered like moths, and Dedé ground them to dust on the floor. She had taken care of the problem, and that was that. Looking up at the mirror, she was surprised by the wild look on her face. The ring on her finger flashed a feverish reminder. She brushed her hair up into a tight ponytail and put on her nightgown. Having blown out the light, she slept fitfully, holding her pillow like a man in her arms.

CHAPTER SIX

Minerva

1949

What do you want, Minerva Mirabal?
Summer

I know the rumor that got started once I'd been living at home a few years. That I didn't like men. It's true that I never paid much attention to the ones around here. But it wasn't that I didn't like them. I just didn't know I was looking at what I wanted.

For one thing, my nose was always in a book. Love was something I had *read* would come. The man I'd love would look like the poet in a frontispiece, pale and sad with a pen in his hand.

For another thing, Papá discouraged boyfriends. I was *his* treasure, he'd say, patting his lap, as if I were a girl in a jumper instead of a woman of twenty-three in the slacks he objected to my wearing in public.

"Papá," I'd say. "I'm too old for that."

One time he offered me anything if I would sit on his lap. "Just come here and whisper it in my ear." His voice was a little thick from drinking. I sat right down and swooped to my prize. "I want to go to the university, Papa, please."

"Now, now," he said as if I were all worked up about something. "You wouldn't want to leave your old Papá, would you?"

"But Papá, you've got Mamá," I argued.

His face went blank. We both listened for Mamá stirring in the front of the house near where we sat. María Teresa was off at school, Dedé was newly married, Patria two times a mother. And here I was, a grown woman sitting on my father's lap. "Your mother and I . . ." he began, but thought better of continuing. Then he added, "We need you around."

Three years cooped at home since I'd graduated from Inmaculada, and I was ready to scream with boredom. The worse part was getting newsy letters from Elsa and Sinita in the capital. They were taking a Theory of Errors class that would make Sor Asunción's hair stand on end even under her wimple. They had seen Tin-Tan in *Tender Little Pumpkins*, and been to the country club to hear Alberti and his band. *And* there were so many nice-looking men in the capital!

I'd get restless with jealousy when Papá brought their letters back from the Salcedo post office. I'd jump in the Jeep and roar off into the countryside, my foot pressing heavily down on the gas as if speed could set me free. I'd drive further and further out, pretending to myself that I was running away to the capital. But something always made me turn the car around and head back home, something I'd seen from the corner of my eye.

One afternoon, I was on one of these getaway rampages, racing down the small side roads that spiderweb our property. Near the northeast cacao groves, I saw the Ford parked in front of a small, yellow house. I tried to figure out what *campesino* family lived there, but I couldn't say I had ever met them.

So I made it my business to take that back road frequently, keeping an eye out. Every time I drove the Ford, these raggedy girls came running after me, holding out their hands, calling for mints.

I studied them. There were three that ran to the road whenever they heard the car, a fourth one sometimes came in the arms of the oldest. Four girls, I checked, three in panties, and the baby naked. One time, I stopped at the side of the road and stared at their Mirabal eyes. "Who is your father?" I asked point blank.

They had been bold, clamoring kids a moment before. Now, spoken to by a lady in a car, they hung their heads and looked at me from the corners of *their* eyes.

"Do you have a brother?" I asked more gently.

It was a delicious revenge to hear them murmur, *"No, señora."* Papá was not going to get the son he wanted, after all!

A little later the woman came sauntering from her house, her hair just combed out from rollers and too much of something on her face. When she saw me, her face fell. She scolded the kids as if that was what she'd come for. "I told you not to bother the cars!"

"They're not bothering anything," I defended them, caressing the baby's cheek.

The woman was looking me over. I suppose she was taking inventory, what I had, what she didn't have, doing the simple arithmetic and, perhaps a few days later, exacting some new promise from Papá.

Everywhere I looked, I kept seeing those four raggedy girls with Papá's and my own deep-set eyes staring back at me. "Give me, give me!" they cried. But when I asked them, "What do you want?" they stood, mute, their mouths hanging open, not knowing where to start.

———

Had they asked me the same thing, I would have stared back, mute, too.

What did I want? I didn't know anymore. Three years stuck in Ojo de Agua, and I was like that princess put to sleep in the fairy tale. I read and complained and argued with Dedé, but all that time I was snoring away.

When I met Lío, it was as if I woke up. The givens, all I'd been taught, fell away like so many covers when you sit up in bed. Now when I asked myself, *What do you want, Minerva Mirabal?* I was shocked to find I didn't have an answer.

All I knew was I was not falling in love, no matter how deserving I thought Lío was. So what? I'd argue with myself. What's more important, romance or revolution? But a little voice kept saying, *Both, both, I want both.* Back and forth my mind went, weaving a yes by night and unraveling it by day to a no.

As always happens, your life decides for you anyway. Lío announced he was seeking asylum out of the country. I was relieved that circumstances would be resolving things between us.

Still, when he left, I was hurt that he hadn't even said goodbye. Then I started worrying that his silence meant he had been caught. Out of the corners of my eyes, I kept seeing Lío himself! He was not a pretty sight. His body was bruised and broken as if he had endured all the tortures in La Fortaleza he had ever described to me. I was sure I was having premonitions that Lío had not escaped after all.

Mamá, of course, noticed the tightening in my face. My bad headaches and asthma attacks worried her. "You need rest," she prescribed one afternoon and sent me to bed in Papá's room, the coolest in the house. He was off in the Ford for his afternoon review of the farm.

I lay in that mahogany bed, tossing this way and that, unable to sleep. Then, something I hadn't planned. I got up and tried the door of the armoire. It was locked, which wasn't all that strange as the hardware was always getting stuck. Using one of my bobby pins, I popped the inside spring and the door sprang open.

I ran my hand along Papá's clothes, releasing his smell in the room. I stared at his new fancy *guayaberas* and started going through the pockets. In the inside pocket of his dress jacket, I found a packet of papers and pulled them out.

Prescriptions for his medicines, a bill for a Panama hat he'd been wearing around the farm, a new, important look for him. A bill from El Gallo for seven yards of gingham, a girl's fabric. An invitation from the National Palace to some party. Then, four letters, addressed to me from Lío!

I read them through hungrily. He hadn't heard from me about his proposal to leave the country. (What proposal?) He had arranged for me to come to the Colombian embassy. I should let him know through his cousin Mario. He was waiting for my answer—next letter. Still no answer, he complained in a third letter. In the final letter, he wrote that he was leaving that afternoon on the diplomatic pouch plane. He understood it was too big a step for me at the moment. Some day in the future, maybe. He could only hope.

It seemed suddenly that I'd missed a great opportunity. My life would have been nobler if I had followed Lío. But how could I have made the choice when I hadn't even known about it? I forgot my earlier ambivalence, and I blamed Papá for everything: his young woman, his hurting Mamá, his cooping me up while he went gallivanting around.

My hands were shaking so bad that it was hard to fold the letters into their envelopes. I stuffed them in my pocket, but his bills and correspondence I put back. I left the doors of the armoire gaping open. I wanted him to know he had been found out.

Minutes later, I was roaring away in the Jeep without a word to Mamá. What would I have said? I'm going to find my good-for-nothing father and drag him back?

I knew where to find him all right. Now that Papá was doing so well, he had bought a second car, a Jeep. I knew damn well he wasn't reviewing the fields if he had taken the Ford, not the Jeep. I headed straight for that yellow house.

When I got there, those four girls looked up, startled. After all, the man they always expected was already there, the car parked in back where it couldn't be seen from the road. I turned into the dirt path and crashed into the Ford, making the bumper curl up and shattering the window in back. Then I came down on that horn until he appeared, shirtless and furious in the doorway.

He took one look at me and got as pale as an olive-skinned man can get. For a long moment, he didn't say anything. "What do you want?" he said at last.

I heard the little girls crying, and I realized my own face was wet with tears. When he came forward, I gave a warning honk and wildly backed out of the path and into the road. A pickup coming around the curve veered and ran into the ditch—plantains, oranges, mangoes, yucca spilling all over the road. That didn't stop me, no. I stepped on the gas. From the corner of my eye I saw him, a figure growing smaller and smaller until I left him behind me.

When I got home, Mama met me at the door. She eyed me, and she must have known. "Next time, you don't leave this house without saying where you're going." We both knew her scold was meaningless. She hadn't even asked where I'd been.

Papá returned that night, his face drawn with anger. He ate his supper in silence as if his review of the farm had not gone well. As soon as I could without making Mamá more suspicious, I excused myself. I had a throbbing headache, I explained, heading for my room.

In a little while, I heard his knock. "I want to see you outside." His voice through the door was commanding. I threw water on my face, combed my hands through my hair, and went out to Papá.

He led me down the drive past the dented Ford into the dark garden. The moon was a thin, bright machete cutting its way through patches of clouds. By its sharp light I could see my father stop and turn to face me. With his shrinking and my height, we were now eye to eye.

There was no warning it was coming. His hand slammed into the side of my face as it never had before on any part of my body. I staggered back, stunned more with the idea of his having hit me than with the pain exploding in my head.

"That's to remind you that you owe your father some respect!"

"I don't owe you a thing," I said. My voice was as sure and commanding as his. "You've lost my respect."

I saw his shoulders droop. I heard him sigh. Right then and there, it hit me harder than his slap: I was much stronger than Papá, Mamá was much stronger. He was the weakest one of all. It was he who would have the hardest time living with the shabby choices he'd made. He needed our love.

"I hid them to protect you," he said. At first, I didn't know what he was talking about. Then I realized he must have discovered the letters missing from his coat pocket.

"I know of at least three of Virgilio's friends who have disappeared."

So he was going to pass this off as my fury over his taking my mail. And I knew that in order to go on living under the same roof, I would have to pretend this was our true difference.

That fancy invitation I found in Papá's pocket caused another uproar— this time from Mamá. It was an invitation to a private party being thrown by Trujillo himself in one of his secluded mansions three hours away. A handwritten note at the end requested that *la señorita* Minerva Mirabal not fail to show.

Now that Papá had become rich, he got invited to a lot of official parties and functions. I always went along as Papá's partner since Mamá wouldn't go. "Who wants to see an old woman?" she complained.

"Come on, Mamá," I argued. "You're in your prime. A *mujerona* of fifty-one." I snapped my fingers, jazzing up Mamá's life. But the truth was, Mamá looked old, even older than Papá with his dapper new hat and his linen *guayaberas* and his high black boots, and a debonair cane that seemed more a self-important prop than a walking aid. Her hair had gone steel gray, and she pulled it back in a severe bun that showed off the long-suffering look on her face.

This time, though, Mamá didn't want me to go either. The note at the end scared her. This wasn't an official *do* but something personal. In fact, after the last big party, a colonel friend had visited Jaimito's family asking after the tall, attractive woman Don Enrique Mirabal had brought along. She had caught El Jefe's eye.

Mamá wanted to get me a medical excuse from Doctor Lavandier. After all, migraines and asthma attacks weren't against the law, were they?

"Trujillo *is* the law," Papá whispered, as we all did nowadays when we pronounced the dreaded name.

Finally, Mamá relented, but she insisted Pedrito and Patria go along to take care of me, and Jaimito and Dedé go to make sure Patria and Pedrito did their job. María Teresa begged to go, too. But Mamá wouldn't hear of it. Expose another young, single daughter to danger, *¡No, señorita!* Besides, María Teresa couldn't go to night parties until her *quinceañera* next year.

Poor Mate cried and cried. As a consolation prize, I offered to bring her back another souvenir. Last time at the party at Hotel Montaña, we all got paper fans with the Virgencita on one side and El Jefe on the other. I kept making María Teresa turn the fan around when she sat in front of me, fanning herself. Sometimes it was El Jefe's probing eyes, sometimes it was the Virgin's pretty face I couldn't stand to look at.

With the party a week away, Papá had to get the Ford fixed. The president of our local branch of Trujillo Tillers couldn't very well arrive at El Jefe's house in a Jeep. It seemed pretty appropriate to me, but having banged up Papá's beauty it wasn't for me to disagree.

While the Ford was at the shop, I drove Papá to his doctor's appointments in San Francisco. It was sad how the richer he got, the more his health deteriorated. He was drinking too much, even I could see that. His heart was weak and his gout made it painful sometimes for him to move around. Doctor Lavandier had him on treatments twice a week. I'd drop him off, then visit with Dedé and Jaimito at their new ice cream shop until it was time to pick him up.

One morning, Papá told me to go on home. He had some errands to run after his appointment. Jaimito would drive him back later.

"We can run them together," I offered. When he looked away, I guessed what he was up to. Several days ago, I had driven out to the yellow house and found it all boarded up. Of course! Papá hadn't broken with this woman but merely moved her off the grounds and into town.

I sat, facing forward, not saying a word.

Finally, he admitted it. "You have to believe me. I only go to see my children. I'm not involved with their mother anymore."

I waited for things to settle down inside me. Then I said, "I want to meet them. They're my sisters, after all."

I could see he was moved by my acknowledging them. He reached over, but I was not ready yet for his hugs. "I'll be back to pick you up."

We drove down narrow streets, past row on row of respectable little houses. Finally we came to a stop in front of a pretty turquoise house with the porch and trim painted white. There they were, awaiting Papá, four little girls in look-alike pale yellow gingham dresses. The two oldest must have recognized me, for their faces grew solemn when I got out of the car.

The minute Papá was on the sidewalk, they darted towards him and dug the mints out of his pockets. I felt a pang of jealousy seeing them treat Papá in the same way my sisters and I had.

"This is my big girl, Minerva," he introduced me. Then, putting a hand on each one's head, he presented them to me. The oldest, Margarita, was about ten, then three more with about three years' difference between them down to the baby with her pacifier on a dirty ribbon round her neck. While Papá went inside the house with an envelope, I waited on the porch, asking them questions they were too shy to answer.

As we were leaving, I saw the mother peeking at me from behind the door. I beckoned for her to come out. "Minerva Mirabal," I said, offering her my hand.

The woman hung her head and mumbled her name, Carmen something. I noticed she was wearing a cheap ring, the adjustable kind that children buy at any street corner from the candy vendors. I wondered if she was trying to pass herself off as a respectable married lady in this, one of the nicer barrios of San Francisco.

As we drove back to Ojo de Agua, I was working out what had been happening ten years back that might have driven Papá into the arms of another woman. Patria, Dedé, and I had just gone away to Inmaculada Concepción, and María Teresa would have been all of four years old. Maybe, I told myself, Papá had missed us so much that he had gone in search of a young girl to replace us? I looked over at him and instantly he looked my way.

"That was very fine of you," he said, smiling hesitantly.

"I know the clouds have already rained," I said, "but, Papá, why did you do it?"

His hands gripped his cane until his knuckles whitened. *"Cosas de los hombres,"* he said. Things a man does. So that was supposed to excuse him, macho that he was!

Before I could ask him another question, Papá spoke up. "Why'd you do what you just did?"

Quick as my reputation said my mouth was, I couldn't come up with an answer, until I remembered his own words. "Things a woman does."

And as I said those words my woman's eyes sprang open.

All the way home I kept seeing them from the corners of my eyes, men bending in the fields, men riding horses, men sitting by the side of the road, their chairs tipped back, nibbling on a spear of grass, and I knew very well I was looking at what I wanted at last.

Discovery Day Dance
October 12

By the time we find the party, we're an hour late. All the way here Papá and Pedrito and Jaimito have been working out the details of their story. "You say how we started out early this morning to give us plenty of time, and then you say we didn't know the way." Papá assigns the different facts to his sons-in-law.

"And you"—he looks around at me in the back seat—"you keep quiet."

"You don't have to plan anything when you're telling the truth," I remind them. But no one listens to me. Why should they? They're probably thinking I got them into this.

Here is the truth. We arrived in San Cristóbal late this afternoon and got a room at the local hotel and changed. By then, our dresses were a mess from riding around on our laps all day. "The worse you look, the better for you," Patria said when I complained that I looked like I'd gotten here on a donkey.

Then we climbed back in the car and drove forever. As a man who *always* knows where he's going, Jaimito couldn't very well stop to ask for directions. Soon we were lost on the back roads somewhere near Baní. At a checkpoint, a *guardia* finally convinced Jaimito that we were going the wrong way. We headed back, an hour late.

Jaimito parks the Ford at the end of the long driveway, facing the road. "In case we have to take off quickly," he says in a low voice. He's been a bundle of nerves about this whole outing. I guess we all have.

It's a hike to the house. Every few steps we have to stop at a checkpoint and flash our invitation. The driveway is well lit, so at least we can see the puddles before we splash into them. It's been raining on and off all day, the usual October hurricane weather. This year, though, the rains seem more severe than ever, everyone says so. My theory is that the god of thunder Huracán always acts up around the holiday of the Conquistador, who killed off all his Taino devotees. When I suggest this to Patria as we walk up the drive, she gives me her pained Madonna look. *"Ay, Minerva, por Dios,* keep that tongue in check tonight."

Manuel de Moya is pacing back and forth at the entrance. I recognize him from the last party, and of course his picture is always in the papers. "Secretary of state," people say, winking one eye. Everyone knows his real job is rounding up pretty girls for El Jefe to try out. How they get talked into it, I don't know. Manuel de Moya is supposed to be so smooth with the ladies, they probably think they're following the example of the Virgencita if they bed down with the Benefactor of the Fatherland.

Papá starts in on our explanation, but Don Manuel cuts him off. "This is not like him. The Spanish ambassador has been waiting." He checks his watch, holding it to his ear as if it might whisper El Jefe's whereabouts. "You didn't see any cars on the way?" Papá shakes his head, his face full of exaggerated concern.

Don Manuel snaps his fingers, and several officers rush forward for instructions. They are to keep a sharp lookout while he escorts the Mirabals to their table. We wonder at this special attention, and Papá begs Don Manuel not to go to so much bother. "This," he says, offering me his arm, "is all my pleasure."

We go down a long corridor, and into a courtyard hung with lanterns. The crowd hushes as we enter. The band leader stands up but then sits back down when he realizes it's not El Jefe. Luis Alberti moved his whole orchestra from the capital just to be on call at *Casa de Caoba.* This is supposed to be El Jefe's favorite party mansion, where he keeps his favorite of the moment. At the last few parties the excited gossip in the powder rooms has been that at present the house is vacant.

Only one reserved table is left in front of the dais. Don Manuel is pulling out chairs for everybody, but when I go to sit down next to Patria, he says, "No, no, El Jefe has invited you to his table." He indicates the head table on the dais where a few dignitaries and their wives nod in my direction. Patria and Dedé exchange a scared look.

"It is really quite an honor," he adds when he notes my hesitation. Across the table Papá is still standing. "Go on, my daughter. You are keeping Don Manuel waiting."

I give Papá an angry look. Has he lost *all* his principles?

From my vantage point at the raised table, I look around. In keeping with Discovery Day, the whole courtyard has been outfitted like one of Columbus' ships. On each table there is a clever centerpiece—a little caravel with tissue sails and lighted candles for masts, a perfect souvenir for Mate. I size it up but decide it won't fit in my purse.

Dedé catches my eye, smiling only after a lag of a second, for we have to seem pleased. She touches her glass and gives me the slightest nod. *Don't drink anything you are offered*, the gesture reminds me. We've heard the stories. Young women drugged, then raped by El Jefe. But what could Dedé be thinking? That Trujillo is going to drug me right here in front of a crowd?! Then what? Manuel de Moya will drag me off to a waiting black Cadillac. Or will there be two waiting black Cadillacs, one with a leering look-alike? That's another story. Security has introduced a double as a protective measure to confuse any would-be assassins. I roll my eyes at Dedé, and then, as she glares at me, I lift my glass in a reckless toast.

As if it were a signal, everyone rises to their feet, lifting their glasses. There is a stir at the entrance, newspapermen swarming, flashbulbs popping. A crowd presses around him, and so I don't see him until he's almost at our table. He looks younger than I remember him from our performance five years ago, the hair darkened, the figure trim. It must be all that *pega palo* we hear he's been drinking, a special brew his *brujo* cooks up to keep him sexually potent.

After the toast, the Spanish ambassador presents this illustrious descendant of the great Conquistador with yet another medal. There is some question about where to pin it on the cluttered sash that crosses his chest. Chapita, the underground boys call him. Lío has told me that the nickname comes from El Jefe's childhood habit of stringing bottle caps across his chest to look like medals.

At long last, we settle down to our plates of cold *sancocho*. Surprisingly, El Jefe does not sit next to me. I feel more and more puzzled as to my role this evening at this table. To my left, Manuel de Moya commences reminiscing about his New York modeling days. The story is Trujillo met him on one of those shopping trips he periodically makes to the States to order his elevator shoes, his skin whiteners and creams, his satin sashes and rare bird plumes for his bicorn Napoleonic hats. He hired the model right on the spot. A tall, polished, English-speaking, white Dominican to decorate his staff.

My right-hand partner, an aging senator from San Cristóbal compliments the stew and points to an attractive, blond woman seated to Trujillo's left. "My wife," he boasts, "half Cuban."

Not knowing what to say, I nod, and lean over to pick up the napkin I dropped when I stood up for El Jefe's entrance. Under the tablecloth, a hand is exploring the inner folds of a woman's thigh. I work it out and realize it is Trujillo's hand fondling the senator's wife.

The tables are pushed back and the music starts, though I wonder that they don't just move the party indoors. There is a strong breeze, announcing rain. Every once in a while, a gust topples a glass or caravel, and there's a loud crash. The soldiers patrolling the edges of the party reach for their guns.

The floor remains empty as it must until El Jefe has danced the first dance.

He rises from his chair, and I am so sure he is going to ask me that I feel a twinge of disappointment when he turns instead to the wife of the Spanish ambassador. Lío's words of warning wash over me. This regime is seductive. How else would a whole nation fall prey to this little man?

God help him! Where is he right now? Was he granted asylum by the embassy or was he caught and locked up in La Fortaleza as my premonitions keep telling me? My head throbs as my imagination dashes here and there, trying to find him safe haven.

"Could I have the honor?" Manuel de Moya is standing at my side.

I shake my head. "Ay, Don Manuel, what a headache I have." I feel a little glee at being able to legitimately refuse him.

A cloud of annoyance crosses his face. But in a flash, he is all good manners. "We must get you a *calmante* then."

"No, no," I wave him off. "It will pass if I sit here quietly." I stress *qui-

etly. I do not want to make conversation with Don Manuel about my headache.

When he goes off, I look over at our table. Patria lifts her eyebrows as if asking, "How are you holding up?" I touch my forehead and close my eyes a moment. She knows how I am suffering from headaches these days. "Tension," Mamá says, and sends me away from the store for extra naps.

Patria comes up to the platform with a whole packet of *calmantes*. Always the mother, that one. She's got a handkerchief in that purse should someone sneeze, a mint to keep a child happy, a rosary in case anyone wants to pray.

I start to tell her about the hanky-panky I saw under the table, but the pervasive Manuel de Moya is beside us again. He has brought a waiter with a glass of water and two aspirin on a little silver tray. I open my hand and disclose my own pills. Don Manuel's face falls.

"But I do need more water," I say to show some gratitude. He presents the glass with so much ceremony, my gratitude dissolves like the pills in my stomach.

Later, at the table, I listen to him make idle conversation with the old senator about the various ailments they have both suffered. Every once in a while he checks to see if my headache is any better. Finally, after the third time, I answer him with what I know he wants. "Let's try the country cure," I say, and I verify that he is not a man to trust when he asks, "What cure is that?"

We dance several sets, and sure enough, as the *campesinos* say, *Un clavo saca otro clavo*. One nail takes out another. The excited rhythm of Alberti's "Fiesta" overwhelms the pulsing throb of my headache. And whatever else he is, Manuel de Moya is a terrific dancer. I keep throwing my head back and laughing. When I look over at our table, Patria is studying me, not quite sure what to make of my pleasure.

Everything happens very fast then. A slow bolero starts, and I feel myself being led towards where Trujillo is now dancing with the attractive, blond wife of the old senator. When we are abreast of them,

Manuel de Moya lets go of my hand and opens up our couple. "Shall we visit?" he asks me, but it is El Jefe who nods. The blond woman pouts as she is whisked away. "A visit is not a long stay," she reminds El Jefe, flashing her eyes at him over Manuel de Moya's shoulder.

I stand a moment, my arms at my sides, feeling the same stagefright of five years back. El Jefe takes my hand. "May I have the pleasure?" He doesn't wait for an answer, but pulls me to him. The smell of his cologne is overpowering.

His hold is proprietary and masculine, but he is not a good dancer. All firmness, and too many flourishes. A couple of times, he steps on my foot, but he does not excuse himself. "You dance very well," he says gallantly. "But then women from El Cibao make the best dancers and the best lovers," he whispers, tightening his hold. I can feel the moisture of his breath on my ear.

"And your last partner, was she from El Cibao?" I ask, encouraging conversation so he has to draw back a little. I have to check myself from saying, A visit is not a long stay, you know.

He holds me out in his arms, his eyes moving over my body, exploring it rudely with his glances. "I am speaking of the national treasure in my arms," he says, smiling.

I laugh out loud, my fear dissipating, a dangerous sense of my own power growing. "I don't feel very much like a national treasure."

"And why not, a jewel like you?" His eyes sparkle with interest.

"I feel like I'm wasting my life in Ojo de Agua."

"Perhaps we can bring you down to the capital," he says archly.

"That's exactly what I'm trying to convince Papá to do. I want to go to the university," I confess, playing this man against my own father. If El Jefe says he wants me to study, Papá will have to let me. "I've always wanted to study law."

He gives me the indulgent smile of an adult hearing an outrageous claim from a child. "A woman like you, a lawyer?"

I play on his vanity, and so, perhaps, become his creature like all the others. "You gave the women the vote in '42. You encouraged the founding of the women's branch of the Dominican party. You've always been an advocate for women."

"That I have." He grins a naughty grin. "A woman with a mind of her own. So you want to study in the capital, eh?"

I nod decisively, at the last minute softening the gesture with a tilt of my head.

"I could see our national treasure then on a regular basis. Perhaps, I could conquer this jewel as El Conquistador conquered our island."

The game has gone too far. "I'm afraid I'm not for conquest."

"You already have a *novio*?" This can be the only explanation. Even so, engagement, marriage—such things make a conquest more interesting. "A woman like you should have many admirers."

"I'm not interested in admirers until I have my law degree."

A look of impatience crosses his face. Our tête-à-tête is not following its usual course. "The university is no place for a woman these days."

"Why not, Jefe?"

He seems pleased by my referring to him by his affectionate title of Chief. By now, we are so immersed in conversation we are barely dancing. I can feel the crowd watching us.

"It's full of communists and agitators, who want to bring down the government. That Luperón mess, they were in back of it." His look is fierce—as if the mere mention had summoned his enemies before him. "But we've been teaching those teachers their lessons all right!"

They must have caught him! "Virgilio Morales?" I blurt out. I can't believe my own ears.

His face hardens, suspicion clouds the gaze. "You know Virgilio Morales?"

What a complete idiot I am! How can I now protect him and myself? "His family is from El Cibao, too," I say, choosing my words carefully. "I know the son teaches at the university."

El Jefe's gaze is withdrawing further and further into some back room of his mind where he tortures meaning out of the words he hears. He can tell I'm stalling. "So, you do know him?"

"Not personally, no," I say in a little voice. Instantly, I feel ashamed of myself. I see now how easily it happens. You give in on little things, and soon you're serving in his government, marching in his parades, sleeping in his bed.

El Jefe relaxes. "He is not a good person for you to know. He and the others have turned the campus into a propaganda camp. In fact, I'm thinking of closing down the university."

"Ay, Jefe, no," I plead with him. "Ours is the first university in the New World. It would be such a blow to the country!"

He seems surprised by my vehemence. After a long look, he smiles again. "Maybe I will keep it open if that will draw you to our side." And then literally, he draws me to him, so close I can feel the hardness at his groin pressing against my dress.

I push just a little against him so he'll loosen his hold, but he pulls me tighter towards him. I feel my blood burning, my anger mounting. I push away, a little more decidedly, again he pulls me aggressively to his body. I push hard, and he finally must let me go.

"What is it?" His voice is indignant.

"Your medals," I complain, pointing to the sash across his chest. "They are hurting me." Too late, I recall his attachment to those *chapitas*.

He glares at me, and then slips the sash over his head and holds it out. An attendant quickly and reverently collects it. El Jefe smiles cynically. "Anything else bother you about my dress I could take off?" He yanks me by the wrist, thrusting his pelvis at me in a vulgar way, and I can see my hand in an endless slow motion rise—a mind all its own— and come down on the astonished, made-up face.

And then the rain comes down hard, slapping sheets of it. The tablecloths are blown off the tables, dashing their cargo onto the floor. The candles go out. There are squeals of surprise. Women hold their beaded evening bags over their heads, trying to protect their foundering hairdos.

In a minute, Manuel de Moya is at our side directing guards to escort El Jefe indoors. A tarp is extended over us. "*Qué cosa, Jefe,*" Don Manuel laments, as if this inconvenience of nature were his fault.

El Jefe studies me as attendants dab at his dripping pancake. Annoyed, he pushes their hands away. I brace myself, waiting for him to give the order. *Take her away to La Fortaleza.* My fear is mixed oddly with excitement at the thought that I will get to see Lío if he, too, has been captured.

But El Jefe has other plans for me. "A mind of her own, this little *cibaeña!*" He smirks, rubbing his cheek, then turns to Don Manuel. "Yes, yes, we will adjourn indoors. Make an announcement." As his private guards close around him, I break away, struggling against the sea of guests rushing indoors out of the rain. Ahead, Dedé and Patria are turning in all directions like lookouts on the mast of a ship.

"We're going," Patria explains, grabbing my arm. "Jaimito's gone to get the car."

"I don't like this one bit," Papá is saying, shaking his head. "We shouldn't go without El Jefe's permission."

"His designs are so clear, Papá." Patria is the oldest, and so in Mamá's absence, her words carry weight. "We're exposing Minerva by staying here."

Pedrito looks up at the blowing lanterns. "The party is breaking up anyway, Don Enrique. This rain is a perfect excuse."

Papá lifts his shoulders and lets them fall. "You young people know what you do."

We make a dash for the covered entryway, passing a table with a caravel still standing. No one will miss it, I think, hiding the little ship in the folds of my skirt. That's when I remember. "*Ay*, Patria, my purse. I left it at the table."

We run back to get it, but can't find it anywhere. "Probably somebody already took it in. They'll send it to you. Nobody is going to steal from El Jefe's house," Patria reminds me. The caravel goes heavy in my hand.

By the time we run back to the entryway, the Ford is idling at the door and the others are already inside. Out on the highway, I recall the slap with mounting fear. No one has mentioned it, so I'm sure they didn't see it. Given everyone's nerves already, I decide not to worry them with the story. Instead, to distract myself—*One nail takes out another*—I go over the contents of my purse, trying to assess exactly what I've lost: my old wallet with a couple of pesos; my *cédula*, which I will have to report; a bright red Revlon lipstick I bought at El Gallo; a little Nivea tin Lío gave me with ashes of the Luperón martyrs not killed at sea.

And then, I remember them in the pocket of the lining, Lío's letters!

All the way home, I keep going over and over them as if I were an intelligence officer marking all the incriminating passages. On either side of me, my sisters are snoring away. When I lean on Patria, wanting the release of sleep, I feel something hard against my leg. A rush of hope goes through me that my purse is not lost after all. But reaching down, I discover the little caravel sunk in the folds of my damp dress.

Rainy Spell

The rain comes down all morning, beating against the shutters, blurring the sounds inside the house. I stay in bed, not wanting to get up and face the dreary day.

A car comes splashing into the driveway. Grim voices carry from the parlor. Governor de la Maza is just now returning from the party. Our absence was noted, and of course, leaving any gathering before Trujillo is against the law. El Jefe was furious and kept everyone till well after dawn—perhaps to show up our early departure.

What to do? I hear their worried voices. Papá takes off with the governor to send a telegram of apology to El Jefe. Meanwhile, Jaimito's father is calling on his colonel friend to see how the fire can be put out. Pedrito is visiting the in-laws of Don Petán, one of Trujillo's brothers, who are friends of his family. Whatever strings can be pulled, in other words, are being yanked.

Now all we can do is wait and listen to the rain falling on the roof of the house.

When Papá returns, he looks as if he has aged ten years. We can't get him to sit down or tell us what exactly happened. All day, he paces through the house, going over what we should do if he is taken away. When hours pass, and no *guardias* come to the door, he calms down a little, eats some of his favorite pork sausages, drinks more than he should, and goes to bed exhausted at dusk. Mamá and I stay up. Every time it thunders we jump as if guards had opened fire on the house.

Next day, early, while Papá is out seeing what damage this last storm has done on the cacao crop, two guardias arrive in a Jeep. Governor de la Maza wants to see Papá and me immediately.

"Why her?" Mamá points to me.

The officer shrugs.

"If she goes, I go," Mamá asserts, but the guard has already turned his back on her.

At the governor's palace, we are met right away by Don Antonio de la Maza, a tall, handsome man with a worried face. He has received orders to send Papá down to the capital for questioning.

"I tried to handle it here"—he shows us his palms—"but the orders have come from the top."

Papá nods absently. I have never seen him so scared. "We . . . we sent the telegram."

"If he goes, I go." Mamá pulls herself up to her full bulk. The *guardias* finally had to let her come this morning. She stood in the driveway refusing to get out of the way.

Don Antonio takes Mamá by the arm. "It will be better all the way around if we follow orders. Isn't that so, Don Enrique?"

Papá looks like he'll agree to anything. "Yes, yes, of course. You stay here and take care of things." He embraces Mamá, who breaks down, sobbing in his arms. It's as if her years and years of holding back have finally given way.

When it's my turn, I give Papá a goodbye kiss as we've gotten out of the habit of hugs since our estrangement. "Take care of your mother, you hear," he whispers to me and in the same breath adds, "I need you to deliver some money to a client in San Francisco." He gives me a meaningful look. "Fifty pesos due at the middle and end of the month until I'm back."

"You'll be back before you know it, Don Enrique," the governor assures him.

I look over at Mamá to see if she's at all suspicious. But she is too upset to pay attention to Papá's business dealings.

"One last thing," Papá addresses the governor. "Why did you want to see my daughter, too?"

"Not to worry, Don Enrique. I just want to have a little talk with her."

"I can trust her then to your care?" Papá asks, looking the governor squarely in the eye. A man's word is a man's word.

"Absolutely. I make myself responsible." Don Antonio gives the *guardias* a nod. The audience is over. Papá is taken out of the room. We listen to their steps in the corridor before they're drowned by the sound of the rain outside, still coming down hard.

Mamá watches Don Antonio like an animal waiting to attack if her young one is threatened. The governor sits down on the edge of his desk and gives me a befriending smile. We have met a couple of times at official functions, including, of course, the last few parties. "Señorita Minerva," he begins, motioning Mamá and me towards two chairs a guard has just placed before him. "I believe there is a way you can help your father."

"¡*Desgraciado!*" Mamá is going on and on. I've never heard such language coming out of her mouth. "He calls himself a man of honor!"

I try to calm her. But I'll admit I like seeing this spunk in Mamá.

We are driving around in the rain in San Francisco, getting our last-minute errands done before we leave for the capital this afternoon to petition for Papá's release. I drop Mamá off at the *clínica* to get extra doses of Papá's medication, and I head for the barrio.

But the turquoise house with the white trim isn't where it used to be. I'm turning here and there, feeling desperate, when I catch a glimpse of the oldest girl, holding a piece of palm bark over her head and wading through the puddles on the street. The sight of her in her wet, raggedy dress tears my own heart to shreds. She must be on an errand, a knotted rag in her free hand, a poor girl's purse. I honk, and she stops, terrified. Probably, she's remembering the time I rammed into our father's car, blowing the horn.

I motion for her to come in the car. "I'm trying to find your mother," I tell her when she climbs in. She stares at me with that same scared look Papá wore only a couple of hours ago.

"Which way?" I ask her, pulling out on the street.

"That way." She motions with her hand.

"Right?"

She looks at me, not understanding. So, she doesn't know directions. Can she read, I wonder? "How do you spell your name, Margarita?" I test her.

She shrugs. I make a mental note that once I'm back, I'm going to make sure these girls are enrolled in school.

In a few turns we are at the little turquoise house. The mother runs out on the porch, clutching the collar of her dress against the rain blowing in. "Is Don Enrique all right?" A doubt goes through my head as to whether my father's assurances that he's no longer involved with this woman are true. That cleaving look in her eye is not just memory.

"He's been called away on urgent business," I tell her more sharply than I meant to.

Then, softening, I hand her the envelope. "I've brought you for the full month."

"You are so kind to think of us."

"I do want to ask you for a favor," I say, though I hadn't meant to ask her now.

She bites her lip as if she knows what I'm going to ask her. "Carmen María, at your orders," she says in the smallest of voices. Her daughter looks up quizzically. She must be used to a much fiercer version of her mother.

"The girls are not in school, are they?" A shake of her head. "May I enroll them when I get back?"

The look on her face is relieved. "You're the one who knows," she says.

"You know as well as I do that without schooling we women have even fewer choices open to us." I think of my own foiled plans. On the other hand, Elsa and Sinita, just starting their third year at the university, are already getting offers from the best companies.

"You are right, señorita. Look at me. I never had a chance." She holds out her empty hands, then looking at her eldest, she adds, "I want better for my girls."

I reach for her hand, and then it seems natural to continue the gesture and give her the hug I've refused Papá all month.

Luckily, the rain lets up for our drive to the capital. When we get there, we stop at each of the three hotels Don Antonio de la Maza wrote down. If no official charge has been made, Papá won't be jailed but put under house arrest at one of these hotels. When we're told at the final stop, Presidente, that no Enrique Mirabal has been registered, Mamá looks as if she is ready to cry. It's late, and the palace offices will be closed, so we decide to get a room for the night.

"We have a special weekly rate," the man offers. He is thin with a long, sad face.

I look over at Mamá to see what she thinks, but as usual, she doesn't say a word in public. In fact, this afternoon with Don Antonio was the first time I ever saw Mamá stand up for herself, or actually, for me and Papá. "We don't know if we'll need it for a whole week," I tell the man. "We're not sure if my father is being charged or not."

He looks from me to my mother and back to me. "Get the weekly rate," he suggests in a quiet voice. "I'll return the difference if you stay a shorter time."

The young man must know these cases are never quickly resolved. I write out the registration card, pressing down hard as he commands. The writing must go through all four copies, he explains.

One for the police, one for Internal Control, one for Military Intelligence, and one last one the young man sends along, not sure where it goes.

A day made in hell, sitting in one or another office of National Police Headquarters. Only the steady pounding of rain on the roof is gratifying, sounding as if old Huracán were beating on the building for all the crimes engineered inside.

We end up at the Office of Missing Persons to report what is now being described as the disappearance of Enrique Mirabal. The place is packed. Most people have been here hours before the office opened to get a good place in line. As the day wears on, I overhear case after case being described at the interrogation desk. It's enough to make me sick. Every so often, I go stand by the window and dab rainwater on my face. But this is the kind of headache that isn't going to go away.

Finally, towards the end of the day, we are the next in line. The petition right before ours is being filed by an elderly man reporting a missing son, one of his thirteen. I help him fill out his form since he isn't any good at his letters, he explains.

"You are the father of thirteen sons?" I ask in disbelief.

"*Sí, señora,*" the old man nods proudly. At the tip of my tongue is the question I burn to ask him, "How many different mothers?" But his troubles make all other considerations fall away. We get to the part where he has to list all his children.

"What's the oldest one's name?" I ask, pencil poised to write.

"Pablo Antonio Almonte."

I write out the full name, then it strikes me. "Isn't this the name of the missing son, and you said he's number three?"

In confidence, the old man tells me that he gave all thirteen sons the same name to try to outwit the regime. Whichever son is caught can swear he isn't the brother they want!

I laugh at the ingenuity of my poor, trapped countryman. I put my own ingenuity to work, coming up with a dozen names from my reading, because, of course, I don't want to give the sons any real Dominican names and get someone in trouble. The head officer has a time reading them. "Fausto? Dimitri? Pushkin? What kind of a name is that?" I'm summoned to help since the old man can't read what I wrote. When I finish, the suspicious officer points to the old man, who is nodding away at the names I've read off. "You say them now."

"My memory," the old man complains. "There are too many."

The officer narrows his eyes at him. "How do you call your sons, then?"

"*Bueno, oficial,*" the cagey old man says, turning and turning his sombrero in his hands, "I call them all, *m'ijo.*" Son, that's what he calls them all.

I smile sweetly, and the decorated chest puffs out. He wants to get on to new game. "We'll do what we can, *compay*," he promises, stamping the form before him and readily accepting the "fee" of rolled-up pesos.

Now it's our turn, but unfortunately, the head officer announces that the office is closing in five minutes. "We've waited so long," I plead to my guard.

"Me, too, all my life to meet you, señorita. So don't break my heart. Come back tomorrow." He looks me up and down, flirting. This time I do not smile back.

I've shot myself in the foot is what I've done by helping out the old Don Juan. Prolonging his audience, I lost us ours today.

Mamá sighs when I tell her that we have to come back tomorrow. *"Ay, m'ijita,"* she says. "You're going to fight everyone's fight, aren't you?"

"It's all the same fight, Mamá," I tell her.

Early next morning, we wake up to a banging at our room door. Four heavily armed guards inform me that I am to be taken to headquarters for questioning. I try to calm Mamá, but my own hands are shaking so bad I can't button up my dress.

At the door, Mamá informs the guards that if I go, she goes, too. But these are a meaner breed than the ones up north. When she tries to follow me out, a guard blocks her way with a thrust of his bayonet.

"No need for that," I say, lifting the bayonet. I reach over and kiss my mother's hand. *"Mamá, la bendición,"* I say, the way I used to as a child before going off to school.

By now, Mamá is sobbing. *"Dios te bendiga,"* she sniffles, then reminds me, "Watch your you-know-what!" I realize she no longer means just my mouth.

I am back at the National Police Headquarters, an office we did not see yesterday. The room is breezy and light, a top floor. Someone in charge.

A courtly, white-haired man comes forward from behind his desk. "Welcome," he says, as if I were here for a social call.

He introduces himself, General Federico Fiallo. And then indicates someone behind me I did not notice when I walked in. I don't know how I could have missed him. He is as close to a toad as a man can look. A heavy-set mulatto with mirrored dark glasses that flash my own scared look back at my face.

"Don Anselmo Paulino," the general introduces him. Everyone knows about Magic Eye. He lost an eye in a knife fight, but his remaining good eye magically sees what everyone else misses. In the last few years, he's risen to be Trujillo's right-hand man by the dirty "security" work he's willing to do.

My empty stomach is churning with dread. I steel myself, recalling face after suffering face I saw yesterday just downstairs. "What do you want with me?"

The general smiles in a kindly way. "I'm keeping you standing, señorita," he apologizes, ignoring my question. The kindness gives way a moment when he snaps his fingers and curtly admonishes the *guardias* for not putting out chairs for his guests. Once the toad and I are seated, the general turns back to his desk. "You must look on me as your protector. Young ladies are the flowers of our country."

He opens the file before him. From where I sit, I can see the pink registration slip from the hotel. Then a number of sheets of paper I recognize as Lío's letters from my purse.

"I am here to ask you some questions about a young man I believe you are acquainted with." He looks squarely at me. "Virgilio Morales."

I feel ready—as I wasn't before—to risk the truth. "Yes, I know Virgilio Morales."

Magic Eye is at the edge of his chair, the veins on his neck showing. "You lied to El Jefe. You claimed you didn't know him, didn't you?"

"Now, now, Don Anselmo," the elderly general soothes. "We don't want to scare the young lady, now do we?"

But Magic Eye doesn't observe such fine distinctions. "Answer me," he orders. He has lit a cigar. Smoke pours from his nostrils like a dark nosebleed.

"Yes, I denied knowing him. I was afraid"— again I choose my words carefully—"of displeasing El Jefe." It is just short of an apology. All I will give.

General Fiallo and Paulino exchange a significant glance. I wonder how there can be any communication between those ancient milky eyes and those dark glasses.

The general picks up a page from the folder and peruses it. "What is the nature of your relationship with Virgilio Morales, Señorita Minerva?"

"We were friends."

"Come, come," he says, coaxing me as if I were a stubborn child. "These are love letters." He holds up a sheaf of papers. *Dios mío*, has everyone in this country been reading my mail except me?

"But you must believe me, we were just friends. If I'd been in love with him, I would have left the country as he wanted me to."

"True," the general concedes. He looks over at Magic Eye, who is stubbing his cigar on the sole of his boot.

"Were you not aware, Señorita Minerva, that Virgilio Morales is an enemy of state?" Magic Eye intervenes. He has put the extinguished cigar back in his mouth.

"I wasn't involved in any treasonous activity if that's what you're asking. He was just a friend, like I said."

"And you are not in communication with him now?" Magic Eye again is taking over the interview. The general raises a perturbed eyebrow. After all this is his breezy office, his top floor, his pretty prisoner.

The truth is that I did write to Lío after I found his letters. But Mario couldn't deliver my note as no one really knows to this day where Lío is. "No, I am not in communication with Virgilio Morales." I address my remark to the general even though the question came from Magic Eye.

"That's what I like to hear." The general turns to Magic Eye. "We have another little matter to discuss, Don Anselmo. Not relating to security." He smiles politely, dismissing him. Magic Eye flashes his dark glasses at the general a second, then stands, and sidles to the door. I notice he has never given his back to us.

General Fiallo now begins chatting about the days he spent posted in El Cibao, the beauty of that region, the lovely cathedral in the square. I am wondering where all this is going, when a door opens across from the one we entered by. Manuel de Moya, tall and dapper, sporting a Prince of Wales ascot.

"Good morning, good morning," he says cheerfully as if we're all about to go on safari. "How are things?" He rubs his hands together. "Don Federico, how are you?" They exchange pleasantries a moment, and then Don Manuel looks approvingly at me. "I had a word with Paulino in the hall as he was leaving. It seems Señorita Minerva has been quite cooperative. I am so glad." He addresses me sincerely. "I hate to see ladies in any kind of distress."

"It must be difficult for you," I acknowledge. He does not catch the sarcasm in my voice.

"So you thought you might be displeasing El Jefe by admitting to a friendship with Virgilio Morales?" I nod. "I'm sure it would mean a great deal to our Benefactor to hear that you have his pleasure in mind."

I wait. I can tell from hanging around these guys that there is bound to be more.

"I believe Don Antonio has already spoken to you?"

"Yes," I say, "he did."

"I hope you will reconsider his offer. I'm sure General Fiallo would agree"—General Fiallo is already nodding before any mention has been made of what he is agreeing to—"that a private conference with El Jefe would be the quickest, most effective way to end all this nonsense."

"*Sí, sí, sí,*" General Fiallo agrees.

Don Manuel continues. "I would like to bring you personally to him tonight at his suite at El Jaragua. Bypass all this red tape." He gestures towards the general, who smiles inanely at his own put-down.

I stare at Manuel de Moya as if pinning him to the wall. "I'd sooner jump out that window than be forced to do something against my honor."

Manuel de Moya plunges his hands in his pockets and paces the room. "I've tried my best, señorita. But you must cooperate a little bit. It can't all be your way."

"What I've done wrong, I'm willing to acknowledge, personally to El Jefe, yes." I nod at the surprised secretary. "But surely, my father and mother can come along as fellow sufferers in my error."

Manuel de Moya shakes his head. "Minerva Mirabal, you are as complicated a woman as . . . as . . ." He throws up his hands, unable to finish the comparison.

But the general comes up with it. "As El Jefe is a man."

The two men look at each other, weighing something heavy in their heads.

Since I am not bedding down with him, it is three more weeks before El Jefe can see us. As far as we can tell, Mamá and I are under arrest since we aren't allowed to leave the hotel to go home and wait there. Pedrito and Jaimito have come and gone a dozen times, petitioning here, visiting a friend with pull there. Dedé and Patria have taken turns staying with us and arranging for our meals.

When the day of our appointment finally arrives, we are at the palace early, eager to see Papá, who has just been released. He is such a pitiful sight. His face is gaunt, his voice shaky; his once fancy *guayabera* is soiled and hangs on him, several sizes too large. He and Mamá and I embrace. I can feel his bony shoulders. "How have they treated you?" we ask him.

His eyes have a strange absence in them. "As well as can be expected," he says. I notice he does not look directly at us when he answers.

We already know from Dedé and Patria's searches that Papá has been in the prison hospital. The diagnosis is "confidential," but we all assumed his ulcers were acting up. Now we learn Papá suffered a heart attack in his cell the Wednesday after he was arrested, but it wasn't till the following Monday that he was allowed to see a doctor. "I'm feeling much better." His thin hands pleat his trousers as he talks. "Much much better. I just hope the music hasn't spoiled the yuccas while I've been gone."

Mamá and I look at each other and then at Papá. "How's that, Enrique?" Mamá asks gently.

"Every time there's a party, half the things in the ground spoil. We've got to stop feeding the hogs. It's all human teeth anyhow."

It's all I can do to keep up the pretense that Papá is making sense. But Mamá's sweetness enfolds him and coaxes him back. "The hogs are doing very well on palm fruit, and we haven't grown yuccas since this one here was a little girl. Don't you remember, Enrique, how we used to be up till all hours on harvest days?"

Papá's eyes light up, remembering. "The first year you wanted to look pretty for me, so you wore a nice dress to the fields. By the time we finished, it looked like the sackcloth the yuccas were in!" He is looking directly at her, smiling.

She smiles at him, her eyes glistening with tears. Her fingers find his hand and hold tight, as if she were pulling him up from an edge she lost him to years back.

El Jefe does not bother to look up as we enter. He is going over a stack of papers with several nervous assistants, his manicured hands following the words being read out to him. He learned his letters late, so the story goes, and refuses to look at anything over a page long. In the offices around him, official readers go through thick reports, boiling the information down to the salient paragraph.

Behind him on the wall, the famous motto: MY BEST FRIENDS ARE MEN WHO WORK. What about the women who sleep with you? I ask in my head.

Manuel de Moya shows us our seats in front of the large mahogany desk. It is a disciplined man's desk, everything in neat stacks, several phones lined up on one side beside a board with labeled buzzers. A panel of clocks ticks away. He must be keeping time in several countries. Right in front of me stands a set of scales like the kind Justice holds up, each small tray bearing a set of dice.

Trujillo scribbles a last signature and waves the assistants out of the room, then turns to his secretary of state. Don Manuel opens a leather folder and reads El Jefe the letter of apology signed by the whole Mirabal family.

"I see Señorita Minerva has signed this," he notes as if I were not present. He reads off Mamá's name and asks if she is related to Chiche Reyes.

"Why Chiche is my uncle!" Mamá exclaims. Tío Chiche has always bragged about knowing Trujillo during their early days in the military. "Chiche worships you, Jefe. He always says even back then he could tell you were a natural leader."

"I have a lot of affection for Don Chiche," Trujillo says, obviously enjoying the homage. He lifts a set of dice from his scales, upsetting the balance. "I suppose he never told you the story of these?"

Mamá smiles indulgently. She has never approved of her uncle's gambling. "That Chiche loves his gambling."

"Chiche cheats too much," Papá blurts out. "I won't play with him." Mamá's eyes are boring a hole in Papá. Our one lifeline in this stormy sea and Papá is cutting the rope she's been playing out.

"I take it you like to play, Don Enrique?" Trujillo turns coldly to Papá.

Papá glances at Mamá, afraid to admit it in her presence. "I know you like to gamble," Mamá squabbles, diverting attention by pretending our real predicament is her naughty husband.

Trujillo returns to the dice in his hands. "That Chiche! He stole a piece of bone from Columbus's crypt and had these made for me when I was named head of the armed forces."

Mamá tries to look impressed, but in fact, she's never liked her troublemaking uncle very much. Every month, it's a knife fight or money trouble or wife trouble or mistress trouble or just plain trouble.

Trujillo puts his dice back on the empty tray. It's then I notice the sides don't balance. Of course, my good-for-nothing uncle would give his buddy loaded dice.

"Human teeth, all of it," Papá mumbles. He looks at the small cubes of bone with a horrified expression on his face.

Mamá indicates her husband with a toss of the head. "You must excuse him, Jefe. He is not well." Her eyes fill, and she dabs at them with the kerchief she keeps balling in her hand.

"Don Enrique will be just fine as soon as he's home for a few days. But may this teach you all a lesson." He turns to me. The cajoling smile of the dance is gone. "You especially, señorita. I've asked that you check in every week with Governor de la Maza in San Francisco."

Before I can say something, Mamá breaks in. "All my daughter wants is to be a good, loyal citizen of the regime."

El Jefe looks my way, waiting for my pledge.

I decide to speak up for what I *do* want. "Jefe, I don't know if you remember what we spoke of at the dance?" I can feel Mamá giving me the eye.

But El Jefe's interest is piqued. "We spoke of many things."

"I mean, my dream of going to law school."

He strokes his short, brush mustache with his fingers, musing. His gaze falls on the dice. Slowly, his lips twist in a wily smile. "I'll tell you what. I'll let you toss for the privilege. You win, you get your wish. I win, I get mine."

I can guess what he wants. But I'm so sure I can beat him now that I know his secret. "I'll toss," I say, my voice shaking.

He laughs and turns to Mamá. "I think you have another Chiche in the family."

Quickly I reach for the heavier set of dice and begin shaking them in my fist. Trujillo studies the wobbling scales. But without my set there, he can't tell which are his loaded pair. "Go ahead," he says, eyeing me closely. "Highest number wins."

I shake the dice in my hand for all they're worth.

I roll a double and look up at Trujillo, trying to keep the glee from my face.

He stares at me with his cold, hard eyes. "You have a strong hand, that I know." He strokes the cheek I slapped, smiling a razor-sharp smile that cuts me down to size. Then rather than using the remaining dice on the tray, he puts his hand out and takes my uncle's set back. He maneuvers them knowingly. Out they roll, a double as well. "We either both get our wishes or we call it even, for now," he adds.

"Even," I say, looking him in the eye, "for now."

"Sign their releases," he tells Don Manuel. "My hellos to Don Chiche," he tells Mamá. Then, we are banished with a wave of his hand.

I look down at the lopsided scales as he puts his dice back. For a moment, I imagine them evenly balanced, his will on one side, mine on the other.

It is raining when we leave the capital, a drizzle that builds to a steady downpour by the time we hit Villa Altagracia. We roll up the windows until it gets so steamy and damp in the car that we have to crack them open in order to see out.

Dedé and Jaimito stayed on in the capital, making some purchases for the new restaurant they've decided to start. The ice cream business is a flop just as Dedé predicted privately to me some time back. Pedrito had to be back yesterday to see about stranded cattle in the flooded fields. He's been taking care of his own farm and ours. So, it's just me and Mamá, and Patria and, of course, Papá mumbling in the back seat of the car.

By Pino Herrado, the rain is coming down hard. We stop at a little cantina until it lets up. Mamá doesn't raise an eyebrow when Papá orders a shot of rum. She's too worried about our audience with El Jefe to fuss at him. "You were asking for it, *m'ija*," she's already told me. We sit silently, listening to the rain on the thatched roof, a numb, damp, fatalistic feeling among us. Something has started none of us can stop.

A soft rain is falling when we reach Piedra Blanca. Ahead, men repair a flooded bridge, so we stop and roll down the windows to watch. *Marchantas* come up to offer us their wares and, tempted by a sample taste of a small, sweet orange, we buy a whole sack of them, already peeled and cut in half. Later, we have to stop to wash our sticky hands in puddles on the roadside.

At Bonao the torrential rains start again and the windshield wipers can't keep pace with the waves of water washing over us. In my head, I start making plans about where we can spend the night if the rain is still this bad once it gets dark.

We pass La Vega, and the rain is lighter now, but shows no sign of letting up. The whole spine of the country is wet. Towards the west, dark clouds shroud the mountains as far as Constanza and on through the whole cordillera to the far reaches of Haiti.

Rain is falling and night is falling in Moca as we pass, the palm roofs sagging, the soil soggy with drowned seeds, the drenched jacarandas losing their creamy blossoms. A few miles after Salcedo, my lights single it out, the ancient anacahuita tree, dripping in the rain, most of its pods gone. I turn into the unpaved road, hoping we won't get stuck in the mud I hear slapping against the underside of the car.

It's raining here, too, in Ojo de Agua. Eye of Water! The name seems ironic given the weather. North to Tamboril and the mountain road to Puerto Plata, the rain drives on, in every *bohío* and small *conuco*, and on out to the Atlantic where it is lost in the waves that rock the bones of martyrs in the deepest sleep. We've traveled almost the full length of the island and can report that every corner of it is wet, every river overflows its banks, every rain barrel is filled to the brim, every wall washed clean of writing no one knows how to read anyway.

CHAPTER SEVEN

María Teresa

1953 to 1958

1953

Tuesday morning, December 15
Fela says rain

I feel like dying myself!

I can't believe she came to the funeral mass with her girls, adding four more slaps to her big blow. One of them looked to be only a few years younger than me, so you couldn't really say, *Ay*, poor Papá, he lost it at the end and went behind the palm trees. He was bringing down coconuts when he was good and hardy and knew what he was doing.

I asked Minerva who invited them.

All she said was they were Papá's daughters, too.

I can't stop crying! My cute cousins Raúl and Berto are coming over, and I look a sight. But I don't care. I really don't.

I hate men. I really hate them.

Wednesday evening, December 16

Here I am crying again, ruining my new diary book Minerva gave me. She was saving it up for my Epiphany present, but she saw me so upset at Papá's funeral, she thought it would help me most now.

Minerva always says writing gets things off her chest and she feels better, but I'm no writer, like she is. Besides, I swore I'd never keep a diary again after I had to bury my Little Book years back. But I'm desperate enough to try anything.

Monday, December 21

I am a little better now. For minutes at a time, I forget about Papá and the whole sad business.

Christmas Eve

Every time I look at Papá's place at the table my eyes fill with tears. It makes it very hard to eat meals. What a bitter end of the year!

Christmas Day

We are all trying. The day is rainy, a breeze keeps blowing through the cacao. Fela says that's the dead calling us. It makes me shiver to hear her say that after the dream I had last night.

We had just laid out Papá in his coffin on the table when a limousine pulls up to the house. My sisters climb out, including that bunch that call themselves my sisters, all dressed up like a wedding party. It turns out I'm the one getting married, but I haven't a clue who the groom is.

I'm running around the house trying to find my wedding dress when I hear Mamá call out to look in Papá's coffin!

The car horn is blowing, so I go ahead and raise the lid. Inside is a beautiful satin gown—in pieces. I lift out the one arm, and then another arm, then the bodice, and more parts below. I'm frantic, thinking we still have to sew this thing together.

When I get to the bottom, there's Papá, smiling up at me.

I drop all those pieces like they're contaminated and wake up the whole house with my screams.

(I'm so spooked. I wonder what it means? I plan on asking Fela who knows how to interpret dreams.)

Sunday afternoon, December 27

Today is the feast day of San Juan Evangelista, a good day for fortunes. I give Fela my coffee cup this morning after I'm done. She turns it over, lets the dregs run down the sides, then she reads the markings.

I prod her. Does she see any *novios* coming?

119

She turns the cup around and around. She shows me where two stains collide and says that's a pair of brothers. I blush, because I guess she can tell about Berto and Raúl. Again, she slowly rotates the cup. She says she sees a professional man in a hat. Then, a *capitaleño*, she can tell by the way he stands.

I am at the edge of my seat, smiling in spite of these sad times, asking for more.

"You'll have to have a second cup of coffee, señorita," she says, setting the cup down. "All your admirers can't fit in one cup of fortune."

¿Berto & Mate?

¿Mate & Raúl ?

¿¿¿¿¿¿¿¿¿forever??????????

Ojo de Agua, Salcedo

30 December 1953

Twenty-third year of the Era of Trujillo

Generalísimo Doctor Rafael L. Trujillo
Benefactor of our Country

Illustrious and well-loved Jefe,

Knowing as I do, the high esteem in which my husband Enrique Mirabal held your illustrious person, and now somewhat less confounded by the irreparable loss of my unforgettable compañero, I write to inform Your Excellency of his death on Monday, the fourteenth day of this month.

I want to take this opportunity to affirm my husband's undying loyalty to Your Person and to avow that both myself and my daughters will continue in his footsteps as your loyal and devoted subjects. Especially now, in this dark moment, we look to your beacon from our troubled waters and count on your beneficent protection and wise counsel until we should breathe the very last breath of our own existence.

With greetings from my uncle, Chiche, I am most respectfully,

Mercedes Reyes de Mirabal

Wednesday late afternoon, December 30

Mamá and I just spent most of the afternoon drafting the letter Tío Chiche suggested she write. Minerva wasn't here to help. She left for Jarabacoa three days ago. Tío Fello dragged her off right after Christmas because he found her very thin and sad and thought the mountain air would invigorate her. Me, I just eat when I'm sad and so I look "the picture of health," as Tío Fello put it.

Not that Minerva would have been much help. She is no good at the flowery feelings like I am. Last October, when she had to give her speech praising El Jefe at the Salcedo Civic Hall, guess who wrote it for her? It worked, too. Suddenly, she got her permission to go to law school. Every once in a while Trujillo has to be buttered up, I guess, which is why Tío Chiche thought this letter might help.

Tomorrow I'll copy it in my nice penmanship, then Mamá can sign it with her signature I've taught her to write.

Sunset

I ask Fela, without mentioning any names, if she has something I can use to spell a certain bad person.

She says to write this person's name on a piece of paper, fold it, and put the paper in my left shoe because that is the foot Eve used to crush the head of the serpent. Then burn it, and scatter those ashes near the hated person.

I'll sprinkle them all over the letter is what I'll do.

What would happen if I put the name in my right shoe? I ask Fela.

The right foot is for problems with someone you love.

So, I'm walking around doing a double spell, Rafael Leonidas Trujillo in one shoe, Enrique Mirabal in the other.

Thursday night, December 31
last day of this old sad year

I can write the saddest things tonight.

Here I am looking out at the stars, everything so still, so mysterious. What does it all mean, anyway?

(I don't like this kind of thinking like Minerva likes. It makes my asthma worse.)

I want to know things I don't even know what they are.

But I could be happy without answers if I had someone to love.

> And so it is of human life the goal
> to seek, forever seek, the kindred soul.

I quoted that to Minerva before she left for Jarabacoa. But she got down our *Gems of Spanish Poetry* and quoted me another poem by the same poet:

> May the limitations of love not cast a spell
> On the serious ambitions of my mind.

I couldn't believe the same man had written those two verses. But sure enough, there it was, *José Martí*, dates and all. Minerva showed me her poem was written later. "When he knew what mattered."

Maybe she's right, what does love come to, anyway? Look at Papá and Mamá after so many years.

I can write the saddest things tonight.

1954

Friday night, January 1

I have been awful really.

I, a young girl in *luto* with her father fresh in the ground.

I have kissed B. *on the lips!* He caught my hand and led me behind a screen of palms.

Oh horror! Oh shamelessness! Oh disgust!

Please make me ashamed, Oh God.

Friday evening, January 8

R. dropped in for a visit today and stayed and stayed. I knew he was waiting for Mamá to leave us alone. Sure enough, Mamá finally stood up, hinting that it was time for people to be thinking about supper, but R. hung on. Mamá left, and R. lit into me. What was this about B. kissing me? I was so mad at B. for telling on us after he promised he wouldn't. I told R. that if I never saw his face or his silly brother's again, it was *perfecto* with me!

Sunday afternoon, January 10

Minerva just got back with a very special secret.

First, I told her my secret about B. and she laughed and said how far ahead of her I am. She says she has not been kissed for years! I guess there are some bad parts to being somebody everybody respects.

Well, maybe she has more than a kiss coming soon. She met somebody VERY special in Jarabacoa. It turns out, this special person is also studying law in the capital, although he's two years ahead of her. And here's something else he doesn't even know yet. Minerva is five years older than he is. She figured it out from something he said, but she says that he's so mature at twenty-three, you wouldn't know it. The only thing, Minerva adds, real breezy and smart the way she can be so cool, is the poor man's already engaged to somebody else.

"Two-timer!" I still hurt so much about Papá. "He can't be a very nice man," I tell Minerva. "Give him up!"

But Minerva's already defending this gallant she just met. She says it's better he look around now before he takes the plunge.

I guess she's right. I know I'm taking a very good look around before I close my eyes and fall in true love.

Thursday, January 14

Minerva is up to her old tricks again. She wraps a towel around the radio and lies under the bed listening to illegal stations.

Today she was down there for hours. There was a broadcast of a speech by this man Fidel, who is trying to overturn their dictator over in Cuba. Minerva has big parts memorized. Now, instead of her poetry, she's always reciting, *Condemn me, it does not matter. History will absolve me!*

I am so hoping that now that Minerva has found a special someone, she'll settle down. I mean, I agree with her ideas and everything. I think people should be kind to each other and share what they have. But never in a million years would I take up a gun and force people to give up being mean.

Minerva calls me her little petit bourgeois. I don't even ask her what that means because she'll get on me again about not continuing with my French. I decided to take English instead—as we are closer to the U.S.A. than France.

Hello, my name is Mary Mirabal. I speak a little English. Thank you very much.

Sunday afternoon, January 17

Minerva just left for the capital to go back to school. Usually I'm the one who cries when people leave, but this time, everyone was weepy. Even Minerva's eyes filled up. I guess we're all still grieving over Papá, and any little sadness brings up that bigger one.

Dedé and Jaimito are staying the night with Jaime Enrique and Baby Jaime Rafael. (Jaimito always brands his boys with his own first name.) Tomorrow we'll head back to San Francisco. It's all settled. I'm going to be a day student and live with Dedé and Jaimito during the week, then come home weekends to keep Mamá company.

I'm so relieved. After we got in trouble with the government and Papá started losing money, a lot of those nose-in-the-air girls treated me awfully. I cried myself to sleep in my dormitory cot every night, and of course, that only made my asthma worse.

This arrangement also helps Dedé and Jaimito, too, as Mamá is paying them for my boarding. Talk about money troubles! Those two have had back luck twice already, what with that ice cream business, now with the restaurant. Even so, Dedé makes the best of it. Miss Sonrisa, all right.

Saturday night, February 6
Home for the weekend

I've spent all day getting everything ready. Next Sunday, the day of *lovers*, Minerva comes to visit and she's bringing her special someone she met in Jarabacoa!!!

Manolo wants to meet you, Minerva wrote us, and then added, *For your eyes only: You'll be pleased to know he broke off his engagement.* Since

I'm the one who reads all our mail to Mamá, I can leave out whatever Minerva marks in the margin with a big EYE.

I'm probably messing up our whole privacy system because I'm teaching Mamá to read. I've been after her for years, but she'd say, "I just don't have a head for letters." I think what convinced her is Papá's dying and me being away at school and the business losing money and Mamá having to mind the store pretty much by herself. There was talk at the dinner table of Dedé and Jaimito moving back out here and running things for Mamá. Dedé joked that they've got a lot of experience with ailing businesses. Jaimito, I could tell, didn't think she was one bit funny.

There's going to be a scene when we get back to San Fran.

Sunday morning, February 14

We're expecting Minerva and Manolo any minute. The way I can't sit still, Mamá says, you'd think it was my own beau coming!

Dinner is *all* in my hands. Mamá says it's good practice for when I have my own house. But she's begged me to stop running everything by her as she's losing her appetite from eating so many imaginary dinners in her head.

So here's my final menu:

(Bear in mind today is the Day of Lovers and so red is my theme.)

Salad of tomatoes and pimientos with hibiscus garnish
Pollo a la criolla (lots of tomato paste in my San Valentín version)
Moors and Christians rice — heavy on the beans for the red-brown color
Carrots — I'm going to shape the rings into little hearts
Arroz con leche

— because you know how the song goes —

Arroz con leche
wants to marry
a clever girl
from the capital
who sews

125

who darns
who puts back her needle
where it belongs!

Night

Manolo just loved my cooking! That man ate seconds and thirds, stopping only long enough to say how delicious everything was. Mamá kept winking at me.

His other good qualities, let's see. He is tall and very handsome and so romantic. He kept hold of Minerva's hand under the table all through the meal.

As soon as they left for the capital, Dedé and Mamá and Patria started in making bets about when the *wedding* would be. "We'll have it here," Dedé said. *Ay, sí,* it's final, Dedé and Jaimito are going to move back to Ojo de Agua. Mamá's told them they can have this house as she wants to build a more convenient "modern" one on the main road. That way she won't be so isolated when all her little chickens have flown. "Just my baby left now," she says, smiling at me.

Oh, diary, how I hate when she forgets I'm already eighteen.

Monday night, February 15
Back in San Fran

I keep hoping that someone special will come into my life soon. Someone who can ravish my heart with the flames of love. (*Gems of Mate Mirabal!*)

I try to put together the perfect man from all the boys I know. It's sort of like making a menu:

Manolo's dimples
Raúl's fairytale-blue eyes
Berto's curly hair & smile
Erasmo's beautiful hands
Federico's broad shoulders
Carlos's nice *fundillos* (Yes, we girls notice them, too!)

And then, that mystery *something* that will make the whole—as we learned in Mathematics—more than the sum of these very fine parts.

Monday night, March 1
San Fran

As *you* well know, diary, I have ignored you *totally*. I hope this will not develop into a bad habit. But I have not been in a very confiding mood.

The night after Manolo came to dinner, I had the same bad dream about Papá. Except when I pulled out all the pieces of wedding dress, Papá's face shifted, and it wasn't Papá anymore, but Manolo!

That started me worrying about Manolo. How he went after Minerva while he was still engaged. Now he's this wonderful, warm, loving man, I say to myself, but will that change with time?

I guess I've fallen into suspicion which Padre Ignacio says is as bad as falling into temptation. I went to see him about my ill feelings towards Papá. "You must not see every man as a potential serpent," he warned me.

And I don't really think I do. I mean, I like men. I want to marry one of them.

Graduation Day!!! July 3

Diary, I know you have probably thought me dead all these months. But you must believe me, I have been too busy for words. In fact, I have to finish writing down Tía's recipe on a card so I can start in on my thank-you notes. I must get them out soon or I shall lose that proper glow of appreciation one feels right after receiving gifts one does not need or even like all that much.

Tía Flor's made a To Die Dreaming Cake for my graduation party. (It's her own special recipe inspired by the drink.) She hauled me into my bedroom to have me write it down, so she said. I had praised it over and over, in word and—I'm afraid—indeed. *Ay, sí*, two pieces, and then some. My hips, my hips! Maybe I should rechristen this To Die Fat Cake?!

In the middle of telling me about beating the batter until it's real foamy (make it look and feel like soap bubbles, she told me) suddenly, straight out, she says, We've got some talking to do, young lady.

Sure, Tía, I say in a little voice. Tía is kind of big and imposing and her thick black eyebrows have scared me since childhood. (I used to call them her mustaches!)

She says Berto and Raúl aren't like brothers anymore, fighting all the time. She wants me to decide which one I want, then let the other one go eat tamarinds. So, she says, which one is it going to be?

Neither one, I blurt out because suddenly I see that what I'm headed for with either one is this mother-in-law.

Neither one! She sits down on the edge of my bed. Neither one? What? Are you too good for my boys?

Wednesday afternoon, July 7

Thank-yous not yet written:

Dedé and Jaimito—my favorite perfume (Matador's Delight). Also, an
    I.O.U. for the new Luis Alberti record when we next go to
    the capital.
Minerva—a poetry book by someone named Gabriela Mistral (?) and
    a pretty gold ring with an opal, my birthstone, set inside four
    cornerstone pearls. We have to get the size fixed in the capi-
    tal. Here's a drawing of it:

Manolo—an ivory frame for my graduation picture. "And for your
    final *beau* when the time comes!" He winks. I'm liking him a
    lot more again.
Tío Pepe and Tía Flor, Raúl, Berto—the cutest little vanity table with
    a skirt the same fabric as my bedspread. Tío made the vanity
    & Tía sewed the skirt for it. Maybe she's not so bad, after all!
    As for Raúl, he offered me his class ring & wanted us to be
    novios. Soon after, Berto cornered me in the garden with his

"Magnet Lips." I told them both I wanted them as friends,
and they both said they understood—it was too soon after
Papá's death. (What I didn't tell either of them was that I met
this young lawyer who did my inheritance transfer this
Friday, Justo Gutiérrez. He's so kind and has the nicest way
of saying, Sign here.)

Patria and Pedrito—a music box from Spain that plays four tunes.
The Battle Cry of Freedom, My Little Sky, There Is Nothing
Like a Mother, and another I can't pronounce—it's foreign.
Also a St. Christopher's for my travels.

Tío Tilo and Tía Eufemia, María, Milagros, Marina—seashell earrings
and bracelet set I would never wear in a thousand years! I
wonder if Tía Eufemia is trying to jinx me so her three old
maid daughters stand a better chance? Everyone knows
seashells keep a girl single, everyone except Tía Eufemia, I
guess.

Mamá—a monogrammed suitcase from El Gallo for taking to the capital. It's settled. I'm going to the university in the fall with
Minerva. Mamá also gave me her old locket with Papá's picture inside. I haven't opened it once. It spooks me on
account of my dream. She has transferred my inheritance to
my name. $10,000!!! I'm saving it for my future, and of
course, clothes & more clothes.

Even Fela gave me a gift. A sachet of magic powders to ward off the
evil eye when I go to the capital. I asked if this also worked as a love
potion. Tono heard me and said, "Somebody has a man in her life."
Then Fela, who delivered me and knows me in and out, burst out
laughing and said, "A man?! This one's got a whole cemetery of them
in her heart! More heartbroken men buried in there than—"

They've both grown careful since we found out about the yardboy
Prieto. Yes, our trusted Prieto has been reporting everything he hears in
the Mirabal household down at Security for a bottle of rum and a couple of pesos. Tío Chiche came and told us. Of course, we can't fire him
or that would look like we have something to hide. But he's been pro-

moted, so we told him, from the yard to the hogpen. Now he hasn't much to report except oink, oink, oink all day.

Friday night, full moon, July 9
Justo María Gutiérrez
Don Justo Gutiérrez and Doña María Teresa Mirabal de Gutiérrez
Mate & Justico, forever!!!

Saturday night, September 18
Tomorrow we leave for the capital.

I'm debating, diary, whether to take you along. As you can see, I haven't been very good about writing regularly. I guess Mamá's right, I *am* awfully moody about everything I do.

But there will be so many new sights and experiences and it will be good to have a record. But then again, I might be too busy with classes and what if I don't find a good hiding place & you fall into the wrong hands?

Oh diary dear, I have been so indecisive about everything all week! Yes, no, yes, no. I've asked everyone's opinion about half a dozen things. Should I take my red heels if I don't yet have a matching purse? How about my navy blue scalloped-neck dress that is a little tight under the arms? Are five baby dolls and nightgowns enough, as I like a fresh one every night?

One thing I was decisive about.

Justo was kind and said he understood. I probably needed time to get over my father's death. I just kept quiet. Why is it that every man I can't love seems to feel I would if Papá hadn't died?

Monday afternoon, September 27
The capital
What a huge, exciting place! Every day I go out, my mouth drops open like the *campesino* in the joke. So many big elegant houses with high walls and *guardias* and cars and people dressed up in the latest styles I've seen in *Vanidades*.

It's a hard city to keep straight, though, so I don't go out much unless Minerva or one of her friends is with me. All the streets are named after Trujillo's family, so it's kind of confusing. Minerva told me this joke about how to get to Parque Julia Molina from Carretera El Jefe. "You take the road of El Jefe across the bridge of his youngest son to the street of his oldest boy, then turn left at the avenue of his wife, walk until you reach the park of his mother and you're there."

Every morning, first thing, we turn to *El Foro Público*. It's this gossip column in the paper signed by Lorenzo Ocumares, a phony name if I ever heard one. The column's really written over at the National Palace and it's meant to "serve notice" to anyone who has been treading on the tail of the rabid dog, as we say back home. Minerva says everyone in the whole capital turns to it before the news. It's gotten so that I just close my eyes while she reads me the column, dreading the mention of our name. But ever since Minerva's speech and Mamá's letter (and my shoe spell) we haven't had any trouble with the regime.

Which reminds me. I must find you a better hiding place, diary. It's not safe carrying you around in my pocketbook on the street of his mother or the avenue of his little boy.

Sunday night, October 3

We marched today before the start of classes. Our *cédulas* are stamped when we come back through the gates. Without those stamped *cédulas*, we can't enroll. We also have to sign a pledge of loyalty.

There were hundreds of us, the women all together, in white dresses like we were his brides, with white gloves and any kind of hat we wanted. We had to raise our right arms in a salute as we passed by the review stand.

It looked like the newsreels of Hitler and the Italian one with the name that sounds like fettuccine.

Tuesday evening, October 12

As I predicted, there is not much time to write in your pages, diary. I am *always* busy. Also, for the first time in ages, Minerva and I are roommates again at Doña Chelito's where we board. So the temptation is always to talk things over with her. But sometimes she won't do at all—like right now when she is pushing me to stay with my original choice of law.

I know I used to say I wanted to be a lawyer like Minerva, but the truth is I always burst out crying if anyone starts arguing with me.

Minerva insists, though, that I give law a chance. So I've been tagging along to her classes all week. I'm sure I'll die either of boredom or my brain being tied up in knots! In her Practical Forensics class, she and the teacher, this little owl-like man, Doctor Balaguer, get into the longest discussions. All the other students keep yawning and raising their eyebrows at each other. I can't follow them myself. Today it was about whether—in the case of homicide—the *corpus delicti* is the knife or the dead man whose death is the actual proof of the crime. I felt like shouting, Who cares?!!!

Afterwards, Minerva asked me what I thought. I told her that I'm signing up for Philosophy and Letters tomorrow, which according to her is what girls who are planning to marry always sign up for. But she's not angry at me. She says I gave it a chance and that's what matters.

Wednesday night, October 13

This evening we went out for a walk, Manolo and Minerva, and a friends of theirs from law school who is very sweet, Armando Grullón.

When we got down to the Malecón, the whole area was sealed off. It was that time of the evening when El Jefe takes his nightly *paseo* by the seawall. That's how he holds his cabinet meetings, walking briskly, each minister getting his turn at being grilled, then falling back, gladly giving up his place to the next one on line.

Manolo started joking about how if El Jefe gets disgusted with any one of them, he doesn't even have to bother to send him to La Piscina to be fed to the sharks. Just elbow him right over the seawall!

It really scared me, him talking that way, *in public*, with guards all around and anybody a spy. I'm just dreading what we'll find in *El Foro Público* tomorrow.

Sunday night, October 17
¡El Foro Privado!
Seen walking in El Jardín Botánico
unchaperoned
Armando Grullón
and
María Teresa Mirabal
Mate & Armando, forever!!!

He put his arms around me, and then he tried to put his tongue in my mouth. I had to say, NO! I've heard from the other girls at Doña Chelito's that one has to be careful with these men in the capital.

Monday morning, October 18
I had the dream again last night. I hadn't had it in such a long time, it upset me all the more because I thought I'd gotten over Papá.

This time Armando played musical faces with Papá. I was so upset I woke up Minerva. Thank God, I didn't scream out and wake up everyone in the house. How embarrassing that would have been!

Minerva just held my hands like she used to when I was a little girl and was having an asthma attack. She said that the pain would go away once I found the man of my dreams. It wouldn't be long. She could feel it in her bones.

But I'm sure what she's feeling is her own happiness with Manolo.

1955

Sunday afternoon, November 20
Ojo de Agua

Diary, don't even ask where I've been for a year! And I wouldn't have found you either, believe me. The hiding place at Doña Chelito's was too good. Only when we went to pack up Minerva's things for her move, did I remember you stashed under the closet floorboards.

Today is the big day. It's been raining since dawn, and so Minerva's plan of walking to the church on foot like Patria did and seeing all the *campesinos* she's known since she was a little girl is out. But you know Minerva. She thinks we should just use umbrellas!

Mamá says Minerva should be glad, since a rainy wedding is suppose to bring good luck. "Blessings on the marriage bed," she smiles, and rolls her eyes.

She is so happy. Minerva is so happy. Rain or no rain, this is a happy day.

Then why am I so sad? Things are going to be different, I just know it, even though Minerva says they won't. Already, she's moved in with Manolo at Doña Isabel's, and I am left alone at Doña Chelito's with new boarders I hardly know.

"I never thought I'd see this day," Patria says from the rocking chair where she's sewing a few more satin rosebuds on the crown of the veil. Minerva at twenty-nine was considered beyond all hope of marriage by old-fashioned people like my sister Patria. That one married at sixteen, remember. *"Gracias, Virgencita,"* she says, looking up at the ceiling.

"Gracias, Manolo, you mean," Minerva laughs.

Then everyone starts in on me, how I'm next, and who is it going to be, and come on, tell, until I could cry.

Sunday evening, December 11
The capital

We just got back from marching in the opening ceremony for the World's Fair, and my feet are really hurting. Plus, the whole back of my dress is drenched with sweat. The only consolation is that if I was hot, "Queen" Angelita must have been burning up.

Imagine, in this heat wearing a gown sprinkled with rubies, diamonds, and pearls, and bordered with 150 feet of Russian ermine. It took 600 skins to make that border! All this was published in the paper like we should be impressed.

Manolo didn't even want Minerva to march. She could have gotten a release, too, since she's pregnant—yes! Those two are not waiting until she's done. But Minerva said there was no way she was going to let all her *compañeras* endure this cross without carrying her share.

We must have marched over four kilometers. As we passed Queen Angelita's review stand, we bowed our heads. I slowed a little when it was my turn so I could check her out. Her cape had a fur collar that rode up so high, and dozens of attendants were fanning her left and right. I couldn't see anything but a little, pouty, sort of pretty face gleaming with perspiration.

Looking at her, I almost felt sorry. I wondered if she knew how bad her father is or if she still thought, like I once did about Papá, that her father is God.

1956

Friday night, April 27
The capital

My yearly entry. I cannot tell a lie. If you look considerably slimmer, diary, it's only because you have been my all-purpose supply book. Paper for letters, shopping lists, class notes. I wish I could shed pounds as readily. I am on a *vast* diet so I can fit into my gown for the festivities. Tomorrow I go over to Minerva's to work on my speech.

Saturday afternoon, April 28
The capital

Honorable Rector, Professors, Fellow Classmates, Friends, Family, I'm really very touched from the bottom of my heart—

Minerva shakes her head. "Too gushy," she says.

I want to express my sincere gratitude for this great honor you have conferred on me by selecting me your Miss University for the coming year—

The baby starts crying again. She's been fussy all afternoon. I think she has a cold coming on. With rainy season here, everyone does. Of course, it could be that little Minou doesn't like my speech much!

135

I will do my very best to be a shining example of the high values that this, the first university in the New World, has instilled in its four hundred years of being a beacon of knowledge and a mine of wisdom to the finest minds that have been lucky enough to pass through the portals of this inspired community—

Minerva says this is going on too long without the required mention of you-know-who. Little Minou has quieted down, thank God. It's so nice of Minerva to help me out—with as much as she has to do with a new baby and her law classes. But she says she's glad I came over. It's kept her from missing Manolo, who couldn't make it down from Monte Cristi again this weekend.

But most especially, my most sincere gratitude goes to our true benefactor, El Jefe Rafael Leonidas Trujillo, Champion of Education, Light of the Antilles, First Teacher, Enlightener of His People.

"Don't overdo it," Minerva says. She reminds me it's going to be a hard crowd to address after this Galíndez thing.

She's right, too. The campus is buzzing with the horror story. Disappearances happen every week, but this time, it's someone who used to teach here. Also, Galíndez had already escaped to New York so everyone thought he was safe. But somehow El Jefe found out Galíndez was writing a book against the regime. He sent agents offering him a lot of money for it—$25,000, I've heard—but Galíndez said no. Next thing you know, he's walking home one night, and he disappears. No one has seen or heard from him since.

I get so upset thinking about him, I don't want to be a queen of anything anymore. But Minerva won't have it. She says this country hasn't voted for anything in twenty-six years and it's only these silly little elections that keep the faint memory of a democracy going. "You can't let your constituency down, Queen Mate!"

We women at this university are particularly grateful for the opportunities afforded us for higher education in this regime.

Minerva insists I stick this in.

Little Minou starts bawling again. Minerva says she misses her *papi*. And almost as if to prove her mother right, that little baby girl starts up a serious crying spell that brings Doña Isabel's soft tap at the bedroom door.

"What are you doing to my precious?" she says, coming in. Doña Isabel takes care of the baby while Minerva's in class. She's one of those pretty women who stay pretty no matter how old they get. Curly white hair like a frilly cap and eyes soft as opals. She holds out her hands, "My precious, are they torturing you?"

"What do you mean?" Minerva says, handing the howling bundle over and rubbing her ears. "This little tyrant's torturing *us!*"

1957

Friday evening, July 26
The capital

I have been a disaster diary keeper. Last year, only one entry, and this year is already half over and I haven't jotted down a single word. I did thumb through my old diary book, and I must say, it does all seem very silly with all the *diary dears* and the *so secretive* initials no one would be able to decipher in a million years!

But I think I will be needing a companion—since from now on, I am truly on my own. Minerva graduates tomorrow and is moving to Monte Cristi to be with Manolo. I am to go home for the rest of the summer—although it's no longer the home I've always known as Mamá is building a new house on the main road. In the fall, I am to come back to finish my degree all on my own.

I'm feeling very solitary and sad and more *jamonita* than a hog.

Here I am almost twenty-two years old and not a true love in sight.

Saturday night, July 27
The capital

What a happy day today looked to be. Minerva was getting her law degree! The whole Mirabal-Reyes-Fernández-González-Tavárez clan gathered for the occasion. It was a pretty important day—Minerva was the first person in our whole extended family (minus Manolo) to have gone through university.

What a shock, then, when Minerva got handed the law degree but not the license to practice. Here we all thought El Jefe had relented against our family and let Minerva enroll in law school. But really what he was planning all along was to let her study for five whole years only to render that degree useless in the end. How cruel!

Manolo was furious. I thought he was going to march right up to the podium and have a word with the rector. Minerva took it best of all of us. She said now she'd have even more time to spend with her family. Something in the way she looked at Manolo when she said that tells me there's trouble between them.

Sunday evening, July 28
Last night in the capital

Until today, I was planning to go back to Ojo de Agua with Mamá since my summer session is also over. But the new house isn't quite done, so it would have been crowded in the old house with Dedé and Jaimito and the boys already moved in. Then this morning, Minerva asked me if I wouldn't come to Monte Cristi and help her set up housekeeping. Manolo has rented a little house so they won't have to live with his parents anymore. By now, I know something is wrong between them, so I've agreed to go along.

Monday night, July 29
Monte Cristi

The drive today was horribly tense. Manolo and Minerva kept addressing all their conversation to me, though every once in a while, they'd start discussing something in low voices. It sounded like treasure hunt clues or something. *The Indian from the hill has his cave up that road. The Eagle has nested in the hollow on the other side of that mountain.* I was so happy to have them talking to each other, I played with little Minou in the back seat and pretended not to hear them.

We arrived in town midafternoon and stopped in front of this little *shack*. Seriously, it isn't half as nice as the house Minerva showed me where Papá kept *that woman* on the farm. I suppose it's the best Manolo can do, given how broke they are.

I tried not to look too shocked so as not to depress Minerva. What a performance that one put on. Like this was her dream house or something. One, two, three rooms—she counted them as if delighted. A zinc roof would be so nice when it rained. What a big yard for her garden and that long storage shed in back sure would come in handy.

The show was lost on Manolo, though. Soon after he unpacked the car, he took off. Business, he said when Minerva asked him where he was going.

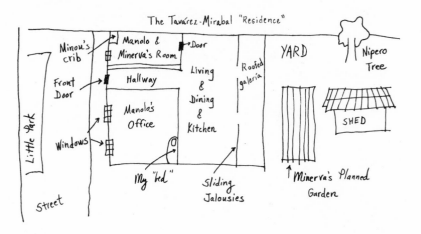

The Tavárez-Mirabal "Residence"

Thursday night, August 15
Monte Cristi

Manolo has been staying out till all hours. I sleep in the front room that serves as his office during the day, so I always know when he comes in. Later, I hear voices raised in their bedroom.

Tonight, Minerva and I were sewing curtains in the middle room where the kitchen, living, dining room, and everything is. The clock struck eight, and still no Manolo. I don't know why it is that when the clock strikes, you feel all the more the absence of someone.

Suddenly, I heard this wracking sob. My brave Minerva! It was all I could do not to start crying right along with her.

From her playpen Minou reached out, offering her mother my old doll I'd given her.

"Okay," I said. "I know something is going on," I said. I took a guess. "Another woman, right?"

Minerva gave me a quick nod. I could see her shoulders heaving up and down.

"I hate men," I said, mostly trying to convince myself. "I really hate them."

Sunday afternoon, August 25
God, it gets hot in M.C.

Manolo and Minerva are on the mend. I mind the baby to give them time together, and they go out walking, holding hands, like newlyweds. Some nights they slip away for meetings, and I can see lights on in the storage shed. I usually take the baby down to Manolo's parents and spend the time with them and the twins, then walk home, accompanied by Manolo's brother, Eduardo. I keep my distance from him. First time I've ever done that with a nice enough, handsome enough young man. Like I said, I've had *enough* of them.

Saturday morning, September 7

A new warm feeling has descended on our little house. This morning, Minerva came into the kitchen to get Manolo his *cafecito*, and her face was suffused with a certain sweetness. She wrapped her arms around me from behind and whispered in my ear, "Thank you, Mate, thank you. The struggle's brought us together again. You've brought us together again."

"Me?" I asked, though I could as easily have said, "What struggle?"

Saturday before sunrise, September 28

This will be a long entry . . . something important has finally happened to me. I've hardly slept a wink, and tomorrow—or really, today, since it's almost dawn—I'm heading back to the capital for the start of fall classes. Minerva finally convinced me that I should finish my degree. But after what happened to her, I'm pretty disillusioned about staying at the university.

Anyhow, as always before a trip, I was tossing and turning, packing and unpacking my bags in my head. I must have finally fallen asleep because I had that dream again about Papá. This time, after pulling out all the pieces of the wedding dress, I looked in and man after man I'd known appeared and disappeared before my eyes. The last one being Papá, though even as I looked, he faded little by little, until the box was empty. I woke up with a start, lit the lamp, and sat listening to the strange excited beating in my heart.

But soon, what I thought was my heartbeat was a desperate knocking on the front shutter. A voice was whispering urgently, "Open up!"

When I got the courage to crack open the shutter, at first I couldn't make out who was out there. "What do you want?" I asked in a real uninviting way.

The voice hesitated. Wasn't this the home of Manolo Tavárez?

"He's alseep. I'm his wife's sister. Can I help you?" By now, from the light streaming from my window, I could see a face I seemed to recall from a dream. It was the sweetest man's face I'd ever seen.

He had a delivery to make, he said, could I please let him in? As he spoke, he kept looking over his shoulder at a car parked right before our front door.

I didn't even think twice. I ran to the entryway, slid the bolt, and pushed open the door just in time for him to carry a long wooden crate from the trunk of the car to the front hall. Quickly, I closed the door behind him and nodded towards the office. He carried the box in, looking all around for a place to hide it.

We finally settled on the space under the cot where I slept. It amazed me even as it was happening how immediately I'd fallen in with this stranger's mission, whatever it was.

Then he asked me the strangest thing. Was I Mariposa's little sister?

I told him I was *Minerva's* sister. I left out the *little*, mind you.

He studied me, trying to decide something. "You aren't one of us, are you?"

I didn't know what *us* he was talking about, but I knew right then and there, I wanted to be a part of whatever he was.

After he left, I couldn't sleep for thinking about him. I went over everything I could remember about him and scolded myself for not having noticed if there was a ring on his hand. But I knew that even if he was married, I would not give him up. Right then, I began to forgive Papá.

A little while ago, I got up and dragged that heavy box out from under. It was nailed shut, but the nails had some give on one side where I could work the lid loose a little. I held the light up close and peered in. I almost dropped that lamp when I realized what I was looking at—enough guns to start a revolution!

Morning—leaving soon—
Manolo and Minerva have explained everything.

A national underground is forming. Everyone and everything has a code name. Manolo is Enriquillo, after the great Taino chieftain, and Minerva, of course, is Mariposa. If I were to say *tennis shoes*, you'd know we were talking about ammunition. The *pineapples* for the picnic are the grenades. *The goat must die for us to eat at the picnic.* (Get it? It's like a trick language.)

There are groups all over the island. It turns out Palomino (the man last night) is really an engineer working on projects throughout the country, so he's the natural to do the traveling and deliveries between groups.

I told Minerva and Manolo right out, I wanted to join. I could feel my breath coming short with the excitement of it all. But I masked it in front of Minerva. I was afraid she'd get all protective and say that I could be just as useful sewing bandages to put in the supply boxes to be buried in the mountains. I don't want to be babied anymore. I want to be worthy of Palomino. Suddenly, all the boys I've known with soft hands and easy lives seem like the pretty dolls I've outgrown and passed on to Minou.

Monday morning, October 14
The capital

I've lost all interest in my studies. I just go to classes in order to keep my cover as a second-year architecture student. My true identity now is Mariposa (# 2), waiting daily, hourly, for communications from up north.

I've moved out of Doña Chelito's with the excuse that I need more privacy to apply myself to my work. It's really not a lie, but the work I'm doing isn't what she imagines. My cell has assigned me, along with Sonia, also a university student, to this apartment above a little corner store. We're a hub, which means that deliveries coming into the capital from up north are dropped off here. And guess who brings them? My Palomino. How surprised he was the first time he knocked, and I opened the door!

The apartment is in a humble part of town where the poorer students live. I think some of them can tell what Sonia and I are up to, and they look out for us. Certainly some must think the worst, what with men stopping by at all hours. I always make them stay for as long as a *cafecito* to give the illusion that they are real visitors. I'm a natural for this, really. I've always liked men, receiving them, paying them attention, listening to what they have to say. Now I can use my talents for the revolution.

But I have eyes for one man only, my Palomino.

Tuesday evening, October 15

What a way to spend my twenty-second birthday! (If only Palomino would come tonight with a delivery.)

I have been a little mopey, I admit it. Sonia reminds me we have to make sacrifices for the revolution. Thank you, Sonia. I'm sure this is going to come up in my *crítica* at the end of the month. (God, it seems like I'll always have a Minerva by my side being a better person than I am.)

Anyhow, I've got to memorize this diagram before we burn the master.

143

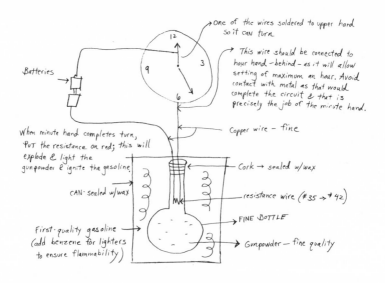

One of the wires soldered to upper hand so it can turn

This wire should be connected to hour hand – behind – as it will allow setting of maximum an hour. Avoid contact with metal as that would complete the circuit & that is precisely the job of the minute hand.

Batteries

When minute hand completes turn, PUT the resistance on red; this will explode & light the gunpowder & ignite the gasoline

Copper wire – fine

CAN· sealed w/wax

Cork → sealed w/wax

resistance wire (#35 → #42)

First-quality gasoline (add benzene for lighters to ensure flammability)

FINE BOTTLE

Gunpowder – fine quality

Thursday night, November 7

Today we had a surprise visitor. We were in the middle of making diagrams to go with the Nipples kits when there was a knock at our door. Believe me, Sonia and I both jumped like one of the paper bombs had gone off. We've got an escape route rigged up a back window, but Sonia kept her wits about her and asked who it was. It was Doña Hita, our landlady, dropping in from downstairs for a little visit.

We were so relieved, we didn't think to clear off the table with the diagrams. I'm still worried she might have spotted our work, but Sonia says that woman has a different kind of contraband in mind. She hinted that if Sonia and I ever get into trouble, she knows someone who can help us. I blushed so dark Doña Hita must have been baffled that this you-know-who was embarrassed at the mention of you-know-what!

Thursday afternoon, November 14

Palomino has been showing up *frequently* and not always with a delivery to make. We talk and talk. Sonia always makes an excuse and goes out to run an errand. She's really a much nicer person than I've made out. Today she left a little bowl of *arroz con leche*—Ahem!— for us to eat. It's a fact, you'll marry the one you share it with.

The funniest thing. Doña Hita bumped into Palomino on the stairs and called him Don Juan! She assumes he's our pimp because he's the one who comes around all the time. I laughed when he told me. But truly, my face was burning at the thought. We hadn't yet spoken of our feelings for each other.

Suddenly, he got all serious, and those beautiful hazel eyes came closer & closer. He kissed me, polite & introductory at first—

Oh God—I am so *deeply* in love!

Saturday night, November 16

Palomino came again today. We finally exchanged real names, though I think he already knew mine. Leandro Guzmán Rodríguez, what a pretty ring it has to it. We had a long talk about our lives. We laid them side by side and looked at them.

It turns out his family is from San Francisco not far from where I lived with Dedé while I was finishing up secondary school. Four years ago he came to the capital to finish a doctorate. That's just when I had come to start *my* studies! We must have danced back to back at the merengue festival in '54. He was there, I was there.

We sat back, marveling. And then our hands reached out, palm to palm, joining our lifelines.

Sunday night, December 1

Palomino stayed last night—on a cot in the munitions room, of course! I didn't sleep a wink just knowing we were under the same roof.

Guess whose name was in my right shoe all day?

He won't come again for a couple of weeks—training up in the mountains, something like that—he can't really say. Then his next delivery will be the last. By the end of the month this location has to be vacated. There have been too many raids in this area, and Manolo is worried.

The munitions room, by the way, is what we've started calling the back room where we keep all deliveries and where, by the way, I keep you, wedged between a beam and the casing of the door. I better not forget you there when we move out. I can just see Doña Hita finding you, opening your covers, thinking she'll discover a whole list of clients, and instead—Lord forbid!—snapping her eyes on the Nipples bomb. Maybe she'll think it's some sort of abortion contraption!

For the hundredth time in the last few months I've wondered whether I shouldn't burn you?

Sunday afternoon, December 15

This weekend has been harder than the last two months put together. I'm too nervous even to write. Palomino has not appeared as I expected. And there is no one to talk to as Sonia has already left for La Romana. I'll be going home in a few days, and all deliveries and pickups have to be made before I leave.

I suppose I'm getting cold feet. Everything has gone without a scrape for months, and I'm sure something will happen now. I keep thinking Doña Hita reported the grenade diagrams we left out in the open that time she surprised us. Then I worry that Sonia's been nabbed leaving town, and I'll be ambushed when my last delivery comes.

I'm a bundle of nerves. I never was any good at being brave all by myself.

Monday morning, December 16

I wasn't expecting Palomino last night, and so when I heard a car pulling up in front of the building, I thought, THIS IS IT! I was ready to escape out the back window, diary in hand, but thank God, I ran to the front one to check first. It was him! I took the stairs two at a time and rushed into the street and hugged and kissed him like the kind of woman the neighbors think I am.

We piled up the boxes he'd brought in the back room, and then we stood a moment, a strange sadness in our eyes. This work of destruction jarred with what was in our hearts. That's when he told me that he didn't like the idea of my being alone in the apartment. He was spending every moment too worried about me to pay careful enough attention to the revolution.

My heart stirred to hear him say so. I admit that for me love goes deeper than the struggle, or maybe what I mean is, love is the deeper struggle. I would never be able to give up Leandro to some higher ideal the way I feel Minerva and Manolo would each other if they had to make the supreme sacrifice. And so last night, it touched me, Oh so deeply, to hear him say it was the same for him, too.

1958

The Day of Lovers, February 14
Cloudy morning, here's hoping for rain.
Blessings on my marriage bed, as Mamá always says.

Doña Mercedes Reyes Viuda Mirabal
announces the wedding of her daughter
María Teresa Mirabal Reyes
to
Leandro Guzmán Rodríguez
son of
Don Leandro Guzmán and Doña Ana Rodríguez de Guzmán
on Saturday, February fourteenth
this nineteen hundred and fifty-eighth year of Our Lord
Twenty-eighth year of the Era of Trujillo
at four o'clock in the afternoon
San Juan Evangelista Church
Salcedo

Mariposa and Palomino, for now!
María Teresa and Leandro, forever!

CHAPTER EIGHT

Patria

1959

Build your house upon a rock, He said, do my will. And though the rain fall and the floods come and the winds blow, the good wife's house will stand.

I did as He said. At sixteen I married Pedrito González and we settled down for the rest of our lives. Or so it seemed for eighteen years.

My boy grew into a man, my girl into her long, slender body like the blossoming mimosa at the end of the drive. Pedrito took on a certain gravity, became an important man around here. And I, Patria Mercedes? Like every woman of her house, I disappeared into what I loved, coming up now and then for air. I mean, an overnight trip by myself to a girlfriend's, a special set to my hair, and maybe a yellow dress.

I had built my house on solid rock, all right.

Or I should say, Pedrito's great-grandfather had built it over a hundred years back, and then each first son had lived in it and passed it on. But you have to understand, Patria Mercedes was in those timbers, in the nimble workings of the transoms, she was in those wide boards on the floor and in that creaky door opening on its old hinges.

My sisters were so different! They built their homes on sand and called the slip and slide adventure.

Minerva lived in a little nothing house—or so Mate had described it to me—in that godforsaken town of Monte Cristi. It's a wonder her babies didn't both die of infections.

Mate and Leandro had already had two different addresses in a year of marriage. Renters, they called themselves, the city word for the squatters we pity here in the country.

Dedé and Jaimito had lost everything so many times, it was hard to keep up with their frequent moves. Now they were in our old house in Ojo de Agua, and Mamá had built her up-to-date cottage on the main road from Santiago, complete with aluminum jalousies and an indoor toilet she called "the sanitary."

And me, Patria Mercedes, like I said, I had settled down for life in my rocksure house. And eighteen years passed by.

My eighteenth year of marriage the ground of my well-being began to give a little. Just a baby's breath tremor, a hairline crack you could hardly see unless you were looking for trouble.

New Year's Eve we gathered in Mamá's new house in Conuco, the sisters and all the husbands, a first since María Teresa's wedding a year ago this February. We stayed late, celebrating being together more than the new year, I think. There wasn't much talk of politics so as not to worry Mamá. Also Jaimito had grown adamant—he didn't want Dedé involved in whatever trouble Minerva and the others were cooking up.

Still, all of us were praying for a change this new year. Things had gotten so bad, even people like me who didn't want anything to do with politics were thinking about it all the time. See, now I had my grown son to nail me to the hard facts. I assigned him to God's care and asked San José and the Virgencita to mind him as well, but still I worried all the time.

It was after one in the morning when Pedrito and Noris and I started back to our house. Nelson had stayed at Mamá's, saying he was going to bring in the new year talking to his uncles. As we rode home, I saw the lamp at the window of the young widow's house, and I knew he'd be bringing it in with more than talk. Rumor had it my "boy" was sowing wild oats along with his father's cacao crop. I had asked Pedrito to talk to our son, but you know how the men are. He was proud of Nelson for proving himself a macho before he was even a grown man.

We hadn't been asleep but a couple of hours when that bedroom was blazing with light. My first thought was of angels descending, their burning brands flashing, their fierce wings stirring up things. But as I came fully awake, I saw it was a car aiming its lights at our bedroom window.

¡Ay, Dios mío! I shook Pedrito awake and flew out of that bed terrified that something had happened to my boy. I know what Pedrito says, that I'm overly protective. But ever since I lost my baby thirteen years ago, my deepest fear is that I will have to put another one in the ground. This time I don't think I could go on.

It was Minerva and Manolo and Leandro and, yes, Nelson, all very drunk. They could hardly contain their excitement till they got inside. They had just tuned into Radio Rebelde to hear the New Year's news, and they had been greeted by the triumphant announcement. Batista had fled! Fidel, his brother Raúl, and Ernesto they call Che had entered Havana and liberated the country. *¡Cuba libre! ¡Cuba libre!*

Minerva started singing our anthem and the others joined in. I kept hushing them, and they finally sobered up when I reminded them *we* were not *libre* yet. The roosters were already crowing as they left to spread the news to all their friends in the area. Nelson wanted to go along, but I put my foot down. Next year when he was eighteen, he could stay out till the cacao needed picking. But this year—he was too dead tired to argue. I walked him to his room and, as if he were still a child, undressed him and tucked him in.

But Pedrito was still wanting to celebrate. And you know him, strong emotion takes him and he knows only one way to express it if I'm close by.

He entered me, and it took some weeks before I realized. But I'd like to think, since my cycles stopped in January, that Raúl Ernesto began his long campaign into flesh the first day of this hopeful new year.

When I told Pedrito I'd missed two months already, he said, "Maybe you're going through the change early, you think?" Like I said, it'd been thirteen years and I hadn't borne fruit. "Let me go in there and see what I can find," he said, leading me by the hand into our bedroom. Our Nelson grinned. He understood now about siestas.

I went on like this another month, and I missed again.

"Pedrito," I said, "I'm pregnant, I'm sure of it."

"How can that be, Mami?" He teased. "We're ready for our grand-children." He indicated our grown son and daughter, playing dominoes, listening in on our secrets.

Noris leapt out of her chair. "*Ay*, Mami, is it true, really?" Fourteen going on fifteen, she had finally outgrown her dolls and was two, three, who knows, ten years away from her own babies. (The way young women wait these days, look at Minerva!) But Noris was like me, she wanted to give herself to things, and at her tender age, she could only imagine giving herself to children.

"Why don't you have one of your own?" Nelson teased, poking his sister where she'd already told him a thousand times it hurt to be poked. "Maybe Marcelino wants to be a daddy?"

"Stop that!" Noris whined.

"Stop that," Nelson mimicked her. Sometimes, I wondered how my son could be with a woman and then come home and nag his sister so miserably.

Pedrito scowled. "That Marcelino gets near you and he won't know what hit him."

"Help me think of a name," I suggested, using the baby to distract them from a silly argument.

I looked down at my belly as if Our Lord might write out the name on my cotton housedress. And suddenly it was as if His tongue spoke in my mouth. On my own, I would never have thought of naming my son after revolutionaries. "Ernesto," I said, "I'm going to name him Raúl Ernesto."

"Ernesto?" Noris said, making a face.

But Nelson's face lit up in a way that made me nervous. "We'll call him Che for short."

"Che!" Noris said, holding her nose. "What kind of a name is that?"

Like I said, it must have been the Lord's tongue in my mouth because back then, I was running scared. Not for myself but for those I loved. My sisters—Minerva, Mate—I was sick sometimes with fear for them, but they lived at a distance now, so I hid the sun with a finger and chose not to see the light all around me. Pedrito didn't worry me. I knew he would always have one hand in the soil and the other somewhere on me. He wouldn't wander far into trouble if I wasn't along. But my son, my first born!

I had tried to shelter him, Lord knows. To no avail. He was always tagging along behind his Tío Manolo and his new Tío Leandro, men of the world who had gone to the university and who impressed him more than his country father. Any chance he got, he was off to the capital "to see Tía Mate and the baby Jacqueline," or to Monte Cristi "to visit Tía Minerva and Minou and the new baby Manolito." Yes, a whole new crop of Mirabals was coming up. That was another possible explanation for my pregnancy—suggestion. After all, whenever we were together for a while under the same roof, our cycles became as synchronized as our watches.

I knew my boy. He wanted to be a man outside the bedroom where he had already proven himself. That widow woman could have started a school in there, the way I understood it. But I didn't resent her, no. She delivered my son gently into manhood from his boyhood, something a mother cannot possibly do.

And so I thought of a way for Nelson to be in the capital, under supervision so he wouldn't be running wild with women or his rebel uncles. I talked to Padre de Jesús López, our new priest, who promised to talk to Padre Fabré about letting Nelson enroll in Santo Tomás de Aquino in the capital. It was a seminary, but there was no obligation to the priesthood.

At first Nelson didn't want to go to a school of pre-priest sissies. But a couple of weeks before the start of classes during the heavy plantings in the yucca field, he had a change of heart. Better to abstain from the gardens of delectable delights than to be stuck planting them, dawn to dusk.

Besides, his weekends would be his own to spend at his aunt María Teresa and his uncle Leandro's house.

Besides, some of those pre-priests were no sissies at all. They talked about *pudenda* and *cunnilingus* as if they were speaking of the body and blood of Christ. How do I know? Nelson came home once and asked me what the words meant, assuming they were liturgical. Young people don't bother with their Latin these days.

Next step was to convince his father, and that was the hardest of all. Pedrito didn't see why we should be spending money sending Nelson to a boarding school in the capital. "His best school is right here beside me learning about his *patrimonio*."

I didn't have the heart to suggest that our son might not want to be a farmer like his father. Recently, Nelson had begun talking to me about going to the university. "It's just for a year, Papi," I pleaded. "It'll be a good finish to his education."

"Besides," I added, "right now, the seminary is the best place for him." It was true. Johnny Abbes and his SIM were dragging young men off the streets, and farms, and from offices, like Herod the boy babies in all of Judea. The church, refusing as it did to get involved in temporal matters, remained the only sanctuary.

Pedrito folded his arms and walked off into his cacao fields. I could see him pacing among the trees. That's where he always went to think, the way I have to get down on my knees to know my own mind. He came back, put his big hands on either side of the door frame his great-grandfather had built over a hundred years ago, and he nodded. "He can go." And then with a gesture indicating the green fields over his shoulders that his great-grandfather, his grandfather, and his father had farmed before him, he added, "If the land can't keep him, I can't make him stay."

So with the help of good Padre de Jesús, Nelson entered Santo Tomás de Aquino last September. Out of harm's way, I thought.

And for a while, you might have said that he was as I was—safe in God's love.

I'll tell you when I panicked. Around Easter my Nelson began to talk about how he would join the liberators once the rumored invasion from Cuba hit our shores.

I sat him down and reminded him what the church fathers were teaching us. God in his wisdom would take care of things. "Promise me

you'll stay out of trouble!" I was on my knees before him. I could not
bear the thought of losing my son. *"Por Dios,"* I pleaded.

"*Ay*, Mamá, don't worry!" he said, looking down at me, embarrassed.
But he gave me a lukewarm promise he'd stay out of trouble.

I did worry all the time. I went to Padre de Jesús for advice. He was
straight out of seminary and brimming with new ideas. He would have
a young way of explaining things I could bring home to my son.

"Padre," I said, kissing the crucifix he offered me, "I feel lost. I don't
know what the Lord requires of us in these hard times." I dared not get
too critical. We all knew there were priests around who would report
you to the SIM if you spoke against the regime.

Still, I hadn't given up on the church as Minerva and María Teresa
had. Ever since I'd had my vision of the Virgencita, I knew spirit was
imminent, and that the churches were just glass houses, or way stations
on our road through this rocky life. But His house was a mansion as big
as the sky, and all you had to do was pelt His window with a pebble-cry,
Open up! Help me, God! and He would let you inside.

Padre de Jesús did not intone vague pronouncements and send me
home with a pat on the head. Not at all. He stood and I could see the
travail of his spirit in how he took off his glasses and kept polishing
them as if they'd never come clean. "Patria, my child," he said, which
made me smile for he couldn't have been but five, six years older than
my Nelson. "We must wait. We must pray." He faced me. "I, too, am lost
so that I can't show you the way."

I was shaking like when a breeze blows through the sacristy and the
votive candles flicker. This priest's frankness had touched me more than
a decree. We knelt there in that hot little rectory, and we prayed to the
Virgencita. She had clung to Jesus until He told her straight out, *Mamá,
I have to be about My Father's business.* And she had to let him go, but it
broke her heart because, though He was God, He was still her boy.

I got braver like a crab going sideways. I inched towards courage the
best way I could, helping out with the little things.

I knew they were up to something big, Minerva and Manolo and
Leandro. I wasn't sure about María Teresa, caught up as she was with

her new baby Jacqueline. But those others, I could feel it in the tension and silence that would come over them when I walked in on one of their conversations. I didn't ask questions. I suppose I was afraid of what I would find out.

But then Minerva came to me with her six-month-old Manolito and asked me to keep him. "Keep him?" I, who treasured my children more than my own life, couldn't believe my sister would leave her son for anything. "Where are you going?" I asked, alarmed.

That tense silence came upon her, and then haltingly, as if wanting to be sure with each step that she was not saying more than she had to, she said, "I'm going to be on the road a lot. And I'll be coming down here for some meetings every week."

"But Minerva, your own child—" I began and then I saw it did hurt her to make this sacrifice she was convinced she needed to make. So I added, "I'd love to take care of my little godson here!" Manolito smiled and came readily to my arms. How delicious to hold him like my own baby five months ahead of time. That's when I told Minerva I was pregnant with a boy.

She was so glad for me. So glad! Then she got curious. "Since when are you a fortune teller to know it's a son?"

I shrugged. But I gave her the best reason I could. "I've got a name all picked out for a boy."

"What are you going to name him?"

I knew then I had brought it up as a way of letting her know I was with her—if only in spirit. "Raúl Ernesto," I said, watching her face.

She looked at me a long moment, and very simply, she said, "I know you want to stay out of trouble, and I respect that."

"If there should come a time—" I said.

"There will," she said.

Minerva and Manolo began coming down every week to Ojo de Agua from Monte Cristi, almost from one end of the island to the other. Now, whenever they were stopped at the interrogation stations, they had a good excuse for being on the road. They were visiting their sickly son at Patria González's house in Conuco. Monte Cristi was too hot, desert really, and their doctor had prescribed healthier air for the little boy.

Every time they came, Leandro drove up from the capital, and this curly-headed man Niño and his pretty wife Dulce came over from San Francisco. They met up with Cuca and Fafa and one named Marién— though sometimes they called each other different, make-believe names.

They needed a place to meet, and so I offered them our land. There was a clearing between the cacao and the *plátano* groves. Pedrito had put some cane chairs and hammocks under a thatched roof, a place for workers to rest or take a siesta during the hot part of the day. Minerva and her group would sit out there for hours, talking. Once or twice when it was raining, I'd invite them to come into the house, but they'd refuse, knowing it was just politeness on my part. And I was thankful to them for sparing me. If the SIM came, Pedrito and I could always swear we knew nothing about these meetings.

It was a problem when Nelson was home from school. He'd go out there, eager to take part in whatever his uncles were plotting. In deference to me, I'm sure, they kept him at a distance. Not in any way that could hurt his young man's pride, but in a comradely way. They'd send him for some more ice or *cigarrillos* or please Nelson, *hombre*, couldn't he take the car down to Jimmy's and see what was up with that radiator since they had to make it back to the capital this very night. Once, they sent the poor boy all the way to Santiago to pick up batteries for the short wave.

When he came back from delivering them, I asked him, "What's going on out there, Nelson?" I knew, but I wanted to hear what he knew.

"Nothing, Mamá," he said.

Then the secret he was keeping became more than he could contain. When it was almost June, he finally confided in me. "They're expecting it this coming month," he whispered. "The invasion, yes!" he added when he saw the excited look on my face.

But you know why that look was there? I'll tell you. My Nelson would be in school in the capital until the very end of June, out of harm's way. He had to study hard if he expected to graduate in time to attend the university in the fall. We had our own little plot cooked up to present to his father—the day before university classes started.

I was the one who was going to be on the road. Mamá couldn't believe it when I asked if she'd keep Manolito those four days. Why, I was five months gone, Mamá exclaimed. I shouldn't be traveling!

I explained that I'd be traveling with Padre de Jesús and the Salcedo group, and this retreat was important for renewing my faith. We were going up to Constanza. That mountain air would be good for my baby. And I'd heard the road was fairly good. I didn't add from whom (Minerva) or why. Troops were patrolling up and down the cordillera just in case any would-be guerrillas inspired by the Cubans were thinking of hiding there.

"Ay, Virgencita, you know what you do with my girls," was all Mamá said. She had become resigned to her daughters' odd and willful ways. And yes, she would keep Manolito. Noris, too.

I had wanted my girl to go along on the retreat, but it was no use. Marcelino's sister had invited Noris to her *quinceañera* party and there was too much to do between now and then.

"But it's two weeks away, *mi amor*." I didn't add that we had already designed and cut her dress, bought her little satin pumps, and tried out how she would wear her hair.

"*¡Ay, Mami!*" she wailed. "*Por favor.*" Why couldn't I understand that getting ready for them was what made parties fun?

How different she was from me at that age! For one thing, Mamá raised us the old-fashioned way where we couldn't go to dances until after our *quinceañeras*. But I was raising my girl modern where she wasn't kept cooped up, learning blind obedience. Still, I wished she'd use her wings to soar up closer to the divine hem of our Blessed Virgin instead of to flutter towards things not worthy of her attention.

I kept praying for her, but it was like Pedrito having to let go of his son. If the Virgencita didn't think it was time for my girl to magnify the Lord, I certainly couldn't talk her into a retreat with "old ladies" and a bunch of bad-breath priests. (Lord forgive her!)

We were a group of about thirty "mature" women—that's how Padre de Jesús described us, bless his heart. We had started meeting a few months back to discuss issues that came up in the gospel and to do Christ's work in the *bohíos* and *barrios*. Now we even had a name, Christian Cultural Group, and we had spread all over the Cibao area. Four priests provided spiritual guidance, Padre de Jesús among them. This retreat was our first, and Brother Daniel had managed to get the Maryknolls to let us use their motherhouse up in the mountains. The theme was the exploration of the meaning of Mary in our lives. I couldn't help thinking that maybe Padre de Jesús or Brother Daniel or one of the others would have an answer for me now about what was required during these troubled times.

"Ha! *Your* church will keep mum till kingdom come," Minerva was always challenging me. Religion was now my belonging she didn't want any part of. "Not a peep to help the downtrodden."

What could I say when I, too, was intent on keeping my own flesh safe. I'd written a letter to Padre Fabré down at Santo Tomás.

Dear Father,

Greetings in the Lord's name from the mother of one of your charges, Nelson González, completing his fourth year, a smart boy on the whole, as you yourself wrote in your last report, but not always the best with self-control. To make sure he studies hard and stays out of trouble, please, do not let my son off the grounds except to come home. He is a country boy not used to the city temptations, and I do not want him getting mixed up with the wrong people.

May this letter be in the strictest of your confidences, Father.
Most faithfully yours, his mother,

Patria Mercedes

But Nelson found out about the letter from his little blabbermouth aunt in the capital. It was unfair, I wasn't letting him become a man. But I stood firm. I'd rather have him stay alive, a boy forever, than be a man dead in the ground.

María Teresa was also hurt. One Saturday morning, she had come to take Nelson out for the weekend, and the director hadn't allowed her.

"Don't you trust me?" she confronted me. Now I had two angry souls to appease with half-truths.

"It isn't you, Mate," I began. I didn't add that I knew from Nelson's remarks that Leandro and Manolo and Minerva were involved in a serious plot.

"Don't worry, I can take care of *your* baby. I've got lots of experience now." Mate was holding pretty Jacqueline, nuzzling her baby's head with little kisses. "Besides, there's nothing happening in the capital Nelson could get into, believe me. The Jaragua's empty. The Olympia has been showing the same movie for a month. No one goes out anymore." And then I heard her say it: "Nothing to celebrate *yet*." I looked her in the eye and said, "You too, Mate?"

She hugged her baby girl close and looked so brave. I could hardly believe this was our tenderhearted little Mate whom Noris resembled so much. "Yes, I'm with them." But then, the hard look faded and she was my baby sister again, afraid of *el cuco* and noodles in her soup. "If anything should happen, promise me you'll take care of Jacqueline."

It seemed I was going to raise all my sisters' babies! "You know I would. She's one of mine, aren't you, *amorcito*?" I took that baby in my arms and hugged her close. Jacqueline looked at me with that wonder the little ones have who still think of the world as a big, safe playroom inside their mother's womb.

Our retreat had been planned for May, the month of Mary. But with the increased rumors of an invasion, El Jefe declared a state of emergency. All through May no one went anywhere without special permission from the SIM. Even Minerva stayed put in Monte Cristi. One day when we hadn't seen his mother for almost a month, Manolito reached up to me from his crib and said, "Mamá, Mamá." It was going to be hard to give him up once this hell on earth was over.

By mid-June, things had quieted down. It looked as if the invasion was not going to come after all. The state of emergency was called off, and so we went ahead with plans for our retreat.

When we got to Constanza, I couldn't believe my eyes. I had grown up in the greenest, most beautiful valley on the island. But you get used to close-by beauty, and Constanza was different, like the picture of a faraway place on a puzzle you hurry to put together. I kept trying to fit it inside me and I couldn't. Purple mountains reaching towards angelfeather clouds; a falcon soaring in a calm blue sky; God combing His sunshine fingers through green pastures straight out of the Psalms.

The retreat house was a little ways out of the village down a path through flower-dotted hillsides. *Campesinos* came out of their huts to watch us pass. A pretty people, golden-skinned, light-eyed, they seemed wary, as if somebody not so kind had come down the road ahead of us. We greeted them and Padre de Jesús explained that we were on a retreat, so if they had any special requests they wanted us to remember in our prayers, please let us know. They stared at us silently and shook their heads, no.

We were each assigned a narrow cell with a cot, a crucifix on the wall, and a fount of holy water at the door. It could have been a palace, I rejoiced so in it all. Our meetings and meals were held in a big airy room with a large picture window. I sat with my back to the dazzling view so as not to be distracted from His Word by His Creation. Dawn and dusk, noon and night we gathered in the chapel and said a rosary along with the little nuns.

My old yearning to be in the religious life stirred. I felt myself rising, light-headed with transcendence, an overflowing fountain. Thank the Lord I had that child in my womb to remind me of the life I had already chosen.

It happened on the last day of our retreat.

The fourteenth of June: how can I ever forget that day!

We were all in that big room having our midafternoon *cursillo.* Brother Daniel was talking of the last moment we knew of in Mary's human life, her Assumption. Our Blessed Mother had been taken up into heaven, body and soul. What did we think of that? We went around the room, everyone declaring it was an honor for a mere mortal. When it came my turn, I said it was only fair. If our souls could go to eternal glory, our hardworking motherbodies surely deserved more. I patted my belly and thought of the little ghost of a being folded in the soft tissues of my womb. My son, my Raulito. I ached for him even more without Manolito in my arms to stanch the yearning.

Next thing I knew, His Kingdom was coming down upon the very roof of that retreat house. Explosion after explosion ripped the air. The house shook to its very foundation. Windows shattered, smoke poured in with a horrible smell. Brother Daniel was shouting, "Fall to the ground, ladies, cover your heads with your folding chairs!" Of course, all I was thinking of was protecting my unborn child. I scrambled to a little niche where a statue of the Virgencita was standing, and begging her pardon, I knocked her and her pedestal over. The crash was drowned out by the thunderous blast outside. Then I crawled in and held my folding chair in front of me, closing the opening, and praying all the while that the Lord not test me with the loss of my child.

The shelling happened in a flash, but it seemed the chaos went on for hours. I heard moans, but when I lowered my chair, I could make out nothing in the smoke-filled room. My eyes stung, and I realized that in my fear I had wet my pants. Lord, I prayed, Lord God, let this cup pass. When the air finally cleared, I saw a mess of glass and rubble on the floor, bodies huddled everywhere. A wall had tumbled down and the tile floor was all torn up. Beyond, through the jagged hole where the window had been, the closest mountainside was a raging inferno.

Finally, there was an eerie silence, interrupted only by the sound of far-off gunfire and the nearby trickle of plaster from the ceiling. Padre de Jesús gathered us in the most sheltered corner, where we assessed our damages. The injuries turned out to look worse than they were, just minor cuts from flying glass, thank the Lord. We ripped up our slips and bandaged the worst. Then for spiritual comfort, Brother Daniel led us through a rosary. When we heard gunfire coming close again, we kept right on praying.

There were shouts, and four, then five, men in camouflage were running across the grounds towards us. Behind them, the same *campesinos* we'd seen on our walk and a dozen or more *guardias* were advancing, armed with machetes and machine guns. The hunted men crouched and careened this way and that as they headed towards the cover of the motherhouse.

They made it to the outdoor deck. I could see them clearly, their faces bloodied and frantic. One of them was badly wounded and hobbling, another had a kerchief tied around his forehead. A third was shouting to two others to stay down, and one of them obeyed and threw himself on the deck.

But the other must not have heard him for he kept on running towards us. I looked in his face. He was a boy no older than Noris. Maybe that's why I cried out, "Get down, son! Get down!" His eyes found mine just as the shot hit him square in the back. I saw the wonder on his young face as the life drained out of him, and I thought, Oh my God, he's one of mine!

Coming down that mountain, I was a changed woman. I may have worn the same sweet face, but now I was carrying not just my child but that dead boy as well.

My stillborn of thirteen years ago. My murdered son of a few hours ago.

I cried all the way down that mountain. I looked out the spider-webbed window of that bullet-riddled car at brothers, sisters, sons, daughters, one and all, my human family. Then I tried looking up at our Father, but I couldn't see His Face for the dark smoke hiding the tops of those mountains.

I made myself pray so I wouldn't cry. But my prayers sounded more like I was trying to pick a fight.

I'm not going to sit back and watch my babies die, Lord, even if that's what You in Your great wisdom decide.

They met me on the road coming into town, Minerva, María Teresa, Mamá, Dedé, Pedrito, Nelson. Noris was weeping in terror. It was after that I noticed a change in her, as if her soul had at last matured and begun *its* cycles. When I dismounted from that car, she came running towards me, her arms out like a person seeing someone brought back from the dead. All of them were sure I had been singed to nothing from what they'd heard on the radio about the bombing.

No, Patria Mercedes had come back to tell them all, tell them all.

But I couldn't speak. I was in shock, you could say, I was mourning that dead boy.

It was all over the papers the next day. Forty-nine men and boys martyred in those mountains. We had seen the only four saved, and for what? Tortures I don't want to think of.

Six days later, we knew when the second wave of the invasion force hit on the beaches north of here. We saw the planes flying low, looking like hornets. And afterwards we read in the papers how one boat with ninety-three on board had been bombed before it could land; the other with sixty-seven landed, but the army with the help of local *campesinos* hunted those poor martyrs down.

I didn't keep count how many had died. I kept my hand on my stomach, concentrating on what was alive.

———

Less than a month before I was due, I attended the August gathering of our Christian Cultural Group in Salcedo. It was the first meeting since our disastrous retreat. Padre de Jesús and Brother Daniel had been down in the capital throughout July conferring with other clergy. To the Salcedo gathering, they invited only a few of us old members whom— I saw later—they had picked out as ready for the Church Militant, tired of the Mother Church in whose skirts they once hid.

They picked right, all right. I was ready, big as I looked, heavy as I was.

The minute I walked into that room, I knew something had changed in the way the Lord Jesus would be among us. No longer was there the liturgical chatter of how San Zenón had made the day sunny for a granddaughter's wedding or how Santa Lucía had cured the cow's pinkeye. That room was silent with the fury of avenging angels sharpening their radiance before they strike.

The priests had decided they could not wait forever for the pope and the archbishop to come around. The time was now, for the Lord had said, I come with the sword as well as the plow to set at liberty them that are bruised.

I couldn't believe this was the same Padre de Jesús talking who several months back hadn't know his faith from his fear! But then again, here in that little room was the same Patria Mercedes, who wouldn't have hurt a butterfly, shouting, "Amen to the revolution."

And so we were born in the spirit of the vengeful Lord, no longer His lambs. Our new name was Acción Clero-Cultural. Please note, action as the first word! And what was our mission in ACC?

Only to organize a powerful national underground.

We would spread the word of God among our brainwashed *campesinos* who had hunted down their own liberators. After all, Fidel would never have won over in Cuba if the *campesinos* there hadn't fed him, hidden him, lied for him, joined him.

The word was, we were all brothers and sisters in Christ. You could not chase after a boy with your machete and enter the kingdom of heaven. You could not pull that trigger and think there was even a needle hole for you to pass through into eternity.

I could go on.

Padre de Jesús walked me out when the meeting was over. He looked a little apologetic when he glanced at my belly, but he went on and asked me. Did I know of any one who would like to join our organization? No doubt he had heard about the meetings Manolo and Minerva were conducting on our property.

I nodded. I knew of at least six, I said, counting Pedrito and Nelson among my two sisters and their husbands. And in a month's time, seven. Yes, once my son was born, I'd be out there recruiting every *campesino* in Ojo de Agua, Conuco, Salcedo to the army of Our Lord.

"Patria Mercedes, how you've changed!"

I shook my head back at him, and I didn't have to say it. He was laughing, putting on his glasses after wiping them on his cassock, his vision—like mine—clean at last.

Next time they gathered under the shade of the thatch, I went out there, carrying my week-old prize.

"*Hola*, Patria," the men called. "That's quite a macho you got there!" When they picked him out of my arms to look him over, my boy howled. He was a crier from the start, that one. "What you call that bawling little he-man?"

"Raúl Ernesto," Minerva said meaningfully, bragging on her nephew.

I nodded and smiled at their compliments. Nelson looked away when I looked at him. He was probably thinking I had come out there to get him. "Come on inside now," I said. "I have something to talk to you about."

He thought I meant him, but I was looking around at the whole group. "Come on."

Minerva waved away my invitation. "Don't you worry about us."

I said, "Come on in, now. I mean it this time."

They looked from one to the other, and something in my voice let them know I was with them. They picked up their drinks, and I could have been leading the children out of bondage, the way they all followed me obediently into my house.

Now it was Pedrito who began to worry. And the worry came where he was most vulnerable.

The same month we met in Padre de Jesús' rectory, a new law was passed. If you were caught harboring any enemies of the regime even if you yourself were not involved in their schemes, you would be jailed, and *everything you owned* would become the property of the government.

His land! Worked by his father and grandfather and great-grandfather before him. His house like an ark with beams where he could see his great-grandfather's mark.

We had not fought like this in our eighteen years of marriage. In that bedroom at night, that man, who had never raised his voice to me, unleashed the fury of three ancestors at me. "You crazy, *mujer*, to invite them into the house! You want your sons to lose their patrimony, is that what you want?"

As if he were answering his father, Raúl Ernesto began to cry. I gave him the breast and long after he was done, I cradled him there to help coax out the tenderness in his father. To remind him there was some for him as well.

But he didn't want me. It was the first time Pedrito González had turned me away. That hurt deep in the heart's tender parts. I was going through that empty period after the baby is born when you ache to take it back into yourself. And the only solace then is the father coming back in, making himself at home.

"If you had seen what I saw on that mountain," I pleaded with him, weeping all over again for that dead boy. "*Ay*, Pedrito, how can we be true Christians and turn our back on our brothers and sisters—"

"Your first responsibility is to your *children*, your *husband*, and your *home!*" His face was so clouded with anger, I couldn't see the man I loved. "I've already let them use this place for months. Let them meet over on your own Mirabal farm from now on!"

It's true, our family farm would have been a logical alternative, but Dedé and Jaimito were living on it now. I had already approached Dedé, and she had come back without Jaimito's permission.

"But you believe in what they're doing, Pedrito," I reminded him. And then I don't know what got into me. I wanted to hurt the man in front of me. I wanted to break this smaller version of who he was and release the big-hearted man I'd married. And so I told him. His first born did not want this patrimony. Nelson had already put in his application for the university in the fall. And what was more, I knew for a fact he was already in the underground along with his uncles. "It's him you'll be throwing to the SIM!"

Pedrito wiped his face with his big hands and bowed his head, resigned. "God help him, God help him," he kept mumbling till my heart felt wrong hurting him as I'd done.

But later in the dark, he sought me out with his old hunger. He didn't have to say it, that he was with us now. I knew it in the reckless way he took me with him down into the place where his great-grandfather and his grandfather and his father had met their women before him.

So it was that our house became the motherhouse of the movement.

It was here with the doors locked and the front windows shuttered that the ACC merged with the group Manolo and Minerva had started over a year ago. There were about forty of us. A central committee was elected. At first, they tried to enlist Minerva, but she deferred to Manolo, who became our president.

It was in this very parlor where Noris had begun receiving callers that the group gave themselves a name. How they fought over that one like schoolgirls arguing over who will hold whose hand! Some wanted a fancy name that would touch all the high spots, Revolutionary Party of Dominican Integrity. Then Minerva moved swiftly through the clutter to the heart of the matter. She suggested we name ourselves after the men who had died in the mountains.

For the second time in her quiet life, Patria Mercedes (alias Mariposa #3) shouted out, "Amen to the revolution!"

So it was between these walls hung with portraits, including El Jefe's, that the Fourteenth of June Movement was founded. Our mission was to effect an internal revolution rather than wait for an outside rescue.

It was on this very Formica table where you could still see the egg stains from my family's breakfast that the bombs were made. Nipples, they were called. It was the shock of my life to see María Teresa, so handy with her needlepoint, using tweezers and little scissors to twist the fine wires together.

It was on this very bamboo couch where my Nelson had, as a tiny boy, played with the wooden gun his grandfather had made him that he sat now with Padre de Jesús, counting the ammunition for the .32 automatics we would receive in a few weeks at a prearranged spot. The one named Ilander we called Eagle had arranged the air drop with the exiles.

It was on that very rocker where I had nursed every one of my babies that I saw my sister Minerva looking through the viewfinder of an M-1 carbine—a month ago I would not have known it from a shotgun. When I followed her aim out the window, I cried out, startling her, "No, no, not the mimosa!"

I had sent Noris away to her grandmother's in Conuco. I told her we were making repairs to her room. And in a way, we were, for it was in her bedroom that we assembled the boxes. It was among her crocheted pink poodles and little perfume bottles and snapshots of her *quinceañera* party that we stashed our arsenal of assorted pistols and revolvers, three .38 caliber Smith and Wesson pistols, six .30 caliber M-1 carbines, four M-3 machine guns, and a .45 Thompson stolen from a *guardia*. I know,

Mate and I drew up the list ourselves in the pretty script we'd been taught by the nuns for writing out Bible passages.

It was in those old and bountiful fields that Pedrito and his son and a few of the other men buried the boxes once we got them loaded and sealed. In among the cacao roots Pedrito lowered the terrible cargo. But he seemed at peace now with the risks he was taking. This was a kind of farming, too, he told me later, one that he could share with his Nelson. From those seeds of destruction, we would soon—very soon—harvest our freedom.

It was on that very coffee table on which Noris had once knocked a tooth out tussling with her brother that the plans for the attack were drawn. On January 21st, the day of the Virgin of Highest Grace, the different groups would gather here to arm themselves and receive their last-minute instructions.

It was down this very hall and in and out of my children's bedrooms and past the parlor and through the back *galería* to the yard that I walked those last days of 1959, worrying if I had done the right thing exposing my family to the SIM. I kept seeing that motherhouse up in the mountains, its roof caving in, its walls crumbling like a foolish house built on sand. I could, by a trick of terror, turn that vision into my own house tumbling down.

As I walked, I built it back up with prayer, hung the door on its creaky hinges, nailed the floorboards down, fitted the transoms. "God help us," I kept saying. "God help us." Raulito was almost always in my arms, crying something terrible, as I paced, trying to settle him, and myself, down.

III

1960

CHAPTER NINE

Dedé

1994
and
1960

When Dedé next notices, the garden's stillness is deepening, blooming dark flowers, their scent stronger for the lack of color and light. The interview woman is a shadowy face slowly losing its features.

"And the shades of night begin to fall, and the traveler hurries home, and the campesino bids his fields farewell," Dedé recites.

The woman gets up hurriedly from her chair as if she has just been shown the way out. "I didn't realize it was this late."

"No, no, I wasn't throwing you an *indirecta*." Dedé laughs, motioning the woman to sit back down. "We have a few more minutes." The interviewer perches at the edge of her chair as if she knows the true interview is over.

"That poem always goes through my head this time of day," Dedé explains. "Minerva used to recite it a lot those last few months when she and Mate and Patria were living over at Mamá's. The husbands were in prison," she adds, for the woman's face registers surprise at this change of address. "All except Jaimito."

"How lucky," her guest notes.

"It wasn't luck," Dedé says right out. "It was because he didn't get directly involved."

"And you?"

Dedé shakes her head. "Back in those days, we women followed

171

our husbands." Such a silly excuse. After all, look at Minerva. "Let's put it this way," Dedé adds. "*I followed my husband. I didn't get involved.*"

"I can understand that," the interview woman says quickly as if protecting Dedé from her own doubts. "It's still true in the States. I mean, most women I know, their husband gets a job in Texas, say, well, Texas it's going to be."

"I've never been to *Tejas,*" Dedé says absently. Then, as if to redeem herself, she adds, "I didn't get involved until later."

"When was that?" the woman asks.

Dedé admits it out loud: "When it was already too late."

The woman puts away her pad and pen. She digs around in her purse for her keys, and then she remembers—she stuck them in the ashtray of the car so she could find them easily! She is always losing things. She says it like a boast. She gives several recent examples in her confused Spanish.

Dedé worries this woman will never find her way back to the main road in the dark. Such a thin woman with fly-about hair in her face. What ever happened to hairspray? Her niece Minou's hair is the same way. All this fussing about the something layer in outer space, and meanwhile, they walk around looking like something from outer space.

"Why don't I lead you out to the anacahuita turn," she offers the interview woman.

"You drive?"

They are always so surprised. And not just the American women who think of this as an "underdeveloped" country where Dedé should still be riding around in a carriage with a mantilla over her hair, but her own nieces and nephews and even her sons tease her about her little Subaru. Their Mamá Dedé, a modern woman, ¡Epa! But in so many other things I have not changed, Dedé thinks. Last year during her prize trip to Spain, the smart-looking Canadian man approached her, and though it'd been ten years already since the divorce, Dedé just couldn't give herself that little fling.

"I'll make it fine," the woman claims, looking up at the sky. "Wow, the light is almost gone."

––––––––––

Night has fallen. Out on the road, they hear the sound of a car hurrying home. The interview woman bids Dedé farewell, and together they walk through the darkened garden to the side of the house where the rented Datsun is parked.

A car nears and turns into the drive, its headlights beaming into their eyes. Dedé and the woman stand paralyzed like animals caught in the beams of an oncoming car.

"Who could this be?" Dedé wonders aloud.

"Your next *compromiso*, no?" the interview woman says.

Dedé is reminded of her lie. "Yes, of course," she says as she peers into the dark. *"¡Buenas!"* she calls out.

"It's me, Mamá Dedé," Minou calls back. The car door slams—Dedé jumps. Footsteps hurry towards them.

"What on earth are you doing here? I've told you a thousand times!" Dedé scolds her niece. She doesn't care anymore if she is betraying her lie. Minou knows, all of her nieces know, that Dedé can't bear for them to be on the road after dark. If their mothers had only waited until the next morning to drive back over that deserted mountain road, they might still be alive to scold their own daughters about the dangers of driving at night.

"Ya, ya, Mamá Dedé." Minou bends down to kiss her aunt. Having taken after both her mother and father, she is a head taller than Dedé. "It just so happens I was off the road an hour ago." There is a pause, and Dedé already guesses what Minou is hesitating to say, for therein awaits another scold. "I was over at Fela's."

"Any messages from the girls?" Dedé says smartly. Beside her, she can feel the eager presence of the interview woman.

"Can't we sit down first," Minou says. There is some emotion in her voice Dedé can't quite make out. She has soured her niece's welcome, scolding her the minute she gets out of her car. "Come, come, you're right. Forgive your old aunt's bad manners. Let's go have a *limonada.*"

"I was just on my way out," the interview woman reminds Dedé. To Minou, she adds, "I hope to see you again—"

"We haven't even met." Minou smiles.

Dedé apologizes for her oversight and introduces the woman to her niece. Oh dear, what a mishmash of gratitude follows. The interview woman is delirious at the good fortune of meeting both sister and daughter of the heroine of the Fourteenth of June underground. Dedé cringes. She had better cut this off. Unlike their aunt, the children won't put up with this kind of overdone gush.

But Minou is chuckling away. "Come see us again," she offers, and Dedé, forced to rise to this politeness, adds, "Yes, now you know the way."

"I went to see Fela," Minou begins after she is settled with a fresh lemonade.

Dedé hears her niece swallow some emotion. What could be wrong? Dedé wonders. Gently now, she prods Minou, "Tell me what the girls had to say today?"

"That's just it," Minou says, her voice still uneven. "They wouldn't come. Fela says they must finally be at rest. It was strange, hearing that. I felt sad instead of glad."

Her last tie, however tenuous, to her mother. So that's what the emotion is all about, Dedé thinks. Then it strikes her. She knows exactly why Fela was getting a blackout this afternoon. "Don't you worry." Dedé pats her niece's hand. "They're still around."

Minou scowls at her aunt. "Are you making fun again?"

Dedé shakes her head. "I swear they've been here. All afternoon."

Minou is watching her aunt for any sign of irony. Finally, she says, "All right, can I ask you anything just like I do Fela?"

Dedé laughs uneasily. "Go on."

Minou hesitates, and then she says it right out, what Dedé suspects everyone has always wanted to ask her but which some politeness kept them from. Trust Minerva's incarnation to confront Dedé with the question she herself has avoided. "I've always wondered, I mean, you all were so close, why you didn't go along with them?"

———————

Certainly she remembers everything about that sunny afternoon, a few days into the new year, when Patria, Mate, and Minerva came over to see her.

She had been preparing a new bed in the garden, enjoying the rare quiet of an empty house. The girl had the day off, and as usual on a Sunday afternoon, Jaimito had gone to the big *gallera* in San Francisco, this time taking all three boys. Dedé wasn't expecting them back till late. From Mamá's house on the main road, her sisters must have seen Jaimito's pickup drive away without her and hurried to come over and pay Dedé this surprise visit.

When she heard a car stop in front of the house, Dedé considered taking off into the cacao grove. She was getting so solitary. A few nights ago Jaimito had complained that his mother had noticed that Dedé wasn't her old lively self. She rarely dropped by Doña Leila's anymore with a new strain of hibiscus she'd sprouted or a batch of *pastelitos* she'd made from scratch. Miss Sonrisa was losing her smiles, all right. Dedé had looked at her husband, a long look as if she could draw the young man of her dreams out from the bossy, old-fashioned macho he'd become. "Is that what your mother says?"

He'd brought this up as he sat in slippers in the *galería* enjoying the cool evening. He took a final swallow from his rum glass before he answered, "That's what my mother says. Get me another one, would you, Mami?" He held out the glass, and Dedé had gone obediently to the icebox in the back of the house where she burst into tears. What she wanted to hear from him was that *he* had noticed. Just his saying so would have made it better, whatever it was. She herself wasn't sure what.

So when she saw her three sisters coming down the path that afternoon, she felt pure dread. It was as if the three fates were approaching, their scissors poised to snip the knot that was keeping Dedé's life from falling apart.

———————

She knew why they had come.

Patria had approached her in the fall with a strange request. Could she bury some boxes in one of the cacao fields in back of their old house?

Dedé had been so surprised. "Why, Patria! Who put you up to this?"

Patria looked puzzled. "We're all in it, if that's what you mean. But I'm speaking for myself."

"I see," Dedé had said, but really what she saw was Minerva in back of it all. Minerva agitating. No doubt she had sent Patria over rather than come herself since she and Dedé were not getting along. It had been years since they'd fought openly—since Lío, wasn't it?—but recently their hot little exchanges had started up again.

What could Dedé say? She had to talk to Jaimito first. Patria had given her a disappointed look, and Dedé had gotten defensive. "What? I should go over Jaimito's head? It's only fair. He's the one farming the land, he's responsible for this place."

"But can't you decide on your own, then tell him?"

Dedé stared at her sister, disbelieving.

"That's what I did," Patria went on. "I joined, and then I talked Pedrito into joining me."

"Well, I don't have that kind of marriage," Dedé said. She smiled to take the huffiness out of her statement.

"What kind of marriage do you have?" Patria looked at her with that sweetness on her face that could always penetrate Dedé's smiles. Dedé looked away.

"It's just that you don't seem yourself," Patria continued, reaching for Dedé's hand. "You seem so—I don't know—withdrawn. Is something wrong?"

It was Patria's worried tone more than her question that pulled Dedé back into that abandoned part of herself where she had hoped to give love, *and* to receive it, in full measure, both directions.

Being there, she couldn't help herself. Though she tried giving Patria another of her brave smiles, Miss Sonrisa burst into tears.

After Patria's visit, Dedé *had* talked to Jaimito. As she expected, his answer was an adamant no. But beyond what she expected, he was furious with her for even considering such a request. The Mirabal sisters liked to run their men, that was the problem. In his house, he was the one to wear the pants.

"Swear you'll keep your distance from them!"

When he got upset, he would just raise his voice. But that night, he grabbed her by the wrists and shoved her on the bed, only—he said later—to make her come to her senses. "Swear!"

Now, when she thinks back, Dedé asks herself as Minou has asked her, Why? Why didn't she go along with her sisters. She was only thirty-four. She could have started a new life. But no, she reminds herself. She wouldn't have started over. She would have died with them on that lonely mountain road.

Even so, that night, her ears still ringing from Jaimito's shout, Dedé had been ready to risk her life. It was her marriage that she couldn't put on the line. She had always been the docile middle child, used to following the lead. Next to an alto she sang alto, by a soprano, soprano. Miss Sonrisa, cheerful, compliant. Her life had gotten bound up with a domineering man, and so she shrank from the challenge her sisters were giving her.

Dedé sent Patria a note: *Sorry. Jaimito says no.*

And for weeks afterwards, she avoided her sisters.

And now, here they were, all three like a posse come to rescue her.

Dedé's heart was beating away as she stood to welcome them. "How wonderful to see you!" She smiled, Miss Sonrisa, *armed* with smiles. She led them through the garden, delaying, showing off this and that new planting. As if they were here on a social call. As if they had come to see how her jasmine shrubs were doing.

They sat on the patio, exchanging the little news. The children were all coming down with colds. Little Jacqueline would be one in a month. Patria was up all hours again with Raulito. That boy was still not sleeping through the night. This gringo doctor she was reading said it was the parents of colicky babies who were to blame. No doubt Raulito was picking up all the tension in the house. Speaking of picking up things: Minou had called Trujillo a bad word. Don't ask. She must have overheard her parents. They would have to be more careful. Imagine what could happen if there were another spying yardboy like Prieto on the premises.

Imagine. An awkward silence fell upon them. Dedé braced herself. She expected Minerva to make an impassioned pitch for using the family farm for a munitions storage. But it was Mate who spoke up, the little sister who still wore her hair in braids and dressed herself and her baby girl in matching dresses.

They had come, she said, because something big, I mean really big, was about to happen. Mate's eyes were a child's, wide with wonder.

Minerva drew her index finger across her throat and let her tongue hang out of her mouth. Patria and Mate burst into nervous giggles.

Dedé couldn't believe it. They'd gone absolutely mad! "This is serious business," she reminded them. Some fury that had nothing to do with this serious business was making her heart beat fast.

"You bet it is," Minerva said, laughing. "The goat is going to die."

"Less than three weeks!" Mate's voice was becoming breathy with excitement.

"On the feast day of the Virgencita!" Patria exclaimed, making the sign of the cross and rolling her eyes heavenward. "*Ay, Virgencita,* watch over us."

Dedé pointed to her sisters. "You're going to do it yourselves?"

"Heavens, no," Mate said, horrified at the thought. "The Action Group does the actual justice, but then all the different cells will liberate their locations. We'll be taking the Salcedo Fortaleza."

Dedé was about to remind her little sister of her fear of spiders, worms, noodles in her soup, but she let Mate go on. "We're a cell, see, and there are usually only three in a cell, but we could make ours four." Mate looked hopefully at Dedé.

As if they were inviting her to join a goddamn volleyball team!

"This is a little sudden, I know," Patria was saying. "But it's not like with the boxes, Dedé. This looks like a sure thing."

"This *is* a sure thing," Minerva confirmed.

"Don't decide now," Patria went on as if afraid what Dedé's snap decision might be. "Think about it, sleep on it. We're having a meeting next Sunday at my place."

"*Ay*, like old times, all four of us!" Mate clapped her hands.

Dedé could feel herself being swayed by the passion of her sisters. Then she hit the usual snag. "And Jaimito?"

There was another awkward silence. Her sisters looked at each other. "Our cousin is also invited," Minerva said with that stiff tone she always used with Jaimito. "But you know best whether it's worth asking him."

"What do you mean by that?" Dedé snapped.

"I mean by that that I don't know what Jaimito's politics are."

Dedé's pride was wounded. Whatever their problems, Jaimito was her husband, the father of her children. "Jaimito's no Trujillista, if that's what you're implying. No more than . . . than Papá was."

"In his own way, Papá *was* a Trujillista," Minerva announced.

All her sisters looked at her, shocked. "Papá was a hero!" Dedé fumed. "He died because of what he went through in prison. *You* should know. He was trying to keep *you* out of trouble!"

Minerva nodded. "That's right. His advice was always, don't annoy the bees, don't annoy the bees. It's men like him and Jaimito and other scared *fulanitos* who have kept the devil in power all these years."

"How can you say that about Papá?" Dedé could hear her voice rising. "How can you let her say that about Papá?" She tried to enlist her sisters.

Mate had begun to cry.

"This isn't what we came for," Patria reminded Minerva, who stood and walked to the porch rail and stared out into the garden.

Dedé raked her eyes over the yard, half-afraid her sister was finding fault there, too. But the crotons were lusher than ever and the variegated bougainvilleas she hadn't thought would take were heavy with pink blossoms. All the beds were neat and weedless. Everything in its place. Only in the new bed where she'd just been working did the soil look torn up. And it was disturbing to see—among the established plantings—the raw brown earth like a wound in the ground.

"We want you with us. That's why we're here." Minerva's eyes as she fixed them on her sister were full of longing.

"What if I can't?" Dedé's voice shook. "Jaimito thinks it's suicide. He's told me he'll have to leave me if I get mixed up in this thing." There, she'd said it. Dedé felt the hot flush of shame on her face. She was hiding behind her husband's fears, bringing down scorn on him instead of herself.

"Our dear cousin," Minerva said sarcastically. But she stopped herself on a look from Patria.

"Everyone has their own reasons for the choices they make," Patria said, defusing the charged atmosphere, "and we have to respect that."

Blessed are the peacemakers, Dedé thought, but she couldn't for the life of her remember what the prize was that had been promised them.

"Whatever you decide, we'll understand," Patria concluded, looking around at her sisters.

Mate nodded, but Minerva could never leave well enough alone. As she climbed in the car, she reminded Dedé, "Next Sunday at Patria's around three. In case you change your mind," she added.

As she watched them drive away, Dedé felt strangely mingled surges of dread and joy. Kneeling at the new bed helped calm the shaking in her knees. Before she had finished smoothing the soil and laying out a border of little stones, she had worked out her plan. Only much later did she realize she had forgotten to put any seeds in the ground.

She would leave him.

Next to that decision, attending the underground meeting over at Patria's was nothing but a small step after the big turn had been taken. All week she refined the plan for it. As she beat the mattresses and fumigated the baseboards for red ants, as she chopped onions for the boys' breakfast *mangú* and made them drink *limonsillo* tea to keep away the cold going around, she plotted. She savored her secret, which tasted deliciously of freedom, as she allowed his weight on her in the dark bedroom and waited for him to be done.

Next Sunday, while Jaimito was at his *gallera*, Dedé would ride over to the meeting. When he came back, he would find the note propped on his pillow.

I feel like I'm buried alive. I need to get out. I cannot go on with this travesty.

Their life together had collapsed. From puppydog devotion, he had moved on to a moody bossiness complicated with intermittent periods of dogged remorse that would have been passion had there been less of his hunger and more of her desire in it. True to her nature, Dedé had made the best of things, eager for order, eager for peace. She herself was preoccupied—by the births of their sons, by the family setbacks after Papá was jailed, by Papá's sad demise and death, by their own numerous business failures. Perhaps Jaimito felt broken by these failures and her reminders of how she had tried to prevent them. His drinking, always social, became more solitary.

It was natural to blame herself. Maybe she hadn't loved him enough. Maybe he sensed how someone else's eyes had haunted her most of her married life.

Lío! What had become of him? Dedé had asked Minerva several times, quite casually, about their old friend. But Minerva didn't know a thing. Last she'd heard Lío had made it to Venezuela where a group of exiles was training for an invasion.

Then, recently, without her even asking, Minerva had confided to Dedé that their old friend was alive and kicking. "Tune into Radio Rumbos, 99 on your dial." Minerva knew Jaimito would be furious if he found Dedé listening to that outlawed station, yet her sister taunted her.

One naughty night, Dedé left Jaimito sleeping heavily after sex and stole out to the far end of the garden to the little shack where she kept the garden tools. There, in the dark, sitting on a sack of bark chips for her orchids, Dedé had slowly turned the dial on Jaimito Enrique's transistor radio. The static crackled, then a voice, very taken with itself, proclaimed, "Condemn me, it does not matter. History will absolve me!"

Fidel's speech was played endlessly at these off hours, as Dedé soon found out. But night after night, she kept returning to the shack, and twice she was rewarded with the unfamiliar, blurry voice of someone introduced as Comrade Virgilio. He spoke his high-flown talk which had never been what had appealed to Dedé. Even so, night after night, she returned to the shed, for these excursions were what mattered now. They were her secret rebellion, her heart hungering, her little underground of one.

Now, planning her exodus, Dedé tried to imagine Lío's surprise at hearing Dedé had joined her sisters. He would know that she, too, was one of the brave ones. His sad, sober eyes that had hung before her mind's eye for so many years melted into the ones that looked back at her now from the mirror. *I need to get out. I cannot go on with this travesty.*

As the day drew closer, Dedé was beset by doubts, particularly when she thought about her boys.

Enrique, Rafael, David, how could she possibly leave them?

Jaimito would never let her keep them. He was more than possessive with his sons, claiming them as if they were parts of himself. Look at how he had named them all with his first name as well as his last! Jaime Enrique Fernández. Jaime Rafael Fernández. Jaime David Fernández. Only their middle names, which perforce became their given names, were their own.

It wasn't just that she couldn't bear losing her boys, although that in itself was a dread large enough to stop her in her tracks. She also couldn't desert them. Who would stand between them and the raised hand when their father lost his temper? Who would make them *mangú* the way they liked it, cut their hair so it looked right, and sit in the dark with them when they were scared and the next morning not remind them she had been there?

She needed to talk to someone, outside her sisters. The priest! She'd gotten lax in her church attendance. The new militancy from the pulpit had become like so much noise in a place you had come to hear soothing music. But now that noise seemed in harmony with what she was feeling inside. Maybe this new young priest Padre de Jesús would have an answer for her.

She arranged for a ride that Friday with Mamá's new neighbors, Don Bernardo and his wife Doña Belén, old Spaniards who had been living down in San Cristóbal for years. They had decided to move to the countryside, Don Bernardo explained, hoping the air would help Doña Belén. Something was wrong with the frail, old woman—she was forgetting the simplest things, what a fork was for, how to button her dress, was it the seed or the meat of the mango you could eat. Don Bernardo was taking her to Salcedo for yet another round of tests at the clinic. "We won't be coming back until late afternoon. I hope that won't inconvenience you very much?" he apologized. The man was astonishingly courtly.

"Not at all," Dedé assured him. She could just be dropped off at the church.

"What have you got to do all day in church?" Doña Belén had a disconcerting ability to suddenly tune in quite clearly, especially to what was none of her business.

"Community work," Dedé lied.

"You Mirabal girls are so civic-minded," Don Bernardo observed. No doubt he was thinking of Minerva, or his favorite, Patria.

It was harder to satisfy Jaimito's suspicions. "If you need to go to Salcedo, I'll take you tomorrow." He had come into the bedroom as she was getting dressed that Friday morning.

"Jaimito, *por Dios!*" she pleaded. He had already forbidden her to go about with her sisters, was he now going to keep her from accompanying a poor old woman to the doctor?

"Since when has Doña Belén been a preoccupation of yours?" Then he said the thing he knew would make her feel the guiltiest. "And what about leaving the boys when they're sick?"

"All they have is colds, for God's sake. And Tinita's here with them."

Jaimito blinked in surprise at her sharp tone. Was it really this easy, Dedé wondered, taking command?

"Do as you please then!" He was giving her little knowing nods, his hands curling into fists. "But remember, you're going over my head!"

Jaimito did not return her wave as they drove away from Ojo de Agua. Something threatening in his look scared her. But Dedé kept reminding herself she need not be afraid. She was going to be leaving him. She told herself to keep that in mind.

———————

No one answered her knock at the rectory, although she kept coming back every half hour, all morning long. In between times, she idled in shops, remembering Jaimito's look that morning, feeling her resolve draining away. At noon, when everything closed up, she sat under a shade tree in the square and fed the pieces of the pastry she'd bought to the pigeons. Once she thought she saw Jaimito's pickup, and she began making up stories for why she had strayed from Doña Belén at the clinic.

Midafternoon, she spotted a green panel truck pulling up to the rectory gates. Padre de Jesús was in the passenger seat, another man was driving, a third jumped out from the back, unlocked the courtyard gates, and closed them after the truck pulled in.

Dedé hurried across the street. There was only a little time left before she had to meet up with Don Bernardo and Doña Belén at the clinic, and she *had* to talk to the priest. All day, the yeses and noes had been swirling inside her, faster, faster, until she felt dizzy with indecision. Waiting on that bench, she had promised herself that the priest's answer would decide it, once and for all.

She knocked several times before Padre de Jesús finally came to the door. Many apologies, he was unloading the truck, hadn't heard the knocker until just now. Please, please come in. He would be right with her.

He left her sitting in the small vestibule while he finished up with the delivery Dedé could hear going on in the adjoining choir room. Over his shoulder as he departed, Dedé caught a glimpse of some pine boxes, half-covered by a tarpaulin. Something about their color and their long shape recalled an incident in Patria's house last fall. Dedé had come over to help paint the baby's room. She had gone into Noris's room in search of some old sheets to lay on the floor, and there, in the closet, hidden behind a row of dresses, she'd seen several boxes just like these, standing on end. Patria had come in, acting very nervous, stammering about those boxes being full of new tools. Not too long after, when Patria had come with her request to hide some boxes, Dedé had understood what tools were inside them.

My God, Padre de Jesús was one of them! He would encourage her to join the struggle. Of course, he would. And she knew, right then and there, her knees shaking, her breath coming short, that she could not go through with this business. Jaimito was just an excuse. She was afraid, plain and simple, just as she had been afraid to face her powerful feelings for Lío. Instead, she had married Jaimito, although she knew she did not love him enough. And here she'd always berated him for his failures in business when the greater bankruptcy had been on her part.

She told herself that she was going to be late for her rendezvous. She ran out of that rectory before the priest could return, and arrived at the clinic while Doña Belén was still struggling with the buttons of her dress.

She heard the terrible silence the minute she walked in the house.

His pickup hadn't been in the drive, but then he often took off after a workday for a drink with his buddies. However, this silence was too deep and wide to be made by just one absence. "Enrique!" she screamed, running from room to room. "Rafael! David!"

The boys' rooms were deserted, drawers opened, rifled through. Oh my God, oh my God. Dedé could feel a mounting desperation. Tinita, who had come to work in the household four years ago when Jaime David was born, came running, alarmed by her mistress's screams. "Why, Doña Dedé," she said, wide-eyed. "It's only Don Jaimito who took the boys."

"Where?" Dedé could barely get it out.

"To Doña Leila's, I expect. He packed bags—" Her mouth dropped open, surprised by something private she wished she hadn't seen.

"How could you let him, Tinita. How could you! The boys have colds," she cried as if that were the reason for her distress. "Have Salvador saddle the mare," Dedé ordered. "Quick, Tinita, quick!" For the maid was standing there, rubbing her hands down the sides of her dress.

Off Dedé rode at a crazy canter all the way to Mamá's. It was already dark when she turned in the drive. The house was all lit up, cars in the driveway, Minerva and Manolo just arriving from Monte Cristi, Mate and Leandro from the capital. Of course, it would be a big weekend. But every thought of the meeting had faded from Dedé's mind.

She had told herself on the gallop over that she must stay calm so as not to alarm Mamá. But the moment she dismounted, she was crying, "I need a ride! Quick!"

"*M'ija, m'ija,*" Mamá kept asking. "What's going on?"

"Nothing, Mamá, really. It's just Jaimito's taken the boys to San Francisco."

"But what's wrong with that?" Mamá was asking, suspicion deepening the lines on her face. "Is something wrong with that?"

By now, Manolo had brought the car around to the door, and Minerva was honking the horn. Off they went, Dedé telling them her story of coming home and finding the house abandoned, the boys gone.

"Why would he do this?" Minerva asked. She was digging through her purse for the cigarettes she could not smoke in front of Mamá. Recently, she had picked up a bad cough along with the smoking.

"He threatened to leave me if I got involved with your group."

"But you're not involved," Manolo defended her.

"Maybe Dedé wants to be involved." Minerva turned around to face the back seat. Dedé could not make out her expression in the dim light. The end of her cigarette glowed like a bright, probing eye. "Do you want to join us?"

Dedé began to cry. "I just have to admit to myself. I'm not you—no really, I mean it. I could be brave if someone were by me every day of my life to remind me to be brave. I don't come by it naturally."

"None of us do," Minerva noted quietly.

"Dedé, you're plenty brave," Manolo asserted in his courtly way. Then, for they were already in the outskirts of San Francisco, he added, "You're going to have to tell me where to turn."

They pulled up behind the pickup parked in front of Doña Leila's handsome stucco house, and Dedé's heart lifted. She had seen the boys through the opened door of the front patio, watching television. As they were getting out of the car, Minerva hooked arms with Dedé. "Manolo's right, you know. You're plenty brave." Then nodding towards Jaimito, who had come to the doorway and was aggressively blocking their way in, she added, "One struggle at a time, sister."

"The liberators are here!" Jaimito's voice was sloppy with emotion. Dedé's arrival with Minerva and Manolo probably confirmed his suspicions. "What do you want?" he asked, hands gripping either side of the door frame.

"My sons," Dedé said, coming up on the porch. She felt brave with Minerva at her side.

"My sons," he proclaimed, "are where they should be, safe and sound."

"Why, cousin, don't you say hello?" Minerva chided him.

He was curt in his greetings, even to Manolo, whom he had always liked. They had together invested their wives' inheritance in that ridiculous project—what was it?—growing onions in some godforsaken desert area where you couldn't even get Haitians to live? Dedé had warned them.

But Manolo's warmth could thaw any coldness. He gave his old business partner *un abrazo*, addressing him as *compadre* even though neither one was godparent to the other's children. He invited himself in, ruffled the boys' hair, and called out, "Doña Leila! Where's my girl?"

Obviously, the boys suspected nothing. They yielded reluctant kisses to their mother and aunt, their eyes all the while trained on the screen where *el gato* Tom and *el ratoncito* Jerry were engaged in yet another of their battles.

Doña Leila came out from her bedroom, ready to entertain. She looked coquettish in a fresh dress, her white hair pinned up with combs. "*¡Manolo, Minerva! ¡Qué placer!*" But it was Dedé whom she kept hugging.

So he hadn't said anything to his mother. He wouldn't dare, Dedé thought. Doña Leila had always doted on her daughter-in-law, so much so that Dedé sometimes worried that Leila's five daughters would resent her. But really it was obvious they adored the sister-in-law-cousin who encouraged them in their small rebellions against their possessive only brother. Seven years ago, when Don Jaime had died, Jaimito had taken on the man-of-the-family role with a vengeance. Even his mother said he was worse than Don Jaime had ever been.

"Sit down, please, sit down." Doña Leila pointed to the most comfortable chairs, but she would not let go of Dedé's hand.

"Mamá," Jaimito explained, "we all have something private to discuss. We'll talk outside," he addressed Manolo, avoiding his mother's eyes.

Doña Leila hurried out to assess the porch. She turned on the garden lights, brought out her good rockers, served her guests a drink, and insisted Dedé eat a *pastelito* snack—she was looking too thin. "Don't let me hold you up," she kept saying.

Finally, they were alone. Jaimito turned the porch lights off, calling out to his mother, that there were too many bugs. But Dedé suspected that he found it easier to address their problems in the dark.

"You think I don't know what you've been up to." The agitation in his tone carried.

Doña Leila called from inside. "You need another *cervecita, m'ijo?*"

"No, no, Mamá," Jamito said, impatience creeping into his voice. "I told Dedé," he addressed his in-laws, "I didn't want her getting mixed up in this thing."

"I can assure you she's never been to any of our gatherings," Manolo put in. "On my word."

Jaimito was silent. Manolo's statement had stopped him short. But he had already gone too far to readily admit that he'd been wrong. "Well, what about her meetings with Padre de Jesús? Everyone knows he's a flaming communist."

"He is not," Minerva contradicted.

"For heaven's sake, Jaimito, I only went to see him once," Dedé added. "And it was in reference to us, if you have to know the truth."

"Us?" Jaimito stopped rocking himself, his bravado deflated. "What about us, Mami?"

Can you really be so blind, she wanted to say. We don't talk anymore, you boss me around, you keep to yourself, you're not interested in my garden. But Dedé felt shy addressing their intimate problems in front of her sister and brother-in-law. "You know what I'm talking about."

"What is it, Mami?"

"Stop calling me Mami, I'm not your mother."

Doña Leila's voice drifted from the kitchen where she was supervising her maid in frying a whole platter of snacks. "Another *pastelito*, Dedé?"

"She's been like that since the minute I got here," Jaimito confided. His voice had grown tender. He was loosening up. "She must have asked me a hundred times, 'Where's Dedé? Where's Dedé?'" It was as close as he could get to admitting how he felt.

"I have a suggestion, *compadre*," Manolo said. "Why don't you two take a honeymoon somewhere nice."

"The boys have colds," Dedé said lamely.

"Their grandmother will take very good care of them, I'm sure." Manolo laughed. "Why not go up to—wasn't it Jarabacoa where you honeymooned?"

"No, Río San Juan, that area," Jaimito said, entering into the plan.

"*We* went to Jarabacoa," Minerva reminded Manolo in a tight voice that suggested she disapproved of the reconciliation he was engineering. Her sister was better off alone.

"They have a beautiful new hotel in Río San Juan," Manolo went on. "There's a balcony with each room, every one with a sea view."

"I hear the prices are reasonable," Jaimito put in. It was as if the two men were working on another deal together.

"So what do you say?" Manolo concluded.

Neither Jaimito nor Dedé said a word.

"Then it's settled," Manolo said, but he must have felt the unsettledness in their silence, for he went on. "Look, everyone has troubles. Minerva and I went through our own rough times. The important thing is to use a crisis like this to grow closer. Isn't that so, *mi amor*?"

Minerva's guard was still up. "Some people can't ever really see eye to eye."

Her statement broke the deadlock, though it was probably the last thing Minerva had intended. Jaimito's competitive streak was reawakened. "Dedé and I see perfectly eye to eye! The problem is other people confusing things."

The problem is when I open my eyes and see for myself, Dedé was thinking. But she was too shaken by the night's events and the long week of indecision to contradict him.

And so it was that the weekend that was to have been a watershed in Dedé's life turned into a trip down memory lane in a rented boat. In and out of the famous lagoons they had visited as a young bride and groom Jaimito rowed, stopping to point with his oar to the swamp of mangroves where the Tainos had fished and later hidden from the Spanish. Hadn't she heard him say so eleven years ago?

And at night, sitting on their private balcony, with Jaimito's arm around her and his promises in her ear, Dedé gazed up at the stars. Recently, in *Vanidades*, she had read how starlight took years to travel down to earth. The star whose light she was now seeing could have gone out years ago. What comfort if she counted them? If in that dark heaven she traced a ram when already half its brilliant horn might be gone?

False hopes, she thought. Let the nights be totally dark! But even that dark wish she made on one of those stars.

––––––––––

The roundup started by the end of the following week.

Early that Saturday Jaimito dropped off Dedé at Mamá's with the two youngest boys. Mamá had asked for Dedé's help planting a crown-of-thorns border, so she said, but Dedé knew what her mother really wanted. She was worried about her daughter after her panicked visit a week ago. She wouldn't ask Dedé any questions—Mamá always said that what went on in her daughters' marriages was their business. Just by watching Dedé lay the small plants in the ground, Mamá would know the doings in her heart.

As Dedé walked up the driveway, assessing what still needed to be done in the yard, the boys raced each other to the door. They were swallowed up by the early morning silence of the house. It seemed odd that Mamá had not come out to greet her. Then Dedé noticed the servants gathered in the backyard, and Tono breaking away, walking briskly towards her. Her face had the burdened look of someone about to deliver bad news.

"What, Tono, tell me!" Dedé found she was clutching the woman's arm.

"Don Leandro has been arrested."

"Only him?"

Tono nodded. And shamefully, in her heart Dedé was thankful that her sisters had been spared before she was frightened for Leandro.

Inside, María Teresa was sitting on the couch, unplaiting and plaiting her hair, her face puffy from crying. Mamá stood by, reminding her that everything was going to be all right. By habit, Dedé swept her eyes across the room looking for the boys. She heard them in one of the bedrooms, playing with their baby cousin Jacqueline.

"She just got here," Mamá was saying. "I was about to send the boy for you." There were no phone lines out where the old house was—another reason Mamá had moved up to the main road.

Dedé sat down. Her knees always gave out on her when she was scared. "What happened?"

Mate sobbed out her story, her breath wheezy with the asthma she always got whenever she was upset. She and Leandro had been asleep just a couple of hours when they heard a knock that didn't wait for an answer. The SIM had broken down the door of their apartment, stormed inside, roughed up Leandro and carried him away. Then they ransacked the house, ripped open the upholstery on the couch and chairs, and drove off in the new Chevrolet. Mate stopped, too short of breath to continue.

"But why? Why?" Mamá kept asking. "Leandro's a serious boy, an engineer!" Neither Mate nor Dedé knew how to answer her.

Dedé tried calling Minerva in Monte Cristi, but the operator reported the line was dead. Now Mamá, who had stood by accepting their shrugs for answers, levelled her gaze at each of them. "What is going on here? And don't try to tell me nothing. I know something is going on."

Mate flinched as if she knew she had misbehaved.

"Mamá," Dedé said, knowing the time had come to offer their mother the truth. She patted a space between them on the couch. "You're going to have to sit down for this."

Dedé was the first to rush out when they heard the commotion in the front yard. What she saw made no sense at first. The servants were all on the front lawn now, Fela with a screaming Raulito in her arms. Noris stood by, holding Manolito's hand, both of them crying. And there was Patria, on her knees, rocking herself back and forth, pulling the grass out of the ground in handfuls.

Slowly, Dedé pieced together the story Patria was telling.

The SIM had come for Pedrito and Nelson who, alerted by some neighbors, had fled into the hills. Patria had answered the door and told the officers that her husband and son were away in the capital, but the SIM overran the place anyway. They scoured the property, dug up the fields, and found the buried boxes full of their incriminating cargo as well as an old box of papers. Inflammatory materials, they called it. But all Patria saw were pretty notebooks written in a girlish hand. Probably something Noris had wanted to keep private from her nosey older brother, and so hidden away in the grove.

They tore the house apart, hauling away the doors, windows, the priceless mahogany beams of Pedrito's old family *rancho*. It was like watching her life dismantled before her very eyes, Patria said, weeping—the glories she had trained on a vine; the Virgencita in the silver frame blessed by the Bishop of Higüey; the wardrobe with little ducks she had stenciled on when Raulito was born.

All of it violated, broken, desecrated, destroyed.

Then they set fire to what was left.

And Nelson and Pedrito, seeing the conflagration and fearing for Patria and the children, came running down from the hills, their hands over their heads, giving themselves up.

"I've been good! I've been good!" Patria was screaming at the sky. The ground around her was bare, the grass lay in sad clumps at her side.

Why she did what she did next, Dedé didn't know. Grief driving her to salvage something, she supposed. Down she got on her knees and began tamping the grass back. In a soothing voice, she reminded her sister of the faith that had always sustained her. "You believe in God, the Father Almighty, Maker of heaven and earth . . ."

Sobbing, Patria fell in, reciting the Credo: "Light of light, who for us men and for our salvation . . ."

"—came down from heaven," Dedé confirmed in a steady voice.

They could not get hold of Jaimito, for he had gone off to a tobacco auction for the day. The new doctor could not come out from San Francisco after they had explained why they needed him. He had an emergency, he told Dedé, but being a connoisseur of fear, she guessed he was afraid. Don Bernardo kindly brought over some of Doña Belén's sedatives, and indiscriminately, Dedé gave everyone a small dose, even the babies, even Tono and Fela, and of course, her boys. A numbed dreariness descended on the house, everyone moving in slow motion in the gloom of Miltown and recent events. Dedé kept trying to call Minerva, but the line was truly, conclusively down, and the operator became annoyed.

Finally, Dedé reached Minerva at Manolo's mother's house. How relieved Dedé felt to hear her voice. It was then she realized that after all her indecisiveness, she had never really had a choice. Whether she joined their underground or not, her fate was bound up with the fates of her sisters. She would suffer whatever they suffered. If they died, she would not want to go on living without them.

Yes, Manolo had been arrested last night, too. Minerva's voice was tight. No doubt Doña Fefita, Manolo's mother, was at her side. Every once in a while Minerva broke into a fit of coughing.

"Are you all right?" Dedé asked her.

There was a long pause. "Yes, yes," Minerva rallied. "The phone's been disconnected but the house is standing. Nothing but books for them to steal." Minerva's laughter exploded into a coughing fit. "Just allergies," she explained when Dedé worried she was ill.

"Put on Patria, please," Minerva asked after giving the grim rundown. "I want to ask her something." When Dedé explained how Patria had finally settled down with a sedative, that maybe it was better if she didn't come to the phone, Minerva point blank asked, "Do you know if she saved any of the kids' tennis shoes?"

"*Ay*, Minerva," Dedé sighed. The coded talk was so transparent even she could guess what her sister was asking about. "Here's Mamá," Dedé cut her off. "She wants to talk to you."

Mamá kept pleading with Minerva to come home. "It's better if we're all together." Finally, she handed the phone back to Dedé. "You convince her." As if Minerva had ever listened to Dedé!

"I am not going to run scared," Minerva stated before Dedé could even begin convincing. "I'm fine. Now can't Patria come to the line?"

A few days later, Dedé received Minerva's panicky note. She was desperate. She needed money. Creditors were at the door. She had to buy medicines because ("Don't tell Mamá") she had been diagnosed with tuberculosis. "I hate to involve you, but since you're in charge of the family finances . . ." Could Dedé advance her some cash to be taken out of Minerva's share of the house and lands in the future?

Too proud to just plain ask for help! Dedé took off in Jaimito's pickup, avoiding a stop at Mamá's to use the phone since Mamá would start asking questions. From the bank, Dedé called Minerva to tell her that she was on her way with the money, but instead she reached a distraught Doña Fefita. Minerva had been taken that very morning, the little house ransacked and boarded up. In the background Dedé could hear Minou crying piteously.

"I'm coming to get you," she promised the little girl.

The child calmed down some. "Is Mamá with you?"

Dedé took a deep breath. "Yes, Mamá is here." The beginning of many stories. Later, she would hedge and say she meant her own Mamá. But for now, she wanted to spare the child even a moment of further anguish.

She rode out to the tobacco fields where Jaimito had said he'd be supervising the planting of the new crop. She had wondered as she was dialing Minerva what Jaimito would do when he came home and found his wife *and* his pickup missing. Something told her he would not respond with his usual fury. Despite herself, Dedé had to admit she liked what she sensed, that the power was shifting in their marriage. Coming home from Río San Juan, she had finally told him, crying as she did, that she could not continue with their marriage. He had wept, too, and begged for a second chance. For a hundredth chance, she thought. Now events were running away with them, trampling over her personal griefs, her budding hopes, her sprouting wings.

"Jaimito!" she called when she saw him from far off.

He came running across the muddy, just-turned field. How ironic, she thought, watching him. Their lives, which had almost gone their separate ways a week ago, were now drawing together again. After all, they were embarking on their most passionate project to date, one they must not fail at like the others. Saving the sisters.

They drove the short distance to Mamá's, debating how to break the news to her. Mamá's blood pressure had risen dangerously after Patria's breakdown on the front lawn. Was it really less than a week ago? It seemed months since they'd been living in this hell of terror and dreadful anticipation. Every day there were more and more arrests. The lists in the newspapers grew longer.

But there was no shielding Mamá any longer, Dedé saw when they arrived at her house. Several black Volkswagens and a police wagon were pulled into the drive. Captain Peña, head of the northern division of the SIM, had orders to bring Mate in. Mamá was hysterical. Mate clung to her, weeping with terror as Mamá declared that her youngest daughter could not leave without her. Dedé could hear the shrieks of Jacqueline calling for her mother from the bedroom.

"Take me instead, please." Patria knelt by the door, pleading with Captain Peña. "I beg you for the love of God."

The captain, a very fat man, looked down with interest at Patria's heaving chest, considering the offer. Don Bernardo, drawn by the commotion from next door, arrived with the bottle of sedatives. He tried to coax Patria back on her feet, but she would not or could not stand up. Jaimito took the captain aside. Dedé saw Jaimito reaching for his billfold, the captain holding up his hand. Oh God, it was bad news if the devil was refusing to take a bribe.

At last, the captain said he would make an exception. Mamá could come along. But out on the drive, after loading the terrified Mate in the wagon, he gave a signal and the driver roared away, leaving Mamá standing on the road. The screams from the wagon were unbearable to hear.

Dedé and Jaimito raced after María Teresa, the small pickup careening this way and that, swerving dangerously around slower traffic. Usually, Dedé was full of admonitions about Jaimito's reckless driving, but now she found herself pressing her own foot on an invisible gas pedal. Still, they never managed to catch up with the wagon. By the time they reached the Salcedo Fortaleza and were seen by someone in authority, they were told the young *llorona* with the long braid had been transferred to the capital. They couldn't say where.

"Those bastards!" Jaimito exclaimed once they were back in the pickup. He kept striking the vinyl seat with his fist. "They're not going to get away with this!" This was the same old violence Dedé had cowered under for years. But now instead of fear, she felt a surge of pity. There was nothing Jaimito or anyone could do. But it touched her that he had found his way to serve the underground after all—taking care of its womenfolk.

Watching him, Dedé was reminded of his fighting cocks which, in the barnyard, appeared to be just plain roosters. But put them in a ring with another rooster, and they sprang to life, explosions of feathers and dagger claws. She had seen them dazed, stumbling, eyes pecked out, still clawing the air at an attacker they could no longer see. She remembered, too, with wonder and some disgust and even an embarrassing sexual rush, how Jaimito would put their heads in his mouth, as if they were some wounded part of him or, she realized, of her that he was reviving.

On the way back to Mamá's, Dedé and Jaimito made plans. Tomorrow early, they would drive down to the capital and petition for the girls, not that it would do any good. But doing nothing could be worse. Unclaimed prisoners tended to disappear. Oh God, Dedé could not let herself think of that!

It was odd to be riding in the pickup, the dark road ahead, a slender moon above, holding hands, as if they were young lovers again, discussing wedding plans. Dedé half expected Minerva and Lío to pop up in back. The thought stirred her, but not for the usual reason of lost opportunity recalled. Rather, it was because that time now seemed so innocent of this future. Dedé fought down the sob that twisted like a rope in her gut. She felt that if she let go, the whole inside of her would fall apart.

As they turned into the driveway, they saw Mamá standing at the end of it, Tono and Patria at her side, trying to hush her. "Take everything, take it all! But give me back my girls, *por Dios!*" she was shouting.

"What is it, Mamá, what is it?" Dedé had leapt out of the pickup before it had even come to a full stop. She already guessed what was wrong.

"Minerva, they've taken Minerva."

Dedé exchanged a glance with Jaimito. "How do you know this, Mamá?"

"They took the cars." Mamá pointed to the other end of the drive and, sure enough, the Ford and the Jeep were gone.

Some of the SIM guards left behind had asked her for the keys. They were confiscating the two vehicles registered under a prisoner's name. Minerva! No one had ever bothered to change those documents since Papá's time. Now they were SIM cars.

"Lord." Mamá looked up, addressing those very stars Dedé had already discounted. "Lord, hear my cry!"

"Let's go talk to Him inside," Dedé suggested. She had seen the hedges move slightly. They were being spied upon and would be from now on.

In Mamá's bedroom, they all knelt down before the large picture of the Virgencita. It was here that all the crises in the family were first addressed—when Patria's baby was born dead, when the cows caught the pinkeye, when Papá had been jailed, and later when he died and his other family had come to light.

Now, in the small room, they gathered again, Patria, Noris, Mamá, even Jaimito, though he hung back sheepishly, unaccustomed to being on his knees. Patria led the rosary, breaking down every now and then, Dedé filling in those breaks with a strong, full voice. But really her heart was not in it. Her mind was thinking over all she must do before she and Jaimito left in the morning. The boys had to be dropped off at Doña Leila's, and Minou had to be sent for in Monte Cristi, and the pickup had to be filled with gas, and some bags packed for the girls in whatever prison held them, and a bag for her and Jaimito in case they had to stay overnight.

The praying had stopped. Everyone was crying quietly now, touching the veil of the Virgin for comfort. Looking up at the Blessed Mother, Dedé saw where Minerva's and Mate's pictures had been newly tucked into the frame that already held Manolo, Leandro, Nelson, Pedrito. She struggled but this time she could not keep down her sobs.

That night as she lay beside Jaimito, Dedé could not sleep. It was not the naughty insomnia that resulted from a trip out to the shed to listen to the contraband station. This was something else altogether. She was feeling it slowly coming on. The dark of a childhood closet, the odor of gasoline she never liked, the feel of something dangerous pawing at her softly to see what she would do. She felt a tickling temptation to just let go. To let the craziness overtake her before the SIM could destroy all she loved.

But who would take care of her boys? And Mamá? And who would coax Patria back if she wandered away again from the still waters and green pastures of her sanity?

Dedé could not run away. Courage! It was the first time she had used that word to herself and understood exactly what it meant. And so, as Jaimito snored away, Dedé began devising a little exercise to distract her mind and fortify her spirit.

Concentrate, Dedé! she was saying. *Remember a clear cool night a lot like this one. You are sitting under the anacahuita tree in the front yard. . . .* And she began playing the happy memory in her head, forcing herself to imagine the scent of jasmine, the feel of the evening on her skin, the green dress she was wearing, the tinkle of ice in Papá's glass of rum, the murmured conversation.

But wait! Dedé didn't make up that memory game the night of the arrests. In fact, she didn't invent it at all. It was Minerva who taught her how to play it after she was released from prison and was living those last few months at Mamá's with Mate and Patria and the children.

Every day Dedé would go over to visit, and every day she would have a fight with Minerva. Dedé would start by pleading, then arguing with Minerva to be reasonable, to stay home. The rumors were everywhere. Trujillo wanted her killed. She was becoming too dangerous, the secret heroine of the whole nation. At the pharmacy, in church, at the *mercado*, Dedé was being approached by well-wishers. "Take care of our girls," they would whisper. Sometimes they would slip her notes. "Tell the butterflies to avoid the road to Puerto Plata. It's not

safe." The butterflies, Lord God, how people romanticized other people's terror!

But Minerva acted unconcerned about her safety. She could not
desert the cause, she'd argue with Dedé, and she would not stay holed
up in Ojo de Agua and let the SIM kill her spirit. Besides, Dedé was giving in to her exaggerated fears. With the OAS clamoring about all the
jailings and executions, Trujillo was not going to murder a defenseless
woman and dig his own grave. Silly rumors.

"*Voz del pueblo, voz del cielo,*" Dedé would quote. Talk of the people,
voice of God.

One time, towards the end, Dedé broke down in tears in the middle
of one of their arguments. "I'm losing my mind worrying about you,
don't you see?" she had wept. But instead of caving in to Dedé's tears,
Minerva offered her an exercise.

"I made it up in La Victoria whenever they'd put me in solitary," she
explained. "You start with a line from a song or a poem. Then you just
say it over until you feel yourself calming down. I kept myself sane that
way." Minerva smiled sadly. "You try it, come on. I'll start you off."

Even now, Dedé hears her sister, reciting that poem she wrote in jail,
her voice raspy with the cold she never got rid of that last year. *And the
shades of night begin to fall, and the traveler hurries home, and the campesino
bids his fields farewell. . . .*

No wonder Dedé has confused Minerva's exercise and her poem
about the falling of night with that sleepless night before their first trip
to the capital. A dark night *was* falling, one of a different order from the
soft, large, kind ones of childhood under the anacahuita tree, Papá
parceling out futures and Mamá fussing at his drinking. This one was
something else, the center of hell maybe, the premonition of which
made Dedé draw closer to Jaimito until she, too, finally fell asleep.

CHAPTER TEN

Patria

January to March 1960

I don't know how it happened that my cross became bearable. We have a saying around here, the humpback never gets tired carrying his burden on his back. All at once, I lost my home, my husband, my son, my peace of mind. But after a couple of weeks living at Mamá's, I got used to the sorrows heaped upon my heart.

That first day was the hardest. I was crazy with grief, all right. When Dedé and Tono walked me into the house, all I wanted to do was lie down and die. I could hear the babies crying far off and voices calming them and Noris sobbing along with her aunt Mate, and all their grief pulled me back from mine. But first, I slept for a long time, days it seemed. When I woke up, Dedé's voice was in my ear, invoking the Lord's name.

And on the third day He rose again . . .

I got up from bed ready to set up housekeeping at Mamá's. I asked for a basin for the baby's bath, and told Noris she had to do something about that hair in her eyes.

Mate and I moved into a front room with the crib for both our babies. I put Noris with Minou and Manolito in the spare room Minerva always used. Mamá, I thought, would do better by herself in her own room.

But past midnight, the sleepers began to shift beds, everyone seeking the comfort of another body. Manolito invariably crawled in with me, and soon after, Raulito would start bawling. That boy was jealous even in his sleep! I'd bring him to my bed, leaving the crib empty, for Jacqueline was already cuddled at her mother's side. In the mornings, I'd find Noris and Minou in Mamá's bed, their arms around each other, fast asleep.

And on the third day He rose again . . .

On my third day at Mamá's, instead of a resurrection, I got another crucifixion. The SIM came for Mate.

It was three months before I laid eyes on her or Minerva or our husbands. Three months before I got to hold my Nelson.

As I said, I recovered. But every now and then, I couldn't get the pictures out of my head.

Over and over again, I saw the SIM approaching, I saw Nelson and Pedrito hurrying out the back way, Noris's stricken face. I saw the throng of men at the door, I heard the stomping, the running, the yelling. I saw the house burning.

I saw tiny cells with very little air and no light. I heard doors open, I saw hands intrusive and ugly in their threats. I heard the crack of bones breaking, the thud of a body collapsing. I heard moans, screams, desperate cries.

Oh my sisters, my Pedrito, oh my little lamb!

My crown of thorns was woven of thoughts of my boy. His body I had talcumed, fed, bathed. His body now broken as if it were no more than a bag of bones.

"I've been good," I'd start screaming at the sky, undoing the "recovery."

And then, Mamá would have to send for Dedé. Together Dedé and I would pray a rosary. Afterwards we played our old childhood game, opening the Bible and teasing a fortune out of whatever verse our hands landed on.

And on the third day He rose again . . .

It was odd living in Mamá's new house. Everything from the old house was here, but all rearranged. Sometimes I'd find myself reaching for a door that wasn't there. In the middle of the night, however fearful I was about waking the children, I had to turn on a light to go to the sanitary. Otherwise, I'd end up crashing into the cabinet that never used to be in the hallway in the old house.

In the entryway hung the required portrait of El Jefe, except it wasn't our old one of Trujillo as a young captain that used to hang next to the Good Shepherd. Mamá had acquired this latest portrait and hung it all by itself, out as far as she could get it from the rest of the house. He was older now—heavier, his jowls thicker, the whole face tired out, someone who had had too much of all the bad things in life.

Maybe because I was used to the Good Shepherd and Trujillo side by side in the old house, I caught myself praying a little greeting as I walked by.

Then another time, I came in from outside with my hands full of anthuriums. I looked up at him, and I thought why not. I set up a vase on the table right under his picture.

It seemed natural to add a nice little lace cloth for the table.

I don't know if that's how it started, but pretty soon, I was praying to him, not because he was worthy or anything like that. I wanted something from him, and prayer was the only way I knew to ask.

It was from raising children I learned that trick. You dress them in their best clothes and they behave their best to match them.

Nelson, my devil! When he was little, he was always tormenting Noris, always getting into things. I'd call him in, give him a bath. But instead of putting him in his pajamas and sending him to bed in the middle of the day where he'd get bored and mean, I'd dress him up in his gabardine trousers and little linen *guayabera* I'd made him just like his father's. And then I'd take him with me to Salcedo for an afternoon novena and a coconut ice afterwards. That dressed-up boy acted like an angel!

So, I thought, why not? Treat *him* like a spirit worthy of my attention, and maybe he would start behaving himself.

Every day I changed the flowers and said a few words. Mamá thought I was just putting on a show for Peña and his SIM who came by often to check on the family. But Fela understood, except she thought I was trying to strike a deal with the evil one. I wasn't at all. I wanted to turn him towards his better nature. If I could do that, the rest would follow.

Jefe, I would say, *remember you are dust and unto dust you shall return.* (That one never worked with him.)

Hear my cry, Jefe. Release my sisters and their husbands and mine. But most especially, I beg you, oh Jefe, give me back my son.

Take me instead, I'll be your sacrificial lamb.

I hung my Sacred Heart, a recent gift from Don Bernardo, in the bedroom. There I offered, not my trick prayers, but my honest-to-God ones.

I wasn't crazy, after all. I knew who was *really* in charge.

I had let go of my hard feelings, for the most part, but there was some lingering bitterness. For instance, I had offered myself to El Jefe to do with as he wanted, but I hadn't extended the same courtesy to God.

I guess I saw it as a clear-cut proposition I was making El Jefe. He would ask for what he always asked for from women. I could give *that*. But there would be no limit to what our Lord would want of Patria Mercedes, body and soul and all the etceteras besides.

With a baby still tugging at my breast, a girl just filling out, and my young-man son behind bars, I wasn't ready to enter His Kingdom.

In the midst of my trials, there were moments. I can't say they were moments of Grace. But they were moments of knowing I was on the right track.

One day soon after Mate was taken, Peña showed up. That man gave me a creepy feeling, exactly the same as the one I'd felt in the presence of the devil in the old days, fooling with my hands at night. The children were out on the patio with me. They kept their distance from Peña, refusing the candies he offered them unless I took them from him, in my hands, first. When he reached for Minou to ride on his knee, all of them ran away.

"Lovely children," he said, to mask the obvious rejection. "Are they all yours?"

"No, the boy and the little girl are Minerva's, and the baby girl is María Teresa's." I said the names very clearly. I wanted it to sink in that he was making these children orphans. "The baby boy and the young girl are mine."

"Don Pedrito must love those children of his."

My blood went cold. "What makes you say so, Captain?" I tried to keep my voice even.

"The SIM made your husband an offer, but he wouldn't take it."

So, he was still alive! Three times, Dedé and Mamá and Jaimito had been down to headquarters, only to be told that there was no record of our prisoners.

"Don't you want to know what the offer was?" Peña seemed miffed. I had noted that he got some thrill out of having me plead for information.

"Yes, please, captain."

"Your husband was offered his freedom and his farm back—"

My heart leapt!

"—if he proved his loyalty to El Jefe by divorcing his Mirabal wife."

"Oh?" I could feel my heart like a hand making a fist in my chest.

Peña's sharp, piglike eyes were watching me. And then he had his dirty little say. "You Mirabal women must be something else"—he fondled himself—"to keep a man interested when all he can do with his manhood is pass water!"

I had to say two Glory Be's to myself before I could speak aloud. Even so, my voice threw sparks. "Captain Peña, no matter what you do to my husband, he will always be ten times the man you are!" That evil man threw back his head and laughed, then picked up his cap from his lap and stood to leave. I saw the lump he'd gotten by working me up to this state.

I went in search of the children to calm myself down. I found Minou digging a hole in the ground and burying all the candies Peña had brought. When I asked her why she was wasting her candies, she said she was burying them like the box her Mamá and Papá had buried in their yard that was bad to touch.

"This is bad candy," she said to me.

"Yes, it is," I said and got down on my knees to help her finish burying it.

Peña's mention of Pedrito was the first news we had had of any of our prisoners. Then, a few days later, Dedé and Mamá came back from another trip to the capital with the "good news" that the girls' names, along with those of the men and my Nelson, had appeared on the latest list of three hundred and seventy-two detained. Oh, how relieved we were! As long as the SIM admitted they were in custody, our prisoners stood less of a chance of being disappeared.

Dark as it was, I went out into the garden with Mamá's scissors. I cut by scent more than sight so that I didn't know exactly what I had until I was back inside. I arranged his spray of jasmine and stems of gardenias in a vase on the little table, then took the rest of the flowers into my bedroom.

And on the third day, He rose again.

We were already working on the third week. Still, there were moments, like I said—resurrection gathering speed.

Sunday, early, we packed ourselves in Jaimito's pickup. Except for a few farm horses over at Dedé's and the old mule at Mamá's, it was the only transportation left us, now that all the cars had been confiscated. Mamá laid out an old sheet in the flatbed and put the children in back with me. She and Dedé and Jaimito rode in front. It was still early morning as we drove towards Salcedo for the first mass. The mist was rising all around us from the fields. As we passed the turnoff to our old house in Conuco, I felt a stab of pain. I looked at Noris, hoping she hadn't noticed, but her pretty face was struggling to be brave.

No one knew that the Voice of God would speak from the pulpit that day. None of us would have expected it from Padre Gabriel, who was, we thought, a stooge substitute sent in after Padre de Jesús was arrested.

When it came, I almost didn't hear it. Raulito was having one of his crying fits and Jacqueline, who is empathic when it comes to tears, had joined in. Then, too, Minou was busy "reading" my upside-down missal to Manolito. Dedé and I were having a time managing the lot, while Mamá was doing her share, casting stern glances from the middle of our pew. As she's all too fond of telling us, we are raising savages with all our new theories about talking, not spanking. "Fighting tyrants and meanwhile creating little ones."

I was headed to the vestibule with the children when I heard what I thought I had misheard. "We cannot remain indifferent to the grievous blows that have afflicted so many good Dominican homes. . . ." Padre Gabriel's voice crackled over the loudspeaker.

"Hush now!" I said, so fiercely the children stopped their fussing and looked at me with full attention.

"All human beings are born with rights derived from God that no earthly power can take away."

The sun was shining through the stained glass window of John the Evangelist, depicted in a loincloth some church ladies had complained was inappropriate, even in our tropical heat. I propped Raulito up on the baptismal font and gave the other children mints to keep them quiet.

"To deny these rights is a grave offense against God, against the dignity of man."

He went on, but I wasn't listening anymore. My heart was beating fast. I knew once I said it I couldn't take it back. *Oh Lord, release my son,* I prayed. And then I added what I'd been holding back. *Let me be your sacrificial lamb.*

When Padre Gabriel was done, he looked up, and there was utter silence in that church. We were stunned with the good news that our Gabriel had delivered unto us. If the church had been a place to clap, we would have drowned out his *"Dóminus vobíscum"* with applause.

We stayed the whole day in Salcedo, sitting in the park between masses, buying treats for the kids as bribes for the next hour-long mass. Their church clothes were soiled by the time the last mass rolled around at six. With each service, the rumor spread, and the crowds grew. People kept coming back, mass after mass. Undercover agents also started showing up. We could spot them easily. They were the ones who knelt with their butts propped on the pew seats and looked about during the consecration. I caught sight of Peña in the back of the church, no doubt taking note of repeaters like me.

Later, we found out this was happening all over the country. The bishops had gathered together earlier in the week and drafted a pastoral letter to be read from every pulpit that Sunday. The church had at last thrown in its lot with the people!

That evening we rode home in high spirits, the babies fast asleep in the arms of the older children. It was already dark, but when I looked up at the sky, I saw a big old moon like God's own halo hung up there as a mark of his covenant. I shivered, remembering my promise.

We were worried about attending mass the following Sunday. All week we heard of attacks on churches throughout the island. Down in the capital, somebody had tried to assassinate the archbishop in the cathedral while he was saying mass. Poor Pittini was so old and blind he didn't even realize what was happening, but kept right on intoning the Kyrie as the assassin was being wrestled to the ground.

Nothing as serious as that happened in our parish. But we had our own excitement. Sunday after the pastoral, we were visited by a contingent of prostitutes. When it was time for communion, there was such sashaying and swaying of hips to the altar rail you'd have thought they were offering *their* body and blood, not receiving His. They lined up, laughing, taunting Padre Gabriel by opening their mouths for the Sacred Host and making lewd gestures with their tongues. Then one of them reached right in his chalice and helped herself.

This was like a gunshot in our congregation. Ten or twelve of us women got up and formed a cordon around our priest. We let in only those we knew had come to the table for salvation, not sacrilege. You can bet those *puticas* lit in to us. One of them shoved me aside, but did Patria Mercedes turn the other cheek? Not on your life. I yanked that scrawny, done-up girl to the back of the church. "Now," I said, "You want to receive communion, you recite the Credo first."

She looked at me as if I had asked her to speak English. Then she gave me a toss of her head and marched off to the SIM to collect whatever her charge was for desecrating.

The following Sunday, we arrived for early mass, and we couldn't get in the door for the stench inside. It took no time at all to find out what the problem was. *¡Sin vergüenzas!* They had come into the church the night before and deposited the contents of latrines inside the confessional.

I sent the children home with Mamá, afraid of some further incident with the SIM. Dedé, Noris, and I stayed to clean up. Yes, Noris insisted, though I fussed that I wanted her home safe with the others. God's house was her house, too, she argued. My prayers to the Virgencita to bring her around had been answered. I had to laugh. It was what Sor Asunción always used to tell us. Beware what you ask God. He might just give you what you want.

———

One morning, close to a month after Mate and Minerva had been taken, I had another visitor. Dedé and Mamá had gone to the capital to make their rounds. Their habit was to drive down every week with Jaimito or with some other prisoner's family. They refused to take me along. They were sure someone at the SIM headquarters would realize they had overlooked me and grab me on the spot.

Before heading home, they always drove out to La Victoria. Out of desperation, I suppose, hoping to catch a glimpse of the girls. Of course, they never saw them. But often there were sheets and towels hanging to dry through the bars of windows, and this touch of domesticity always gave them hope.

I was in the parlor, teaching Noris how to appliqué monograms just as I had once taught Mate. The children were busy building their block palaces on the floor. Tono came in and announced there was a visitor. Instantly, my heart sank, for I assumed it was Peña again. But no, it was Margarita, no last name given, wanting to see the *doña* of the house, though she couldn't say in relation to what.

The young woman sitting on the stoop out back looked vaguely familiar. She had a sweet, simple face and dark, thick hair held back with bobby pins. The eyes, the brows, the whole look had Mirabal written all over it. *Ay, no*, I thought, not now. She stood up the minute she saw me, and bowed her head shyly. "Could we speak privately?"

I wasn't sure what to expect. I knew Minerva had stayed in touch with them over the years, but I had always kept my distance. I did not want to be associated with the issue of a *campesina* who had had no respect for the holy banns of matrimony or for the good name of Mirabal.

I nodded towards the garden where no one could overhear our talk.

When we were a little ways down the path, she reached in her pocket and offered me a folded note.

My hands began to shake. "God be praised," I said, looking up. "Where did you get this?"

"My mother's cousin works in La Victoria. He doesn't want his name mentioned."

I unfolded the note. It was the label off a can of tomato paste. The back had been written on.

We're in Cell # 61, Pavilion A, La Victoria—Dulce, Miriam, Violeta, Asela, Delia, Sina, Minerva, and me. Please notify their families. We are well but dying for news of home and the children. Please send Trinalin as we are all down with a bad grippe & Lomotil for the obvious. Any food that keeps. Many kisses to all but especially to my little darling.

And then, as if I wouldn't recognize that pretty hand in a million years, the note was signed, *Mate.*

My head was spinning with what needed to be done. Tonight with Mamá and Dedé, I would write a reply and fix up a package. "Can we send something back with your relative?"

She nodded, lingering as if she had something else to say. I realized I had forgotten there was always a charge for such services. "Wait here, please," I said, and ran to the house to get my purse.

She looked pained when I offered her the bills. "No, no, we wouldn't take anything from you." Instead, she handed me a card with the name of the pharmacy I always went to in Salcedo; her own name was written on the back. "Margarita Mirabal, to serve you."

That *Mirabal* was something of a shock. "Thank you, Margarita," I said, offering her my hand. Then I added the words I found hard to wrench from my prideful heart. "Patria Mercedes, to serve you."

When she had left, I read Mate's note over and over as if with each reading, new information would surface. Then I sat down on the bench by the birds of paradise, and I had to laugh. Papá's other family would be the agents of our salvation! It was ingenious and finally, I saw, all wise. He was going to work several revolutions at one time. One of them would have to do with my pride.

———————

That night, Dedé, Mamá, and I stayed up late preparing the package. We made sweet potato biscuits with molasses, which would have a lot of nutrition, and filled a bag full of little things that wouldn't spoil. We packed a change of underwear for each of them, and socks, and inside the socks I stuck a comb and brush for them to share. I couldn't imagine how Mate was taking care of that long hair.

Our little pile of things grew, and we began arguing over what was necessary. Mamá thought it would be a mistake to send Mate her good black towel she had made the week she was home—to save her nerves. She had finished appliquéing the *M* in gold satin, but had not gotten to the *G* yet. "The more you send the more chances someone along the way will steal the whole thing."

"*Ay*, Mamá, have a little faith."

She put her hands on her hips and shook her head at me. "Patria Mercedes, you should be the first one to know . . ." We kept our sentences incomplete whenever we were criticizing the government inside the house. There were ears everywhere, or at least we imagined them there. "That is no towel for a jail cell," Mamá finished, as if that was what she had been about to say from the start.

Dedé convinced her. She used the same argument about the manicure set, the case with lipstick and face powder, the little bottle of Matador's Delight. These little touches of luxury would raise the the girls' spirits. How could Mamá argue with that!

Tucked inside Mate's prayerbook, I put some money and our note.

Dearest Minerva and Mate, we are petitioning at headquarters, and God willing, some door will open soon. The children are all well, but missing you terribly. Please advise us of your health and any other needs. Also, what of the men, and dear Nelson? Send any news, and

*remember you are in the hearts and prayers of Patria and Dedé, and
your loving mother.*

Mamá wrote her own name. I couldn't keep back my tears when I
saw her struggling with the pen and then ruining her signature by running the ink with her tears.

After Mamá went to bed, I explained to Dedé who had brought the
note over. I had been vague with Mamá, so as not to open old wounds.
"She looks like Mate," I reported. "She's quite pretty."

"I know," Dedé admitted. It turned out she knew a lot more.

"Back when Papá died, Minerva asked me to take out of her inheritance for those girls' education." Dedé shook her head, remembering.
"I got to thinking about it, and I decided to put in half. It wasn't all that
much," she added when she saw my face. I was a little hurt not to be
included in this charitable act. "Now the oldest has her pharmacy
degree and is helping out the others."

"A fine girl," I agreed.

"There isn't any other kind of Mirabal girl," Dedé said, smiling. It was
a remark Papá used to make about *his* girls. Back then, we had assumed
he was talking just about us.

Something wistful and sisterly hung in the air. Maybe that's why I
went ahead and asked her. "And you, Dedé, how are you doing?"

She knew what I meant. I could read a sister's heart even if it was
hidden behind a practiced smile. Padre de Jesús had told me about an
aborted visit Dedé had made to his rectory. But since the girls' arrest,
we were all too numb to feel or talk of any other grief.

"Jaimito is behaving himself very well. I can't complain," she said.
Behave? What a curious word for a wife to use about her husband.
Often now, Dedé slept over at Mamá's with the two younger boys. To
keep an eye on us, so she said.

"Things are all right then?"

"Jaimito's been great," Dedé went on, ignoring my question. "I'm very
grateful, since I know he didn't want any part of this mess."

"None of us did," I observed. And then, because I could see her drawing in, I turned away from any implied criticism of Jaimito. Actually—

unlike Minerva—I liked our blustery cousin. Under all his swagger, that man had a good heart.

I took her hand. "When all this is over, please get some counsel from Padre de Jesús. Faith can strengthen a marriage. And I want you both to be happy together."

Suddenly she was in tears. But then, she always got weepy when I spoke to her that way. I touched her face, and motioned for us to go outside. "What's wrong, you can tell me," I asked as we walked up the moon-lit drive.

She was looking up at the sky. The big old moon of a few days back had shrunk to something with a big slice of itself gone. "Jaimito's a good man, whatever anyone thinks. But he would have been happier with someone else, that's all." There was a pause.

"And you?" I prodded.

"I suppose," she admitted. But if she had a ghost in her heart, she didn't give out his name. Instead, she reached up as if that moon were a ball falling into her empty hands. "It's late," she said. "Let's go to bed."

As we made our way back down the drive, I heard a distinct cough.

"We've got visitors again," I whispered.

"I know," she said, "ghosts all over the place."

The minute Jaimito's pickup turned onto the road in the mornings for daily mass, the little toy-engine sound of a VW would start up. All night, we smelled their cigarettes in the yard and heard muffled coughs and sneezes. Sometimes, we would call out, "God bless you!" As the days wore on, we began taking our little revenges on them.

There was a nook where one side of the house met another, and that was their favorite after-dark hiding place. Mamá put some cane chairs out there along with a crate with an ashtray so they'd stop littering her yard. One night, she set out a thermos full of ice water and a snack, as if the three Kings were coming. They stole that thermos and glasses and the ashtray, and instead of using the path Mamá had cleared for them, they trampled through her flowers. The next day, Mamá moved her thorn bushes to that side of the yard. That night when she heard them out there, she opened up the bathroom window and dumped Jacqueline's dirty bathwater out into the yard. There was a surprised cry, but they didn't dare come after us. After all, they were top secret spies, and we weren't supposed to know they were out there.

Inside, Dedé and I could barely contain our hilarity. Minou and Jacqueline laughed in that forced way of children imitating adult laughter they don't really understand. Next morning, we found bits of fabric and threads and even a handkerchief caught on the thorns. From then on when they spied on us, they kept a respectful distance from the house.

Getting our packet to Margarita took some plotting.

The morning after her visit, we stopped at the pharmacy on the way back from daily mass. While the others waited in the pickup, I went in. I was holding Raulito in such a way that his blanket covered up the package. For once, that little boy was quiet, as if he could tell I needed his good behavior.

It was strange going into that pharmacy now that I knew she worked there. How many times in the past hadn't I dropped in to buy aspirin or formula for the baby. How many times hadn't the sweet, shy girl in the white jacket taken care of my prescriptions. I wondered if she'd known all along who I was.

"If it's any problem—" I began, handing her the package. Quickly, she slipped it under the counter. She looked at me pointedly. I should not elaborate in this public place.

Margarita scowled at the large bill I pressed into her hand. In a whisper, I explained it was for the Lomotil and Trinalin and vitamins I wanted her to include in the package. She nodded. The owner of the pharmacy was approaching.

"I hope this helps," Margarita said, handing me a bottle of aspirin to disguise our transaction. It was the brand I always bought.

That week, Mamá and Dedé came back elated from their weekly trip. They had seen a black towel hanging out of a window of La Victoria! Dedé couldn't be sure, but she thought she saw a zigzag of something in the front, probably the monogram. And who else would have a black towel in prison?

"I know, I know," Mamá said. "I already heard it several times coming home." She mimicked Dedé: "*See, Mamá, what a good idea it was to send that towel.*"

"The truth is," Mamá continued—it was her favorite phrase these days—"I didn't think it'd get to her. I've gotten so I suspect everyone."

"Look at this!" Jaimito called us over to where he was sitting at the dining room table, reading the papers he'd bought in the capital. He pointed to a photograph of a ghostly bunch of young prisoners, heads bowed, as El Jefe wagged his finger at them. "Eight prisoners pardoned yesterday at the National Palace." He read off the names. Among them, Dulce Tejeda and Miriam Morales, who, according to Mate's note, shared a cell with her and Minerva.

I felt my heart lifting, my cross light as a feather. All eight pardoned prisoners were either women or *minors*! My Nelson had only turned eighteen a few weeks ago in prison. Surely, he still counted as a boy?

"My God, here's something else," Jaimito went on. Capitán Victor Alicinio Peña was listed in the real estate transactions as having bought the old González farm from the government for a pittance. "He stole it is what he did," I blurted out.

"Yes, the boy stole the mangoes," Dedé said in a loud voice to conceal my indiscretion. Last week, Tono had found a little rod behind Mama's wedding picture—a telltale sign of bugging. Only in the garden or riding around in a car could we speak freely with each other.

"The truth is . . ." Mamá began, but stopped herself. Why give out the valuable truth to a hidden microphone?

———

Peña owed me was the way I saw it. The next day, I put on the yellow dress I'd just finished and the black heels Dedé had passed on to me. I talcumed myself into a cloudy fragrance and crossed the hedge to Don Bernardo's house.

"Where are you going, Mamá?" Noris called after me. I'd left her tending the children. "Out," I said, waving my hand over my shoulder, "to see Don Bernardo." I didn't want Mamá or Dedé to know about my outing.

Don Bernardo really was our next door angel disguised as an old Spaniard with an ailing wife. He had come to the island under a refugee program Trujillo had instituted in the forties "to whiten the race." He had not been much help to the dictator in that regard, since he and Doña Belén had never had any children. Now he spent most of his days reminiscing on his porch and tending to an absence belted into a wheelchair. From some need of his own, Don Bernardo pretended his wife was just under the weather rather than suffering from dementia. He conveyed made-up greetings and apologies from Doña Belén. Once a week, the old man struggled to get behind the wheel of his old Plymouth to drive Doña Belén over to Salcedo for a little checkup.

He was a true angel all right. He had come through for us as a godfather for all the little ones—Raulito, Minou, and Manolito—at a time when most people were avoiding the Mirabals.

Then, after the girls were taken, I realized that Jacqueline hadn't been christened. All my children had been baptized the country way, within the first cycle of the moon after their birth. But María Teresa, who always loved drama and ceremony, had kept postponing the christening until it could be done "properly" in the cathedral in San Francisco with the bishop officiating and the girls' choir from Inmaculada singing "Regina Coeli." Maybe pride ran in more than one set of veins in the family.

One afternoon when I was still a little crazy with grief, I ran out of Mamá's house, barefoot, with Jacqueline in my arms. Don Bernardo was already at his door with his hat on and his keys in his hand. "So you're ready to be a fish in the waters of salvation, eh, my little snapper?" He chucked Jacqueline under her little chin, and her tears dried up like it was July in Monte Cristi.

Now I was at Don Bernardo's door again, but this time without a baby in my arms. "What a pleasure, Patria Mercedes," he greeted me, as if it were the most natural thing in the world to have me drop in at any hour of the day or night, barefoot *or* dressed up, with a favor to ask.

"Don Bernardo, here I am bothering you again," I said. "But I need a ride to Santiago to Captain Peña's office."

"A visit to the lion's den, I see."

I caught a glimpse of a smile in the curve of his thick, white mustache. Briefly, he entered the bedroom where Doña Belén lay harnessed

215

in her second childhood. Then out he came, crooking his elbow as my escort. "Doña Belén sends her greetings," he said.

Captain Victor Alicinio Peña received me right away. Maybe it was my nerves, but his office had the closed-in feeling of a jail cell, metal jalousies at the windows and fluorescence the only light. An air conditioner gave out a violent mechanical sound, as if it were about to give out. I wished I were outside, waiting under the almond trees in the square with Don Bernardo.

"It's a pleasure to see you, Doña Patria." Captain Peña eyeballed me as if he had to be true to his verb and *see* every part of me. "How can I be of help?" he asked, motioning for me to sit down.

I had planned to make an impassioned plea, but no words came out of my mouth. It wouldn't have been exaggerating to say that Patria Mercedes had been struck dumb in the devil's den.

"I must say I was a little surprised to be told you were here to see me," Peña went on. I could see he was growing annoyed at my silence. "I am a busy man. What is it I can do for you?"

Suddenly, it all came out, along with the tears. How I had read in the papers about El Jefe excusing minors, how my boy had just turned eighteen in prison, how I wondered if there was anything at all Peña could do to get my boy pardoned.

"This matter is outside my department," he lied.

That's when it struck me. This devil might seem powerful, but finally I had a power stronger than his. So I used it. Loading up my heart with prayer, I aimed it at the lost soul before me.

"This came down from above," he continued. But now, he was the one growing nervous. Absently, his hands fiddled with a plastic card on his key ring. It was a prism picture of a well-stacked brunette. When you tilted it a certain way, her clothes dropped away. I tried not to be distracted, but to keep right on praying.

Soften his devil's heart, oh Lord. And then, I said the difficult thing, *For he, too, is one of your children.*

Peña lay down his pathetic key ring, picked up the phone, and dialed headquarters in the capital. His voice shifted from its usual bullying bark to an accommodating softness. "Yes, yes, General, absolutely." I wondered if he would ever get to my petition. And then it came, so smoothly buttered, it almost slipped right by me. "There's a little matter I've got sitting here in my office." He laughed uproariously at something said on the other end. "No, not exactly *that* little matter."

And then he told what I was after.

I sat, my hands clutched on my lap. I don't know if I was praying as much as listening intently—trying to judge the success of my petition from every pause and inflection in Peña's voice. Maybe because I was watching him so closely a funny thing started to happen. The devil I was so used to seeing disappeared, and for a moment, like his tilting prism, I saw an overgrown fat boy, ashamed of himself for kicking the cat and pulling the wings off butterflies.

I must have looked surprised because as soon as he hung up, Peña leaned towards me. "Something wrong?"

"No, no," I said quickly, bowing my head. I did not want to be pushy and ask him directly what he had found out. "Captain," I pleaded, "can you offer me any hope?"

"It's in the works," he said, standing up to dismiss me. "I'll let you know what I find out."

"*¡Gracias, ay, muchas gracias!*" I kept saying, and I wasn't just thanking Peña.

The captain held on to my hand too long, but this time I didn't pull away. I was no longer his victim, I could see that. I might have lost everything, but my spirit burned bright. Now that I had shined it on him, this poor blind moth couldn't resist my light.

It was time to tell him what I'd be doing for him. "I'll pray for you, Captain."

He laughed uneasily. "What for?"

"Because it's the only thing I have left to repay you with," I said, holding his gaze. I wanted him to understand that I knew he had taken our land.

We waited, and weeks went by. A second, and then a third, pastoral was read from the pulpits. The regime responded with a full-force war against the church. A campaign began in the papers to cancel the concordat with the Vatican. The Catholic church should no longer have a special status in our country. The priests were only stirring up trouble. Their allegations against the government were lies. After all, our dictator was running a free country. Maybe to prove himself right, Trujillo was granting more and more pardons and visiting passes.

Every day or so, I stopped at the portrait with a fresh flower and a little talk. I tried to pretend he was my boy, too, a troubled one in need of guidance. "You know as well as I do that casting out the church won't do you a bit of good," I advised him. "Besides, think of your future. You're no spring chicken at sixty-nine, and very soon, you're going to be where you don't make the rules."

And then more personally, I reminded him of the pardon I'd asked for.

But nothing came through for us. Either Peña had forgotten or—God forbid!— something terrible had happened to Nelson. I started having bad days again and long nights. Only the thought of Easter just around the corner kept Patria Mercedes inching along. The blossoms on the flame trees were about to burst open.

And on the third day He rose again . . .

The little notes kept streaming in. From the few hints Mate could drop into them, I pieced together what the girls were going through in prison.

They asked for food that would keep—they were hungry. Bouillon cubes and some salt—the food they got had no flavor. Aspirin—they had fevers. Ephedrine—the asthma was acting up. Ceregen—they were weak. Soap—they were able to wash themselves. A dozen small crucifixes? That I couldn't make out. One or two, yes, but a dozen?! I believed they were feeling more peace of mind when they asked for books. Martí for Minerva (the poems, not the essay book) and for Mate, a blank book and a pen. Sewing materials for both, plus the children's recent measurements. *Ay, pobrecitas,* they were missing their babies.

I spent hours with Don Bernardo and Doña Belén next door, wishing my mind could fade like hers into the past. I would have gone all the way back, all the way back to the beginning of—I wasn't sure of what.

Finally, when I'd almost given up hope, Peña arrived at the house in his big showy white Mercedes, wearing an embroidered *guayabera* instead of his uniform. Oh dear, a personal visit.

"Capitán Peña," I welcomed him. "Please come inside where it's cool." I made a point of stopping at the entryway so he could see the fresh flowers under the portrait. "Shall I make you a rum coke?" I was gushing shamelessly all over him.

"Don't bother yourself, Doña Patria, don't bother yourself." He indicated the chairs on the porch. "It's nice and cool out there." He looked at the road as a car slowed, the driver taking in who had dropped in on the Mirabal family.

Right then and there, I realized this visit was as much for him as for me. I'd heard that he was having trouble at our place—I will never call that farm anything else. All the *campesinos* had run off, and there wasn't a neighbor willing to lend a hand. (What could he expect? That whole area was full of González!) But being seen conversing with Doña Patria sent out the message—I didn't hold him responsible for my loss. All he had done was buy a cheap farm from the government.

Mamá did, however, hold him responsible. She locked herself in her bedroom with her grandbabies and refused to come out. She would never visit with the monster who had torn her girls from her side. She didn't care that he was trying to help us now. The truth was the devil was the devil even in a halo. But I knew it was more complicated than that. He was both, angel and devil, like the rest of us.

"I have good news for you," Peña began. He folded his hands on his lap, waiting for me to gush a little more over him.

"What is it, Captain?" I leaned forward, playing my pleading part.

"I have the visiting passes," he said. My heart sunk a little, I had wanted the pardon most of all. But I thanked him warmly as he counted out each one. "Three passes," he concluded when he was done.

Three? "But we have six prisoners, Captain," I tried to keep my voice steady. "Shouldn't it be six passes?"

"It *should* be six, shouldn't it?" He gave me little righteous nods. "But

Manolo's in solitary, and Leandro's still deciding on a job for El Jefe. So! They're both—shall we say—unavailable."

A job for El Jefe? "And my Nelson?" I said right out.

"I talked with headquarters," Peña spoke slowly, delaying the news to increase my anticipation. But I stayed unruffled, praying my Glory Be's, one right after the other. "Seeing as your boy is so young, and El Jefe has been pardoning most minors . . ." He swilled his drink around so the ice tinkled against the glass. "We think we can get him in with the next round."

My first born, my little ram. The tears began to flow.

"Now, now, Doña Patria, don't get like that." But I could tell from Peña's tone that he loved seeing women cry.

When I had controlled myself, I asked, "And the girls, Captain?"

"The women were all offered pardons as well."

I was at the edge of my chair. "So the girls are coming home, too?"

"No, no, no," he said, wagging his finger at me. "They seem to *like* it in prison. They have refused." He raised his eyebrows as if to say, what can *I* do about such foolishness? Then he returned us to the subject of his little coup, expecting more of my gratitude. "So, how shall we celebrate when the boy comes home?"

"We'll have you over for a *sancocho*," I said before he could suggest something rude.

As soon as he was gone, I rushed to Mamá's bedroom and delivered my good news.

Mamá went down on her knees and threw her hands up in the air. "The truth is the Lord has *not* forgotten us!"

"Nelson is coming home?" Noris rushed forward. Since his imprisonment, Noris had moped horribly, as if Nelson were a lost love instead of "the monster" who had tortured her all her childhood.

The younger children began to chant, "Nelson home! Nelson home!"

Mamá looked up at me, ignoring the racket. "And the girls?"

"We have passes to see them," I said, my voice dropping.

Mamá stood up, stopping the clamor short. "And what does the devil want in return?"

"A *sancocho* when Nelson comes home."

"Over my dead body that man is going to eat a *sancocho* in my house."

I put my hand on my lips, reminding Mamá that she had to watch what she said.

"I mean it, over my dead body!" Mamá hissed. "And that's the truth!"

By the time she said it the third time, she and I both knew she was resigned to feeding Judas at her table. But there would be more than one stray hair in that *sancocho,* as the *campesinos* liked to say. No doubt Fela would sprinkle in her powders and Tono would say an Our Father backwards over the pot, and even I would add some holy water I'd bottled from Jacqueline's baptism to give to her mother.

That night as we walked in the garden, I admitted to Mamá that I had made an indiscreet promise. She looked at me, shocked. "Is that why you snuck out of the house a few weeks ago?"

"No, no, no. Nothing like that. I offered Our Lord to take me instead of my Nelson."

Mamá sighed. "*Ay, m'ija,* don't even say so. I have enough crosses." Then she admitted, "I offered Him to take me instead of any of you. And since I'm the mother, He's got to listen to me first."

We laughed. "The truth is," Mamá continued, "I have everything in hock to Him. It'll take me another lifetime to fulfill all the *promesas* I've made once everybody comes home.

"As for the Peña *promesa,*" she added, "I have a plan." There was that little edge of revenge in her voice. "We'll invite all the neighbors."

I didn't have to remind her that we weren't living among our kin anymore. Most of these new neighbors wouldn't come, afraid of being seen socializing with the blackmarked Mirabals. That was part of Mamá's plan. "Peña will show up, thinking the *sancocho* is meant just for him."

I started laughing before she was through. I could see which way her revenge was going.

"All those neighbors will look out their windows and kick themselves when they realize they slighted the head of the northern SIM!"

"*Ay,* Mamá," I laughed. "You are becoming *la jefa* of revenge!"

"Lord forgive me," she said, smiling sweetly. There wasn't a bit of sorry in her voice.

"That makes two of us," I said, hooking my arm with hers.

"Good night," I called out to the cigarette tips glowing like fireflies in the dark.

Monday, Peña telephoned. The audience with El Jefe was set in the National Palace for the next day. We were to bring a sponsor. Someone willing to give the young offender work and be responsible for him. Someone who had not been in trouble with the government.

"Thank you, thank you," I kept saying.

"So when is my *sancocho*?" Peña concluded.

"Come on, Mamá," I said when I got off the line and had given her our good news. "The man isn't all that bad."

"Humpf!" Mamá snorted. "The man is smart is what he is. Helping with Nelson's release will do what twenty *sancochos* couldn't do. Soon the González clan will have him baptizing their babies!"

I knew she was right, but I wished she hadn't said so. I don't know, I wanted to start believing in my fellow Dominicans again. Once the goat was a bad memory in our past, that would be the real revolution we would have to fight: forgiving each other for what we had all let come to pass.

We made the trip to the capital in two cars. Jaimito and I rode down in the pickup. He had agreed to sponsor his nephew, giving him his own parcel to farm. I always said our cousin had a good heart.

Mamá, Tío Chiche and his son, Blanco, a young colonel in the army, followed in Don Bernardo's car. We wanted a show of strength—our most respectable relations. Dedé was staying behind to take care of the children. It was my first excursion out of the Salcedo province in three months. My mood was almost festive!

At the last minute, Noris stole into the pickup and wouldn't come out. "I want to go get my brother," she said, her voice breaking. I couldn't bring myself to order her out.

Somehow, in our excitement, our two cars lost each other on the road. Later we found out that Don Bernardo's old Plymouth had a flat near the Constanza turnoff, and when Blanco went to change it, there was no jack or spare in the trunk. Instead, Mamá described a whole library that Don Bernardo confessed he had hidden there. In her forgetful rages, Doña Belén had taken it into her head to rip up her husband's books, convinced there were love letters hidden in those pages.

Because we had backtracked, looking for them, we got to the National Palace with only minutes to spare. Up the front steps we raced—there must have been a hundred of them. In Dedé's tight little heels, I suffered my Calvary, which I offered up to my Nelson's freedom. At the entrance, there was a checkpoint, then two more friskings inside. Those were my poor Noris's Calvary. You know how girls are at that age about any attention paid their bodies, and this was out and out probing of the rudest kind. Finally, we were escorted down the hall by a nervous little functionary, who kept checking his watch and motioning for us to hurry along.

With all the rushing around, I hadn't stopped to think. But now I began worrying that our prize would be snatched away at the last minute. El Jefe was going to punish us Mirabals. Just like with Minerva's degree, he would wait till I had my hands on my Nelson and then say, "Your family is too good to accept pardons, it seems. I'm so sorry. We'll have to keep the boy."

I could not let myself be overcome by fears. I hung on to the sound of my girl's new heels clicking away beside me. My little rosebud, my pigseye, my pretty one. Suddenly, my heart just about stopped. *¡Ay, Dios mío!* What could I be thinking, bringing her along! Everybody knew that with each passing year the old goat liked them younger and younger. I had offered *myself* as a sacrificial lamb for Nelson. Certainly not my darling.

I squeezed my Noris's hand. "You stay by me every second, you hear! Don't drink anything you're offered, and it's no to any invitation to any party."

"Mamá, what are you talking about?" Her bottom lip was quivering.

"Nothing, my treasure. Nothing. Just stay close."

It was like asking the pearl to stay inside its mother oyster. All the way down that interminable hall, Noris held tight to my hand.

I needed her touch as much as she needed mine. The past was rushing down that long corridor towards me, a flood of memories, sweeping me back as I struggled to keep up with the little official. We were on our way to the fateful Discovery Day dance, Minerva and Dedé, Pedrito, Papá and Jaimito and I, and nothing bad had happened yet. I was climbing up to the shrine of the Virgencita in Higüey to hear her voice for the first time. I was a bride, promenading down the center aisle of San Juan Evangelista twenty years back to marry the man with whom I would have our dear children, dearer than my life.

The room was a parlor with velvet chairs no one would dream of sitting on even if invited, which we weren't. Doors led in from three sides, and posted at each one was a fine-featured guard from El Jefe's elite all-white corps. A few other families stood by, in clumps, looking solemn, the women in black, the men in suits or formal *guayaberas*. My yellow dress stood out like a shout I tried to quiet by draping my black mantilla over my shoulders. Still, I was glad I had worn it. I was going to greet my boy dressed in the sunshine he hadn't seen in a month.

A crowd of journalists was let in one of the doors. A tall American draped with cameras approached and asked us in his accented Spanish what our feelings were today. We looked to the little man, who nodded his permission. The audience was as much for the press as for us. We were part of a stage show.

El Jefe entered in a wash of camera flashes. I don't know what I thought I'd see— I guess after three months of addressing him, I was sure I'd feel a certain kinship with the stocky, overdressed man before me. But it was just the opposite. The more I tried to concentrate on the good side of him, the more I saw a vain, greedy, unredeemed creature. Maybe the evil one had become flesh like Jesus! Goosebumps jumped all up and down my bare arms.

El Jefe sat down in an ornate chair on a raised platform and spoke directly to the families of the prisoners to be released. We had better do a better job of controlling our young people. Next time, we shouldn't expect such mercy. As a group, we thanked him in chorus. Then we were to name ourselves for him, one by one, and thank him again with little personalized comments. I couldn't think of anything to add to my thank-you, but I was hoping that Jaimito would come up with something.

When our turn came, El Jefe nodded for me to speak first. I had a momentary cowardly thought of not giving him my complete name.

"Patria Mercedes Mirabal de González, to serve you."

His bored, half-lidded eyes showed a spark of interest. "So you are one of the Mirabal sisters, eh?"

"Yes, Jefe. I'm the oldest." Then, to emphasize what I was here for, I added, "Mother of Nelson González. And we're very grateful to you."

"And who is that little flower beside you?" El Jefe smiled down at Noris.

The journalists noted the special attention we were receiving and came forward with their cameras.

Once everyone's particular thanks had been given, El Jefe turned and spoke to an aide beside him. A hush went through the room like a crack through a china cup. Then talk resumed. El Jefe moved closer to Noris to ask what flavor ice cream she liked. I kept her hand tight in mine while I scanned every door. This might be some sort of roulette game in which I had to guess correctly which one Nelson would come through in order to win his freedom. The American journalist threw out questions to El Jefe about his policies regarding political prisoners and the recent OAS charges of human rights abuses. El Jefe waved them away. He had managed to get out of Noris that she liked chocolate and strawberry if it wasn't too strawberryish.

A door swung open. A cortege of guards in dress whites came through, followed by a handful of sorry-looking boys, their skulls visible under their shaven heads, their eyes big and scared, their faces swollen with bruises. When I saw Nelson, I cried out and dropped to my knees.

Lord, I remember praying, *thank you for giving me my son again.*

I didn't need to remind Him what I had offered in return. Still, I didn't expect Him to come right out and claim it. Later Jaimito said it was just

Trujillo calling me to receive my prisoner. But I know a godly voice when I hear one. I heard Him all right, and He called my name.

Next day, we were famous. On the front page of *El Caribe*, the two photographs were side by side: Noris giving her hand to a smiling Jefe (*Young Offender Softens El Jefe's Heart*); and me, kneeling, my hands clutched in prayer (*Grateful Madre Thanks Her Benefactor*).

CHAPTER ELEVEN

María Teresa

March to August 1960

Wednesday, March 16 (55 days)

I just got the notebook. Santicló has had to be very careful this time around, smuggling in just a couple of things every few days.

Security measures are stepped up after the second pastoral, he says. You're safer in here than out there, bombs and what not.

He tries to say helpful things.

But can he really believe we're safer in here? Maybe *he* is, being a guard and all. But we politicals can be snuffed out just like that. A little visit to La 40, that's all it takes. Look at Florentino and Papilín— I better stop. I know how I get.

Thursday, March 17 (56 days)

The fear is the worse part. Every time I hear footsteps coming down the hall, or the clink of the key turning in the lock, I'm tempted to curl up in the corner like a hurt animal, whimpering, wanting to be safe. But I know if I do that, I'll be giving in to a low part of myself, and I'll feel even less human. And that is what they want to do, yes, that is what they want to do.

Friday, March 18 (57 days)

It feels good to write things down. Like there will be a record.

Before this, I scraped on the wall with our contraband nail. A mark for each day, a line through a week. It was the only record I could keep, besides the one in my head where I would remember things, store them.

The day we were brought here, for instance.

They marched us down the corridor past some of the men's cells. We looked a sight, dirty, uncombed, bruised from sleeping on the hard floor. The men started calling out their code names so we'd know who was still alive. (We kept our eyes averted, for they were all naked.) I listened hard but I didn't hear, *"¡Palomino vive!"* I'm trying not to worry about it as we didn't hear a lot of names because the guards commenced beating on the bars with their nightsticks, drowning out the men's cries. Then Minerva began singing the national anthem, and everyone joined in, men and women. That time Minerva got solitary for a week.

The rest of us "women politicals" were locked up in a cell no bigger than Mamá's living and dining room combined. But the real shock was the sixteen other cellmates we found here. "Nonpoliticals," all right. Prostitutes, thieves, murderers—and that's just the ones who have confided in us.

Saturday, March 19 (58 days)
Three bolted steel walls, steel bars for a fourth wall, a steel ceiling, a cement floor. Twenty-four metal shelves ("bunks"), a set of twelve on each side, a bucket, a tiny washbasin under a small high window. Welcome home.

We're on the third floor (we believe) at the end of a long corridor. Cell # 61 facing south towards the road. El Rayo and some of the boys are in Cell # 60 (next to the *guardia* station), and # 62 on our other side is for nonpoliticals. Those guys *love* to talk dirty through the walls. The other girls don't mind, they say, so most of them have taken bunks on that side.

Twenty-four of us eat, sleep, write, go to school, and use the bucket—everything—in a room 25 by 20 of my size 6 feet. I've walked it back and forth many times, believe me. The rod in the middle helps, on account of we hang our belongings and dry towels there, and it kind of divides the room in two. Still, you lose your shame quickly in this horrid place.

All us politicals have our bunks on the east side, and so we've asked for the southeast corner to be "ours." Minerva says that except for closed meetings, anyone can join our classes and discussions, and many have. Magdalena, Kiki, América, and Milady have become regulars. Dinorah sometimes comes, but it's usually to criticize.

Oh yes, I forgot. Our four-footed Miguelito. He shows up for any occasion that involves crumbs.

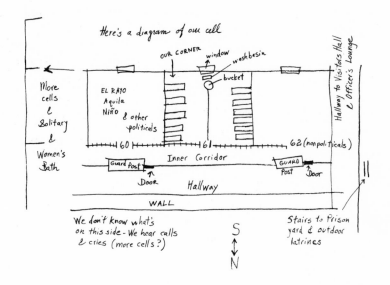

Sunday, March 20 (59 days)

Today I took my turn at our little window, and everything I saw was blurry through my tears. I had such a yearning to be out there.

Cars were speeding east to the capital, north towards home; there was a donkey loaded down with saddlebags full of plantains and a boy with a switch making him move along; lots and lots of police wagons. Every little thing I was eating up with my eyes so I lost track of time. Suddenly, there was a yank at my prison gown. It was Dinorah, who keeps grumbling about us "rich women" who think we are better than riffraff.

"That's enough," she snapped. "We all want to have a turn."

Then the touchingest thing happened. Magdalena must have seen I'd been crying because she said, "Let her have my turn."

"And mine," Milady added.

Kiki offered her ten minutes, too, and soon I had a whole other half hour to stand on the bucket if I wanted to.

Of course, I immediately stepped down, because I didn't want to deny anyone their ten minutes of feasting on the world. But it raised my spirits so much, the generosity of these girls I once thought were below me.

Monday, March 21 (60 days)

I keep mentioning the girls.

I have to admit the more time I spend with them, the less I care what they've done or where they come from. What matters is the quality of a person. What someone is inside themselves.

My favorite is Magdalena. I call her our little birdseed bell. Everybody comes peck-peck-pecking what they want off her, and she gladly gives it. Her ration of sugar, her time at the sink, her bobby pins.

I don't know what she's in for, since there's a sort of unwritten courtesy here that you're not supposed to ask anyone—though a lot of the girls blurt out their stories. Magdalena doesn't say much about herself, but she has a little girl, too, and so we are always talking about our daughters. We don't have any pictures, but we have thoroughly described our darlings to each other. Her Amantina sounds like a doll girl. She's seven years old with hazel eyes (like my Jacqui) and light brown curls that used to be blond! Strange . . . since Magdalena herself is pretty dark with quite a kink in her hair. There's a story there, but I didn't dare come right out and ask who the father was.

Tuesday, March 22 (61 days)

I broke down last night. I feel so ashamed.

It happened right before lights out. I was lying on my bunk when the call went round, *¡Viva Trujillo!* Maybe it was that call or maybe it was all finally getting to me, but suddenly the walls were closing in,

and I got this panicked feeling that I would never *ever* get out of here.
I started to shake and moan, and call out to Mamá to take me
home.

Thank God, Minerva saw in time what was going on. She crawled
in my bunk and held me, talking soft and remindful to me of all
the things I had to live and be patient for. I settled down, thank
God.

It happens here all the time. Every day and night there's at least one
breakdown—someone loses control and starts to scream or sob or
moan. Minerva says it's better letting yourself go—not that *she* ever
does. The alternative is freezing yourself up, never showing what
you're feeling, never letting on what you're thinking. (Like Dinorah.
Jailface, the girls call her.) Then one day, you're out of here, free, only
to discover you've locked yourself up and thrown away the key somewhere too deep inside your heart to fish it out.

Wednesday, March 23 (62 days)

I'm learning a whole new language here, just like being in our
movement. We've got code names for all the guards, usually some feature of their body or personality that lets you know instantly what to
expect from them. Bloody Juan, Little Razor, Good Hair. I never could
figure out Tiny, though. The man is as big as a piece of furniture you
have to move in a truck. Tiny what? I asked Magdalena. She explained
that Tiny is the one with the fresh fingers, but according to those who
have reason to know, he has very *little* to brag about.

Every day we get the "shopping list" from the knockings on the
wall. Today bananas are 5 cents each (*tiny* brown ones); a piece of ice,
15 cents; one cigarette, 3 cents; and a bottle of milk that is really
half water, 15 cents. Everything is for sale here, everything but your
freedom.

The code name for these "privileges" is turtle, and when you want
to purchase a privilege, you tell the *guardia* in charge that you'd like to
throw some water on the turtle.

Today, I threw a whole bucket on the creature and bought rounds
of cassava for everyone in our cell with the money Santicló brought us

231

from Mamá. Ten cents a stale round, and I couldn't even keep mine down.

Thursday, March 24 (63 days)

Periodically, we are taken downstairs to an officers' lounge and questioned. I've only been twice. Both times I was scared so witless that the guards had to carry me along by the arms. Then, of course, I'd get one of my asthma attacks and could barely breathe to talk.

Both times, I was asked gruff questions about the movement and who my contacts were and where we'd gotten our supplies. I always said, *I have already said all I know,* and then they'd threaten me with things they would do to me, to Leandro, to my family. The second time, they didn't even threaten that much except to say that it was too bad a pretty lady would have to grow old in prison. Miss out on . . . (A bunch of lewd comments I won't bother to repeat here.)

The ones they take out a lot are Sina and Minerva. It isn't hard to figure out why. Those two always stand up to these guys. Once, Minerva came back from one of the interrogation sessions laughing. Trujillo's son Ramfis had come special to question her because Trujillo had said that Minerva Mirabal was the brain behind the whole movement.

I'm very flattered, Minerva said she said. But my brain isn't big enough to run such a huge operation.

That worried them.

Yesterday, something that could have been awful happened to Sina. They took her into a room with some naked men prisoners. The guards stripped off her clothes in front of the prisoners. Then they taunted Manolo, setting him up on a bucket and saying, Come now, leader, deliver one of your revolutionary messages.

What did he do? Minerva wanted to know, her voice all proud and indignant.

He stood up as straight as he could and said, *Comrades, we have suffered a setback but we have not been beaten.*

Death or Liberty!

That was the only time I saw Minerva cry in prison. When Sina told that story.

Friday, March 25 (64 days)

Bloody Juan beats on the bars with an iron bar at five, ¡*Viva Trujillo!* and we are rudely woken up. No chance of mistaking—even for a minute—where I am. I hide my face in my hands and cry. This is how every day starts out.

Lord forbid Minerva should see me, she'd give me one of her talks about morale.

It's my turn to empty the bucket, but Magdalena offers to do it. Everybody's been so kind about relieving me because of the way my stomach's been.

Right before *chao* comes, Minerva leads us in singing the national anthem. We know through knocking with our neighbor cell that our "serenades" really help raise the men's spirits. The guards don't even try to stop us anymore. What harm are we doing? Minerva asks. In fact, we're being patriotic, saying good morning to our country.

Today we sing, *Adiós con el corazón,* since this is Miriam's and Dulce's last day. Most of us are crying.

I end up vomiting my breakfast *chao.* Anything can set me off these days. Not that my stomach needs an excuse for rejecting that watery paste. (What *are* those little gelatin things I sometimes bite down on?)

Saturday, March 26 (65 days)

We just had our "little school," which Minerva insists on every day, except Sundays. I guess Fidel did this when he was in prison in the Isle of Pines, and so we have to do it, too. Minerva started us off by reciting some Martí and then we all talked about what we thought the words meant. I was daydreaming about my Jacqui—wondering if she was walking yet, if she was still getting the rash between her little fingers—when Minerva asked what I thought. I said I had to agree with what everyone was saying. She just shook her head.

Then, we politicals gathered in our corner and rehearsed the three cardinal rules:

Never believe them.
Never fear them.
Never ask them anything.

Even Santicló? I asked. He is so good to me, to all of us really.

Especially Santicló, Sina said. I don't know who is tougher, Minerva or her.

Both of them have warned me about getting too fond of the enemy.

Sunday, March 27 (66 days)

Yesterday night, Santicló brought us the last of the contents of Mamá's package, including some Vigorex. Maybe now this stomach of mine will settle down. The smelling salts will also help. Mamá and Patria outdid themselves. We have everything we need and then some luxuries. That is, if Minerva doesn't give it all away.

She says we don't want to create a class system in our cell, the haves and have nots. (We don't? What about when Tiny gave Dinorah a *dulce leche* as payment for her favors, and she didn't offer anyone a crumb, even Miguelito?)

Minerva gives me her speech about how Dinorah's a victim of our corrupt system, which we are helping to bring down by giving her some of our milk fudge.

So everyone's had a Bengay rub and a chunk of fudge in the name of the Revolution. At least I get this notebook to myself.

Or so I think, till Minerva comes around asking if I couldn't spare a couple of pages for América's statement for her hearing tomorrow.

And can we borrow the pen? Minerva adds.

Don't I have *any* rights? But instead of fighting for them, I just burst out crying.

[pages torn out]

Monday, March 28 (67 days)

I left my *chao* untouched. Just a whiff of that steamy paste, and I didn't even want to take a chance. I'm lying on my bunk now, listening to the Little School discussing how a woman revolutionary should handle a low remark by a comrade. Minerva excused me from class. I feel like my insides are trying to get out.

I've gotten so thin, I've had to take in the waistbands of all my panties and stuff the cups of my brassiere with handkerchiefs. We were fooling the other day about whose were bigger. Kiki made a low remark about how the men are probably doing the same thing with their you-know-whats. First month I was here, I was shocked by such dirty talk. Now I laugh right along with everybody.

Tuesday late night, March 29 (68 days)

I can't even fall asleep tonight remembering Violeta's prayer at the close of our group rosary: *May I never experience all that it is possible to get used to.*

How it has spooked me to hear that.

Wednesday, March 30 (69 days)

I am trying to keep a schedule to ward off the panic that sometimes comes over me. Sina brought it up during Little School. She had read a book written by a political prisoner in Russia who was locked away for life, and the only way he kept himself from going insane was to follow a schedule of exercises in his head. You have to train your mind and spirit. Like putting the baby on a feeding schedule.

I think it's a good idea. Here's my schedule.

—The Little School every morning—except Sundays.

—Writing in my book during guard change as I can get away with twenty minutes at a time. Also after lights-out if there is a bright enough moon.

—Going to the "movies" in my head, imagining what is happening at home right this moment.

—Doing some handiwork. The guards are always bringing us the prison mending.

—Helping clean up the cell—we've got a rotating list of duties Sina wrote up.

—I also try to do one good thing for a cellmate every day, from giving Delia massages for her bad back to teaching Balbina, who's deaf, and some of the others, too, how to write their names.

—And finally, the thing that gets me the most kidding, I try to "walk" for half an hour every day. Twenty-five feet down and back, twenty feet across and back.

Where are you going? América asked me yesterday.

Home, I replied without stopping my walk.

Thursday, March 31 (70 days)

Day by day goes by and I begin to lose courage and wallow in dark thoughts. I'm letting myself go. Today I didn't even braid my hair, just wound it in a knot and tied a sock around it. My spirits are so low.

Our visiting privileges were cancelled again. No explanation. Not even Santicló knows why. We were marched down the hall and then brought back—what a mean trick.

And it's certain now—Leandro is not here with the rest of us. Oh God, where could he be?

Friday, April 1 (71 days)

Minerva and I just had a talk about morale. She says she's noticed how upset I've been lately.

I *am* upset. We could have been out with Miriam and Dulce a whole week ago. But no, we Mirabals had to set a good example. Accepting a pardon meant we thought we had something to be pardoned for. Also, we couldn't be free unless everyone else was offered the same opportunity.

I argued all up and down, but it was like the time Minerva wanted to do the hunger strike. I said, Minerva, we're already half-starved, what more do you want?

She held my hands and said, Then do what *you* think is right, Mate.

Of course, I ended up on a hunger strike, too. (Santicló snuck me in some chocolates, thank God, and rounds of cassava or I *would* have starved.)

This time, too, I'd have taken that pardon. But what was I supposed to do? Leave Minerva behind to be a martyr all by herself?

I start to cry. I can't take it anymore, I tell Minerva. Every day, my little girl is growing up without me.

Stop thinking like that, Minerva says. Then she tries all over again to lead me through this exercise where I concentrate on nice thoughts so as not to get desperate—

I have to stop and hide this. They're coming in for some sort of check.

Saturday, April 2 (72 days)

There was a row here yesterday. As a consequence, there have been extra guards patrolling the hall outside our cell, so I didn't dare write until tonight.

Minerva is back in solitary, this time for three weeks.

When they came in to remove our crucifixes, we sort of expected it because of what's been going on.

The officials call it the Crucifix Plot. Minerva and El Rayo cooked up this idea that everyone without exception was to wear a crucifix as a symbol of our solidarity. Patria sent us a dozen little wooden ones Tío Pepe made for those who didn't already have one. Soon, even the meanest prostitutes were dangling crosses above their bosoms. The naked men all wore them, too.

Whenever someone was taken for a "visit" to La 40 or got desperate and began shouting or crying, we'd all start singing "O Lord, My Sturdy Palm When Cyclone Winds Are Blowing."

We kept this up for a week. Then the chief warden, Little Razor, went from cell to cell, announcing the new regulations, no more hymn singing, no more crucifixes. Especially after this second pastoral Santicló told us about, Trujillo was sure the priests were out to get him. Our crucifix wearing and praying was a plot.

A sorry-looking Santicló and a not so sorry-looking Tiny and Bloody Juan came in with four other guards to confiscate our crucifixes. When I handed Santicló my little gold one from my First Communion I'd always worn, he gave me a quick wink and slipped it in his pocket. He was going to save mine for me. Gold crucifixes were bound to get "lost" in Little Razor's safekeeping.

Everyone complied except for Minerva and Sina. They managed to get Sina's off her because all she did was stand real straight with her chin up. But when they grabbed Minerva, she started kicking and

swinging her arms. Santicló's cap flew across the room and Tiny was
smacked in the face. Bloody Juan got a bloody nose when he tried to
intervene.

Where does that sister of mine get her crazy courage?

As she was being marched down the hall, a voice from one of the
cells they passed called out, *Mariposa does not belong to herself alone.
She belongs to Quisqueya!* Then everyone was beating on the bars, calling out, *¡Viva la Mariposa!* Tears came to my eyes. Something big and
powerful spread its wings inside me.

Courage, I told myself. And this time, I felt it.

[pages torn out]

Thursday, April 7 (77 days)

Today, at long last, I got to see Mamá and Patria, and Pedrito—at a
distance. Jaimito and Dedé didn't come up because we're only allowed
one visitor. But Santicló let Patria sit at my table after prisoner # 49
was taken back. That's what Pedrito's called. And something I didn't
know till today, I'm # 307.

Mamá was so upset about Minerva being in solitary, I decided not
to bring up the way I've been feeling and worry her even more.
Besides, I didn't want to take up time I could be hearing about my
precious. She's got two new teeth, and has learned to say, *Free Mamá,
Free Papá*, every time she passes Trujillo's picture in the entryway.

Then Patria gave me the best news so far—Nelson is free! He was
offered and accepted a pardon. *Ay*, how it made me wish all over
again we hadn't turned ours down.

As for Leandro. He and some of the others are still being held in La
40. I'm so relieved just to know he's alive. Patria heard from Peña up
in Salcedo about Leandro being pressured to do some job for Trujillo.
They sure picked the wrong guy. My gentle Palomino has the iron will
of a stallion.

Mamá said she's going to bring Jacqueline next week. Not inside for
a visit, of course. It's not allowed. But Jaimito can park on the road,
and I can take a peek out my window—

How can Mamá tell our window looks out on the road? I asked her.

Mamá laughed. There's a certain black flag flown from a certain
window.

How ingenious of Mamá! I always wondered why she sent me my
good towel.

Friday, April 8 (78 days)

Magdalena and I had a long talk about the real connection between
people. Is it our religion, the color of our skin, the money in our
pockets?

We were discussing away, and all of a sudden, the girls started con-
gregating, one by one, including the two new ones who have replaced
Miriam and Dulce, everybody contributing their ideas. And it wasn't
just the usual, Sina and Asela and Violeta and Delia, the educated
women, talking. Even Balbina knew something was up and came and
sat right in front of me so she could watch my mouth. I spoke real
slow for her to understand that we were talking about love, love
among us women.

There is something deeper. Sometimes I really feel it in here, especially late at night, a current going among us, like an invisible needle
stitching us together into the glorious, free nation we are becoming.

Saturday, April 9 (79 days)

I am very low. The rain doesn't help. The days drag on.

This morning, I woke up with the thought, Jacqui has to get some
new shoes! And that's been going around and around in my head all
day. The old ones are probably pinching her toes and she'll learn to
walk pigeon-toed, and then we'll have to get her some corrective
braces, on and on and on.

You get a thought in your head in this crazy place and it looms so
big. But let it be her shoes I worry about instead of the other thing
tugging at my mind now all the time.

Sunday, April 10 (80 days)

I've got a big worry, and Minerva isn't here for me to talk to.

I go back and calculate. Leandro and I were trying like crazy in
December and January. I wanted another one soon, since I've enjoyed

having my Jacqui so much. Also, I admit, I wanted an excuse to stay home. Like Dedé, I just didn't have the nerves for revolution, but unlike her, I didn't have the excuse of a bossy husband. Not that my Leandro wouldn't have preferred for me to be just his wife and his little girl's mother. More than once he said one revolutionary in the family was enough.

I missed January, then February, and now most definitely March. I know almost everyone here has stopped menstruating. Delia says stress can do this to a woman; she's seen it before in her practice. Still, this queasiness is all too familiar.

If I am and the SIM find out, they'll make me carry it to full term, then give it to some childless general's wife like the story Magdalena told me. That *would* kill me.

So, if there really is no chance I'll be out soon, then I want to release this poor creature from the life it might be born to.

The girls all know home remedies, since most of them have had to get rid of unwanted side effects of their profession. And Delia is a woman doctor, so she can help, too.

I'm giving it till Minerva gets back to decide.

Not sure what day it is

Still very weak, but the bleeding has stopped.

I can't bear to tell the story yet.

Just this—I've either bled a baby or had a period. And no one had to do a thing about it after the SIM got to me.

Another day

Magdalena has been nursing me. She feeds me broth with crunched-up saltines Santicló brings me. She says he's smuggled in a little gift every day. Today, it was this blue ribbon she used to tie my braid and a little packet of honeyballs.

Balbina has also been so sweet. She rubs my feet, and the way she kneads the soles and pats the heels, it's like she's talking to me with her touching. Saying, *Get well, get well, get well.*

And I wiggle my toes back and smile wanly at her, *I will, I will, I hope I will.*

240

Friday (I think)

You think you're going to crack any day, but the strange thing is
that every day you surprise yourself by pulling it off, and suddenly
you start feeling stronger, like maybe you are going to make it through
this hell with some dignity, some courage, and most important—
never forget this, Mate—with some love still in your heart for the
men who have done this to you.

Saturday, April 16

I've got to get a note written to Mamá. She must have been worried
sick when I didn't show up Thursday. What a pity I missed seeing my
little girl!

But that loss seems small now compared to what has happened.

[pages torn out]

Easter Sunday

Minerva came back this afternoon. They released her five days early
on account of Easter. How Christian of them.

We had a little welcome party for her with some of the saltines Santicló had brought me and a hunk of white cheese Delia managed to
get by throwing lots of water on the turtle. Miguelito, of course,
showed up for the crumbs.

I try to be lighthearted, but it takes such effort. It's as if I am so
deep inside myself, I can't come to the surface to be with anyone. The
easiest to be with is Magdalena. She holds my head in her lap and
strokes my forehead just like Mamá.

It's only her I've told what happened.

Wednesday, April 20 (90 days)

Minerva keeps asking me. I tell her I can't talk about it yet. I
know I've told Magdalena, but somehow telling Minerva is
different. She'll make some protest out of it. And I don't want
people to know.

Minerva says, Write it down, that'll help, Mate.

I'll try, I tell her. Give me a few more days.

Tuesday, April 26 (96 days)

Minerva has excused me from the Little School today so I can write this.

Here is my story of what happened in La 40 on Monday, April 11th.

[pages torn out]

Saturday, April 30 (100 days)

After you lose your fear, the hardest thing here is the lack of beauty. There's no music to listen to, no good smells, ever, nothing pretty to look at. Even faces that would normally be pretty like Kiki's or beautiful like Minerva's have lost their glow. You don't even want to look at yourself, afraid what you'll see. The little pocket mirror Dedé sent is kept in our hiding place for anyone who wants a look. A couple of times, I've dug it up, not on account of vanity, but to make sure I am still here, I haven't disappeared.

Wednesday, May 25 (125 days—1,826 days to go—Oh God!)

I have not been able to write for a while. My heart just hasn't been in it.

Monday, Minerva and I got arraigned. It was my first time out of here since that other Monday in April I don't want to remember, and Minerva's first since we got here in February. The guards told us to put on our street clothes, so we knew right off we weren't going to La 40.

I rubbed rosewater in my hair, then braided it with Santicló's ribbon, humming the whole while the little boat song my Jacqui loves to clap to. I was so sure we were going to be released. Minerva wagged her finger at me and reminded me of the new cardinal rule she's added to her other three: Stay hopeful but do not expect anything.

And she was right, too. We were driven down to the courthouse for our joke of a trial. No one was there to represent us and we couldn't talk or defend ourselves either. The judge told Minerva if she tried one more time, she would be in contempt, and the sentence and fine would be increased.

Five years and a fine of five thousand pesos for each of us. Minerva just threw her head back and laughed. And of course, I bowed mine and cried.

[pages torn out]

Wednesday, June 15 (I've decided to stop counting—it's just too depressing!)
My journal has stayed in our hiding place, everyone helping themselves to clean pages when they need paper. I haven't minded. Not much has mattered for days on end.

Minerva says I'm understandably depressed. The sentence on top of what I went through. She read what I wrote, and she wants me to tell the OAS (when and if they ever come) about what happened at La 40. But I'm not sure I can do that.

You have nothing to be ashamed of! Minerva says, all fierce. She is doing my face in sculpture so I'm supposed to sit still.

Yes, the authorities are now encouraging us to start hobbies— again, the OAS on their backs. Minerva has taken up sculpture, in prison of all places. She had Mamá bring her some plaster and tools. After each session, Santicló is supposed to collect them, but he's pretty lenient with us.

So we now have a couple of little scalpels in our hiding place along with our other contraband, the knife, the sewing scissors, the pocket mirror, four nails, and the file, and of course, this *diario*.

What is this arsenal for? I ask Minerva. What are we going to do with it?

Sometimes I think revolution has become something like a habit for Minerva.

Friday, June 24, hot as hell in here
We now have two new women guards. Minerva thinks they've been assigned to us to impress the OAS with the prison system's delicacy towards women prisoners.

Delicacy! These women are as tough or tougher than the men, especially the fat one Valentina. She's nice enough to us politicals but a real witch to the others, seeing as the OAS won't be investigating their treatment. The nonpolitical girls have such wonderful, foul mouths. Here's their little chant when Valentina is out of earshot:

> Valentina, *la guardona*,
> stupid bloody fool
> went to suck milk from a cow
> but got under the bull.

The guards are all worried about the rumored coming of the OAS. We've heard that if a political complains, the guards in charge of that cell will be in very hot water indeed—maybe even shot! El Jefe cannot afford any more international trouble right now.

During our Little School, Minerva warns us not to be swayed by these rumors or manipulated by "fine" treatment. We must let the Committee know the real situation or this hell will go on. She gives me a pointed look as she says this.

Monday, June 27, midafternoon

I've told myself, Mate, don't pay them any attention. But with so few distractions in this place, what else am I supposed to think of?

There's quite a gossip underground in this place. It relies mostly on our knocking system, but notes are also passed, and brief exchanges sometimes take place in the visitors' hall on Thursdays. News travels. And it really has hurt to hear the ugly rumor going around. My Leandro—along with Valera, Fafa, Faxas, Manzano, and Macarrulla—is being accused of being a traitor.

Minerva says, Mate, don't listen to evil tongues. But sometimes she gets so angry herself at what comes through the wall that she says she is going to tell the whole world what happened to me, what persuasion was used on poor Leandro.

Oh please, Minerva, I plead. Please.

The movement is falling apart with all this mistrust and gossip. Manolo is so worried, he has tapped out a communiqué that has come all the way down the line. The comrades had his permission to work on that book. There is nothing in it but information the SIM had already collected after months of tortures. Manolo admits even he talked, giving names of those who were already caught or had escaped abroad.

Compañeros y compañeras. We must not fall prey to petty divisions, but concentrate on our next point of attack — the OAS members when they come. If sanctions are imposed, the goat will fall.

We are suffering a setback but we have not been beaten.

Death or Liberty!

But the terrible rumors continue.

Tuesday morning, June 28 (a bad night)

I couldn't sleep all night for how worked up I was about the rumors. Then to top it off, the stench kept everyone else up, too. We're all angry at Dinorah for going in the bucket. Especially after we made our agreement to use the outdoor latrine at night so the whole cell wouldn't have to endure bad smells while we're trying to sleep. And except for Bloody Juan, the guards are willing to take us out. (Especially Tiny, who gets his chance to "frisk" us in the dark.)

It certainly comes out, living in such close quarters with people, which ones are only looking out for themselves and which ones are thinking about the whole group. Dinorah is a perfect example of the selfish kind. She steals into our food "locker," she swipes our underwear from the central rod when we aren't looking, and she has been known to report us for wall tapping with Cell # 60. At first, Minerva made excuses about how Dinorah learned bad civic habits from a corrupt system. But ever since Dinorah turned in Minerva's treasured packet of little notes from Manolo, my open-minded sister has become quite guarded around this so-called victim.

I know I've been reluctant to share certain things, but I usually reflect a moment and end up giving most of my things away. I always check with everyone to see if no one else wants the lamp a certain night, and I never hog my turn at the window for fresh air or drying laundry.

If we made up the perfect country Minerva keeps planning, I would fit in perfectly. The only problem for me would be if self-serving ones were allowed in. Then I believe I'd turn into one of them in self-defense.

> *Thursday night, June 30, heat unbearable,*
> *Santicló brought us some paper fans*

We've found a great new hiding place, my hair!

This is how it happened. Patria slipped me a clipping today, and I knew I'd be checked—like we always are—going in and out of the vsitors' hall. It's a pretty serious offense if you're caught with contraband. You might lose visiting privileges for as long as a month or even be put in solitary. I tried slipping it back to her, but Bloody Juan was our patrol, and his hawk eyes weren't going to miss twice.

I was getting more and more anxious as the time was almost up. That newspaper clipping was burning a hole in my lap. Minerva made a hand sign we learned from Balbina that means, *Give it to me*. But I was not going to let her be caught and take the blame. Then I felt the heaviness of my braid down my back, and I got the idea. I'm always fooling with my hair, plaiting it, unplaiting it, a nervous habit of mine that's gotten worse here. So I folded that piece of paper really small, and, pretending I was neatening up my braid, I wound it into my hair.

And that's how the whole prison found out about the assassination attempt.

BETANCOURT ACCUSATIONS UNFOUNDED

Ciudad Trujillo, R.D. Spokesman Manuel de Moya expressed his outrage at the vicious and unfounded accusations of President Rómulo Betancourt of Venezuela. Betancourt has accused the Dominican government of being involved in the attempt on his life that occurred in the capital city of Caracas, June 24. The President was injured when a parked car exploded as his own limousine paraded by. Speaking from his hospital bed, Betancourt announced he has again filed charges with the Organization of American States. When asked why a small, peace-loving island would strike out against him, President Betancourt confabulated a plot against his life by the Dominican government: "Ever since I brought charges of his human rights abuses before the OAS, Trujillo has been after me." De Moya regretted these insults to the virgin dignity of our Benefactor and expressed the openness of our government to any and all investigations from member nations who wish to ascertain the falsity of these malicious charges. The OAS has accepted the invitation, and a five-member committee is due here by the end of July.

Friday night, July 1, no one can sleep, and not just because of the heat!
The mood here has changed overnight. Our divided movement is pulling together, gossip and grievances cast aside. The walls have been nothing but knockings all day long. The latest news I smuggled in!

Trujillo is in hot water now, and he knows it. He has to put on a good show when the OAS comes. There are all kinds of rumors that we are *all* to be pardoned. Everyone is so hopeful! Except, of course, the *guardias*.

When the gringos come, Santicló asks us this evening, you girls aren't going to complain about me, now are you?

Yes, Santicló, Delia teases him. We're going to say you had a soft heart for certain prisoners. You didn't treat us all equally. I never got mints or a ribbon for my hair.

Santicló looks a little frightened, so I say, She's just teasing you, Santicló. You've been a real friend. I say that to be polite, but then I get to thinking about it, and it is true.

That's why we nicknamed him Santicló after the big, jolly American "saint" who brings gifts even to those who don't believe in Jesus or the three Kings.

Sunday night, July 10 (Mamá sent us a flashlight)
No OAS yet, but lots *more* rumors. The beginning of last week, everyone thought they'd be here by the end of the week. But now the rumor is they're waiting to see if Betancourt will live. Also they're working out how they'll conduct their investigations.

Just lock them in here with us, Sina says. We'll give them an earful.

Yes, Dinorah says. You girls give them an earful, then the rest of us will give them something else.

Everybody bursts out laughing. We've talked openly about it, and I can't say I really miss it, but some of the girls are ready to scream, they want a man so. And, I should add, it's not just the dubious "ladies" saying this. Minerva is the biggest surprise of all.

These girls can be *so* vulgar. Lord, in six months my ears have heard what they hadn't known about in twenty-four years. For instance, the girls have an elaborate system of body clues by which they can tell what kind of a man you're suited for. Say, your thumb is fat and kind of short, then you're bound to like men with a similar endowment elsewhere. I happen to have a short but slender thumb, and that proves I'm really compatible with a short, slender man with "average" endowments. Phew!

Some of these girls are sleeping together, I know. That's the only thing Santicló won't allow. He says it's just not right. Once a woman is with a woman, she's ruined for a man.

I myself had a close encounter that turned out to be all right. With Magdalena the other night after our talk.

—Valentina just went by on her sneaky feet.

I better put this away and not try the devil twice. To be continued.

Monday afternoon, July 11, quiet time

I mentioned the close encounter I had with Magdalena. This is what happened.

She was visiting over here one night, and we got to talking about ourselves, and finally she told me her whole life story. I'll say this, it's enough to break my heart. I've been going around for months thinking no one has suffered like I have. Well, I'm wrong. Magdalena has taught me more about how privileged I really am than all of Minerva's lectures about class.

When Magdalena was thirteen, her mother died, and she didn't have any place to go, so she took a job as a maid for a rich, important family. (The de la Torres, real snobs.) Night after night, she was "used" by the young man of the house. She said she never reported it to her mistress, since she thought it was part of her job. When she got pregnant, she did go to the *doña*, who accused her of being an ungrateful, lying whore, and threw her out on the street.

Magdalena gave birth to a baby girl, Amantina, and for years they lived hand to mouth. Magdalena says the trash heap near the old airport was their *bodega*, and their home an abandoned shed near the runway.

Pobrecitas, I kept saying.

At some point, the de la Torres must have caught sight of the blond-headed, hazel-eyed little girl. They decided she was related to their son. They drove over to the new house where Magdalena was working and took the poor, screaming child away.

Tears brimmed in my eyes. Any story of a separated mother and daughter can get me started these days.

That's when Magdalena gave me this real serious look—like she was grateful to me for understanding. But then the gratitude turned into something else. She came forward like she was going to tell me a secret and brushed her lips to mine. I pulled back, shocked.

Ay, Magdalena, I said, I'm not *that* way, you know.

She laughed. Girl, I don't know what you mean by *that way,* like it's a wrong turn or something. My body happens to also love the people my heart loves.

It made sense the way she said that.

Still, I felt really uncomfortable in my narrow bunk. I wanted her knee touching my knee not to mean anything, but it did. I wanted her to leave, but I didn't want to hurt her feelings. Thank goodness, she got the hint and went on with the rest of her story.

—Quiet time is over. Minerva's hollering for us all to come do exercises.

I'll finish this tonight.

later

The rest of the story is that Magdalena tried to get Amantina back. One night, she stole into the de la Torre house and climbed the same back stairs the young man used to climb down, and she got as far as the upstairs hall, where she was caught by the *doña* coming out of her bedroom in her nightdress. Magdalena demanded her child back and pulled out a knife to show she meant business.

Instead of shock I felt glee. Did you succeed?

What do you think I'm doing here? she said. I got twenty years for attempted murder. When I get out, she continued, my little girl will be my age when I came in. Then Magdalena began to cry like her tears were spilling out of her broken heart.

I didn't even think about her kissing me earlier. I just reached out and took her in my arms like Mamá always does me.

Saturday afternoon, July 23

Leandro is finally here with us! El Rayo says he's in Pavilion B with Manolo and Pedrito and the rest of the central committee.

Also, the ridiculous book is out. *¡Complot Develado!* No one here has seen it yet, but we've heard it's an album of all our photographs with a description of how the movement got started. Nothing that hasn't been in the papers for months already.

I hope all those who wagged their tongues feel ashamed of themselves.

Wednesday evening, August 3— we got real chicken and rice tonight!

Minerva and Sina have been talking strategy to me since the news was announced this morning. It's as final as anything can be around here. The OAS Peace Committee comes this Friday. Only one prisoner from each pavilion will be interviewed. The head guards were given the choice. And they picked me.

Minerva says it's because they don't think I'll complain. And you have to, she says. You have to, Mate.

But they haven't done anything, I protest. They're victims, too, like you say.

But victims that can do a lot of harm. And this isn't personal, Mate, she adds. This is principle.

I never was good at understanding that difference so crucial to my sister. Everything's personal to me that's principle to her, it seems.

We've heard that the interviews won't be supervised, but that doesn't mean a thing here. The hall will be bugged with secret microphones, no doubt. It would be suicide to talk openly. So, Minerva and Sina have written up a statement I must somehow slip to the committee, signed by the Fourteenth of June Movement.

There is something else, Minerva says, looking down at her hands. We need someone to write a personal statement.

What about what Sina went through? I say. Have Sina write up something.

It's not the same, please, Mate. You don't even have to write it up, she adds. We can just tear out the pages in your journal and put them in with our statement.

There are other considerations, I tell her. What about Santicló? If the statements are traced to me, he'll be shot.

Minerva holds me by the arms. Revolution is not always pretty, Mate. Look at what they did to Leandro, to Manolo, what they did to Florentino, to Papilín, to you, for God's sake. It won't stop unless we stop it. Besides, those are just rumors about the *guardias* being shot.

I'll see, I say at last, I'll see.

Ay, Mate, promise me, she says, looking in my eyes, please promise me.

So I say to her the only thing I can say. I promise you this, I'll be true to what I think is right.

Minerva has never heard such talk from me. Fair enough, she says, fair enough.

Saturday, August 6

Minerva has asked me a dozen times what happened. A dozen times I've told her and the others the story. Rather, I've tried to keep up with their questions.

How many members were in the committee. (Seven in all, though two looked like they were there just to translate.) Where was the session? (In the visitors' hall—that's why we didn't have visiting hours Thursday. The authorities spared themselves the trouble of having to bug a new place.) How long was my session? (Ten minutes—though I waited two hours outside the door with a very nervous Santicló.) Then, most importantly. Did I get a chance to slip the papers to a member of the committee?

Yes, I did. When I was leaving, a serious young man came forward to thank me and lead me out. He spoke a very polite, pretty Spanish. Probably Venezuelan or maybe Paraguayan. By the way he was looking me over, I could tell he wanted a closer look. Checking for scars or skin pallor—something. I had given La Victoria a good report and said that I had been treated fairly. What everyone else from the other cells had probably told them as well.

Just as he was turning away, I loosened my braid and let the first folded note fall on the floor. When he saw it, he seemed surprised and went to pick it up. But then he thought better of it and kicked it under the table instead. He gave me this pointed look. I returned him a slight nod.

Santicló met me right outside the door. His jolly, round face looked so afraid. As he was walking me back down the corridor, he wanted to know how it went.

Don't worry, I said, and I smiled at him. It was actually his blue ribbon that I had used to hold both notes twisted in my braid. I unwound that ribbon just enough so the first note with the statement Minerva and Sina had drafted slipped out. It was signed *The Four-teenth of June Movement* so it can't be traced to any one cell. And what are they going to do, shoot *all* the prison guards?

The second note with my story was lodged further up in my braid. Maybe it was the sight of that ribbon Santicló had given me when I was so broken, I don't know. But right then and there, I decided not to drop the second note. I just couldn't take a chance and hurt my friend.

As far as Minerva is concerned, I kept my promise to her. I did what *I* thought was right. But I think I'll wait till sometime in the future to tell her *exactly* what that was.

Sunday afternoon, August 7—we're having a little party later
We have been told to be ready for our release tomorrow!

None of the men are being freed, though, only the women. Gallantry to impress the OAS is what Minerva guesses.

I was so afraid she was going to get high-minded on me again. But she's agreed to go, since this is not a pardon but a release.

I think Minerva is close to her own breaking point. She has been acting funny. Sometimes, she just turns to me and says, What? as if I had asked her something. Sometimes her hand goes to her chest as if she is making sure she has a heartbeat. I am glad we will soon be out of here.

What hurts is thinking of those I'm leaving behind.

Every time I look at Magdalena I have to look away.

I've learned so much from you, I tell her. This has been the most meaningful experience of my whole life, I tell her.

I'm going to start crying before the party even starts.

late night

The moonlight is streaming in through our little window. I can't sleep. I am sitting up in my bunk, writing my last entry in the little space left, and sobbing in the quiet way you learn in prison so you don't add to anyone else's grief.

I feel sad to be leaving. Yes, strange as it sounds, this has become my home, these girls are like my sisters. I can't imagine the lonely privacy of living without them.

I tell myself the connection will continue. It does not go away because you leave. And I begin to understand the revolution in a new way.

At our "farewell party," I took a chance Dinorah might report me and had all of them sign my book like an autograph book. Some of them I'd taught how to write their names, so this is a real memento of my time here.

As for the book itself—Santicló is going to smuggle it out for me. We will be inspected thoroughly, I'm sure, when we leave.

Then we passed around our little hoard of sugar cubes and crackers and peanuts. I had a couple of bars of chocolates left and I cut those in thin slices. Even Dinorah added some guava paste she'd been hoarding. Then we looked at each other, and there was such a sad heartfelt feeling among us. Minerva started to say something, but she couldn't get it out. So we just held each other, and one by one, we wished each other well and then goodbye.

For the OAS Committee investigating Human Rights Abuses.

This is a journal entry of what occurred at La 40 on Monday, April 11th, 1960, to me, a female political prisoner. I'd rather not put my name. Also, I have blotted out some names as I am afraid of getting innocent people in trouble.

Please don't put it in the papers either, as I am concerned for my privacy.

When they came for me that morning, I thought that maybe I was being taken to the officers' lounge for questioning.

But instead, Bloody Juan escorted me down the stairs and outside. There was a wagon waiting. It took me only a minute to realize where we were going.

I kept looking out the window, hoping I'd be seen by someone who might recognize me and tell my family they had spotted me in a police wagon headed towards La 40. How strange that the sun was shining so innocently. That people were walking around as if there were no such thing in the world as poor souls in my predicament.

I tried getting some explanation as to why I was being taken in. But Bloody Juan is not one to explain things.

By the time we got to La 40, I was shaking so bad I couldn't get out of the wagon. I felt ashamed that they had to carry me in like a sack of beans.

There was a bunch of them already waiting in the interrogation room, tall fat Johnny with his Hitler mustache. The one called Cándido with the curly hair. Then a bug-eyed one that kept cracking his knuckles to make the sound of breaking bones.

They stripped me down to my slip and brassiere and made me lie down on this long metal table, but they didn't buckle the belts I saw dangling down the sides. I have never known such terror. My chest was so tight I could barely breathe.

Johnny said, Hey, pretty lady, don't get all excited.

We're not going to hurt you, the one called Cándido said.

That made me shake all the more.

When the door opened, and ██████████ was brought in, I didn't immediately recognize him. A walking skeleton, that's what he looked like, shirtless, his back covered with blisters the size of dimes.

I sprang up, but Bloody Juan pushed me back down on the table. You lay down nice like you're in bed waiting for him, Bug Eye said. Then he said something gross about what torture does to the necessary organ. Johnny told him to shut up.

What do you want with her? ███████ shouted. I could tell he was scared.

We want her to help us persuade you, Johnny said in a voice that was too calm and rational for this eerie place.

She has nothing to do with this, ███████ cried.

Are you saying you've reconsidered, Johnny asked.

But ███████ stood his ground. I'm not discussing the matter further unless you let her go.

That's when Bug Eye slammed him with a fist, knocking him down. How dare scum dictate terms to the captain! Then all of them joined in kicking ███████ until he was writhing in agony on the floor.

I was screaming for them to stop. It felt like my very own stomach was being punched, and that's when the pains as bad as contractions began.

Then Johnny asked me if I couldn't persuade ███████. After all, ███████, ███████, ███████, ███████ and ███████ had all reconsidered.

I was so tempted to say, Ay, ███████, save yourself, save us. But I couldn't. It was as if that would have been the real way to let them kill us.

So I told those monsters that I would never ask ███████ to go against what his conscience told him was right.

Two of a kind, the one called Cándido said. We'll have to use stronger persuasions.

I guess, Johnny said. Tie her down.

Bug Eye stood before me, holding a rod with a little switch. When he touched me with it, my whole body jumped with exquisite pain. I felt my spirit snapping loose, soaring above my body and looking down at the scene. I was about to float off in a haze of brightness when ███████ cried out, I'll do it, I'll do it!

And down I went, sucked back into the body like water down a drain.

Next thing I knew, ██████ was calling out my name and shouting, Tell them I had to do it, as he was being dragged away.

Johnny seemed in a bad mood at all this commotion. Get him out of here, he said. Then to Bloody Juan, Get her dressed and take her back.

I was left alone in that room with a handful of guards. I could tell they were all ashamed of themselves, avoiding my eyes, quiet as if Johnny were still there. Then Bloody Juan gathered up my clothes, but I wouldn't let him help me. I dressed myself and walked out to the wagon on my own two feet.

CHAPTER TWELVE

Minerva

August to November 25, 1960

House Arrest
August and September

All my life, I had been trying to get out of the house. Papá always complained that, of his four girls, I should have been the boy, born to cut loose. First, I wanted to go to boarding school, then university. When Manolo and I started the underground, I traveled back and forth from Monte Cristi to Salcedo, connecting cell with cell. I couldn't stand the idea of being locked up in any one life.

So when we were released in August and put under house arrest, you'd have thought I was getting just the punishment for me. But to tell the truth, it was as if I'd been served my sentence on a silver platter. By then, I couldn't think of anything I wanted more than to stay home with my sisters at Mamá's, raising our children.

Those first few weeks at home took some getting used to.

After seven months in prison, a lot of that time in solitary, the overload was too much. The phone ringing; a visitor dropping by (with permission from Peña, of course); Peña himself dropping by to see about the visitor; Don Bernardo with guavas from his tree; rooms to go in and out of; children wanting their shoelaces tied; the phone ringing again; what to do with the curdled milk.

In the middle of the day when I should have been out soaking up sun and getting good country air in my infected lungs, I would seek the quiet of the bedroom, slip out of my dress and lie under the sheets watching the sun speckling the leaves through the barely opened jalousies.

But as I lay there, the same overload would start happening in my head. Bits and pieces of the past would bob up in the watery soup of my thoughts those days—Lío explaining how to hit the volleyball so there was a curve in its fall; the rain falling on our way to Papá's funeral; my hand coming down on Trujillo's face; the doctor slapping her first breath into my newborn baby girl.

I'd sit up, shocked at what I was letting happen to me. I had been so much stronger and braver in prison. Now at home I was falling apart.

Or, I thought, lying back down, I'm ready for a new life, and this is how it starts.

I grew stronger gradually and began taking part in the life of the household.

None of us had any money, and the dwindling income from the farm was being stretched mighty thin across five families. So we started up a specialty business of children's christening gowns. I did the simple stitching and seam binding.

The pneumonia in my lungs cleared up. I got my appetite back and began to regain the weight I'd lost in prison. I could wear again my old clothes Doña Fefita had brought down from Monte Cristi.

And, of course, my children were a wonder. I'd swoop down on them, showering them with kisses. "Mami!" they'd shriek. How lovely to be called mother again; to have their little arms around my neck; their sane, sweet breath in my face.

And pinto beans—were they always so colorful? "Wait, wait, wait," I'd cry out to Fela before she dunked them in the water. I'd scoop up handfuls just to hear the soft rattle of their downpour back in the pot. Everything I had to touch. Everything I had to taste. I wanted everything back in my life again.

But sometimes a certain slant of light would send me back. The light used to fall just so at this time of day on the floor below my top bunk.

And once, Minou got hold of a piece of pipe and was rattling it against the *galería* rail. It was a sound exactly recalling the guards in prison running their nightsticks against the bars. I ran out and yanked the pipe from her hand, screaming, "No!" My poor little girl burst out crying, frightened by the terror in my voice.

But those memories, too, began to fade. They became stories. Everyone wanted to hear them. Mate and I could keep the house entertained for hours, telling and retelling the horrors until the sting was out of them.

––––––––––

We were allowed two outings a week: Thursdays to La Victoria to visit the men, and Sundays to church. But for all that I was free to travel, I dreaded going out of the house. The minute we turned onto the road, my heart started pounding and my breathing got shallow.

The open vistas distressed me, the sense of being adrift in a crowd of people pressing in on all sides, wanting to touch me, greet me, wish me well. Even in church during the privacy of Holy Communion, Father Gabriel bent down and whispered "*¡Viva la Mariposa!*"

My months in prison had elevated me to superhuman status. It would hardly have been seemly for someone who had challenged our dictator to suddenly succumb to a nervous attack at the communion rail.

I hid my anxieties and gave everyone a bright smile. If they had only known how frail was their iron-will heroine. How much it took to put on that hardest of all performances, being my old self again.

––––––––––

My best performances were reserved for Peña's visits. He came often to supervise our house arrest. The children got so used to his toad face and grabby hands, they began calling him Tío Capitán and asking to hold his gun and ride on his knee horse.

I myself could not get used to him. Whenever that big white Mercedes turned into our narrow driveway, I ran to my bedroom and shut the door to give myself time to put on my old-self face.

In no time, someone was sent back there to get me. "It's Peña. You've got to come!" Even Mamá, who once refused to receive him, now buttered him up whenever he was over. After all, he had let her have her babies back.

One afternoon I was out trimming the laurel in the front yard. Manolito was "helping" me. After cutting the branches, all but a sliver, I held him up to pull them off. From his perch on my shoulders, he reported all he saw out on the road. "Tío's car!" he cried out, and sure enough, I saw the flash of white through a break in the hedge. It was too late to tune up for my performance. I went directly to the carport to receive him.

"What a rare occasion, Doña Minerva. The last few times I've come you haven't been well." In other words, I've noticed your rudeness. All of it is filed away. "You must be feeling better," he observed, without a question mark.

"I saw your car, I saw your car," sang Manolito.

"Manolito, my boy, you are all eyes. We could use men like you in the SIM."

Oh God, I thought.

———

"Ladies, it's nice to have you all here," Peña noted, when Mate and Patria joined us on the patio. Dedé had appeared with her shears to work on the hedge and keep her eye on "things." Whenever she didn't like my tone, she would clip the crown of thorns violently, scattering a spray of leaves and red petals in the air.

For the umpteenth time, Peña reminded us how lucky we were. Our five-year sentence had been commuted to house arrest. Instead of the restrictions of prison, we had only a few rules to obey. (We called them Peña's commandments.) He rehearsed them each time he came: No trips, no visitors, no contact with politicals. Any exceptions only by his permission. "Clear?"

We nodded. I was tempted to bring out the broom and set it by the door, the country way to tell people it was time to go.

Peña dunked the bobbing ice cubes with a fat finger. Today he had come for more than the recital of his rules. "El Jefe has not visited our province for a while now," he began.

Of course not, I thought. Most families in Salcedo had at least one son or daughter or husband in prison.

"We are trying to get him to come. All loyal citizens are writing letters."

Clip-clip went Dedé's shears, as if to drown out anything I might be thinking.

"El Jefe has been very generous to you girls. It would be nice if you composed a letter of thanks for his leniency."

He glanced at me and Mate, resting his eyes on Patria last. We gave him nothing with our faces. Poor nervous Dedé, who had edged up the patio towards us and was rewatering all the plants, said that yes, that would be wise. "I mean nice," she corrected herself quickly, and Patria, Mate, and I bowed our heads to hide our smiles.

After Peña left there was a fight. The others wanted to go ahead and write the damn letter. But I was against it. Thank Trujillo for punishing us!

"But what harm can a little letter do?" Mate argued. It was no longer so easy for me to talk that one into anything.

"People look to us to be an example, we've got a responsibility!" I spoke so fiercely, they looked a little sheepish. My old self was putting on quite a show.

"Now, Minerva," Patria reasoned. "You know if he publishes the silly thing everyone will know why we wrote it."

"Just go along with us this one time," Mate pleaded with me.

It reminded me of that time in Inmaculada when I had not wanted to perform for Trujillo with my friends. But I had given in to them, and we had almost met our end, too, with Sinita's bow-and-arrow assassination attempt.

What finally convinced me was Patria's argument that the letter might help free the men. A grateful note from the Mirabal sisters might just soften El Jefe's heart towards our husbands.

"Heart?" I said, making a face. Then, sitting down to our task, I made it perfectly clear: "This is against my better principles."

"Someone needs to have less principles and more sense," Dedé murmured, but without much fight in her voice. I think she was relieved to see a little spark of the old Minerva again.

Afterwards I felt small with what I'd done. "We've got to do something," I kept muttering.

"Calm down, Minerva. Here," Dedé said, pulling down Gandhi from the shelf. Elsa had given me this book when I first got out of prison to show me, she said, that being passive and gentle could be revolutionary. Dedé had approved wholeheartedly.

Today, Gandhi would not do. What I needed was a shot of Fidel's fiery rhetoric. He would have agreed with me. We had to do something, soon!

"We have to accept this cross is what we have to do," Patria said.

"Like hell we do!" I said. I was on a rampage.

It lasted only until the end of that day.

We were already in bed when I heard them talking loudly on the porch. They were everywhere—the dark glasses, the ironed pants, the pomaded hair. They stayed on the road until night, when they drew close to the house like moths drawn towards the light.

Usually I covered my head with my pillow and after a while fell asleep. But tonight I couldn't ignore them. I got up from bed, not even bothering to throw a shawl over my nightgown.

Dedé caught me going out the door. She tried to hold me back, but weak though I still was, I pushed her aside easily. Dedé was still Dedé, without much conviction in her fighting.

Two SIM agents were sitting on our rockers as comfortable as you please. "*Compañeros*," I said, startling them in mid-rock with the revolutionary greeting. "I'm going to have to ask you to please keep your voices down. You're right under our bedroom windows. Remember, you are guards, not guests here."

Neither of them said a word.

"Well, if there's nothing else, good night then, *compañeros*."

I had turned back towards the door when one of them called out, "*¡Viva Trujillo!*" the "patriotic" way of beginning and closing the day. But I wasn't going to invoke the devil's name in my own yard.

After a short pause in which she was probably waiting to see if I'd answer, Dedé called from inside the house, "*¡Viva Trujillo!*"

"¡Viva Trujillo!" Mate took it up.

And then a couple of more voices added their good wishes to our dictator, until what had been a scared compliance became, by the exaggeration of repetition, a joke. But I could feel the men listening specifically for my loyalty call.

"Viva—" I began and felt ashamed as I took a deep breath and pronounced the hated name.

Just in case I should go on a rampage again, Mamá confiscated the old radio. "What we need to know, we'll know soon enough!" And she was right, too. Little bits of news leaked in, sometimes from the least likely people.

My old friend Elsa. She had married the journalist Roberto Suárez, who was assigned to the National Palace and, though critical of the regime, wrote the flowery feature articles required of him. One night long ago, he had kept Manolo and me, as well as Elsa, in stitches with tales of his journalistic escapades. He had been held in prison once for three days for printing a picture in which Trujillo's bare leg showed between the cuff of his pants and the top of his sock. Another time, in a misprint he hadn't caught, Roberto's article had stated that Senator Smathers had delivered an elegy, instead of a eulogy, of Trujillo before the joint members of the United States Congress. That time Roberto was put in jail for a month.

I had thought for sure the Suarezes would join our movement. So when Leandro moved to the capital to coordinate the cells there, I mentioned the Suarezes to him as a likely couple. Elsa and Roberto were contacted and declared themselves "friendly," but did not want to join.

Now, in my hard times, my old friend sprang to my side. Every week since our release in August, Elsa had driven up from the capital to visit her elderly grandfather in La Vega. She would then swing up to Santiago, butter up Peña (she was good at this), and get a pass to come see me. Knowing we were in straitened circumstances, she brought bags of "old" clothes that looked fairly new to me. She claimed she couldn't fit into anything after her babies had been born and she'd gotten big as a cow.

Elsa . . . always exaggerating. She had the same good figure as always—as far as I could tell. "But look at these hips, please, just look at these legs!" she'd remind me.

Once she asked me, "How do you stay so trim?" Her eyes ran over my figure in an appraising way.

"Prison," I said flatly. She didn't mention my figure again.

Elsa and Roberto owned a boat, and every weekend they took it out. "To fish." Elsa winked. At sea they picked up Swan broadcasts from a little island south of Cuba as well as Radio Rebelde in Cuba and Radio Rumbos from Venezuela. "It's a regular newsroom out there," said Elsa, every visit catching me up on the latest news.

One day Elsa appeared, her face flushed with excitement. She couldn't sit down for a minute, not even for her favorite *pastelito* snack. She had news to tell me that required an immediate walk in the garden. "What is it?" I said, clutching her arm when we were halfway down the anthuriums.

"The OAS has imposed sanctions! Colombia, Peru, Ecuador, Bolivia, Venezuela," Elsa counted them off with her fingers, "even the gringos. They've all broken relations!" She and Roberto had been out on the boat Sunday and seen an American warship on the horizon.

"The capital is like this!" Elsa rubbed her fingers together. "Roberto says by next year—"

"Next year!" I was alarmed. "By then, who knows what can happen."

We walked a little while in silence. Far off, I could hear the shouts of the children playing with the big, bright beach ball their Tía Elsa had brought them from the capital. "Dedé tells me I shouldn't talk to you about all this. But I said to her, Dedé, it's in Minerva's blood. I told her about that time you almost shot Trujillo with a toy arrow, remember? I had to step in and pretend it was part of our play."

I wondered which of us had revised the past to suit the lives we were living now. "Ay, Elsa, that's not how it happened."

"Well, anyhow, she told me about the time you freed your father's rabbits because you didn't think it was right to have them caged."

That story was remembered my way, but I felt diminished hearing it. "And look at me now."

"What do you mean? You've gained a little weight. You're looking great!" She ran her eyes over me, nodding in approval. "Minerva, Minerva, I am so proud of you!"

How much I wanted at that moment to unburden myself to my old friend. To confess that I didn't feel the same as before prison. That I wanted my own life back again.

But before I could say a thing, she grabbed my hands. *"¡Viva la Mariposa!"* she whispered with feeling.

I gave her the bright brave smile she also required of me.

Our spirits were so high with the good news we couldn't wait for Thursday to tell the men. The night before, we were almost festive as we rolled our hair in the bedroom so it would curl for our men the next day. We always did this, no matter how gloomy we were feeling. And they noticed it, too. It was a fact—we had all compared notes—that our men got more romantic the longer they were in prison. Patria claimed that Pedrito, a man of few words if there ever was one, was composing love poems for her and reciting them during visiting hours. The most embarrassing part, she admitted, was that this made her start feeling *that* way right there in the middle of the prison hall surrounded by guards.

Dedé sat by, watching our preparations with displeasure. She had gotten into the habit of staying over the nights before our visits. She said she had to be at Mamá's early the next day anyhow to help with all the children once we left. But really, she was there to convince us not to go.

"You're exposing yourselves to an accident by going down all together," Dedé began, "that's what you're doing."

We all knew what kind of accident she meant. Just a month ago Marrero had been found at the foot of a cliff, having supposedly lost control of his car.

"Bournigal's drivers are very reliable," Patria reassured her.

"Think of how many orphans you'd be leaving behind, how many widowers, a mother in *luto* for the rest of her life." Dedé could really pour on the tragedy.

I don't know if it was nerves or what, but all three of us burst out laughing. Dedé stood up and announced she was going home. "Come on, Dedé," I called as she headed out the door. "There's a curfew. Be reasonable."

"Reasonable!" Her voice was seething with anger. "If you think I'm going to sit by and watch you all commit suicide, you're wrong."

She didn't make it past the front gate. The SIM sent her back. She slept on the couch and the next morning wouldn't talk to us all through breakfast. When she turned away as we went to kiss her goodbye, I decided to use her own fears on her. "Come on, Dedé. Think how sorry you'd be if something should happen to us and you didn't say goodbye." She stiffened with resistance. But the second the driver turned on the engine, she ran to the car, sobbing. She blurted out the one loss she hadn't mentioned the night before, "I don't want to have to live without you."

————————

The atmosphere in prison was bright with hope. The voices in the visitors' hall had a lift to them, now and then there was laughter. The news had spread there already: sanctions had been imposed, the gringos were closing down their embassy.

Only Manolo, like Dedé, was not convinced. He seemed gloomier than ever.

"What is it?" I asked between passings of the guard. "Isn't it good news?"

He shrugged. Then seeing my worried face, he smiled, but it was a smile for my benefit, I could tell. I noticed for the first time that some of his front teeth were broken off.

"We'll be home soon!" I always tried to raise his spirits with the thought of our little nest in Monte Cristi. The owners, old friends of Manolo's parents, were allowing us to keep our things there until the day they should find a new tenant. Strangely enough, it gave me hope to know our little house, the only home we'd ever shared, was still intact.

Manolo leaned towards me, his lips grazing my cheek. A kiss to mask what he had to say. "Our cells, are they ready?"

So that's what was worrying him. He didn't know that the revolution was out of our hands. Others were now in charge.

"Who?" he persisted.

I hated to tell him I didn't know. That we were totally disconnected at Mamá's. The guard was passing by, so I remarked instead about the plantain fritters we'd eaten the night before. "Nobody knows who they are," I mouthed when the guard was safely down the row.

Manolo eyes grew big in his pale face. "This could be a plant. Find out who's left." His grip tightened until my hands felt numb, but I would never tell him to let go.

We were watched around the clock, our visits supervised, even food vendors had their baskets checked at the gate. When and how and whom was I to contact? And if I tried, I'd only be risking more lives.

But it was more than that. I had put on too good a show for Manolo as well. He didn't know the double life I was leading. Outwardly, I was still his calm, courageous *compañera*. Inside, the woman had got the upper hand.

And so the struggle with her began. The struggle to get my old self back from her. Late in the night, I'd lie in bed, thinking, You must gather up the broken threads and tie them together.

Secretly, I hoped that events would settle the matter for me and, along with everyone else, I honestly believed we were seeing the last days of the regime. Shortages were everywhere. Trujillo was doing all the crazy things of a trapped animal. In church in a drunken stupor, he had seized the chalice and dispensed communion to his frightened attendants. The pope was talking about excommunication.

But with everyone against him and no one left to impress, Trujillo didn't have to hold himself back anymore. One morning, soon after sanctions went into effect, we woke up to the sound of sirens on the road. Trucks were roaring by, full of soldiers. Dedé did not appear that morning, and since that one was like clockwork, we knew something was wrong.

The next day Elsa brought the very news we'd been waiting for, with the conclusion we had dreaded. Two nights ago after dark, a group of young men had run through Santiago, distributing leaflets under doors, urging an uprising. Every last one of them had been caught.

"'They will find out what it is to run a comb through tangled hair,'" Elsa quoted Trujillo's reaction to the young rebels' capture.

Peña came by late that afternoon. All further visits to La Victoria were cancelled.

"But why?" I blurted out. And then bitterly I added, "We wrote the letter!"

Peña narrowed his eyes at me. He hated to be asked questions that implied he wasn't in charge of things. "Why don't you write another letter to El Jefe and ask him to explain himself to you!"

"She's just upset. We all are," Patria explained. She made a pleading face for me to be nice. "Aren't you just upset, Minerva?"

"I'm very upset," I said, folding my arms.

It was the end of September before visiting days were reinstated at La Victoria, and we got to see the men. That morning when we picked up our passes, Peña gave us a warning look, but we were all so relieved, we answered him with smiles and too many thank-yous. All the way down in the car we rented with a driver, we were giddy with anticipation. Mate told some of her favorite riddles we all pretended not to know she could have the pleasure of answering them herself. The thing Adam had in front that Eva had in back was the letter A. The thing that's put in hard and comes out soft were the beans in the boiling water. That one had gotten a taste for spicy humor in prison.

Our mood changed considerably when we were finally ushered into that dim, familiar hall. The men looked thinner, their eyes desperate in their pale faces. Between passings of the increased *guardia* patrol, I tried to find out from Manolo what was going on.

"It's over for us." Manolo clutched my hands.

"You can't think like that. We'll be back in our little house before the year is up."

But he insisted on goodbyes. He wanted me to know how deep was his love for me. What to say to the children. What kind of burial he wanted if I got a body, what kind of memorial service if I didn't.

"Stop this!" I said in an annoyed voice. My heart was in my mouth. On the drive home, we all wept, unable to console each other, for my sisters had heard the same grim news from Pedrito and Leandro. The men in their cells were being taken out at night in small groups and killed.

The driver, a man about our age who had already driven us down twice, looked in his rearview mirror. "The butterflies are sad today," he noted.

That made me sit up and dry my tears. The butterflies were not about to give up! We had suffered a setback but we had not been beaten.

In the long days that followed, we expected Peña to appear every morning with the horrible news. Now I was the one waiting out on the *galería* to intercept him if he came. I did not want anyone else to have to bear the first blow.

Clearly, the tide had turned. The failed uprising plunged the whole country into despair again. At home, everyone walked around with the look of people at a funeral. "We cannot give up," I kept saying.

They marveled at my self-control—and so did I. But by now in my life I should have known. Adversity was like a key in the lock for me. As I began to work to get our men out of prison, it was the old Minerva I set free.

Saving the Men
October

We could see them, chugging along behind us in their little Volkswagen. They would have a heyday reporting to Peña that we had visited another political. "Rufino," I said, "turn down Pasteur, quick."

Rufino had become our favorite driver. Every time we rented from Bournigal, we asked for him. Ever since the trip home from our last visit to the prison, we had felt his unspoken allegiance to us. Just this morning, when Dedé had worried about us leaving the house, Rufino had spoken up. "*A Dio'*, Doña Dedé, you think I'll let anything happen to the butterflies? They'll have to kill me first."

"And they will, too!" she had muttered.

He was peering into the rearview mirror. "We've lost them."

I checked out the back window myself. Then I turned to my sisters as if to say, See, you didn't believe me.

"Maybe this'll be just the excuse they need." Mate was tearful. We had just come from seeing the men. Leandro and Manolo had been told they would be going on a little trip—what all the prisoners were told before they were killed. They were desperate, grim, taking the Miltown we had smuggled in to them, and still not sleeping.

"They're in God's hands." Patria made the sign of the cross.

"Now listen to me, you two. We have a good excuse," I reminded them. "Delia is a female doctor and we have plenty of reason to see her." Neither Mate nor I had had a period for months.

Delia was nervous as she let us into her small office, her eyes full of signals. Before I could say a thing, she held up her hand to her lips and gestured towards the wall where her diplomas hung. We cannot talk here.

"We came about our cycles," I began, searching the wall for the telltale little rod. Wherever it was, all the SIM got at first was an earful about our women problems. Delia relaxed, thinking that was truly why we were here. Until I concluded a little too unmetaphorically, "So is there any activity in our old cells?"

Delia gave me a piercing look. "The cells in your systems have atrophied and are dead," she said sharply.

I must have looked stricken, for Delia's manner softened, "A few of them are still active, to be sure. But most importantly, new cells are filling in all the time. You need to give your bodies a rest. You should see menstrual activity by the beginning of next year."

Next year! I reached for the prescription pad on her desk and wrote down Sina's name with a big question mark.

"Gone. Asylum," she wrote back.

So Sina had abandoned our struggle. But then, I reminded myself, I had too, in effect, under house arrest for the last two months.

I listed six more names of members I knew had been released. Then I watched Delia draw a line through each one.

Finally I wrote, Who's left in our area?

Delia bit her lip. Throughout our meeting her manner had been guarded, as if we were being watched as well as bugged. Now she wrote down a name hurriedly, held it up for us to read, then tore all the used pages in half, over and over again. She stood, eager to have us gone.

The name Delia held up for us to see was unknown to us, a Dr. Pedro Viñas. When we got home, we asked Mamá, who went through a whole family tree of Viñas, only to declare she didn't know this particular one. We grew suspicious, for a stranger in our midst probably meant a SIM plant with a fabricated name. But Don Bernardo banished our doubts. Dr. Pedro Viñas was a urologist in Santiago, a very good one, who had attended Doña Belén several times. I called up and made an appointment for early next week. The woman's voice on the other end spoke to me as if I were a young child. "What is the little problem we're having?"

I had to think what a urologist was for. The only doctors I knew were Delia, Dr. Lavandier, and the doctor in Monte Cristi who had delivered my babies. "Just a little problem," I said, stalling.

"Oh, that," she said. And gave me a time.

Permission from Peña was next. That was not going to be easy. The morning after our unauthorized detour, he appeared at the house. We could tell by the bang of his car door that we were in for it.

For a full minute he shouted threats and obscenities at us. I sat on my hands as if they were extensions of my mouth. It took all my self-control not to order him and his filthy mouth out of our house.

Finally Peña calmed down enough to ask us what we had been up to. He was looking straight at me, for I was usually the one to do the talking.

But we had already settled it among us. I was to keep my mouth shut, and Patria, his favorite, was to do the explaining. "We had to see the doctor about a private matter."

"*¿Qué mierda privado?*" Peña's face was so red, it looked ready to explode.

Patria blushed at the obscenity. "We had to consult about some women's problems."

"Why didn't you just ask my permission?" Peña was softening. By now, Patria had got him to sit down in a rocker and at least accept a glass of guanabana juice—good for the nerves, Mamá always said. "I wouldn't keep you from medical care. But you know very well"—he looked straight at me—"that Delia Santos is on the political list. The rules clearly state, no contact with politicals."

"We weren't seeing her in her political capacity," I protested. Patria coughed a reminder of our agreement. But once I got started, it was hard to shut me up. "In fact, Captain, I'm glad to hear that you wouldn't stand in the way of our medical care—"

"Yes," Patria swiftly cut in. "You have been very kind to us." I could feel her eyes scouring me.

"I have been referred to Dr. Viñas in Santiago—"

"And you would be very grateful for the captain's leniency in allowing you to go," Patria reminded me, embedding my request in her scold.

Patria and Mate dropped me off in front of the small house on their way to El Gallo. A black Volkswagen was already parked across the street. It was hard to believe this was a doctor's office, but the sign in the window insisted. The lawn was overgrown, not in that neglected way that makes a place look shabby, but with nice abandon, as if to say, there's room in this house for everything, even a lot of grass.

How Patria had managed this was beyond me. Mamá always said Patria's sweetness could move mountains, and monsters, obviously. Not only had she gotten Peña to grant me permission for this visit, she had also secured a pass for herself and Mate to go shopping for supplies in the meanwhile. Our little dressmaking business was doing well. We were already working on November's orders and here it was only the middle of October. We couldn't sleep nights, so we sewed. Sometimes Patria started a rosary, and we all joined in, stitching and praying so as not to let our minds roam.

The genial little man who met me at the door seemed more like an uncle than a professional man or, Lord knows, a revolutionary. "We're having a little problem," he chuckled. Some chickens had gotten into the office from his house next door, and the maid was chasing them out with a broom. Dr. Viñas entered into the fun, teasing the maid to the delight of several small children who seemed to be his. He had gotten hold of some eggs and kept pulling them out of unlikely places, the children's ears, his own underarms, the boiler for his syringes. "Look what the hens left me," he said each time. His children screamed with delight.

Finally, the hens were out of view and the children were sent along with the maid to tell their Mamita to bring over a *cafecito* for the señorita. The diminutives were killing me. Lord, I thought, so this is what we've come to. But the minute Dr. Viñas closed the door of his consulting room, he was a different man, intent, serious, down to business. He seemed to know exactly who I was and why I had come.

"This is an honor," he said, motioning for me to sit down. He turned on the raspy air conditioner—the place was not bugged, he was pretty sure—but just in case. We spoke in whispers.

"The boys," I began, "we believe they're all about to be killed." I heard myself strangely demoting our men to the more helpless boys. Another diminutive—and from me.

Dr. Viñas sighed. "We tried our best. The problem was getting the ingredients for the picnic—" He looked at my face for a moment to see if I understood. "We were all set to go, the whole party assembled. But the gringos pulled out on their promise of pineapples. Some of the boys went ahead anyway." He made a gesture of broadcasting pamphlets.

"Why did the gringos pull out?" I wanted to know.

"They got cold feet. Afraid we're all communists. They say they don't want another Fidel. They'd rather have a dozen Trujillos."

I could feel dread rising in my chest. The men were not going to be saved after all. My old prison cough started up. Dr. Viñas reached for a thermos and poured me iced water in a glass cup that had measurement marks on the side. When my coughing had subsided, he went on, "The gringos are flirting with another group now."

That was hopeful news. "The MPDs?"

Dr. Viñas laughed, and briefly I saw the family doctor inside this toughened revolutionary. "No, they're idealists, too, and all of us idealists are dirty communists. These are people the gringos feel are safer. Some of Trujillo's old cronies who are tired of the old man. Their only ideology is, well, you know." He patted his pockets.

"Then why do you say there's hope?"

"Let them bring down the old man, and then we'll take over." Dr. Viñas grinned, his fat little cheeks lifting his glasses.

"It's not what we planned," I reminded him.

"One must have a left hand," he said, showing me his left hand.

I found I was wringing both of my hands, swallowing to keep the tickle in my throat from erupting into another coughing fit. "Isn't there anything we can do?"

He nodded, one sure, deep nod. "What you can do is keep our hopes up. You're an example, you know. The whole country looks to you."

When I made a face, he frowned. "I'm quite serious," he said.

There was a knock at the door. We both jumped.

"*Amorcito,*" a sweet voice called, "I have your little *cafecito* here."

And the world of diminutives closed in again on us.

———————

For Manolo, I lifted out the bad news like a fish bone, and gave him the promising tidbit—that the gringos were working with a group to slaughter the goat for the picnic.

Manolo had not heard this. His face tensed up. "I don't like it. The gringos will take over the revolution."

They'll take over the country, I thought to myself. I didn't say it out loud. No use depressing him any more than he already was. And at this point I didn't care enough. I was so desperate for Trujillo to be gone. Like Viñas said, we could fix the future later.

"Tell Viñas—" Manolo began.

I rolled my eyes to indicate the guard approaching behind him. Out loud, I went on, "The children miss you so much. The other day I asked them what they wanted for Benefactor's Day, and they said, 'Bring Papi home!' Manolo?" He was not listening, I could tell. His eyes had a faraway look I recognized from my own days in this horrible place.

I touched his face to bring him back. "Mi *amor*, just remember, soon, soon . . . Monte Cristi." I hummed the song.

"No singing," the guard announced. He had stopped in front of us.

"Sorry, soldier." I recognized Good Hair under the brim of his cap. I nodded at him, but his eyes were cold and flat, as if he did not know me. "We were just saying goodbye."

Today our interview was shorter than usual, since I was sharing my twenty minutes with Manolo's mother, who had driven down from Monte Cristi. Just before I came upstairs, we spoke briefly in the warden's office. She had a surprise she promised to tell me later.

I waited alone in the car with the radio on low. (No music allowed.) Just being in the prison yard was bringing back waves of that old panic. To distract myself, I fiddled with the radio dials, hoping Rufino would get back soon so I'd have someone to talk to. He was making the rounds, distributing the cigarettes and pesos we always brought the guards to encourage them to treat our prisoners right.

The visitors started filing past the checkpoint at the big exit door. Suddenly, Doña Fefita appeared, weeping, Mate and Patria on either side of her. My heart sank, remembering how depressed Manolo had been today.

I hurried up to them. "What's wrong?"

Mate and Patria shrugged—they didn't know—and before Doña Fefita could say, the guards shouted for us to move along.

We were not allowed to "congregate" in the prison yard, but down the road we stopped both cars. Doña Fefita began crying again as she recounted what had happened. She had arranged to buy the little house Manolo and I had lived in. But instead of being pleased, Manolo had snapped at her. Didn't she know that the only way he was going to come home was in a box?

This made my legs go weak beneath me. But I couldn't let my own devastation show. "Now Doña Fefita, he's just worn out. That place—" I cast a glance over her shoulder.

My sisters joined in with their reassurances. "We've got to keep our spirits up for the men." But when our eyes met, it was not a look of optimism that we exchanged.

Doña Fefita finally calmed down. "So, should I buy it, Minerva? Should I?"

It was hard for me to go against Manolo's wishes. We had always decided things together. "Maybe . . . you should wait."

She heard the hesitation in my voice and went on, more determined. "I'll take it upon myself. I want you to have a place to go to when this is all over."

She had put my feeling in words exactly. A place to go to when this is all over.

But her generosity was not allowed. A very short time later, I received notice to remove our possessions from the premises. The SIM were opening a new office in Monte Cristi.

And so Dedé and I set out in the pickup on Monday morning to do as we were bid. Rufino was our driver, since Jaimito, short-handed, couldn't take time off from the cacao harvest. He had not wanted Dedé to accompany me either, but she said she could not allow me to dismantle my house alone. We planned to be back Wednesday afternoon, in time for me to go with Mate and Patria to La Victoria the next day. Ah, the busy life of house arrest! Peña had immediately granted me permission for the trip to Monte Cristi. After all, as head of the Northern SIM, he knew exactly why my old house needed to be vacated. He was probably the mastermind.

The drive north turned out to be one of those sunny moments that come even in the darkest days. My gloominess fell away as if we were on holiday. I hadn't spent time alone with Dedé since we were cooped up in Ojo de Agua together, two young girls waiting for their lives to happen.

I knew she had mustered up all her courage to come along, the way she kept looking behind us when we first hit that isolated stretch of highway. But she soon settled down and was lively and talkative—as if to distract us from the sad mission we were on.

"Rufino," I said, "wouldn't Dedé make a great *gavillera*?" We were having a whistling contest, and Dedé had just won with a piercing trill.

"*Gavillera*, me! Are you crazy." Dedé laughed. "I wouldn't have lasted a day up in those hills. I would have given myself up to those good-looking gringos."

"Gringos, good-looking? ¡*Mujer*!" I made a face. All I could think of was how they had deserted Viñas and his men. "They look like somebody stuck them in a bucket of bleach and forgot they were there. That goes for their passion, too!"

"How would you know about their passion?" Dedé challenged. "You've never even known a gringo. Or have you kept something from me, my dear?" She gave her shoulders a saucy shimmy. Rufino looked away.

"Why not let Rufino decide," I said. "What do you think, Rufino? Are gringos good-looking?"

He smiled. Lines deepened on either side of his mouth. "A man doesn't know if another man is handsome," he said at last.

I found a way around that by invoking his wife. "Would Delisa say gringos are good-looking?"

His jaw tightened. "She had better keep her eyes to herself!"

Dedé and I looked at each other and smiled.

Feeling happy, I congratulated myself on asking Dedé to come along. Now she'd see that her fears were unfounded. The roads were not full of murderers. As unreal as it seemed in the midst of our troubles, that glorious ordinary life went on without us. There was a *campesino* with his donkey loaded down with charcoal. There was a truck with its flatbed full of girls giggling and waving at us. There under the blue sky was the turquoise sea, sparkling with holiday promises.

Suddenly and incomprehensibly to us in our carefree state—just around a curve, a car was parked across the road. Rufino had to slam on the brakes, and Dedé and I were thrown against each other. Five *calíes* in dark glasses swarmed around the pickup and ordered us out of the cab.

I will never forget the terror on Dedé's face. How she reached for my hand. How, when we were asked to identify ourselves, what she said was—I will never forget this—she said, "My name is Minerva Mirabal."

In Monte Cristi we were taken into a dim little guardhouse in back of the fort. I could see why they needed new quarters. The nervous man with worried eyes apologized for any discomfort. The escort had been a precaution. People had heard that Minerva Mirabal was coming to town today, and there were rumors that there might be some sort of commotion.

"Which one of you is Minerva Mirabal?" he asked, watching us through his cigarette smoke. The little finger on his left hand had a long, clawlike nail. I found myself wondering what it was for.

"I'm Minerva," I said, looking firmly at Dedé. That old man at Missing Persons we'd met years back flashed through my head. If he could give all fifteen sons the same name, why not two Minervas in the Mirabal family?

Our interrogator glanced suspiciously from one to the other, then addressed Dedé. "Why did you tell my men you were Minerva?"

Dedé could barely talk. "I . . . I . . . She's my little sister. . . ."

Little sister, indeed! I had never been Dedé's little sister as far as character was concerned. It had always been the big problem between us.

The man watched us, waiting.

"She's Minerva," Dedé finally agreed.

"You're certain of this, now?" the man asked without humor. He had sat back down, and was nervously flicking a lighter that would not light. Sizing him up, I employed a skill I had acquired in prison with my interrogators. I decided this jumpy little man could be cowed. He was trying too hard.

I pulled out our pass signed by Peña from my purse. As head of the Northern Division of the SIM, he was certainly this man's superior. "Captain Peña has authorized this trip. I hope there will be no problems for us to report back to him."

The paroxysm of blinking made me pity the poor man. His own terror was a window that opened onto the rotten weakness at the heart of Trujillo's system. "No problems, no problems. Just precautions."

As we waited outside for Rufino to bring the pickup around, I could see him through the door of his office. He was already on the phone—probably reporting our arrival to Peña. While he spoke, he was cleaning the wax out of his ear with his little finger. I felt somehow relieved to know what that nail was for.

At the little house, Dedé had us all organized: this bunch of boxes to store at Doña Fefita's; this bunch to take back with us; this pile to give away. I had to smile—she was still the same old Dedé, who stocked the shelves of the family store so neatly I always regretted having to sell anything.

Now she was in the kitchen-living room, making a clatter with the pots and pans. Every once in a while she'd come in with something in her hand. Mamá had given me some of her furnishings when she had moved to the new house.

"I didn't know you had this." Dedé held up the dainty oil lamp, its pale rose chimney fluted like the petals of a flower. "Our old bedroom lamp, remember?" I had forgotten that Dedé and I once shared a room before Mate and I paired up.

Reminiscing with Dedé was better than facing the flood of memories in the front room. Law books lay piled in a corner. Everything had been strewn on the floor—the porcelain donkey, our framed law degrees, the seashells Manolo and I had found on Morro Beach. I had not anticipated how hard this would be. I kept wishing the SIM had ransacked the place the way they had Patria's and carted off everything. This way was much crueler, making me face the waste of my life before me.

Here was the book of Martí's poems Lío had dedicated to me. ("In memory of my great affection . . .") And the little ship I had stolen for Mate. (What was it doing among my things?) And here was a yellowing newspaper with a picture of Lina Lovatón captioned with a poem by Trujillo. And a holy card from our pilgrimage to Higüey the time Patria claimed to have heard a voice. And a Nivea tin full of smelly ashes, probably from some Ash Wednesday when Mamá had dragged me to church. I went to the door for a swallow of fresh air.

Early evening it was, the cool of the day. The little square looked like a tree full of crows. There must have been over a hundred people strolling, sitting on benches, idling in front of the little gazebo where rallies were held, and contests on holidays. It could have been Benefactor's Day all over again except that everyone was dressed in black.

As I stood at the door, not fully comprehending the sight, the trucks began to roll in. *Guardias* unloaded. The clicking of their boots as they went into formation was the only sound. They surrounded the square.

I stepped out on the sidewalk. I don't know what I thought I was going to do. All strolling stopped. Suddenly, everyone faced me, and one totally quiet moment passed. Then almost as if at a signal, the crowd disbanded. Little groups began walking towards the side streets. In minutes the square was empty.

Not a shot had been fired, not a word said. The *guardias* stood uselessly around the empty square for a while longer. Finally, they climbed back into their trucks and roared away.

When I turned to go back inside, I was surprised to find Dedé at the door, a frying pan in her hand. I had to smile to myself. My big sister had been ready to march right out and bang a few heads if a massacre got started.

Back inside, the rooms were getting too dark to see. We wandered through the house, bumping into boxes, trying light switches, hoping to get a little more packing done. But the electricity had been cut off, and the oil lamp that had once lit the dark between our beds had already been packed away.

———

Wednesday evening when we got back, we found Mate in a bad state. She had had her bad dream from Papá's death. But this time, when she opened the lid of the coffin, Leandro and Manolo and Pedrito were inside. Every time she recounted it, she began to sob.

"You're going to look awful tomorrow," I warned, hoping to appeal to her vanity.

But Mate didn't care. She cried and cried until at last we were all spooked.

To make matters worse, Tío Pepe appeared right after supper. His pickup was decked with paper flags and a banner proclaiming, WELCOME, JEFE, TO SALCEDO PROVINCE. The SIM let him right in.

"Quite a getup you have there," I noted.

Tío Pepe nodded wordlessly. When the nieces and nephews began clamoring for the little flags on the pickup, he snapped at them. Their mouths dropped. They had never seen their jolly uncle cross.

"Time for bed," Mamá said, ushering her brood of grandchildren towards the bedrooms.

"Let's get some air," Tío Pepe suggested. Patria, Mate, and I grabbed our shawls and followed him outside.

Deep in the garden where we always went to talk, he told us about the gathering he'd just come from. There had been a reception honoring El Jefe at the mayor's house. A list of all the people that Trujillo wanted to see there had been published in the local paper. Tío Pepe's name had been on it.

"¡Epa, tío!" I said. "Hobnobbing with the big guys."

"He wanted me there because he knows I'm related to you." Tío Pepe's voice was only a whisper above the trilling of the cicadas.

From the house we could hear Mamá getting the children ready for bed. "Put on your pajama bottoms right this minute!" No doubt she was scolding my little hellion. Without his father, that boy was growing up a handful.

"He's by the big punch bowl, surrounded by his flies—you know how shit attracts flies. Forgive my foul mouth, girls, but nothing else fits this devil in human form. Surrounded by those men— you know, Maldonado and Figueroa and Lomares, and that Peña fellow. They're all saying, 'Ay, Jefe, you've done so much good for our province.' 'Ay, Jefe, you've raised strong morale after sanctions.' 'Ay, Jefe,'" Tío Pepe crooned to imitate the cronies. "El Jefe keeps nodding at this pile of horse shit, and finally he says, looking right at me— I'm standing at my post by the Salcedo farmers, filling up on those delicious *pastelitos* Florín makes— and he says, 'Well, boys, I've really only got two problems left. If I could only find the man to resolve them.'

"Then he goes quiet, and I know and everyone else knows, we're supposed to ask him what are those problems, and can we please be the men to resolve them. Sure enough, the biggest shit lover of all, Peña, says, 'Jefe, I am at your service. Just tell me your problems and I'll give my life if need be—blah blah blah.' So El Jefe says, brace yourselves now. He says, looking straight at me, he says, 'My only two problems are the damn church and the Mirabal sisters.'"

I felt the hair rising on my arms. Mate began to cry.

"Now, now, it's no reason to get alarmed." Tío Pepe tried to sound like his usual cheerful self. "If he was really going to do something, he wouldn't have announced it. That's the whole point. He was giving me a warning to deliver back to you."

"But we aren't doing anything," Mate said in a weary voice. "We're locked up here all week except for visiting the men. And it's not like we don't have permission from Peña himself."

"Maybe—for a while, anyhow—you should think about not going out at all."

So Trujillo was no longer saying Minerva Mirabal was a problem, but that all the Mirabal sisters were. I wondered whether Dedé would be implicated now that I had dragged her with me to Monte Cristi.

Patria hadn't said a word the whole time. Finally she spoke up. "We can't desert the men, Tío."

Just then, the light from the children's bedroom that gave on the garden went out. As we stood in the dark a while longer, calming ourselves, I had this eerie feeling that we were already dead and looking longingly at the house where our children were growing up without us.

The next morning, Thursday, we stopped as required at SIM headquarters on our way down to La Victoria. Rufino came back to the car without the papers. "He wants to see you."

Inside, Peña was waiting for us, the fat spider at the center of his web.

"What's wrong?" I asked the minute we sat down where he pointed. I should have kept my mouth shut and let Patria do the talking.

"You don't want to make a useless trip, do you?" He waited a long second for the grim possibilities of his statement to sink in.

My nerves were worn thin after the bad night we'd spent. I leapt up—and thank God, Peña's desk was in the way, for I could have slapped the fat, smug look off his face. "What have you done to our husbands?"

The door opened, a guard peeked in. I recognized Albertico, our village mechanic's youngest boy. The look of concern was for us, not Peña. "I heard shouts," he explained.

Peña whirled about at that. "What do you think, *pendejo*? That I can't manage a bunch of women by myself?" He shouted obscenities at the scared boy, and ordered him to close the door and to pay attention to his business or he'd have business on his hands he wouldn't want to pay attention to.

The door closed immediately in a flurry of apologies.

"Sit, sit." Peña motioned me impatiently towards the bench where my two sisters already sat, rigid, clutching their hands in silent prayer.

"You have to understand," Patria said in a placating voice. "We're worried about our husbands. Where are they, Captain?"

"Your husband"—he pointed to her—"is at La Victoria, I have your pass right here."

With a trembling hand Patria took the paper he offered her. "And Manolo and Leandro?"

"They are being moved."

"Where?" Mate asked, her pretty face perking up with ridiculous hope.

"To Puerto Plata—"

"Why on earth?" I confronted Peña. I felt Patria squeezing my hand as if to say, watch that tone of voice, girl.

"Why, I thought you would be pleased. Less distance for *the butterflies* to travel." Peña spoke with sarcastic emphasis. I wasn't all that surprised he knew our code name the way people were bruiting it about. Still, I didn't like the sound of it in his mouth. "Visiting days in Puerto Plata are Fridays," Peña was explaining to the others. "If you women want to see your men more often, we can arrange for other days as well."

Certainly there was something suspicious in his granting us these privileges. But all I felt was numb, resigned, sitting in that stuffy office. Not only was there nothing in the world we could do to save the men, there was nothing in the world we could do to save ourselves either.

Talk of the people, Voice of God
November 25, 1960

The soldier was standing on the side of the road with his thumb out, dressed in a camouflage uniform and black, laced-up boots. The sky was low with clouds, a storm coming. On this lonely mountain road, I felt sorry for him.

"What do you say?" I asked the others.

We were evenly divided. I said yes, Mate said no, Patria said whatever.

"You decide," we told Rufino. He was fast becoming our protector and guide. None of Bournigal's other drivers would take us over the pass.

Mate had grown suspicious of everyone since Tío José's visit. "He is a soldier," she reminded us. On my side of the argument I added, "So? We'll be all the safer."

"He's so young," Patria noted as we approached the shoulder where he stood. It was just an observation, but it tipped the scales, and Rufino stopped to offer the boy a ride.

He sat in front with Rufino, twisting his cap in his hands. The uniform was too large, and the starched shoulders stuck out in crisp, unnatural angles. For a minute, it worried me that he seemed so uncomfortable, maybe he was up to something. But as I studied the closely cropped head and the boyish slenderness of his neck, I decided he was just not used to riding around with ladies. So I made conversation, asking him what he thought of this and that.

He was headed back to Puerto Plata after a three-night furlough to meet his newborn son in Tamboril. We offered him our congratulations, though I thought he was much too young to be a father. Or a soldier, for that matter. Someone was going to have to take in that uniform. Maybe we could do alterations in our new shop.

I remembered the camouflage fatigues I'd sewn for myself last November. Ages ago, it seemed now. The exercises I used to do to get in shape for the revolution! Back then, we believed we'd be in these mountains as guerrillas before the year was over.

And here it was late November, a year later, and we were riding over the pass in a rented Jeep to visit our husbands in prison. The three butterflies, two of them too skittish to sit next to the windows facing the steep drop just inches from the slippery road. One of them, just as scared, but back to her old habits of pretending there was nothing to fear, as *el señor* Roosevelt had said, but being afraid.

I made myself look down the side of the mountain at the gleaming rocks below. The dangerous possibilities, the fumes from the bad muffler, the bumpiness of the road—I felt a queasiness in my stomach. "Give me one of those Chiclets, after all," I asked Mate. She'd been chomping on hers ever since we started to climb the mountain on this curving stretch of road.

It was our fourth trip to see them since their transfer to Puerto Plata. We had left the children home this time. They'd already been on the previous Friday to see their daddies, and every one of them had gotten car sick on the way there and back. This mountain road made everyone queasy.

"Tell me something," I asked the young soldier in the front seat. "What's it like being posted in Puerto Plata?" The fort there was one of the biggest, most strategic in the country. Its walls stretched out gray and ominous for miles, and its spotlights beamed even into the Atlantic. It was a popular coast for invasions, therefore heavily guarded. "Have you seen any action yet?"

The young soldier half turned in his seat, surprised that a woman should interest herself in such things. "I just joined last February when the call went out. So far I've only done prison detail."

I exchanged a glance with my sisters in the back seat. "You must get some important prisoners from time to time?"

Patria dug her elbow in my ribs, biting her lip so as not to smile.

He nodded gravely, wanting to impress us with his own importance as their guard. "Two politicals came just this last month."

"What'd they do?" Mate asked in an impressed voice.

The boy hesitated. "I'm not really sure."

Patria took both Mate's and my hands in her own. "Are they going to be executed, you think?"

"I don't believe so. I heard they were going to be moved back to the capital in a few weeks."

How odd, I thought. Why go to all the trouble of transferring the boys up north only to ship them back in a month? We had already decided on moving to Puerto Plata and opening a store, and this news would ruin that plan. But then, this was just a boy in a too-big uniform. What did he know?

The storm started up about then. Rufino let down the canvas flaps and told the soldier how to do his side. We snapped the back panels in place. The inside of the Jeep grew dark and stuffy.

285

Soon the downpour was upon us. The heavy rain hit the canvas top with the sound of slaps. I could barely hear Patria or Mate talking, much less Rufino and the young soldier up front.

"Maybe we should think it over," Patria was saying.

Before our prison visit today, we had planned to look at some rental houses Manolo's friend Rudy and his wife Pilar had lined up for us. It had all been decided. We would be moving to Puerto Plata with the children by the first of December, opening up a little store at the front of the house. The reaction to our traveling had finally become too disturbing. Every time we left the house, people came out on the road and blessed us. When we got back, we felt obliged to blow the horn, as if to say, "We're here, safe and sound!"

Dedé and Mamá got weepy every time we started out.

"Those are just rumors," I'd say, trying to comfort them.

"Talk of the people, voice of God," Mamá would answer, reminding me of the old saying.

"Rufino, if it's too bad, and you want to stop—" Patria had come forward in her seat. We could see that there was nothing to be seen out the front but sheets of water. "We can wait till the storm's over."

"No, no, don't preoccupy yourselves." Rufino was almost shouting to be heard above the pounding rain. Somehow, a yelled reassurance did not sound very reassuring. "We'll be in Puerto Plata by noon."

"Si Dios quiere," she reminded him.

"Si Dios quiere," he agreed.

It was reassuring to see the young soldier's head nod in agreement—until he added, "God and Trujillo willing."

This was Patria's first visit to see Manolo and Leandro since they'd been moved. Usually, on Thursdays, she was headed down to La Victoria to visit Pedrito with a regular ride that didn't return until Friday midday. By that time Mate and I had already left for Puerto Plata, accompanied by one or the other of our mothers-in-law. Since the rumors had gotten so bad, both of them had virtually moved in with us. Their sons had made them promise they wouldn't let us out of their sight. Those poor women.

The night before, Mate and I had been readying ourselves for our trip today, talking away, just the two of us. Patria was still in the capital, and Dedé's little one was sick, and so she was home, taking care of him. Mate was doing my nails when we heard the sound of a car pulling into the driveway. Mate's hand jerked, and I could see that she had painted the whole top of my thumb red.

We both tiptoed down the hall to the living room and found Mamá angling the jalousie just so. We all sighed with relief when we heard Patria's voice, thanking her ride.

"And what are you doing traveling at this time of night!" Mamá scolded before poor Patria was even in the door.

"I got a ride back tonight with Elsa," Patria explained. "There were five already in the car. But she was nice enough to squeeze me in. I've been wanting to go see the boys."

"We'll discuss that in the morning," Mamá said in her nonnegotiable voice, herding us out of the room by flipping off the lights.

In our bedroom, Patria was full of talk about Pedrito. "*Ay, Dios mío,* that man was so romantic today." She raised her arms over her head and stretched in that full-bodied way of cats.

"*¡Epa!*" Mate egged her on.

She smiled a pleased, dreamy smile. "I told him I wanted to see the boys tomorrow, and he gave me his permission."

"Patria Mercedes!" I was laughing. "You asked for his permission? What can he do from prison to stop you?"

Patria gave me a quizzical look, as if the answer were obvious. "He could have said, no, you can't go."

Next morning, we had Mamá almost convinced that the three of us would be just fine traveling by ourselves when Dedé rushed in, breathless. She looked around at the signs of our imminent departure. Her eye fell on Patria, putting on her scarf. "And what are you doing here?" she asked. Before Patria could explain, Rufino was at the door. "Any time you ladies are ready. Good day," he said, nodding towards Mamá and Dedé. Mamá murmured her good days, but Dedé gave the chauffeur the imperious look of a mistress whose servant has disobeyed her wishes.

"All three of you are going?" Dedé was shaking her head. "What about Doña Fefita? Or Doña Nena?"

"They need a rest," I said. I didn't add that we'd be house-hunting today. We hadn't told our mothers-in-law or Mamá or—Lord knows!—Dedé about our plans yet.

"Why, Mamá, with all due respect, are you mad to let them go alone?" Mamá threw up her hands. "You know your sisters," was all she said.

"How handy," Dedé said with heavy sarcasm, pacing the room. "How very very handy for the SIM to have all three of you sitting pretty in the back seat of that rundown Jeep with a storm brewing in the north. Maybe I should just give them a call. Why not?"

Rufino was at the door again.

"We should go," I said, to spare him having to say it again.

"La bendición," Patria called, asking for Mamá's blessing.

"La bendición, mis hijas." Mamá turned abruptly, as if to hide the worry on her face. She headed towards the bedrooms. As we went out, I could hear her scolding the children, who were wailing with disappointment at not being taken on our outing.

Dedé stood by the Jeep, blocking our way. "I'm going crazy with worrying. I'll be the one locked up forever, you'll see. In the madhouse!" There was no self-mockery in her voice.

"We'll come visit you, too," I said, laughing. But then seeing her teary, unhappy face, I added, "Poor, poor Dedé." I took her face in my two hands. I kissed her goodbye and then climbed into the Jeep.

We were at the counter paying for the purses. The very correct young salesclerk was taking his time, and the manager had already been by once to hurry him along. With infinite patience the clerk folded the straps just so, located each purse at the center of the brown parcel paper he painstakingly tore from the roll, and commenced creasing the edges. I watched his hands working, mesmerized. This must be how God does things, I thought, as if He has all the time in the world.

We had asked permission for this brief detour to El Gallo on our way to Puerto Plata today. Our sewing supplies were low again, and we needed thread in several colors, seam bindings, and ribbons to complete November's orders. The drive over the mountain was long. If our nerves cooperated, we could catch up on some of the hand sewing today.

When we went to pay, the salesclerk showed us a new shipment of Italian purses. Mate mooned over one in red patent leather with a snap in the shape of a heart. But of course, she wouldn't think of such an extravagance. "Unless—" She looked up at us. Patria and I were also examining the display case. There was a practical black bag with innumerable zippered pockets and compartments just perfect for Patria's goodwill supplies. Then I spotted a smart leather envelope that would be exactly the thing for a young lawyer to carry. An investment in hope, I thought.

"Shall we?" We looked at each other like naughty schoolgirls. We hadn't bought ourselves a single thing since before prison. We should, Mate decided. She did not want to be the only one splurging. I didn't need much talking into, but at the last minute, Patria desisted. "I just can't. I don't really need it." I felt a flicker of anger at her for her goodness that I didn't want—at this moment—to live up to.

As he wrapped Mate's first, the man kept his head bowed. But for one fleeting instant, I caught his eyes on us and a look of recognition dawning on his face. How many people—on the street, in church, on the sidewalks, in shops like this one—knew who we were?

"New purses. A sign of good luck coming!" Somebody else waiting for the future, I thought. I felt a flush of embarrassment to be caught shopping when I should have been plotting a revolution.

Rufino came in the store from the sidewalk where he was parked. "We better get started. The rainstorm looks like it's coming and I want to be over the worse part of the pass by then."

The young man looked up from his wrapping. "You aren't planning to go over the pass today, are you?"

My stomach clenched. But then, I thought, the more people know, the better. "We always go Fridays to Puerto Plata to see the men," I told him.

The floor manager came forward, smiling falsely at us, but throwing meaningful looks his attendant's way. "Finish up there, you don't want to delay the ladies." The young man hurried off and was back momentarily with our change. He finished wrapping my purse.

As he handed it over, the attendant gave me an intent look. "Jorge Almonte," he said, or something like that. "I put my card in your purse if there should ever be any need."

The rain let up just as we came upon La Cumbre, the lonely mountain village that had grown up around one of Trujillo's seldom-used mansions. Too isolated, some people said. El Jefe's two-story concrete house sat on top of the mountain above a cluster of little palm huts that seemed to be barely holding on to the cliff. We craned our necks every time we went by. What did we think we'd see? A young girl brought here for a forced rendezvous? The old man himself walking around his grounds, beating the side of his shiny boots with a riding crop.

The iron gateway blazed its five stars above the gleaming T. As we passed, our young soldier passenger saluted, though no guards were in sight.

We drove by shabby palm huts. The one time we had stopped here to stretch our legs the whole little village had gathered, offering to sell us anything we might want to buy. "Things are bad," the villagers complained, looking up towards the big house.

Rufino pulled over and rolled up the side flaps. A welcome breeze blew in, laden with the smells of damp vegetation. "Ladies," Rufino asked us, before climbing back in, "if you'd like to stop?"

Patria was sure she did not want to stop. This was her first time, and the road was a little spooky until you got used to it.

Just as we were rounding the curve—on that stretch where the house shows the most from the road, I glanced up. "Why, look who's there!" I said, pointing to the big white Mercedes that sat by the front door.

All three of us knew at the same instant what it meant. An ambush lay ahead! Why else was Peña at La Cumbre? We had seen him just this morning in Santiago when we picked up our permissions. Patria's chatty friend had made no mention of being headed in our direction.

We could not turn around now. Were we being followed? We stuck our heads out the window to see what lay behind as well as ahead.

"I give myself to San Marco de León," Patria intoned, repeating the prayer for desperate situations. I found myself mouthing the silly words.

Panic was rising up from my toes, through my guts, into my throat. The thunder in my chest exploded. Mate was already wheezing, searching through her purse for her medication. We sounded like a mobile sanatorium.

Rufino slowed. "Shall we stop at the three crosses?" Up ahead on a shoulder were three white crosses marking the casualties from a recent accident. Suddenly, it loomed in my head as the place for an ambush. The last place we should stop.

"Keep on going, Rufino," I said, and I took great swallows of the cool air that was blowing in on us.

———————

To divert ourselves, Mate and I began moving the contents of our old purses into our new ones. The card of Jorge Almonte, Attendant, EL GALLO, found its way to my hand. The gold rooster logo crowed from the upper right-hand corner. I turned the card over. The words were written in big block letters in a hurried hand: "Avoid the pass." My hand shook. I would not tell the others. It could only make things worse, and Mate's asthma had just begun to calm down.

But in my own head I was working it all out: it was a movie scene that became suddenly, terrifyingly real. This soldier was a plant. How foolish we'd been, picking him up on this lonely country road.

I began chatting him up, trying to catch him in a lie. What time was he due at the fort and why had he hitched rather than caught a ride in an army truck? Finally, he turned around halfway in his seat. I could see that he was afraid to speak.

I'll coax it out of him, I thought. "What is it? You can tell me."

"You ask more questions than *mi mujer* when I get home," he blurted out. His color deepened at the rude suggestion that I could be like his wife.

Patria laughed and tapped my head with a gloved hand. "That *coco* fell right on your head." I could see she, too, felt surer of him now.

The sun broke through the clouds, and shafts of light shone like blessings on the far valley. The arc of His covenant, I thought. I will not destroy my people. We had been silly, letting ourselves believe all those crazy rumors.

To entertain us, Mate began telling riddles she was sure we hadn't heard. We humored her. Then Rufino, who collected them, knowing how much Mate loved them, offered a new one to her. We began to descend towards the coast, the roadside growing more populous, the smell of the ocean in the air. The isolated little huts gave way to wooden houses with freshly painted shutters and zinc roofs advertising Ron Bermúdez on one side, *Dios y Trujillo* on the other.

Our soldier had been laughing loudly at the riddles he always guessed wrong. He had one of his own to contribute. It turned out to be much nastier than any of Mate's!

Rufino was indignant. "A Dio', are you forgetting there are ladies in the car?"

Patria leaned forward, patting a hand on each man's shoulder. "Now, Rufino, every egg needs a little pepper." We all laughed, glad for the release of the pent-up tension.

Mate crossed her legs, jiggling them up and down. "We're going to have to stop soon unless you quit making me laugh." She was famous for her tiny bladder. In prison, she'd had to practice holding it in since she didn't like going out to the latrine with strange guards in the middle of the night.

"Everybody serious," I ordered, "because we sure can't stop here."

We were at the outskirts of the city now. Brightly colored houses sat prettily in their kempt plots, side by side. The rain had washed the lawns, and the grasses and hedges shone emerald green. Everything was a fresh joy to see. Groups of children played in puddles on the street, scattering as the Jeep approached, so as not to be sprayed. An impulse seized me. I called out to them, "We're here, safe and sound!"

They stopped their play and looked up. Their baffled little faces did not know what to make of us. But I kept waving until they waved back.

I felt giddy, as if I'd been granted a reprieve from my worse fears. When Mate needed a piece of paper for her discarded Chiclet, I pulled out Jorge's card.

Manolo was upset at his mother for letting us come alone. "She promised me she wouldn't let you out of her sight."

"But, my love," I said, folding my hands over his, "reason it out. What could Doña Fefita do to protect me even if I were in danger?" I had a brief, ludicrous picture of the old, rather heavy woman banging a SIM *calié* over the head with her ubiquitous black purse.

Manolo pulled and pulled at his ear, a nervous habit he had developed in prison. It moved me to see him so nakedly affected by his long months of suffering. "A promise is a promise," he concluded, still aggrieved. Oh dear, there would be words next time, and then Doña Fefita's tears all the way home.

Manolo's color had started to come back. This was definitely a better prison, brighter, cleaner than La Victoria. Every day, our friends Rudy and Pilar sent over a hot meal, and after they ate, the men were allowed to walk around in the prison yard for a half hour. Leandro, the engineer, joked that he and Manolo could have mashed at least a ton of sugarcane by now if they'd been rigged up with a harness like a team of oxen.

We sat around in the little yard where they usually brought us during our visits if the weather was good. Unaccountably, after the bad storm, the sun had come out in the late afternoon. It shone on the barracks, painted a pea-green, amoeba-shaped camouflage that looked almost playful; on the storybook towers with flags flying in a row; on the bars gleaming brightly, as if someone had taken the time to polish them. If you didn't let yourself think what this place was, you could almost see it in a promising light.

Tentatively, Patria brought up the topic. "Have you been told anything about being moved back?"

Leandro and Manolo looked at each other. A worried look passed between them. "Did Pedrito hear something?"

"No, no, nothing like that," Patria soothed them. And then she looked to me to bring up what the young soldier had reported in the car, that two "politicals" would be going back to La Victoria in a few weeks.

But I did not want to worry them. Instead I began to describe the perfect little house we'd seen earlier. Patria and Mate joined in. What we didn't tell the men was that we had not rented the house, after all. If they were going to be moved back to La Victoria, there was no use. The big white Mercedes parked at the door of La Cumbre crossed my mind. I leaned forward, as if to leave its image physically at the back of my mind.

We heard the clanging of doors in the distance. Footsteps approached, there were shouted greetings, the click and slap of gun salutes. The guard was changing.

Patria opened her purse and withdrew her scarf. "Ladies, the shades of night begin to fall, the wayfarer hurries home . . ."

"Nice poetry." I laughed to lighten the difficult moment. I had such a hard time saying goodbye.

"You're not going back tonight?" Manolo looked shocked at the idea. "It's too late to start out. I want you to stay with Rudy and Pilar and head back tomorrow."

"I touched his raspy cheek with the back of my hand. He shut his eyes, giving himself to my touch. "You mustn't worry so. Look how clear that sky is. Tomorrow we'll probably have another bad storm. We're better off going home this evening."

We all looked up at the deepening, golden sky. The few low-lying clouds were moving quickly across it—as if heading home themselves before it got too dark.

I didn't tell him the real reason why I didn't want to stay with his friends. Pilar had confided in me as we drove around looking at houses that Rudy's business was about to collapse. She did not have to say it, but I guessed why. We had to put more distance between us, for their sake.

Manolo held my head in both his hands. I wanted to lose myself in his sad dark eyes. "Please, *mi amor.* There are too many rumors around."

I reasoned with him. "If you gave me a peso for every premonition, dream, admonition we've been told this month, we'd be able to—"

"Buy ourselves another set of purses." Mate held hers up and nodded for me to hold up mine.

Then, there was the call, "Time!" The guards closed in, their flat, empty faces showing us no consideration. "Time!"

We stood, said our hurried goodbyes, our whispered prayers and endearments. Remember . . . Don't forget . . . *Dios te bendiga, mi amor.* A final embrace before they were led away. The light was falling quickly. I turned for a last look but they had already disappeared into the barracks at the end of the yard.

We stopped at the little restaurant-gas pump on the way out of town. The umbrellas had all been taken down in preparation for night, and only the little tables remained. Since Mate and Patria were thirsty and wanted a refreshment, I went and made the call. The line was busy.

I paced back and forth in front of the phone the way one does to remind someone ahead that others are waiting. But neither Mamá nor Dedé could know that I was waiting for them to get off the line.

"Still busy," I came back and told my sisters.

Mate picked up her new purse and mine from the extra chair. "Sit with us, come on." But I couldn't see how I could sit. I guess it was getting to me, listening to everyone's worries.

"Give it another five minutes," Patria suggested. It seemed reasonable enough. In five minutes whoever was on would be off the line. If not, it was a sure sign that one of the children had left the phone off the hook and who knew when Tono or Fela would discover it.

Rufino leaned against the back of the Jeep, his arms crossed. Every so often, he'd look up at the sky—checking the time.

"I think maybe I will have a beer," I said at last.

"*¡Epa!*" Mate said. She was drinking her lemonade through a straw, daintily like a girl, trying to make the sweet pleasure last. We would be stopping at least once more on the road. I could see that.

"Rufino, can I get you one?" He looked away, a sign that indeed he would like a cold beer but was too shy to say so. Off I went to the bar for our two Presidentes. I tried the number again while the obliging proprietor dug up his two coldest ones from the bottom of the deep freeze.

"Still busy," I told our little table when I got back.

"Minerva!" Patria shook her head. "That wasn't five minutes."

The afternoon was deepening towards evening. I felt the cooler air of night blowing off the mountain. We had not brought our shawls. I imagined Mamá just now seeing them, draped brightly on the backs of chairs, and going to the window once again to watch for car lights.

Undoubtedly, she would pass the phone. She would see it was off the hook. She would heave a sigh and replace it in its cradle. I went back to try one more time.

"I give up," I said when I came back. "I think we should just go."

Patria looked up at the mountain. Behind it was another one and another one, but then we would be home. "I feel a little uneasy. I mean that road is so—deserted."

"It's always that way," I informed her. The veteran mountain-pass traveler.

Mate finished the last of her drink and sucked the sugar through the straw, making a rude sound. "I promised Jacqui I'd tuck her in tonight." Her voice had a whiny edge. Mate had not been separated from her baby overnight since we'd come home from prison.

"What do you say, Rufino?" I asked him.

"We can make it to La Cumbre before dark, for sure. From there, it's all downhill. But it's up to you," he added, not wanting to express a preference. Surely, his own bed with Delisa curled beside him was better than a little cot in the tiny servant's room at the back of Rudy and Pilar's yard. He had a baby, too. It struck me I had never asked him how old the child was, boy or girl.

"I say we go," I said, but I still read hesitancy in Patria's face.

Just then, a Public Works truck pulled into the station. Three men got out. One veered off behind the building to the smelly toilet we had been forced to use once and swore never again. The other two came up to the counter, shaking their legs and pulling at their crotches, the way men getting out of cars do. They greeted the proprietor warmly, giving him half-arm *abrazos* over the counter. "How are you, *compadre*? No, no, we can't stay. Pack us up a dozen of those pork fries over there—in fact, hand us a couple to eat right now."

The proprietor talked with the men as he filled their order. "Where you headed at this hour, boys?"

The driver had taken a large bite of the fried rind in his hand. "Truck needs to be in Tamboril by dark." He spoke with his mouth full, licking his greasy fingers when he was done and then tweezing a handkerchief out of his back pocket to wipe himself. "Tito! Where is that Tito?" He turned around and scanned the tables, his eye falling on us. We smiled, and he took his cap off and held it to his heart. The flirt. Rufino straightened up protectively from his post next to the car.

When Tito came running from behind the pumps, his buddies were already inside the truck, gunning the motor. "Can't a man shit in peace?" he called out, but the truck was inching forward, and he had to execute a tricky mount on the passenger's running board. I was sure they had performed the maneuver before for a lady or two. They honked as they pulled out into the road.

We looked at each other. Their lightheartedness made us all feel safer somehow. We'd be following that truck all the way to the other side of the mountains. Suddenly, the road was not so lonesome.

"What do you say?" I said, standing up. "Shall I try one more time?" I looked towards the phone.

Patria closed her purse with a decisive snap. "Let's just go."

We moved quickly now towards the Jeep, hurrying as if we had to catch up with that truck. I don't know quite how to say this, but it was as if we were girls again, walking through the dark part of the yard, a little afraid, a little excited by our fears, anticipating the lighted house just around the bend—

That's the way I felt as we started up the first mountain.

Epilogue

Dedé

1994

L ater they would come by the old house in Ojo de Agua and insist on seeing me. Sometimes, for a rest, I'd go spend a couple of weeks with Mamá in Conuco. I would use the excuse that the monument was being built, and the noise and dust and activity bothered me. But it was really that I could bear neither to receive them nor turn them away.

They would come with their stories of that afternoon—the little soldier with the bad teeth, cracking his knuckles, who had ridden in the car with them over the mountain; the bowing attendant from El Gallo who had sold them some purses and tried to warn them not to go; the big-shouldered truck driver with the husky voice who had witnessed the ambush on the road. They all wanted to give me something of the girls' last moments. Each visitor would break my heart all over again, but I would sit on this very rocker and listen for as long as they had something to say.

It was the least I could do, being the one saved.

And as they spoke, I was composing in my head how that last afternoon went.

───────

It seems they left town after four-thirty, since the truck that preceded them up the mountain clocked out of the local Public Works building at four thirty-five. They had stopped at a little establishment by the side of the road. They were worrying about something, the proprietor said, he didn't know what. The tall one kept pacing back and forth to the phone and talking a lot.

The proprietor had had too much to drink when he told me this. He sat in that chair, his wife dabbing at her eyes each time her husband said something. He told me what each of them had ordered. He said I might want to know this. He said at the last minute the cute one with the braids decided on ten cents' worth of Chiclets, cinnamon, yellow, green. He dug around in the jar but he couldn't find any cinnamon ones. He will never forgive himself that he couldn't find any cinnamon ones. His wife wept for the little things that could have made the girls' last minutes happier. Their sentimentality was excessive, but I listened, and thanked them for coming.

———————

It seems that at first the Jeep was following the truck up the mountain. Then as the truck slowed for the grade, the Jeep passed and sped away, around some curves, out of sight. Then it seems that the truck came upon the ambush. A blue-and-white Austin had blocked part of the road; the Jeep had been forced to a stop; the women were being led away peaceably, so the truck driver said, *peaceably* to the car. He had to brake so as not to run into them, and that's when one of the women— I think it must have been Patria, "the short, plump one"—broke from the captors and ran towards the truck. She clung to the door, yelling, "Tell the Mirabal family in Salcedo that the *calíes* are going to kill us!" Right behind her came one of the men, who tore her hand off the door and dragged her away to the car.

It seems that the minute the truck driver heard the word *calíe*, he shut the door he had started opening. Following the commanding wave of one of the men, he inched his way past. I felt like asking him, "Why didn't you stop and help them?" But of course, I didn't. Still, he saw the question in my eyes and he bowed his head.

———————

Over a year after Trujillo was gone, it all came out at the trial of the murderers. But even then, there were several versions. Each one of the five murderers saying the others had done most of the murdering. One of them saying they hadn't done any murdering at all. Just taken the girls to the mansion in La Cumbre where El Jefe had finished them off.

The trial was on TV all day long for almost a month.

Three of the murderers did finally admit to killing one each of the Mirabal sisters. Another one killed Rufino, the driver. The fifth stood on the side of the road to warn the others if someone was coming. At first, they all tried to say they were that one, the one with the cleanest hands.

I didn't want to hear how they did it. I saw the marks on Minerva's throat; fingerprints sure as day on Mate's pale neck. They also clubbed them, I could see that when I went to cut her hair. They killed them good and dead. But I do not believe they violated my sisters, no. I checked as best I could. I think it is safe to say they acted like gentlemen murderers in that way.

After they were done, they put the dead girls in the back of the Jeep, Rufino in front. Past a hairpin curve near where there were three crosses, they pushed the car over the edge. It was seven-thirty. The way I know is one of my visitors, Mateo Núñez, had just begun listening to the Sacred Rosary on his little radio when he heard the terrible crash.

He learned about the trial of the murderers on that same radio. He walked from his remote mountain shack with his shoes in a paper sack so as not to wear them out. It must have taken him days. He got a lift or two, here and there, sometimes going the wrong way. He hadn't traveled much off that mountain. I saw him out the window when he stopped and put on his shoes to show up proper at my door. He gave me the exact hour and made the thundering noise of the tumbling Jeep he graphed with his arcing hand. Then he turned around and headed back to his mountain.

He came all that way just to tell me that.

The men got thirty years or twenty years, on paper. I couldn't keep straight why some of the murderers got less than the others. Likely the one on the road got the twenty years. Maybe another one was sorry in court. I don't know. But their sentences didn't amount to much, anyway. All of them were set free during our spell of revolutions. When we had them regularly, as if to prove we could kill each other even without a dictator to tell us to.

After the men were sentenced, they gave interviews that were on the news all the time. What did the murderers of the Mirabal sisters think of this and that? Or so I heard. We didn't own a TV, and the one at Mamá's we turned on only for the children's cartoons. I didn't want them to grow up with hate, their eyes fixed on the past. Never once have the names of the murderers crossed my lips. I wanted the children to have what their mothers would have wanted for them, the possibility of happiness.

Once in a while, Jaimito brought me a newspaper so I could see all the great doings in the country. But I'd roll it up tight as I could get it and whack at the house flies. I missed some big things that way. The day Trujillo was assassinated by a group of seven men, some of them his old buddies. The day Manolo and Leandro were released, Pedrito having already been freed. The day the rest of the Trujillo family fled the country. The day elections were announced, our first free ones in thirty-one years.

"Don't you want to know all about it?" Jaimito would ask, grinning, trying to get me excited. Or more likely, hopeful. I'd smile, grateful for his caring. "Why? When I can hear it all from you, my dear?"

Not that I was really listening as he went on and on, recounting what was in the papers. I pretended to, nodding and smiling from my chair. I didn't want to hurt his feelings. After all, I listened to everyone else.

But the thing was, I just couldn't take one more story.

In her mother's old room, I hear Minou, getting ready for bed. She keeps a steady patter through the open window, catching me up on her life since we last talked. The new line of play clothes she designed for her store in the capital; the course she is teaching at the university on poetry and politics; Jacqueline's beautiful little baby and the remodeling of her penthouse; Manolito, busy with his agricultural projects—all of them smart young men and women making good money. They aren't like us, I think. They knew almost from the start they had to take on the world.

"Am I boring you, Mamá Dedé?"

"Not at all!" I say, rocking in pleasing rhythm to the sound of her voice.

The little news, that's what I like, I tell them. Bring me the little news.

Sometimes they came to tell me just how crazy I was. To say, "Ay, Dedé, you should have seen yourself that day!"

The night before I hadn't slept at all. Jaime David was sick and kept waking up, feverish, needing drinks of water. But it wasn't him keeping me up. Every time he cried out I was already awake. I finally came out here and waited for dawn, rocking and rocking like I was bringing the day on. Worrying about my boy, I thought.

And then, a soft shimmering spread across the sky. I listened to the chair rockers clacking on the tiles, the isolated cock crowing, and far off, the sound of hoof beats, getting closer, closer. I ran all the way around the *galería* to the front. Sure enough, here was Mamá's yardboy galloping on the mule, his legs hanging almost to the ground. Funny, the thing that you remember as most shocking. Not a messenger showing up at that eerie time of early dawn, the dew still thick on the grass. No. What shocked me most was that anybody had gotten our impossibly stubborn mule to gallop.

The boy didn't even dismount. He just called out, "Doña Dedé, your mother, she wants you to come right away."

I didn't even ask him why. Did I already guess? I rushed back into the house, into our bedroom, threw open the closet, yanked my black dress off its hanger, ripping the right sleeve, waking Jaimito with my piteous crying.

When Jaimito and I pulled into the drive, there was Mamá and all the kids running out of the house. I didn't think *the girls*, right off. I thought, there's a fire, and I started counting to make sure everybody was out.

The babies were all crying like they had gotten shots. And here comes Minou tearing away from the others towards the truck so Jaimito had to screech to a stop.

"Lord preserve us, what is going on?" I ran to them with my arms open. But they hung back, stunned, probably at the horror on my face, for I had noticed something odd.

"Where are they!?" I screamed.

And then, Mamá says to me, she says, "*Ay*, Dedé, tell me it isn't true, *ay*, tell me it isn't true."

And before I could even think what she was talking about, I said, "It isn't true, Mamá, it isn't true."

There was a telegram that had been delivered first thing that morning. Once she'd had it read to her, Mamá could never find it again. But she knew what it said.

There has been a car accident.

Please come to José María Cabral Hospital in Santiago.

And my heart in my rib cage was a bird that suddenly began to sing. Hope! I imagined broken legs strung up, arms in casts, lots of bandages. I rearranged the house where I was going to put each one while they were convalescing. We'd clear the living room and roll them in there for meals.

While Jaimito was drinking the cup of coffee Tono had made him— I hadn't wanted to wait at home while the slow-witted Tinita got the fire going—Mamá and I were rushing around, packing a bag to take to the hospital. They would need nightgowns, toothbrushes, towels, but I put in crazy things in my terrified rush, Mate's favorite earrings, the Vicks jar, a brassiere for each one.

And then we hear a car coming down the drive. At our spying jalousie—as we called that front window—I recognize the man who delivers the telegrams. I say to Mamá, wait here, let me go see what he wants. I walk quickly up the drive to stop that man from coming any closer to the house, now that we had finally gotten the children calmed down.

"We've been calling. We couldn't get through. The phone, it's off the hook or something." He is delaying, I can see that. Finally he hands me the little envelope with the window, and then he gives me his back because a man can't be seen crying.

I tear it open, I pull out the yellow sheet, I read each word.

I walk back so slowly to the house I don't know how I ever get there.

Mamá comes to the door, and I say, Mamá, there is no need for the bag.

At first the guards posted outside the morgue did not want to let me in. I was not the closest living relative, they said. I said to the guards, "I'm going in there, even if I have to be the latest dead relative. Kill me, too, if you want. I don't care."

The guards stepped back. "Ay, Dedé," the friends will say, "you should have seen yourself."

I cannot remember half the things I cried out when I saw them. Rufino and Minerva were on gurneys, Patria and Mate on mats on the floor. I was furious that they didn't all have gurneys, as if it should matter to them. I remember Jaimito trying to hush me, one of the doctors coming in with a sedative and a glass of water. I remember asking the men to leave while I washed up my girls, and dressed them. A nurse helped me, crying, too. She brought me some little scissors to cut off Mate's braid. I cannot imagine why in a place with so many sharp instruments for cutting bones and thick tissues, that woman brought me such teeny nail scissors. Maybe she was afraid what I would do with something sharper.

Then some friends who had heard the news appeared with four boxes, plain simple pine without even a latch. The tops were just nailed down. Later, Don Gustavo at the funeral parlor wanted us to switch them into something fancy. For the girls, anyhow. Pine was appropriate enough for a chauffeur.

I remembered Papá's prediction, *Dedé will bury us all in silk and pearls.* But I said no. They all died the same, let them all be buried the same. We stacked the four boxes in the back of the pickup.

We drove them home through the towns slowly. I didn't want to come inside the cab with Jaimito. I stayed out back with my sisters, and Rufino, standing proud beside them, holding on to the coffins whenever we hit a bump.

People came out of their houses. They had already heard the story we were to pretend to believe. The Jeep had gone off the cliff on a bad turn. But their faces knew the truth. Many of the men took off their hats, the women made the sign of the cross. They stood at the very edge of the road, and when the truck went by, they threw flowers into the bed. By the time we reached Conuco, you couldn't see the boxes for the wilting blossoms blanketing them.

When we got to the SIM post at the first little town, I cried out, "Assassins! Assassins!"

Jaimito gunned the motor to drown out my cries. When I did it again at the next town, he pulled over and came to the back of the pickup. He made me sit down on one of the boxes. "Dedé, *mujer*, what is it you want—to get yourself killed, too?"

I nodded. I said, "I want to be with them."

He said—I remember it so clearly—he said, "This is *your* martyrdom, Dedé, to be alive without them."

"What are you thinking, Mamá Dedé?" Minou has come to the window. With her arms folded on the sill, she looks like a picture.

I smile at her and say, "Look at that moon." It is not a remarkable moon, waning, hazy in the cloudy night. But as far as I'm concerned, a moon is a moon, and they all bear remarking. Like babies, even homely ones, each a blessing, each one born with—as Mamá used to say—its loaf of bread under its arm.

"Tell me about Camila," I ask her. "Has she finished growing that new tooth?"

With first-time-mother exactitude Minou tells me everything, down to how her little girl feeds, sleeps, plays, poops.

Later the husbands told me their stories of that last afternoon. How they tried to convince the girls not to go. How Minerva refused to stay over with friends until the next morning. "It was the one argument she should have lost," Manolo said. He would stand by the porch rail there for a long time, in those dark glasses he was always wearing afterwards. And I would leave him to his grief.

This was after he got out. After he was famous and riding around with bodyguards in that white Thunderbird some admirer had given him. Most likely a woman. Our Fidel, our Fidel, everyone said. He refused to run for president for those first elections. He was no politician, he said. But everywhere he went, Manolo drew adoring crowds.

He and Leandro were transferred back to the capital the Monday following the murder. No explanation. At La Victoria, they rejoined Pedrito, the three of them alone in one cell. They were extremely nervous, waiting for Thursday visiting hours to find out what was going on. "You had no idea?" I asked Manolo once. He turned around right there, with that oleander framing him. Minerva had planted it years back when she was cooped up here, wanting to get out and live the bigger version of her life. He took off those glasses, and it seemed to me that for the first time I saw the depth of his grief.

"I probably knew, but in prison, you can't let yourself know what you know." His hands clenched the porch rail there. I could see he was wearing his class ring again, the one that had been on Minerva's hand.

Manolo tells how that Thursday they were taken out of their cell and marched down the hall. For a brief moment they were hopeful that the girls were all right after all. But instead of the visitors' room, they were led downstairs to the officers' lounge. Johnny Abbes and Cándido Torres and other top SIM cronies were waiting, already quite drunk. This was going to be a special treat, by invitation only, a torture session of an unusual nature, giving the men the news.

I didn't want to listen anymore. But I made myself listen—it was as if Manolo had to say it and I had to hear it—so that it could be human, so that we could begin to forgive it.

There are pictures of me at that time where even I can't pick myself out. Thin like my little finger. A twin of my skinny Noris. My hair cropped short like Minerva's was that last year, held back by bobby pins. Some baby or other in my arms, another one tugging at my dress. And you never see me looking at the camera. Always I am looking away.

But slowly—how does it happen?—I came back from the dead. In a photo I have of the day our new president came to visit the monument,

I'm standing in front of the house, all made up, my hair in a bouffant style. Jacqueline is in my arms, already four years old. Both of us are waving little flags.

Afterwards, the president dropped in for a visit. He sat right there in Papá's old rocker, drinking a frozen *limonada*, telling me his story. He was going to do all sorts of things, he told me. He was going to get rid of the old generals with their hands still dirty with Mirabal blood. All those properties they had stolen he was going to distribute among the poor. He was going to make us a nation proud of ourselves, not run by the Yanqui imperialists.

Every time he made one of these promises, he'd look at me as if he needed me to approve what he was doing. Or really, not me, but my sisters whose pictures hung on the wall behind me. Those photos had become icons, emblazoned on posters—already collectors' pieces. *Bring back the butterflies!*

At the end, as he was leaving, the president recited a poem he'd composed on the ride up from the capital. It was something patriotic about how when you die for your country, you do not die in vain. He was a poet president, and from time to time Manolo would say, "*Ay*, if Minerva had lived to see this." And I started to think, maybe it was for something that the girls had died.

Then it was like a manageable grief inside me. Something I could bear because I could make sense of it. Like when the doctor explained how if one breast came off, the rest of me had a better chance. Immediately, I began to live without it, even before it was gone.

I set aside my grief and began hoping and planning.

When it all came down a second time, I shut the door. I did not receive any more visitors. Anyone had a story, go sell it to *Vanidades*, go on the *Talk to Félix Show*. Tell them how you felt about the coup, the president thrown out before the year was over, the rebels up in the mountains, the civil war, the landing of the marines.

I overheard one of the talk shows on the radio Tinita kept turned on in the outdoor kitchen all the time. Somebody analyzing the situation. He said something that made me stop and listen.

"Dictatorships," he was saying, "are pantheistic. The dictator manages to plant a little piece of himself in every one of us."

Ah, I thought, touching the place above my heart where I did not yet know the cells were multiplying like crazy. So this is what is happening to us.

Manolo's voice sounds blurry on the memorial tape the radio station sent me, *In memory of our great hero. When you die for your country, you do not die in vain.*

It is his last broadcast from a hidden spot in the mountains. "Fellow Dominicans!" he declaims in a grainy voice. "We must not let another dictatorship rule us!" Then something else lost in static. Finally, "Rise up, take to the streets! Join my comrades and me in the mountains! When you die for your country, you do not die in vain!"

But no one joined them. After forty days of bombing, they accepted the broadcast amnesty. They came down from the mountains with their hands up, and the generals gunned them down, every one.

I was the one who received the seashell Manolo sent Minou on his last day. In its smooth bowl he had etched with a penknife, *For my little Minou, at the end of a great adventure,* then the date he was murdered, December 21, 1963. I was furious at his last message. What did he mean, *a great adventure*. A *disgrace* was more like it.

I didn't give it to her. In fact, for a while, I kept his death a secret from her. When she'd ask, I'd tell her, "*Sí, sí,* Papi is up in the mountains fighting for a better world." And then, you see, after about a year or so of that story it was an easy next step for him to be up in heaven with her Mami and her Tía Patria and her Tía Mate living in a better world.

She looked at me when I told her this—she must have been eight by then—and her little face went very serious. "Mamá Dedé," she asked, "is Papi dead?"

I gave her the shell so she could read his goodbye for herself.

"That was a funny woman," Minou is saying. "At first I thought you were friends or something. Where did you pick her up, Mamá Dedé?"

"Me? Pick her up! You seem to forget, *mi amor,* that the museum is just five minutes away and everyone shows up there wanting to hear the story, firsthand." I am rocking harder as I explain, getting angrier. Everyone feels they can impose. The Belgian movie maker who had me pose with the girls' photos in my hands; the Chilean woman writing a book about women and politics; the schoolchildren who want me to hold up the braid and tell them why I cut it off in the first place.

"But, Mamá Dedé," Minou says. She is sitting on the sill now, peering out from her lighted room into the *galería* whose lights I've turned off against the mosquitoes. "Why don't you just refuse. We'll put the story on cassette, a hundred and fifty pesos, with a signed glossy photograph thrown in for free."

"Why, Minou, the idea!" To make our tragedy—because it is *our* tragedy, really, the whole country's—to make it into a money-making enterprise. But I see she is laughing, enjoying the deliciously sacrilegious thought. I laugh, too. "The day I get tired of doing it, I suppose I'll stop."

My rocking eases, calmed. Of course, I think, I can always stop.

"When will that be, Mamá Dedé, when will you have given enough?"

When did it turn, I wonder, from my being the one who listened to the stories people brought to being the one whom people came to for the story of the Mirabal sisters?

When, in other words, did I become the oracle?

My girlfriend Olga and I will sometimes get together for supper at a restaurant. We can do this for ourselves, we tell each other, like we don't half believe it. Two divorced *mujeronas* trying to catch up with what our children call *the modern times*. With her I can talk over these things. I've asked her, what does she think.

"I'll tell you what I think," Olga says. We are at El Almirante, where— we have decided—the waiters must be retired functionaries from the old Trujillo days. They are so self-important and ceremonious. But they do let two women dine alone in peace.

"I think you deserve your very own life," she is saying, waving my protest away. "Let me finish. You're still living in the past, Dedé. You're in the same old house, surrounded by the same old things, in the same little village, with all the people who have known you since you were this big."

She goes over all these things that supposedly keep me from living my own life. And I am thinking, Why, I wouldn't give them up for the world. I'd rather be dead.

"It's still 1960 for you," she concludes. "But this is 1994, Dedé, *1994!*"

"You're wrong," I tell her. "I'm not stuck in the past, I've just brought it with me into the present. And the problem is not enough of us have done that. What is that thing the gringos say, if you don't study your history, you are going to repeat it?"

Olga waves the theory away. "The gringos say too many things."

"And many of them true," I tell her. "Many of them." Minou has accused me of being pro-Yanqui. And I tell her, "I am pro whoever is right at any moment in time."

Olga sighs. I already know. Politics do not interest her.

I change the subject back to what the subject was. "Besides, that's not what I asked you. We were talking about when I became the oracle instead of the listener."

"Hmm," she says. "I'm thinking, I'm thinking."

So I tell her what I think.

"After the fighting was over and we were a broken people"—she shakes her head sadly at this portrait of our recent times—"that's when I opened my doors, and instead of listening, I started talking. We had lost hope, and we needed a story to understand what had happened to us."

Olga sits back, her face attentive, as if she were listening to someone preach something she believes. "That's really good, Dedé," she says when I finish. "You should save that for November when you have to give that speech."

———

I hear Minou dialing, putting in a call to Doroteo, their goodnight tête-à-tête, catching up on all the little news of their separated hours. If I go in now, she'll feel she has to cut it short and talk to her Mamá Dedé instead.

And so I come stand by the porch rail, and the minute I do, of course,

I can't help thinking of Manolo and of Minerva before him. We had this game called Dark Passages when we were children. We would dare each other to walk down into the dark garden at night. I only got past this rail once or twice. But Minerva, she'd take off, so that we'd have to call and call, pleading for her to come back. I remember, though, how she would stand right here for a moment, squaring her shoulders, steeling herself. I could see it wasn't *so* easy for her either.

And when she was older, every time she got upset, she would stand at this same rail. She'd look out into the garden as if that dark tangle of vegetation were the new life or question before her.

Absently, my hand travels to my foam breast and presses gently, worrying an absence there.

"*Mi amor,*" I hear Minou say in the background, and I feel goose bumps all up and down my arms. She sounds so much like her mother. "How's our darling? Did you take her to Helados Bon?"

I walk off the porch onto the grass, so as not to overhear her conversation, or so I tell myself. For a moment I want to disappear. My legs brushing fragrances off the vague bushes, the dark growing deeper as I walk away from the lights of the house.

The losses. I can count them up like the list the coroner gave us, taped to the box of things that had been found on their persons or retrieved from the wreck. The silliest things, but they gave me some comfort. I would say them like a catechism, like the girls used to tease and recite "the commandments" of their house arrest.

One pink powder puff.

One pair of red high-heeled shoes.

The two-inch heel from a cream-colored shoe.

Jaimito went away for a time to New York. Our harvests had failed again, and it looked as if we were going to lose our lands if we didn't get some cash quick. So he got work in a *factoría*, and every month, he sent home money. I am ashamed after what came to pass to say so. But it was gringo dollars that saved our farm from going under.

And when he came back, he was a different man. Rather, he was more who he was. I had become more who I was, too, locked up, as I said, with Mamá and the children my only company. And so, though we lived under the same roof until after Mamá died, to spare her another sadness, we had already started on our separate lives.

One screwdriver.

One brown leather purse.

One red patent leather purse with straps missing.

One pair of yellow nylon underwear.

One pocket mirror.

Four lottery tickets.

We scattered as a family, the men, and later the children, going their separate ways.

First, Manolo, dead within three years of Minerva.

Then Pedrito. He had gotten his lands back, but prison and his losses had changed him. He was restless, couldn't settle down to the old life. He remarried a young girl, and the new woman turned him around, or so Mamá thought. He came by a lot less and then hardly at all. How all of that, beginning with the young girl, would have hurt poor Patria.

And Leandro. While Manolo was alive, Leandro was by his side, day and night. But when Manolo took off to the mountains, Leandro stayed home. Maybe he sensed a trap, maybe Manolo had become too radical for Leandro, I don't know. After Manolo died, Leandro got out of politics. Became a big builder in the capital. Sometimes when we're driving through the capital, Jacqueline points out one impressive building or another and says, "Papá built that." She is less ready to talk about the second wife, the new, engrossing family, stepbrothers and sisters the age of her own little one.

One receipt from El Gallo.

One missal held together with a rubber band.

One man's wallet, 56 *centavos* in the pocket.

Seven rings, three plain gold bands, one gold with a small diamond stone, one gold with an opal and four pearls, one man's ring with garnet and eagle insignia, one silver initial ring.

One scapular of our Lady of Sorrows.

One Saint Christopher's medal.

Mamá hung on twenty years. Every day I wasn't staying over, I visited

her first thing in the morning and always with an orchid from my garden for the girls. We raised the children between us. Minou and Manolito and Raulito, she kept. Jacqueline and Nelson and Noris were with
me. Don't ask me why we divided them that way. We didn't really. They
would wander from house to house, they had their seasons, but I'm
talking about where they most often slept.

What a time Mamá had with those teenage granddaughters. She
wanted them locked up like nuns in a convent, she was always so afraid.
And Minou certainly kept her—and me—in worries. She took off, a
young sixteen-year-old, by herself to study in Canada. Then it was Cuba
for several years. ¡Ay, Dios! We pinned enough Virgencitas and *azabaches*
and hung enough scapulars around that girl's neck to charm away the
men who were always wanting to get their hands on that young beauty.

I remember Minou telling me about the first time she and Doroteo
"got involved"—what she called it. I imagined, of course, the bedside
scene behind the curtain of that euphemism. He stood with his hands
under his arms as if he were not going to give in to her charms. Finally,
she said, "Doroteo, what's wrong?" And Doroteo said, "I feel like I'd be
desecrating the flag."

He had a point there. Imagine, the daughter of two national heroes.
All I said to Minou was "I like that young man."

But not Mamá. "Be smart like your mother," she kept saying. "Study
and marry when you're older." And all I could think of was the hard
time Mamá had given Minerva when she had done just that!

Poor Mamá, living to see the end of so many things, including her
own ideas. Twenty years, like I said, she hung on. She was waiting until
her granddaughters were past the dangerous stretch of their teen years
before she left them to fend for themselves.

And then fourteen years ago this last January, I came into her bedroom one morning, and she was lying with her hands at her waist,
holding her rosary, quiet, as if she were praying. I checked to make sure
she was gone. It was strange how this did not seem a real death, so
unlike the others, quiet, without rage or violence.

I put the orchid I had brought the girls in her hands. I knew that,
unless my destiny was truly accursed and I survived my children, this

was the last big loss I would have to suffer. There was no one between me and the dark passage ahead—I was next.

The complete list of losses. There they are.

And it helps, I've found, if I can count them off, so to speak. And sometimes when I'm doing that, I think, Maybe these aren't losses. Maybe that's a wrong way to think of them. The men, the children, me. We went our own ways, we became ourselves. Just that. And maybe that is what it means to be a free people, and I should be glad?

———————

Not long ago, I met Lío at a reception in honor of the girls. Despite what Minou thinks, I don't like these things. But I always make myself go.

Only if I know he will be there, I won't go. I mean our current president who was the puppet president the day the girls were killed. "Ay, Dedé," acquaintances will sometimes try to convince me. "Put that behind you. He's an old, blind man now."

"He was blind when he could see," I'll snap. Oh, but my blood burns just thinking of shaking that spotted hand.

But most things I go to. "For the girls," I always tell myself.

Sometimes I allow myself a shot of rum before climbing into the car, not enough to scent the slightest scandal, just a little thunder in the heart. People will be asking things, well meaning but nevertheless poking their fingers where it still hurts. People who kept their mouths shut when a little peep from everyone would have been a chorus the world couldn't have ignored. People who once were friends of the devil. Everyone got amnesty by telling on everyone else until we were all one big rotten family of cowards.

So I allow myself my shot of rum.

At these things, I always try to position myself near the door so I can leave early. And there I was about to slip away when an older man approached me. On his arm was a handsome woman with an open, friendly face. This old fool is no fool, I'm thinking. He has got himself his young nurse wife for his old age.

I put out my hand, just a reception line habit, I guess. And this man reaches out both hands and clasps mine. "Dedé, *caramba*, don't you know who I am?" He holds on tight, and the young woman is beaming beside him. I look again.

"¡Dios santo, Lío!" And suddenly, I have to sit down.

The wife gets us both drinks and leaves us alone. We catch up, back and forth, my children, his children; the insurance business, his practice in the capital; the old house I still live in, his new house near the old presidential palace. Slowly, we are working our way towards that treacherous past, the horrible crime, the waste of young lives, the throbbing heart of the wound.

"Ay, Lío," I say, when we get to that part.

And bless his heart, he takes my hands and says, "The nightmare is over, Dedé. Look at what the girls have done." He gestures expansively.

He means the free elections, bad presidents now put in power properly, not by army tanks. He means our country beginning to prosper, Free Zones going up everywhere, the coast a clutter of clubs and resorts. We are now the playground of the Caribbean, who were once its killing fields. The cemetery is beginning to flower.

"Ay, Lío," I say it again.

I follow his gaze around the room. Most of the guests here are young. The boy-businessmen with computerized watches and walkie-talkies in their wives' purses to summon the chauffeur from the car; their glamorous young wives with degrees they do not need; the scent of perfume; the tinkle of keys to the things they own.

"Oh yes," I hear one of the women say, "we spent a revolution there."

I can see them glancing at us, the two old ones, how sweet they look under that painting of Bidó. To them we are characters in a sad story about a past that is over.

All the way home, I am trembling, I am not sure why.

It comes to me slowly as I head north through the dark countryside—the only lights are up in the mountains where the prosperous young are building their getaway houses, and of course, in the sky, all the splurged wattage of the stars. Lío is right. The nightmare is over; we are free at last. But the thing that is making me tremble, that I do not want to say out loud—and I'll say it once only and it's done.

Was it for this, the sacrifice of the butterflies?

"Mamá Dedé! Where are you?" Minou must be off the phone. Her voice has that exasperated edge our children get when we dare wander from their lives. *Why aren't you where I left you?* "Mamá Dedé!"

I stop in the dark depths of the garden as if I've been caught about to do something wrong. I turn around. I see the house as I saw it once or twice as a child: the roof with its fairytale peak, the verandah running along three sides, the windows lighted up, glowing with lived life, a place of abundance, a magic place of memory and desire. And quickly I head back, a moth attracted to that marvelous light.

I tuck her in bed and turn off her light and stay a while and talk in the dark.

She tells me all the news of what Camila did today. Of Doroteo's businesses, of their plans to build a house up north in those beautiful mountains.

I am glad it is dark, so she cannot see my face when she says this. *Up north in those beautiful mountains where both your mother and father were murdered!*

But all this is a sign of my success, isn't it? She's not haunted and full of hate. She claims it, this beautiful country with its beautiful mountains and splendid beaches—all the copy we read in the tourist brochures.

We make our plans for tomorrow. We'll go on a little outing to Santiago where I'll help her pick up some fabrics at El Gallo. They're having a big sale before they close the old doors and open under new management. A chain of El Gallos is going up all over the island with attendants in rooster-red uniforms and registers that announce how much you are spending. Then we'll go to the museum where Minou can get some cuttings from Tono for the atrium in her apartment. Maybe Jaime David can have lunch with us. The big important senator from Salcedo better have time for her, Minou warns me.

Fela's name comes up. "Mamá Dedé, what do you think it means that the girls might finally be at rest?"

That is not a good question for going to bed, I think. Like bringing up

319

a divorce or a personal problem on a postcard. So I give her the brief, easy answer. "That we can let them go, I suppose."

Thank God, she is so tired and does not push me to say more.

Some nights when I cannot sleep, I lie in bed and play that game Minerva taught me, going back in my memory to this or that happy moment. But I've been doing that all afternoon. So tonight I start thinking of what lies ahead instead.

Specifically, the prize trip I've as good as won again this year.

The boss has been dropping hints. "You know, Dedé, the tourist brochures are right. We have a beautiful paradise right here. There's no need to travel far to have a good time."

Trying to get by cheap this year!

But if I've won the prize trip again, I'm going to push for what I want. I'm going to say, "I want to go to Canada to see the leaves."

"The leaves?" I can just see the boss making his professional face of polite shock. It's the one he uses on all the *tutumpotes* when they come in wanting to buy the cheaper policies. *Surely your life is worth a lot more, Don Fulano.*

"Yes," I'll say, "leaves. I want to see the leaves." But I'm not going to tell him why. The Canadian man I met in Barcelona, on last year's prize trip, told me about how they turn red and gold. He took my hand in his, as if it were a leaf, spreading out the fingers. He pointed out this and that line in my palm. "Sugar concentrates in the veins." I felt my resolve to keep my distance melting down like the sugar in those leaves. My face I knew was burning.

"It is the sweetness in them that makes them burn," he said, looking me in the eye, then smiling. He knew an adequate Spanish, good enough for what he had to say. But I was too scared yet to walk into my life that bold way. When he finished the demonstration, I took back my hand.

But already in my memory, it has happened and I am standing under those blazing trees—flamboyants in bloom in my imagination, not having seen those sugar maples he spoke of. He is snapping a picture for me to bring back to the children to prove that it happens, yes, even to their old Mamá Dedé.

It is the sweetness in them that makes them burn.

———————

Usually, at night, I hear them just as I'm falling asleep.

Sometimes, I lie at the very brink of forgetfulness, waiting, as if their arrival is my signal that I can fall asleep.

The settling of the wood floors, the wind astir in the jasmine, the deep released fragrance of the earth, the crow of an insomniac rooster.

Their soft spirit footsteps, so vague I could mistake them for my own breathing.

Their different treads, as if even as spirits they retained their personalities, Patria's sure and measured step, Minerva's quicksilver impatience, Mate's playful little skip. They linger and loiter over things. Tonight, no doubt, Minerva will sit a long while by her Minou and absorb the music of her breathing.

Some nights I'll be worrying about something, and I'll stay up past their approaching, and I'll hear something else. An eerie, hair-raising creaking of riding boots, a crop striking leather, a peremptory footstep that makes me shake myself awake and turn on lights all over the house. The only sure way to send the evil thing packing.

But tonight, it is quieter than I can remember.

Concentrate, Dedé, I say. My hand worries the absence on my left side, a habitual gesture now. My pledge of allegiance, I call it, to all that is missing. Under my fingers, my heart is beating like a moth wild in a lamp shade. Dedé, concentrate!

But all I hear is my own breathing and the blessed silence of those cool, clear nights under the anacahuita tree before anyone breathes a word of the future. And I see them all there in my memory, as still as statues, Mamá and Papá, and Minerva and Mate and Patria, and I'm thinking something is missing now. And I count them all twice before I realize—it's me, Dedé, it's me, the one who survived to tell the story.

A Postscript

On August 6, 1960, my family arrived in New York City, exiles from the tyranny of Trujillo. My father had participated in an underground plot that was cracked by the SIM, Trujillo's famous secret police. At the notorious torture chamber of La Cuarenta (La 40), it was just a matter of time before those who were captured gave out the names of other members.

Almost four months after our escape, three sisters who had also been members of that underground were murdered on their way home on a lonely mountain road. They had been to visit their jailed husbands who had purposely been transferred to a distant prison so that the women would be forced to make this perilous journey. A fourth sister who did not make the trip that day survived.

When as a young girl I heard about the "accident," I could not get the Mirabals out of my mind. On my frequent trips back to the Dominican Republic, I sought out whatever information I could about these brave and beautiful sisters who had done what few men—and only a handful of women—had been willing to do. During that terrifying thirty-one-year regime, any hint of disagreement ultimately resulted in death for the dissenter and often for members of his or her family. Yet the Mirabals had risked their lives. I kept asking myself, What gave them that special courage?

It was to understand that question that I began this story. But as happens with any story, the characters took over, beyond polemics and facts. They became real to my imagination. I began to invent them.

And so it is that what you find in these pages are not the Mirabal sisters of fact, or even the Mirabal sisters of legend. The actual sisters I never knew, nor did I have access to enough information or the talents and inclinations of a biographer to be able to adequately record them. As for the sisters of legend, wrapped in superlatives and ascended into myth, they were finally also inaccessible to me. I realized, too, that such deification was dangerous, the same god-making impulse that had created our tyrant. And ironically, by making them myth, we lost the Mirabals once more, dismissing the challenge of their courage as impossible for us, ordinary men and women.

So what you will find here are the Mirabals of my creation, made up but, I hope, true to the spirit of the real Mirabals. In addition, though I had researched the facts of the regime, and events pertaining to Trujillo's thirty-one-year depotism, I sometimes took liberties—by changing dates, by reconstructing events, and by collapsing characters or incidents. For I wanted to immerse my readers in an epoch in the life of the Dominican Republic that I believe can only finally be understood by fiction, only finally be redeemed by the imagination. A novel is not, after all, a historical document, but a way to travel through the human heart.

I would hope that through this fictionalized story I will bring acquaintance of these famous sisters to English-speaking readers. November 25th, the day of their murder, is observed in many Latin American countries as the International Day Against Violence Towards Women. Obviously, these sisters, who fought one tyrant, have served as models for women fighting against injustices of all kinds.

To Dominicans separated by language from the world I have created, I hope this book deepens North Americans' understanding of the nightmare you endured and the heavy losses you suffered—of which this story tells only a few.

¡Vivan las Mariposas!

To those who helped me write this book

Bernardo Vega
Minou
Dedé
Papi

Fleur Laslocky
Judy Yarnall

Shannon Ravenel
Susan Bergholz

Bill

La Virgencita de Altagracia

mil gracias

William Galvan's *Minerva Mirabal*, Ramon Alberto Ferreras's *Las Mirabal*, as well as Pedro Mir's poem "Amén de Mariposas," were especially helpful in providing facts and inspiration.

Octavío de la Maza Vázquez • Antonio de la Maza Váz
• Altagracia Almánzar de Martínez • David Vidal R
Abigail Montalvo • Rafael Patiño • Rafael Aníbal Pat
• Gustavo Adolfo Patiño • Andrés Perozo • Alfonso
Perozo • José Luis Perozo • Santiago Lazano • Jos
Tomás Ceballos Martínez • Gerardo Ellis Cambiaso
Cantizano Flores • Carlos Russo Victoria • Ramón
Cerda Anico • Olegario Vargas • Miguel Hormazá
Silverio • Victor Capellán • Roberto Capellán • Tanc
• Juan Morales • **María Teresa Mirabal de Guzmár**
Salvador Cobián Parra • Juan Canto Rosario • Jo
• Cipriano Bencosme • Donato Bencosme • Sergio
Panchito Madera • Enrique Blanco • Federico Rojas
• Freddy Valdez • Mauricio Báez • Luis Escotto Go
Israel Rodríguez • Salvador Reyes • José Manuel Peña
• Manuel Tejada Florentino • Sixto Hernández • Ca
• Juda Odalis Cepeda • Doroteo Rodríguez • C
(Tavitín) • Maraño García • Pedro Jaime Tineo •
Pedro Vega • José Almonte • Ramón Marrero Ari
Padre Barnett • Aníbal Vallejo • Juan Steffani • Al Du
• Vico Garris • Rudy Garris • Roque Peña • Jorge
Franco • Federico Henríquez (Gugú) • Manuel Ca
Castillo Díaz • José Daniel Ariza • Ramón A. Castro
Oca • Fulvio Liz • Manuel Valera • Saúl Domíngue
Guillermo Mauritz • Pedro Julio Báez • Prin Ramírez A
• **Patria Mirabal de González** • Pablo Martínez •
Roberto Pastoriza (Fifí) • Salvador Estrella • Luis M
Sanabia Valverde • José Tavárez Cabrera • José Tavár
• Miguel Vallejo • Conrado Martínez Hernández • I
Vallejo • Guarionex Contreras • Nelson Peguero
Méndez Cohén • Rafael Reynoso • Arturo Canario • Fa